Tyler Anne Snell genuinely loves all genres of the written word. However, she's realised that she loves books filled with sexual tension and mysteries a little more than the rest. Her stories have a good dose of both. Tyler lives in Alabama with her same-named husband and their mini 'lions.' When she isn't reading or writing, she's playing video games and working on her blog, Almost There. To follow her shenanigans, visit tylerannesnell.com

Addison Fox is a lifelong romance reader, addicted to happily-ever-afters. After discovering she found as much joy writing about romance as she did reading it, she's never looked back. Addison lives in New York with an apartment full of books, a laptop that's rarely out of sight and a wily beagle who keeps her running. You can find her at her home, on the web at addisonfox.com or on Facebook Facebook.com/addisonfoxauthor and Twitter @addisonfox

Also by Tyler Anne Snell

Uncovering Small Town Secrets
Searching for Evidence
Surviving the Truth
Accidental Amnesia
Reining in Trouble
Credible Alibi
Identical Threat
Last Stand Sheriff
Manhunt
Toxin Alert

Also by Addison Fox

The Cowboy's Deadly Mission
Special Ops Cowboy
Under the Rancher's Protection
Undercover K-9 Cowboy
Colton's Covert Witness
Deadly Colton Search
The Colton Sheriff

Discover more at millsandboon.co.uk

COLD CASE CAPTIVE

TYLER ANNE SNELL

UNDERCOVER COLTON

ADDISON FOX

MILLS & BOON

First Published in Great Britain 2022
by Mills & Boon, an imprint of HarperCollins*Publishers* Ltd
1 London Bridge Street, London, SE1 9GF

www.harpercollins.co.uk

HarperCollins*Publishers*
1st Floor, Watermarque Building,
Ringsend Road, Dublin 4, Ireland

Special thanks and acknowledgement are given to Addison Fox for her
contribution to *The Coltons of Colorado* series.

ISBN: 978-0-263-30343-8

0522

MIX
Paper from
responsible sources
FSC® C007454

This book is produced from independently certified FSC™
paper to ensure responsible forest management.

For more information visit: www.harpercollins.co.uk/green

Printed and Bound in Spain using 100% Renewable electricity at
CPI Black Print, Barcelona

COLD CASE
CAPTIVE

TYLER ANNE SNELL

This book is for Regan. Your daily support during this book meant the absolute world. Without your ear, without your encouragement, Lily and Ant would probably still be sleuthing somewhere in my head. You're the absolute best.

Prologue

"The truth is, everyone has forgotten the truth. One of them, at least."

Lillian Howard had her accordion folder tucked beneath one arm, her hair wrapped up in a tight bun, and a tone that was equal parts respectful and professorial.

Detective Kenneth Gray, decidedly not a student but head of the department's cold case task force, kept her stare with rapt attention. He had, as a matter of fact, been the one who had originally called her in for an interview. They'd already gotten the technical parts out of the way— her resume of working at a sheriff's department in north Alabama after deciding to forgo a career at the FBI, even though he didn't ask why she denied the job and she didn't offer an explanation—and now they had arrived at the chit-chat part. The human element.

The *let's see if you'll fit in here* back-and-forth.

Too bad for her that she rarely abided by normal social conventions.

Even when she really wanted the job.

All Kenneth had had to do was open the floor for some polite conversation after leaving the meeting room and going to his office and she'd bowled into it, trying her best to get a strike.

"And what truth is that?" he asked.

Lily was glad to hear that there was no condescension in his words. Her former colleagues had been less than welcoming. It probably hadn't helped matters that she was on the younger side and had an intense love for order, which had gotten her labeled as a control freak. Though she preferred "type A" instead.

Then there was her memory. It stretched as long as it did far.

Lily finally took her seat across the desk from him. She put the accordion folder on her lap and recited a speech she'd given countless times in her much younger years.

The ball was now gliding down the alley.

"That Annie McHale wasn't the first young girl to go missing in Kelby Creek."

She unwrapped the worn string from around the folder's latch but decided not to open it yet. The folder was filled with papers, pictures and her own notes. Some were newer, some were in slightly smudged pen written by a seventeen-year-old Lily.

"Annie McHale was taken five years ago," she continued. "Ida Perez was taken fourteen years ago at the age of sixteen."

Lily fought the urge to adjust how she was sitting in the chair. She knew she was rigid—she often became that way when she was focused—but this time it was from the memory of the cold that day. The lingering but still-powerful effect of seeing the police lights strobe against the trees, feeling the chill of the creek against her soaked skin, and knowing by the look on the adults' faces that there would probably be no happy ending.

It was a hard pull to the past that Lily had tried to distance herself from as the years had gone by.

Yet Kelby Creek, Alabama's past had proven to be extremely persuasive.

That's why she was here.

That's why she'd agreed to come back.

That's why she hoped Detective Gray listened.

For now, at least, he didn't stop her. So she gave him the facts.

Concise, emotionless facts.

"Ida Perez was outside talking with her brother, Anthony, when, after he looked away for a second, she disappeared. Shortly after he realized she was gone, a teenaged neighbor heard Ida scream a few houses down. Together they followed the sound through the back end of the neighborhood until they made it to the beginning of the woods. The neighbor managed to see that Ida was with an adult male but it had started to get dark and rain. They couldn't make anything else out." Lily fought the urge to move again. She reached deep inside herself and threw every switch that controlled her emotions to Off. "Ida and her captor went deeper into the woods after that. The neighbor and her brother followed until they got to the creek, where the man attacked Anthony. The kidnapper knocked him unconscious with a rock from the creek bed and then dragged him into the water. It forced the neighbor to make a decision. Drag him out and save him, or chase after Ida. The neighbor chose to save Anthony. Ida and the man were never seen again."

There.

Concise.

Factual.

Detective Gray leaned forward. He ran a hand across his jaw and nodded.

"It's not lost on me the connection between Annie and Ida. Just like it's not lost on me that this town seems to have glazed over Ida's disappearance and not Annie's."

Lily pushed her shoulders back, not that they weren't already in perfect posture.

"Before what happened to Annie made national news, this entire town dropped everything to try and find her," she reminded him. "It shouldn't matter if you come from a rich family or not. That's what you're supposed to do when a child is taken or goes missing. This town failed Ida Perez."

She hadn't meant to sound as bitter as she had.

Lily reeled herself back in so it wouldn't happen again.

Detective Gray simply nodded one more time.

"Well, as you know, a lot of things were mishandled from a lot of different directions in the past. Closed cases, ongoing investigations, evidence logs, false statements, intimidation… It's why this department *now* is fighting so hard to make sure that never happens again. And it's why the cold case task force was formed."

"To make sure old cases were properly handled," she said, quoting him from the press release almost a year before when the unit was announced.

He nodded.

"It's a job we—and I—take very seriously. Just like the hiring of detectives to the task force." He threaded his fingers together and looked thoughtful. "Our job can be hard, can be difficult, and we can find answers that we don't want. Hell, most of the time we're looking for broken needles in a soggy haystack and then *if* we find them, we're returning them to still-broken families."

"But finding answers can bring closure," she interrupted.

Detective Gray was solemn.

"It can bring closure," he agreed. "And that's the best thing some people can hope to get."

He didn't mention his personal experiences in the matter, even though everyone in Kelby Creek knew about his journey to find answers and justice after his first wife was murdered and her case left cold for years.

"The drive and the desire to find that for families, for loved ones, and to seek justice and a sense of peace for the victims, is what I want the most in the people on this team," he continued. "I *need* intelligent, compassionate and driven detectives, especially since there's still a lot of people who are against the department. Most notably anyone in this department poking around the past."

It was Lily's turn to nod.

"I agree," she finally said when it was clear Detective Gray was waiting for a response. "It's the only thing I've ever been interested in doing. Finding answers. Trying to bring closure."

"It also helps to have a personal connection for this kind of job," he mused. "It's not needed for everyone but it certainly helps those who have it. And I'm guessing that you have one you're trying to sidestep saying. To Ida Perez's case. Can I ask what that connection is?"

Lily turned tight-lipped.

She knew this part was coming, yet it still felt uncomfortable to answer.

She took a moment, something she didn't often do.

Then her voice came out with more emotion than she realized it would.

"I was the neighbor," she said. "I saved Ida Perez's brother from the creek and I'm the last person who saw her alive."

Chapter One

Anthony Perez was staring at the scar next to his hairline while he waited for a call. He ran his finger along the small line and marveled again at how something so thin could be all that was left of so much damage.

Like a drop of water sitting on the ground after a flood destroyed the world around it.

It didn't seem like much to the people who were looking at the puddle but hadn't been around for the flood.

Ant tapped the skin for good measure and then ran his hands back through his black hair. It caused some to cascade over his forehead and hide the scar.

Maybe that's why his hair was a bit longer than seemed appropriate for a thirty-year-old man trying his damnedest to lead a straitlaced, simple life.

Or maybe he knew it had an effect on most women and kept it that way.

His last date had called his hairstyle "yummy."

She'd also spoken in hashtags and asked if he'd been in a fraternity in college.

Ant wasn't knocking a woman who spoke her mind, or in hashtags, but he had to admit he wasn't a fan of how much *she* wasn't a fan of him saying no to the fraternity question.

And a double no to college in general.

He hadn't had the time for college. He'd barely had the time for high school and the only reason he'd passed that was thanks to a girl who probably had never even said the word "yummy."

Ant checked his reflection one more time before deciding to head back out to the mechanic's floor.

He was one of five who worked at Slaggerman's Auto on the corner of Kinderman and 5th. Despite not being thrilled about living in Justice, North Carolina, he didn't mind the shop. It was work he knew how to do and work that kept him away from others. Mostly.

With one look toward the open garage doors, Ant knew one of the rare interactions he was about to have with their head mechanic, Martin, wasn't going to be a good one.

"Hey, Ant, I just got a call from Tonya out at Fortner and *she* had some interesting things to say about your work." Martin huffed his way through his words all the way to where Ant was standing. Then he took an inadvertent step back. Martin might have been who Ant answered to but that didn't change the blaring fact that Ant was a good foot taller than him. That and Martin was built like a twig while Ant never skipped a workout on his makeshift home gym back at his apartment.

"What did Tonya *out at Fortner* say about my work?" Ant slid back, dipping heavily into sarcasm where he shouldn't have.

Martin didn't seem to appreciate the tone. His face became red as he answered.

"She said not only did you *not* charge her the right amount for her brand-new transmission but you didn't charge her *at all* for her tire rotation and oil change." He put his hands on his hips. The power move still didn't match up to Ant's natural stance. "Is that true? Are you

giving away work for free? You do know this isn't a charity, right?"

Ant sighed. Not at all respectful. Then again, he hadn't
liked Martin from the first day.

"Tonya is in her seventies, a widow and, according to
her ungrateful grandkid who came in with her, she's going
to a home in the next year or two," Ant said. "She's also
one of Slaggerman's most loyal customers. She's been
coming here for almost twenty years. So I did the transmission work fast and cut down on the price because of
it. The cost of the oil change and tire rotation I took out
of my paycheck. You can check with your wife. She's the
one who approved it."

Martin went from a shade of crimson to the color of a
stop sign.

"If Tonya is one of our most loyal customers then it
should stand to reason she's not going to complain about
full price," Martin bit out. "Like you said yourself, she's
been paying it for twenty years."

Ant looked down his nose at the smaller man. It was
time he crossed his arms over his chest. Martin eyed the
move with visible hesitancy.

Now they were at a crossroads. Ant knew this song and
dance as well as he knew the first thing he was doing when
he got home was putting on his jogging shorts and going
right back out to run through his frustration. He'd been
here before, with other jobs. With other men like Martin.
He could de-escalate, sure, and say what Martin wanted
to hear. Keep his job and come back the next day pretending everything was square.

Or he could say exactly what was on his mind and be
back in his apartment before lunch, another job search in
his future.

Ant might not have gone to college but he was educated enough to understand that everyone followed a pattern.

His was giving lip to people who deserved to receive it.

"I assumed we don't reward our customers' loyalty by taking a leak all over them for twenty years straight." Ant shrugged. "But I guess that's just me."

Martin opened his mouth, shut it, and then opened it again.

Ant imagined if they were in a cartoon, smoke would be coming out of Martin's ears by this point. Instead the other man finally let all of his anger come out in a string of expletives.

Ant didn't pay much mind to it. He'd been cussed out of a job before. In fact, he had a bit of a track record. Some people had Employee of the Month awards. Ant collected You're Fired tirades. So he decided to tune out the angry Martin.

It was how he picked up that his phone was vibrating in his pocket so quickly.

"You know what, I'm going to take this," he interrupted Martin. "But how about I clean out my locker when I'm done and then we can call it a day?"

Ant didn't wait for an answer and walked outside, pulling out his phone as he went.

He might have played it cool to the small man behind him but he couldn't deny that cool turned into a shake-up in his stomach at the caller ID that was across his screen.

Ant cleared his throat and answered.

"Perez."

There was audible movement on the other side of the phone but the voice was crystal clear over it.

"Hi, Ant, it's Lillian. Lily. I'm assuming you got my voice mail last night?"

Ant nodded then felt foolish since she couldn't actually see him.

"Yeah, uh, I mean, yes, I got it," he answered. "I had a long day so I crashed early. Sorry I missed your call."

"That's fine. I was—" More movement. "Sorry, I'm going through some boxes. Um, yeah, I shouldn't have called so late."

There was a pause between them.

Ant opened his mouth and then closed it again. He bounced from one foot to the other.

Lily broke the small silence.

"The reason I called is— Wait, are you in the middle of anything?"

That he could answer quickly. In the background he could still hear Martin raving.

"Not anymore."

"Okay. Well, good, I guess." A sigh, so deep and genuine, came across the airwaves. It was a sound that Ant hadn't heard in a long, long time. Whatever Lily had called about she was about to bottom-line it. Ant prepared himself the best he could.

Which wasn't enough.

"The reason I called was because I think I might have found something," she said, her voice flat but firm.

His heartbeat sped up.

"You found something?"

They both knew what she was talking about but Lily spelled it out for him.

"Ida's case," she clarified. "Anthony, I think I found a new lead."

Chapter Two

Lily slipped the phone into her jacket pocket and stepped out into the rain. Her detective's badge swung against her chest at the movement. Her heartbeat was on a downward slope. She couldn't believe she'd called him. Yet she hadn't hesitated. Just like she didn't hesitate now.

Lily stilled her badge with one hand and waved an acknowledgment to the interim sheriff, Blake Bennet. Her long red hair was braided down her back, tight and unmoving. She'd been on the job two months longer than Lily had but had adjusted quickly, despite being from the city. Now she went back to eyeing the deep hole dug into the dark, wet dirt of the woods.

"It's a hole," Sheriff Bennet said in greeting.

Her Southern twang was deep but steady. She'd spent her thirty-four years between north Florida, east Georgia and south Alabama and could make a two-syllable word into five real quick. Lily had grown up in Kelby Creek and done a stint a little up north but had shaken the Southern accent.

Most of the time, at least. When she let out any foul language there was always a curve and syrupy swoop to it.

The sheriff motioned to where the dirt should have been flat and covered in grass and underbrush. Instead there was, true as she said it, a hole. Deep and narrow. Maybe six feet down, give or take.

Lily traced the space with her eyes.

"Yep. That's a hole, all right."

There was nothing in it.

Sheriff Bennet laughed.

"Not the call you were expecting while you were knee-deep in files, huh?"

The rain slacked off a little. Lily shrugged into her jacket.

"Not exactly. Though not the first time I've been called to look at a hole in the ground. I'm just excited that there's no one in it."

Lily wasn't kidding. Her last job had put her in the position to find a man buried in a ditch, killed by his brother. She'd also had the misfortune of being the detective on call who'd interrupted a man trying to actively bury a poor woman who'd simply been in the wrong place at the wrong time. Lily still had nightmares about that hole. She also still had the scar from the man when she'd fought him into custody.

Sheriff Bennet took a deep drink of her coffee. Her demeanor changed to no-nonsense quickly after.

"I know you're cold case task force so I thought I'd make sure this isn't any kind of—I don't know—Kelby Creek thing that, as an outsider, I wouldn't get." She motioned to the woods around them. "My only other thought was that it might be a hunter's trap. A poorly and incorrectly made hunter's trap."

Lily crouched down and inspected the edges of the hole. The weather had done a number on the dirt but she bet the hole was made with a shovel, not a human hand or animal paw. Not machinery, either. There were no tire tracks leading up to the spot from the dirt road behind them.

"If this is a hunter's trap, I'd agree it's a bad one," Lily decided after a moment. She rubbed her hands along her denim-clad thighs. "It's not far enough into the woods to be useful, never mind how deep and narrow it is."

"Any cold cases with something similar I should know about?"

Lily didn't have a photographic memory but she was damned good at remembering the details when it came to her work. To the men and women who'd been reduced to files on her desk through no fault of their own. It was the least she could do to sit up and pay attention when their stories were in her hands.

"There's nothing in the cold cases I've seen that deals with dug-out holes," Lily answered. "The only one that I've read that even has a mention of a hole was Jessica Tamblin's attack about seven years ago."

The sheriff's eyebrow went up at that. She'd made it clear to Lily that the cold case task force was under the supervision of Detective Gray and, unless it was pertinent to current cases, she was staying out of it. Not her circus, not her monkeys. A refreshing stance given that the cold case task force had been started because of rampant corruption among the higher-ups years ago.

Lily was glad for the extra space to go through the cases in her own way. It was something Detective Gray respected as well. She only gave him updates at their weekly morning meetings. Then she'd go back to her desk and dig in. She liked working solo, after all. A sentiment not shared by her coworker and desk mate, Detective Kathryn Juliet.

She was a chatterbox compared to Lily's relative quiet.

"Jessica Tamblin was floating the creek with some friends and lost her necklace. She went back the next day to look for it and found a man named Albert Johnson shooting up instead. He didn't appreciate the interruption and tried to attack her. She ran but didn't get far after stumbling across a hole. It was only mentioned in the report because the responding deputy tripped over it too and twisted his ankle pretty good."

The two women gazed down as the rain pitter-pattered off their jackets. It was light and had been part of a consistent rain that Kelby Creek had been entertaining for almost two weeks straight. It didn't bother Lily but made her dog, Cook, very grumpy.

"So maybe this is just a hole, then," Sheriff Bennet said. "Not some kind of serial killer's MO."

That got a snort from Lily.

"Of all the issues Kelby Creek has had, serial killers have thankfully not been a part of them."

The sheriff shook her head.

"You better knock on wood with that one. The second we rule something out, there's a good chance in the next second we'll be proven wrong."

Sheriff Bennet took a long pull of her coffee and then stretched.

"Either way I'm going to have someone come out and check on this thing in a few hours," she continued. "If only to satisfy the man who called it in. He was a bucket and a half of anxiety over it. He even made Deputy Park nervous."

The Flood, a nickname for the town-wide corruption investigation that followed Annie McHale's kidnapping, may have happened five years ago, but that didn't stop Kelby Creek as a whole from being anxious. It was as if the entire town had an itchy trigger finger. They could spend their whole lives holding that gun and never use it but, still, it was in their hands ready the second they were scared enough.

Lily didn't blame anyone. How could she after what happened?

Sheriff Bennet waited as Lily took notes, snapped a few pictures on her phone for good measure, before both walked back to the sheriff's truck. She hopped in and rolled down the window. The rain started to hit the black interior as she spoke.

"First night of the fair is tomorrow. I'm not sure what Gray told you but the department is setting up a booth along the thoroughfare. We're parking one of the deputy cruisers there so kids and curious adults alike can crawl through or take pictures with it. The fire department's doing the same. Since you're Cold Case I'm not going to ask you to go but it would be nice if you stopped by. Especially since this'll be the first time in a long while that the fair is actually back around here."

Lily had already known her answer before the sheriff had stopped speaking. Still she tried to look thoughtful before saying no.

"I've got a lot of work to do, but don't worry. I'm sure the rest of the department will have enough fun for me."

Sheriff Bennet snorted but she didn't try to dissuade her.

"Let us know if you change your mind." The sheriff started to roll up her window but paused. Her brow was creased in question. "What happened with Jessica Tamblin?"

Lily didn't pretend to ponder this question.

"She ended up making it to the creek and a fisherman who was nearby. Her attacker ran and was caught at his home later that night. Jessica, if I'm not mistaken, lives in Kipsy now. She has a kid and two dogs. Seems happy."

Sheriff Bennet nodded.

"It's nice to hear the wins sometimes."

Lily kept her mouth shut. When the headlights had disappeared past the trees, she went back to the hole.

It was nice to hear the wins.

It was impossible to forget the losses.

Her gaze lifted against the rain to the woods around her.

The weight of her phone in her pocket felt like it was pulling down her entire body.

She would never admit it but sometimes in the quiet of rain and in the kiss of darkness, Lily would see her there.

Arms outstretched, fingers trying to grasp anything—everything. Mouth open but only a strangled sound escaping around gasps for breath. The rain water between the tips of her fingers and the pounding of Lily's heart terrifyingly loud.

The boy drowning beneath its surface punctuating a life-altering choice.

Anthony or Ida?

The rain hitting the leaves of the trees around her back then quieted into the soft rain against Lily now.

She stared into the woods a little longer.

She heard the coughing in her mind. The man, coughing. Now she hoped it would be enough.

Enough to finally get some answers.

Enough to finally find him.

Lily didn't stare into the woods any longer.

She looked down at the hole, trying to dig herself out of the past.

Then she left.

A GREAT EXODUS had taken place during and after The Flood. When Lily came back to town a few months ago she had half expected Kelby Creek to be a partial ghost town. She'd been surprised to see that it was growing, and had been during her absence. She drove away from the sheriff's department that afternoon and headed toward the only bar in town, Rosewater Inn. Once a failing motel, it had been remodeled and expanded. Its parking lot was always full after her shift and tonight she counted fifteen cars in the parking lot as she stopped at a nearby light.

Depending on who rode with whom that was fifteen or so patrons inside.

Fifteen people Lily could connect with, talk to, become friends with.

Fifteen or more chances to expand a social group that no longer existed.

Fifteen people to question.

Fifteen people to wonder about.

Fifteen people to tell her they didn't remember Ida Perez.

Lily's foot pressed down on the gas the second the light went green. She took the street behind Rosewater and followed it to the far corner of Holly Grove. She hadn't been picky when house hunting but couldn't deny she liked the seclusion that being at the end of the last street in the neighborhood gave her. No one came her way unless they had an invitation. Or just needed to turn their car around.

The property also had a bigger yard, something her shiny black three-year-old Labrador, Cook, seemed to appreciate.

What he didn't appreciate was more rain.

Cook met Lily with a frenzy of tail wagging, tongue licking, and runs between her and the back door as soon as she was inside the two-story house.

"Since we have a dog door and you're more than proficient in using it, I'm going to assume you've already discovered it's still raining," she told him, taking care to scan him for any mud. Thankfully, Cook rarely dug, which helped keep the mud and dirt to hardwood floor and tile ratio at an acceptable level. If the rain got any harder, and kept on for two more weeks, then even Cook's good behavior wouldn't help.

Lily opened the baby gate she had latched at the bottom of the staircase, letting him know he was safe to go between floors. It was enough to make him forget all about going outside. He bounded up the stairs, yipping in excitement as he went.

"You'd think you don't sleep up there every single night by the way you fuss when I get home."

Cook gave her a well-timed bark. She shook her head and laughed.

Lily made her one-person dinner from a box and ate it on the couch with the TV on. *House Hunters* showed a family trying to find an old Colonial in Washington. She would have chosen the third house since it was closest to the wife's work but the family ended up going with the first home, something bigger so they could add onto their family in the coming years.

Lily twisted her fork around her "healthy" vegan pasta and thought about the two bedrooms upstairs. One was the master suite. The other was an office. She couldn't imagine it any other way.

It worked for her.

Her job wasn't just a job after all.

Lily finished her food and was debating going up to that same office when Cook jumped up from his spot on the floor next to her feet. He was gentle but flipped to defensive on a dime when it came to guarding Lily and their home. He ran to the door, emitting a low growl, before Lily even heard the doorbell.

"Cook, calm," she said, dipping her voice down. Lily

had her service weapon in hand by the time a knock followed the first ring. She looked into the peephole, already running through a list of people it could be.

When she saw the slightly blurred image of the man, she realized she hadn't included him as a possibility at all.

It couldn't be him.

Lily faced her service weapon down.

"Cook, go to your bed."

Cook listened. He went to his bed with a whine but settled.

It wasn't as easy for Lily. Her heartbeat had gone from an even keel to an all-out run. It thumped so hard in her chest she bet her shirt moved.

There was no way it was him.

Right?

Lily opened the door as if it was the first time she'd ever done so. Her inner voice was in total disbelief.

"Ant?"

It had been fourteen years since Anthony Perez had been close enough to touch. The time between felt like a lifetime and it felt like a minute. There was the man—and, goodness, what a man he was—standing on her front doorstep, dripping rain water onto the space where she needed a welcome mat. He was tall but broad, with well-defined muscles she guessed from the way his clothes fit him. The dark hair that had blended in with the night was longer and his face was covered in matching stubble and there was a look to him that let anyone with good eyesight know he wasn't some teenager anymore.

Yet, that was what Lily felt wash over her next. That familiar feeling of standing across from a teenaged Ant. Eyes dark and wild, chaotic energy barely contained in the way he moved and spoke. A boy who was on the cusp of being a man, despite the fact that they'd both been through more than most adults would ever experience.

Ant, the brother.

Ant, the broken.

Ant, the boy drowning in the creek.

There were just some things that time couldn't change— no matter if it was a minute or fourteen years.

For Lily, she was standing in front of a man and seeing the face of a boy in her lap, coughing up water and trying to make sense of the dark world around him.

The logical part of her brain knew that not only was he now a man, he was a man who that morning hadn't been in Kelby Creek.

"What are you doing here?"

Ant hadn't been smiling. He looked even unhappier now.

"What do you mean, *why am I here*?" His tenor caught her off guard, despite having heard it over the phone. It was brass and grit and so distinctly Ant Perez. It also sent a small shiver through her. She didn't have the time to figure out why.

"You're the one who called me about a new lead," he continued, all pointed syllables. "What was I supposed to do? Just sit around and wait for you to call again?"

Shiver or no shiver, fourteen years or not, Lily jutted out her hip in exasperation.

"Yes! Exactly that."

Ant shook his head. Water shucked off him.

"No way," he shot back. "I don't think so. You can't just call after all these years with a possible new lead and not expect me to run back here, ready to help. I'm part of this."

A boom of thunder put Lily further on edge.

"I said I thought I found a potential lead and that I'd call the moment I knew something," she countered. "I told you I'd keep you updated, not loop you into the investigation. I definitely didn't say for you to come back to Kelby Creek and directly to my home."

Lily's words were professional, analytical.

It was the only way she could handle seeing Ant in person.

Flip the emotional switch was her mantra when it came to work.

And when it came to what happened in the woods when they were teens.

She couldn't *feel* or she'd be overwhelmed.

Overwhelmed with guilt and shame and anger.

None of which would do them any good.

Ant didn't seem to be struggling in the holding-back department. His brow drew in, angry. He pointed a finger at her.

"I may not have a badge or some fancy desk at the department but this is *my* case, Lily. She was my sister. My responsibility. That makes anything new about this case something I need to know. So I'm here. And I'm not leaving town until you can prove to me that the lead is a dead end." His gaze switched to over her shoulder. It seemed to cool Ant a little. His anger transformed into stubbornness. That old familiar chaotic energy was swirling out of him as his parting words came out low and hard.

"I'll be back in the morning, and every morning, until then."

Chapter Three

Anthony was heated going back to his old Camaro at the curb. He could feel it beneath the collar of his shirt and in the tips of his fingers when opening the driver's side door.

Heat.

All-consuming heat.

It always happened when something about Ida's case didn't go his way. Not that there was a right way for it to go. There would never be a right way. Whatever answers he'd eventually get, Ant was realistic enough to know what the outcome would be.

Ida hadn't been seen in fourteen years.

No trace. No hints or even rumors about her or the man who had taken her.

Nothing.

She was gone. Ant knew it, Lily knew it, but that didn't mean he was going to stop looking for the who and why of it all.

Looking for justice.

Looking for vengeance.

Ant turned over his engine and sped out of the neighborhood, a feral growl of frustration mixing in with the rain beating against his windshield. He took a left at the first stoplight and parked in the lot for Rosewater Inn.

He stared at the neon open sign in the bar portion's window.

"Drinking isn't going to solve anything," he told himself. "It's just gonna give you a tab and a headache in the morning. That's all."

Anthony took a deep breath. He sank back in his seat when he let it out.

He hadn't expected his first in-person with Lily in years to go the way it had. After her call about a potential lead he had felt a pull back to town that was so strong that he'd up and left a half hour after their call had ended.

A pull from her.

A pull to the past.

Anthony had expected that to be met with some kind of feeling from Lily. He hadn't expected her to not want him there a lick. Every bit of her looked twisted at the sight of him. It had made his own twisted insides tighten.

He'd walked up that sidewalk to her front porch with each step collecting something new to feel.

The first step had excitement pulsing through his body. They had something. It was a potential lead. A path they hadn't traveled down yet. Not back then, not since. Something new.

Then that excitement turned to something heavy. He was about to see the only other person who understood what it had been like that night in the woods by the creek. Shared trauma and tragedy and commiseration he'd never been able to get from another person in fourteen years.

The nerves had set in next. A few steps of wading through the reality that Lily had obviously been doing things in her life that he hadn't. She'd taken her experience and turned it into a career of helping others. He'd… gone down a different path. One he wasn't always proud of.

Would she see that in him?

Would she look down her nose at his mistakes?

Those nerves had then melted into an anxiousness that had been a powder keg with a quickly burning fuse.

And when Lily had opened the door?

Anthony had felt everything all at once.

Shame, excitement, anxiety, pain, and then utter appreciation.

Lily Howard wasn't just all grown up, she was all grown up and beautiful.

Her hair was longer but still the caramel swirl of light brown and reddish-blond that framed a teardrop face full of focus, freckles, and with eyes that were the color of the forest beneath the moonlight. She was still well below his height but the way she held herself had been more noticeable. More prominent and filled with confidence. Lily Howard wasn't a woman that blended in with the crowd.

She was also no longer the girl by the creek, hair hanging down into her face, telling him to breathe while the rain danced around them.

She was a woman who hadn't wanted him there. Something about that had been too much. He'd been rude because of it. Abrasive. He'd all but ambushed her. There was no way around it. The only reason he'd come to his senses was because of the baby gate at the bottom of the stairs behind her.

She wasn't the girl by the creek.

She was a woman, at night, standing in her home with a life he was interrupting.

Anthony ran a hand through his hair, heat seeping out like a balloon deflating.

His anger, his frustration. He hadn't meant to aim them at her of all people.

He'd apologize tomorrow. When he was outside her home in the morning.

Because no matter what he felt for Lily Howard, Ant was still back in town for Ida.

Ant sat there a few minutes more trying to decide whether to go into the bar or head to the hotel just outside Kelby Creek. It wasn't the greatest place but he didn't need much. He never did. Ant was always acutely aware that what he had was just one more thing Ida never would. It made appreciating the small things easy. It made missing the big things a passing feeling.

The rain lessened after a few minutes. Ant took it as a sign. He started his car again and was hoping the hotel wasn't full up when he pulled out of the lot.

Another sign came his way before he could even turn onto the road.

On the other side of the intersection was none other than Lily in her car. No one was in the passenger seat but she kept turning toward the back. In between the turn-arounds Ant could see she wasn't exactly riding easy. Her eyebrows were drawn in and her mouth twisted down. She was focused. And it didn't seem like a good thing she was focusing on.

Ant waved in her direction but the light turned green and she was gone the second it did.

She wasn't just driving. She was heading somewhere with purpose greasing her pedals.

Ant's light turned green a bit later.

He didn't need any more signs.

He pulled out his phone and dialed the number Lily had called him from earlier that morning.

She didn't pick up.

Ant stared down the straightaway she'd just taken.

Not a car in sight.

Wherever she was going, she was going there fast.

COOK WAS HAVING a good ol' time in the back seat. He was a dog born to ride in the car. Never was the boy happier than when he was pressed against worn cloth and staring outside as the world flashed by. It didn't matter that it was raining and dark. Or that his human was in a foul mood.

Lily hadn't handled Ant's sudden appearance with the most grace. Berating him wouldn't have been her first choice but, at the same time, she wasn't about to be talked down to on her own front porch.

Watching him walk away in a well-deserved huff had only put her in a mood. She'd scrapped her earlier plan of showering and heading straight to bed and was ready to head to her office when her phone had gone off. It had been one of the new hires at the Dawn County Sheriff's Department. A deputy named Sterling Costner. He couldn't find the hole in the ground that Lily and Sheriff Bennet had been pontificating over earlier that day.

Deputy Costner wasn't new to town by any means but he had admitted that his time in that stretch of the woods in Kelby Creek had been limited. He'd looked for the hole, found nothing, looked a little more, then had gotten a call from his wife, Mel. His words were drenched in worry when he admitted that she wasn't just pregnant but the kind of pregnant that had her throwing up most hours of any waking day. He also didn't step around the fact that her seasickness bands that he was supposed to take home to help her were locked in his truck instead. Lily hadn't needed anything past that. Sure, she wasn't jonesing to go out into the woods at night to look for a hole but what else did she have going for her as an alternative?

Nothing but thinking about Ant, Ida and how she hadn't managed to help either.

Lily had assured Sterling that she could more than handle the task and invited her sidekick Cook along for the ride. It would, at the very least, work out some of their excess energy.

Plus, it was no secret that Lily Howard had once known every part of the woods in Kelby Creek. That went double for the creek itself.

The road was a little washed out but she got to the point where she had parked her car earlier without issue. She parked back a little farther than before so her headlights could illuminate what her flashlight couldn't. The trees lit up like an eerie Christmas. Cook whined in the back seat as she parked.

"I'm not leaving you in the car," she assured him as she got out. "Don't worry."

Lily opened up the back door and patted her leg. Cook bounded out in a flash, yipping playfully. She caught his collar and connected his leash to it. Nine times out of ten the leash wouldn't be needed but Lily wasn't taking her chances with the location.

Kelby Creek's woods ate people whole and those they didn't, they spat out with missing pieces.

"I'll let you run wild at the house," she told him after another loud whine. "Here, you're with me."

Cook stayed at her side and followed her and the beam of her flashlight away from the car. The trees around them stood sentry against the rain and wind. The dirt beneath their feet was now a mass of mush. Lily still followed the landscape with ease.

Yet where there was supposed to be a hole, there was nothing but mud and leaves.

Lily blinked down at the spot for a few moments. Her flashlight beam skittered along the ground like a scanner after a tricky barcode. Lily backtracked to the car, checked for the subtle landmarks she'd followed in before—the tree on the other side of the road that must have been struck by lightning, and the dip in the dirt that had been made from water runoff—and then went back to the same spot.

Still no hole.

"I guess someone filled it," she told Cook.

Even as she said the words, Lily didn't like them. They didn't feel right. They didn't sit right. A creeping feeling trickled down her back. The dark around her, the rain against her slicker and the mud beneath her feet fused together to make a pit in her stomach.

A pit she'd more than felt before.

For all the things Lily knew of the victims in her cold cases, very few of the living knew about what she'd become after Ida's kidnapping. Sure, professionally her life fit neatly on paper. She'd become determined, singularly focused, and driven to law enforcement after a traumatic event.

But personally? Emotionally? That had been a challenge.

She'd gone to counseling at the insistence of her parents and had been treated for post-traumatic stress and triggers. Gotten tips on how to avoid, deal with, and cope with both. She'd had setbacks and breakthroughs and had gotten the okay from her counselor to make it her choice whether to seek further treatment. Years later and that same counselor was why Cook had come into her life. He'd begun training as a PTSD service dog but, due to budget cuts, hadn't completed the training. Still, he was a companion. A smart, well-behaved friend who could pull Lily out of her own head when she went too deep.

Like when she was standing in the darkness. In the rain. In the mud.

Her hand clutched the flashlight. Her heartbeat sped up. The rain became louder, her breathing with it.

"Just because I'm here doesn't mean that he is, too."

Lily spoke the words softly, a mantra that she had to recite on occasion. Cook, already sensing her rising anxiety, licked her hand. If that didn't work she knew he'd nudge her next, trying to get her to pet him. If that didn't work he'd try to bring her something to play fetch with.

She didn't know what happened if those three methods failed. She'd been lucky enough to snap out of her episodes before finding out.

Lily felt the warmth of Cook's fur against her fingertips. She focused on it.

"Thanks," she said after a moment. "I'm—"

A stick cracked a few feet behind her.

The word *okay* flew back down her throat and ran into her heart there.

She spun around.

It was a man. Or, rather, a silhouette of one standing just inside the beams of her headlights. That silhouette was alarmingly tall. He also had his hands in the air.

The details filtered in next.

Dark hair, a low-slung vehicle parked on the road just behind her car.

Anthony.

"I tried calling," he yelled out. "You weren't answering."

"So you followed me?" Lily's voice cracked. It caught her by surprise. "First my house and now this?"

Ant was nonplussed by her anger. Maybe because it wasn't true anger at all. Her heart was still racing and the rain was still loud. He didn't move a muscle.

"I saw you driving and you looked a little freaked. When I saw you pull in here, I wanted to make sure you were okay."

Lily made a loud noise of strangled frustration.

"I'm fine," she exclaimed, rain running down her nose from the wet tangles of her hair.

Ant was obviously not convinced.

His voice was calm and even when he responded.

"Then why do you still have your gun pointing at me?"

It was as if someone had thrown back a curtain. All at once Lily saw her service weapon aimed at Ant and felt her viselike grip on it and the flashlight she'd tucked beneath the butt.

She hadn't even realized that she'd pulled the weapon out.

"That's what happens when you get surprised by someone stalking you," she responded hotly. Lily returned her weapon to the holster at her hip. "At night. For the second time."

Ant lowered his hands.

At the sound of Cook barking, Lily realized she had dropped his leash when she'd gotten gun-happy.

"Cook, come!"

But the Lab stayed behind her, just outside the trees. He kept barking.

It wasn't at them.

Lily pointed her flashlight's beam down and hurried over. Cook's nose was in the dirt.

Right where the hole was supposed to be.

"What is it?" Ant appeared at her side, eyes on the ground.

"There was a hole here earlier today. Someone called it in but we didn't find anything weird other than the hole itself. The sheriff wanted us to come back out and check on it." Lily crouched down. Cook was insistent on something. He wasn't just touching the dirt. He was nosing it hard enough that it was displacing. More concerning was he hadn't even alerted to Ant's presence. "I came out here because the deputy that was supposed to check on it couldn't find it."

Lily placed the flashlight on the ground. She put her hand on the damp dirt. This only seemed to rally Cook. He started digging with his front paws.

That feeling, that pit in her stomach, started to tighten.

Her body must have registered something her mind hadn't yet caught up to. Lily lowered her head and turned her ear to the ground.

It was only the second after she'd done it that she understood why.

"I—I can hear something."

The world around her seemed to fade away.

Then she heard it again.

A scream.

Muffled, but definitely a scream.

And it was coming from beneath her hand.

Lily looked up, ice filling her veins.

"Anthony, I think someone's buried under here."

Chapter Four

Ant had big hands. Big, calloused hands from manual labor and years of hard work. When he left Kelby Creek, he didn't set out to pursue one single trade. He just aimed to survive for a while. Survive until he could find the truth. Then, maybe, he could start really living.

There was also real power behind his hands. Years of surviving came right up along years of preparing.

He'd made a promise to himself the day after Ida had been taken.

He wouldn't give another attacker the satisfaction of besting him in a fight and he certainly would never again be that boy with his eyes closed in the creek water.

In the end it all added up to big, strong hands ready for anything.

That included digging into the wet earth.

Ant plunged his fingers down into the mud and threw back the dirt, knees sinking down into the ground a little with each handful. Lily was right beside him, digging in a frenzied rush. Even her dog was doing his part.

It wasn't long before he hit something hard.

Anthony's fingers stubbed against the immovable object less than a foot down.

"Flashlight!"

Lily moved the beam over his shoulder and into the hole they'd made.

Ant brushed the dirt aside. "It's wood."

Lily's hair brushed against his shoulder as she peered over into the circle of light.

"That wasn't here this morning."

On cue another scream sounded.

This time he could make out a word.

"Help!"

Anthony dug back in, scooping out the dirt until the wood stopped.

"It's a box," he yelled. "She's buried in a box!"

Lily dropped back to her knees as they furiously tried to move more dirt aside to open the top of the container. Ant could make out one hinge on the side but the top had no openings. No handles. He ran his fingers along where there should have been a lip, looking for a latch or something he could undo to open it.

There was nothing.

If the box opened, it wasn't from the direction they were looking down on.

"We're going to have to break it open."

He shook his head trying to get a purchase on the corner. There were no slats or holes. Whoever was inside had to be low on oxygen and only getting lower.

"I can't get it," he grunted out.

The wood was firm.

There was nothing he could do with his bare hands.

"I might have something in the car," Lily said. "I'll call this in, too."

Lily was up and running. Her dog went with her, barking.

The rain continued to fall, not caring about their situation.

"Hang on," Ant yelled down to the woman in the box. "We'll get this open!"

Ant got lower and threw all of his strength into digging out one side. It wasn't a successful move. There was no way he could dig it out by hand in time. He needed a shovel. The box had to have been standing straight up. That meant if there was a latch on the side or the bottom it would be a while before they could get to it.

A while the woman probably didn't have.

"Can you hear me?" he called out.

He waited for the woman to answer.

She just kept screaming for help.

It was a haunting sound.

Ant tried to pull at the box again. He slipped and a splinter tore into his hand.

"Hurry, Lily!"

Ant balled his fist. If they couldn't find something to break into it, he'd have to make his fists do the job. A few broken knuckles was a worthy price to pay for freeing someone buried alive.

He flexed his hand, ready, but Lily's dog's barks became noticeably louder.

Then the growling started.

Ant spun around at the sound. So did Lily right next to the car.

Together they saw what her dog was alerting them to.

It was the only reason she had time to throw herself to the side as a man in a yellow rain slicker lunged at her, a shovel swinging down in his hand.

LILY DIDN'T HAVE time to make a noise. She barely had time to move as the shovel crashed into the ground next to her. The wind from the swing was as unsettling as Cook's snarling.

Lily's shoulder connected with the ground as she went down. Her cheek hit the dirt next. There wasn't even a breath of time to dwell on the pain as her attacker recovered instantly from his missed hit.

He swung the shovel back up like a human pendulum and put the force of both hands around the wood. It was going to be a devastating blow, no matter where it hit her. Lily struggled to move enough so that the shovel wouldn't be the last thing she saw. With the heels of her boots she tried to push herself backward.

The mud was unforgiving.

One boot slipped along the wet ground and that was enough. She lost her only opening to avoid a painful fate. And the attacker knew it. He brought the shovel down with startling quickness.

Somehow it stopped in midair.

In the glow of the flashlight that had fallen to the ground, Ant appeared, his hand wrapped around the wood of the shovel, holding it back with apparent ease.

Lily gaped up at him, awestruck.

He said only one word to the man in the rain slicker before turning the tide.

"No."

The shovel came out of Rain Slicker's hand just as Cook's growls turned into a bite. The man roared in pain. He kicked out on what must have been reflex. Or pragmatism. Fight the thing dealing you current damage, not the thing that's coming next.

And boy, was Ant coming next.

The man kicked out at Cook again. Lily was pulled to her feet by Cook's yelp right as Ant put the mystery man on his tail with a momentum-infused arc of the shovel. The metal thunked against the man's arm with audible force.

He stumbled back. Cook kept his distance but was back to growling.

Ant readied for another swing while Lily went for her gun.

Neither had the chance to follow through.

The man might have been outnumbered but he was deceptively fast. One second he was fighting for footing among the mud, the next he was spinning. He did a 180 and charged Ant.

Momentum won out again. This time not in their favor.

The men collided and hit the ground. Ant made a noise at the impact and the shovel fell to the mud. Rain Slicker started to wail fists against him. Enraged, Lily sprang into action. Instead of going for the gun and possibly shooting the very man she was trying to help, Lily scooped up the shovel.

It only seemed fair since she was the only one who hadn't used it yet.

Thunder clapped overhead, rain kept falling, and Lily brought the shovel down on their attacker's back like she was gunning for a prize at the fair.

He roared in pain. Gut-twisting, can't-get-out-of-your-head pain.

Lily tried to use that pain. She went for his wrist to attempt a pin. Ant seemed to pick up on the attempt and tried to flip the man, grunting at the effort.

But once again, Rain Slicker was a surprise and a half.

He pulled Lily forward. The second she fell was the second he threw a punch.

Pain lit up behind her eyes as his fist collided with her jaw. She clenched her teeth, willing herself not to pass out, but she knew she was going to feel it in the morning.

Ant made an ugly noise and charged the attacker, connecting several blows. The man in the slicker became the man on his back.

After a few more hits the man went limp, his hands slapping the wet ground beneath him.

Lily held her breath, waiting for another attack.

It didn't come.

Instead Cook ran up and licked at her cheek.

"Are you okay?" Ant looked down to meet Lily's eyes. There was blood dripping down from his eyebrow and lip.

Lily shook herself. "Yeah. Yeah, I'm okay. You?"

Ant nodded but he wasn't staying put long.

"He's out. Can you restrain him with something? Cuffs or ties?"

Lily reached out and touched Cook. He seemed okay, too.

She nodded.

"I have ties in my car."

Ant pushed himself off the ground and grabbed the discarded shovel. He ran over back to their original goal.

The woman buried in the box.

Lily struggled to her feet. She threw Cook into the back seat and shut the car door quickly behind the dog. She backtracked to where she'd dropped her phone when Rain Slicker had first attacked. Their night dispatcher, Janet Kim, took her hurried call in stride. A marvel considering she'd already called in their earlier situation and that had been dire enough.

"I need both hands so I'm hanging up," she told Janet. "The guy in yellow is the baddie. Don't touch the man with the black hair."

Lily ended the call and grabbed the crowbar from her trunk. Her ties came next.

She made quick work of hog-tying Rain Slicker before binding his hands and feet. The adrenaline from the fight started to fade as she went through the motions. It ushered in more pain. It also put an extra urgency on the noise behind her. If she was hurting, she couldn't imagine what the woman in the box was going through.

A shovel biting into dirt. A man grunting with exertion. Rain continuing to make the effort more difficult.

Ant trying to save a woman who Rain Slicker must not have wanted saved.

Lily bypassed the urge to do more than a quick search to see that he wasn't carrying any weapons and high-tailed it to Ant. It was amazing how much he'd shoveled out around the box in the short time she'd been at the car.

"This thing opens from the side," he huffed at her as he dug and flung the dirt over his shoulder. The blood on his face mixed with the rain but the dripping water could not wash away his determined expression. "Like a coffin standing up. It's gonna be hard to break open without being dug all the way out."

But that didn't stop him from trying. Ant took the crowbar after digging out some more space. He'd uncovered, she guessed, half of the box. True to his own guess, there was an obvious gap that ran up to the corner next to the top. It was a lid.

Ant jammed the head of the crowbar into the small opening.

"Move away from my voice," he yelled out to the woman inside. "I'm breaking the box!"

He pushed against the bar. Nothing happened for a moment. Then the wood made a cracking sound.

Lily grabbed the shovel and put the metal blade into the small opening the crowbar was making. When it caught, she also started to push against it. For a moment that was all they did.

Using leverage and gravity to try to break the box open while a woman screamed for help over and over again.

Not at all what Lily had expected of the night.

Not at all what she'd expected to deal with during her career.

That didn't mean she felt any less grateful when the slow cracking became a fast break.

The box splintered open at the top, breaking at the force of their tools. Lily fell back onto the dirt outside the hole. Ant went in the other direction. He dropped the crowbar and started pulling at the remaining wood with his bare hands.

The next board wasn't as quick to snap but it eventually gave way. Lily scrambled over to see into the new opening, ready to assess how hurt the woman was, who she was, and to assure her that she was all right.

But when Ant pulled back the board, the yelling didn't skip a beat.

Which was confusing, considering there was no woman in the box at all.

"What in the—" Ant reached his hand through the opening and snaked it downward. He got a hold of something and pulled it back out, hands covered in dirt, rain and blood.

The woman's yells were louder now.

Ant turned to her, holding something slightly bigger than his hand up in the rain between them. The screams for help were coming out of it with a crispness that was disarming.

Lily took the object from Ant's hand.

"It's a tape recorder," she said. "The play button is taped down. It's on a loop."

Ant looked from it and then back to the box.

His voice was loud and angry when he spoke.

"What the hell is going on here?"

Chapter Five

Ant was leaning against the break room counter, Cook lying asleep at his feet. Lily Howard was standing tall and absolutely in her element, though soaked to the bone.

"I need to question our attacker. I have a list of questions I want answered," she told Detective Foster Lovett. A man who Ant was actually familiar with but hadn't seen since they were teens. "And that's why I want to investigate this," Lily continued, her voice as even as a tightrope. "I'm motivated to find the answers."

Foster opened his mouth to probably buck Lily's demand again but paused when a dark-skinned woman with a round, very pregnant belly walked in. Ant recognized her from a story in the local paper a few years back. It was Millie, Foster's wife. Someone else who had dealt with a sibling disappearing.

Lucky for both of them they'd gotten a happy ending.

Millie had a small bag of ice packs she'd gotten from the drugstore. The gel kind that felt nice no matter how bad a shiner you were rocking. Millie handed him the biggest of the bunch. He nodded to her but then handed it to Lily. She took it without a word, her eyes still on Foster. Ant took a smaller pack for his eyebrow. It had stopped bleeding but he knew his skin was still stained from it.

"You're going to give a statement but you aren't going

to talk to him now," Foster stated when Lily pressed the pack to her jaw. "You're dripping wet, bloodied and tired. We can handle questioning the guy. Detective Reiner is already at the site with Sheriff Bennet. You can go home and tomorrow we can go over your questions."

"We were there from go to stop," Ant piped up. "Lily should be asking that guy questions before any of you even introduce yourselves. Sidelining her because she's got mud on her boots and a little blood on her clothes makes as much sense as a recorder being buried in a box."

Lily didn't look at him but Ant saw her give a little nod. Foster wasn't convinced.

"We have protocols that we need to stick to now," he tried again. "Ones that go into effect after a law enforcement—involved altercation."

"I wasn't on the clock," Lily said.

Foster shook his head. "Doesn't mean you're a civilian. And it doesn't mean we're going to let you talk to the man." Foster pinched his nose and sighed. "Go home. Come back in the morning. That's the best I'm going to do, especially since our perp is currently being evaluated at the hospital. Instead of rattling around here, waiting, at least get that dog a bone and yourself some dry clothing. Okay?"

Ant knew that Lily wasn't happy with her options but she gave a curt nod all the same.

"Do I need to call Detective Gray or have you already notified him?" Lily's voice had changed a little but Ant couldn't figure out which end of the emotional spectrum it had gone toward.

Foster nodded. "We were actually with him and his wife, Willa, when I got the call. He'll be here bright and early tomorrow, too."

If there was any more hesitation in Lily, it seemed to leave at that. Ant pushed off the counter and whistled.

Cook was up and alert in a flash. His tail was wagging as they followed Lily out.

"I need to go by my office really quick," she said over her shoulder. Ant turned with her and soon they were in a somewhat large room with three desks, several filing cabinets and a few boxes neatly organized.

Lily glanced back at the door. She went to one of the two desks butted up against each other and bent low. Ant got the impression that whatever she was doing, she didn't want the head detective or his wife to see. He stepped back to block the door. Cook sat next to him, tail still wagging.

Lily pulled an accordion folder from a drawer. She tucked it under her arm, despite still being wet from the rain. Ant eyed her desk as she looked in another drawer. The top was neat. Just an orderly set of pens and a computer monitor.

That was it.

No framed pictures. No knickknacks.

Just order.

It fit her.

"All right. I'm ready."

Lily was pressing the folder tight against her while they made their exit out of the sheriff's department. She didn't offer any explanation when they stopped next to her car in the parking lot and let Cook into the back seat.

He wasn't going to pry.

Not after the night they'd had.

"That's a good dog," Ant said instead. "He was one heck of an alarm and then a fighting buddy when we needed him."

Lily was hovering between their cars. She nodded but it was easy to see she wasn't all there. The parking lot's lone light showed a woman with a jaw that was bruised and wet hair that was dark from the rain. Ant reached out, ducking his chin down a little for a better angle to see the other mark on her cheek. He skimmed the scratched area with his thumb, careful not to apply too much pressure.

"I guess getting the equivalent of rug burn from the ground is better than getting a shovel to the back," he reasoned. Then he made a face. "But still, I'm not happy seeing it. Does it sting?"

Lily took a step back, just out of reach. She shook her head.

"Only when I focus on it so I'm not going to focus on it. What about you?" She didn't touch him, or even reach for him. Her eyes were the only thing that moved.

"I've had much worse than a busted lip and a split eyebrow before. Nothing some more ice and maybe a beer can't handle."

If Lily had been someone else, maybe a woman he'd dated in the past, he thought she might follow up to make sure he wasn't putting on a brave face. But Lily was, well, Lily. She took him at his word. The silence that followed didn't leave a nice taste in his mouth, though. He broke it quickly.

"I think it's a load of crock you aren't at the hospital now, talking to that guy," he said. "You've already proven you can handle yourself. Plus, we found the box and, considering he had the shovel, I'm assuming he dug the hole. Not hard math for anyone, and baby stuff for a detective like you."

Ant thought he saw a smile try to show itself on her face. He wasn't sure if it was his imagination or not. Either way, Lily made a noise that sounded dangerously close to contempt.

"I'm too emotionally close to this," she said. "Sometimes it's hard to keep yourself in line during something like this. It was the right call. Even if we don't like it."

Ant thought of Ida.

He knew Lily went there, too.

If she was too emotionally invested in the man in the slicker and the buried box, what did that mean for Ida's investigation? Had Lily stripped out her feelings for what had happened? Had she moved on but was just trying to see it through for him?

Ant could have asked her—he could have asked her several times over throughout the years—but, like always, he kept his mouth shut.

They could talk about Ida's case but they never talked about what happened. Not in detail. Not about the creek.

He wasn't going to start now.

Lily sighed. She wrung out her hair over her shoulder.

"It's late," she said. "And Foster isn't wrong. We're all in dire need of a change and a shower. Everything else we can talk about tomorrow. Where are you staying?"

Ant had been thinking about a hotel earlier. Now his mind went to the Camaro.

"It's between a hotel and my car," he said, honestly. "I'm not picky about where I sleep and I'm not sure I'm up to driving out of Kelby Creek tonight."

He refrained from telling her that he really wasn't up for leaving her. Ant could no more get the image of the man bringing down the shovel on Lily out of his head than he could bring himself to call the hotel to see if there were any vacancies. Instead he shrugged. It wasn't a big deal to sleep in his car. He'd done it before.

"What about your cousin?" Lily asked. "Don't you normally stay with her when you come to town?"

It surprised Ant that Lily knew he came to town on occasion. Then again, hadn't they talked on the phone a few years back when he'd been with Shandra? Maybe her memory was just that good. Ant did get the feeling that Lily had a knack for being detail-oriented. It was part of the job, right?

He nodded. The pain in his brow throbbed at the movement.

"I do but it's a full house now that her father-in-law is bunking there along with the kids. I don't want to get in the way, especially since I didn't call ahead and it's late."

Lily eyed him in a way she hadn't before. Like she was tallying up invisible data. She cocked her head to the side a little.

"If you don't mind bunking on my couch, you can stay with me tonight," she said, simply. "Me and Cook, that is. He sleeps in a crate in my room so he wouldn't bother you."

Ant wanted to say that there was nothing that Cook could do to bother him after what the dog had done out in the woods. Instead he asked if she was sure.

"I really don't mind hanging in my car," Ant added. "You were right earlier. You didn't ask for me to come to town and you definitely weren't expecting me, either."

He recalled the baby gate at the stairs. He also, not for the first time, tried to peek at her hand to see if a ring was on it, but Lily nodded and that was that.

"You stopped a shovel from ruining my day. Offering my couch is the least I can do."

Ant ignored the excitement that stirred in him. He wasn't in Kelby Creek for Lily, after all. Only for her lead. Her small lead she hadn't explained to him yet.

Now he wouldn't have to wait on her doorstep in the morning for that conversation.

Now all he had to do was wake up in her living room.

That's why he was excited.

Right?

"Okay, then," he said after a moment. "Lead the way."

COOK WASN'T THE only one shaking off when they were stopped at the garage door leading into the house. Lily's clothes were still soaked and her jeans had adhered to her skin by means of mud. Both had her feeling all kinds of ick. Cook, though, didn't seem to mind his new weight. His tail was wagging as he nosed the door.

"If you think for a second that I'm going to let you run around wearing all of that mud, you have another think coming, buddy."

Lily slid her rain jacket off and hung it up on one of the hooks next to the door. She took her boots off next, deciding the wet socks would just have to stay in the garage for the night. Her hair was already up in a messy bun and she was sure the light makeup she'd been wearing was now washed away. She rolled her neck around to dispel some of the tension and started to slip her fingers under the hem of her shirt. She caught herself before she could lift it over her stomach.

For once, she wasn't alone.

A car door shut in the distance. The security light outside the garage came to life.

Ant made his way through the circle of light with a backpack. It was the only thing he was wearing from his waist up.

He was just a man in his jeans and shoes, bloodied and bruised.

And looking every bit as strong as Lily had suspected him to be.

His torso didn't move as he walked up to meet her. It was a wall of hardened muscle.

She wasn't exactly sure what all Anthony Perez had been up to over the past fourteen years but she'd put money on the fact that he definitely worked out.

"My shirt didn't even make the drive. I had to chuck it

in the parking lot trash can before I followed you," he explained, motioning to his chest.

Lily felt her face heat. She adjusted her gaze to the key ring in her hand and cleared her throat. Then tried to play it off as a small cough. She wasn't sure if she hit the mark.

"I'm definitely going to have to start a new load of laundry ASAP if I have any hope of saving mine." Cold air burrowed into her wet clothes as the door to the house opened. It was all Cook needed to begin his own personal race. He was off into the dark house with excited yips and the sound of nails on hardwood. "I'm also going to have to give that one a bath before he destroys the house!"

Cook had the zoomies. There was no denying that. He went from lapping up some water from his bowl in the kitchen to running full speed into the living room. Despite the pain pulsing through various parts of her body, Lily had to give chase.

"Crap! I forgot to put up the gate! He's going to go straight to my bed!"

Lily followed the Lab through the hall, around a quick loop in the guest bathroom, and was hot on his heels when he barked excitedly through the living room. She was already imagining the additional laundry she'd have to do once the mud-covered dog rocketed himself onto her clean bed.

"Not so fast there, buddy!"

Ant was at the foot of the stairs, crouched and with his arms held open wide. The baby gate was secured behind him, blocking the steps.

Cook crashed into him, giving off a stray bark for good measure. Despite the gate, the dog couldn't have been happier to have a fresh face to lick. His tail thudded against the hardwood like a ticking clock.

Lily took a second to catch her breath, listening to Ant laugh at the dog trying to lap up his face.

"Thanks," Lily breathed out. "You just saved my bed-spread."

"Not a problem." Ant found a good spot behind Cook's ear to scratch. "Want me to help you corral him into the bathroom?"

Lily wasn't going to say it but she was surprised at Cook's trust in Ant, a relative stranger. Maybe it had to do with the fact that Ant had helped them in the fight.

Either way Lily was grateful for the offer. Together they got Cook into the guest bathroom without any fuss. Lily motioned to upstairs when they were settled.

"You can take the baby gate down and head upstairs to the bathroom for your own shower," she offered. "Cook is a great dog but this might take a bit."

"You sure? I don't mind helping."

"You've already helped a lot tonight," she said with a quick shake of her head. "Showering is your reward."

Ant laughed and the motion lit up his eyes. It was quite the contrast to his bloodied eyebrow and split lip. As they'd wrestled with Cook a moment ago, she'd finally caught a glimpse of his knuckles, busted and caked in blood, and wanted nothing more than for him to rest.

"All right. I won't be long. Reward or not, I'm not a shower hog."

He disappeared upstairs while Cook received a quick but thorough bath. Lily brushed her hand over his fur and skin and examined both. As far as she could tell there were no injuries from their attacker. Still, it boiled her blood and hurt her soul to hear her dog whimper during the fight. Had she known there was even a remote possibility that going to check on the hole would lead to him being in danger...

Lily dropped the towel she'd been using to dry the dog. She buried her head in the fur of his neck.

"You're definitely sleeping with me tonight, wet or not," she whispered.

Cook just kept wagging his tail.

Lily emerged from the bathroom, exhausted. Cook went to the baby gate and sat down next to it, as if he knew what she'd just offered. Ant was already back in the living room, this time with a shirt on.

The bruising on his face was easier to see now that he was cleaned up.

Lily wasn't a fan of it, either. She wanted to say something, a lot of something, but the world of what had happened between them felt too large.

And she was tired.

"I'll grab some blankets and pillows," was all she said before going to the linen closet.

Ant was quiet when she handed them over. He stayed quiet when she finally spoke.

"Help yourself to any food, drink or ice packs in the kitchen. I'm going to shower now and try to get some sleep. You should, too."

Ant stared at her for a second. No words, just dark eyes on her.

Lily saw him standing there one second, then saw him stopping the shovel in the next.

"No."

It would have sent a shiver through her had she not felt her body being dragged down by pain and the need to rest.

She also didn't want to think about what would have happened had he not been there. If she'd been caught by the man, alone.

Then, as it often did, the present dissolved into a memory of the past.

Ant wasn't in Kelby Creek to save her.

And Lily could tell that he'd remembered that fact, too.

Ant's words were low but calm. He took a step forward, the pillow still in his hand.

"We've had a night of it, I'll give you that, but the world could stop spinning and it wouldn't keep me from asking about her. About Ida. You of all people should know that."

Lily did. She said as much.

"I do."

Ant took another step closer. As if being near her would help transfer what she knew right into him.

"This morning you said you had a potential lead and then you asked me if I remembered Ida's abductor coughing when we were in the woods." He shook his head a little. His stare never wavered from her. "You've asked me a lot of questions through the years...but you've never asked me that. Why? What changed?"

Lily didn't want to answer; she didn't want to lie. So she simplified her response, for brevity's sake.

"A man named Bryant Lautner was pulled over for speeding an hour before Ida was taken. The deputy let him go with a warning because he couldn't stop coughing and the deputy didn't want to get sick." Lily felt the slight adrenaline surge she'd gotten when first reading the report. The memory of that horrible night pushed in next. "When we first chased after the man and Ida into the woods, I couldn't find them for a second. It was too dark. The rain was in my eyes. But then I heard him coughing. That's how I knew which direction to run in."

If Ant had been sitting, Lily bet dollars to doughnuts he would have jumped up at that. His entire body went taut. Cook alerted to him with a nudge at his hand.

"And this Bryant Lautner, where is he now?"

Lily held up her hands to stop him. He had already

jumped down the rabbit hole, no questions asked. She didn't need that from him. Not right now.

"That's what I've been trying to find out. You were going to be my first call after I did."

Ant's look of skepticism stung at that. He didn't believe her.

She wasn't sure she believed her, either.

It was such a small lead and they'd been burned before. If she hadn't needed his answer—to know if he remembered the man coughing for reassurance that she was remembering right—Lily might not have included Ant in it at all.

Why give him the burden of reliving the heartbreak of losing his sister all over again? She hadn't wanted to, unless it was necessary.

Right now, it wasn't.

Before he could wind up, Lily walked to the stairs.

"I'll see you in the morning, Ant," she said, voice hard. "Try to get some sleep."

She was done talking. By the look in his eye, he knew it, too. He accepted it but not without his lips deepening into a frown.

"You too."

His voice was far-off.

Lily went up the stairs. A world of pain and memories stretched between them.

She doubted either one of them would get a good sleep tonight.

Chapter Six

The sheets were cold. Smooth and cold.

Light from the hallway plug-in reached through the space of the open door. The blackout curtains were doing their job, though the darkness from the rain hitting the roof above definitely helped.

Lily rolled over and stretched her hand out. There was no fur or wiggle of warmth next to her. She opened her eyes wider and tried to focus in the mostly dark room.

Cook wasn't on the bed.

She rolled over and peered down at his crate. She'd left it open the night before in case Cook wanted to fall into routine. Then she'd promptly fallen asleep with him at her side. He wasn't in either spot now.

Which meant he was downstairs.

And so was Ant.

Lily's stomach tightened on reflex.

Anthony Perez was in her house. On her couch. All these years later.

She didn't know how to feel about that. So she switched her focus to something she understood well.

Pain.

There was throbbing in various places across her body. Most notably her shoulder. Nothing was broken but everything felt bruised. Her muddy romp with Rain Slicker had indeed left a mark.

Lily felt along her nightstand until she found the bottle of ibuprofen. She took two with a sip from a water bottle before even sitting up all the way.

If she was in pain, she had to guess Ant was swimming in it.

Lily padded to the small en suite bathroom and went through her morning routine. She pulled half of her hair up and dressed in a white tank top, a pair of black jeans and a blazer. She was deeply fond of the coat given how lightweight it was in the Southern humidity and the fact that it hid her shoulder holster well. Lily's boots were still in the garage so she left the room in her socks. She felt weirdly naked doing so.

She also felt bare without lipstick on so she put that on, too.

Then she stopped by her dresser to rub it off on her discarded sleep shirt.

She was about to see Anthony Perez. Not go on some date.

Lily straightened her blazer and checked her phone. Six thirty. One unread text.

It was from Detective Gray. The time stamp was right after midnight.

I'll be in the office at start of shift. If you need time off, take it.

Lily wasn't going to accept that offer. There was no need for her to skip out on interrogating their attacker. She only hoped the big bosses agreed. If not, maybe bringing Ant with her wouldn't be such a bad idea. He *had* defended her the night before. And he hadn't just been talking. He'd believed what he was saying. She deserved to be in there more than the rest. She could handle her own, after all.

It was nice to hear the confidence. In her last job the bullpen had been male-dominated and, of those men, several had shown animosity toward her, a younger woman well on her way up the ladder. Fighting for her spot, her right, wasn't something she liked doing. Though she would, it had still been a good feeling to hear someone standing behind her, defending her.

It was still such a bizarre feeling to know that it had been Ant's voice rallying her.

They weren't even friends, really. Apart from a few conversations over the phone through the years, they hadn't spoken with much depth to each other. Hadn't made plans to catch up. Didn't talk about anything that wasn't Ida-related.

They were just two people who had shared an awful day together. One that had obviously followed them into the lives they'd led since.

But as she descended the stairs, careful not to make too much noise, she couldn't help but want to know more. How had he left North Carolina so fast? Did his boss understand? Did his girlfriend, if he had one, care? Had he listened to music on the ride down or was he an audiobook kind of guy? Maybe he'd taken to podcasts, playing them off his phone as he ate up the miles.

Or had he used the road and silence to think about the woods? The creek?

Lily misjudged her attention span. With her thoughts on Ant she forgot to step lightly on the second-to-last step on the stairs. Its whine was as loud as it was unforgiving. Lily cringed and braced for Cook to round the corner and a sleepy Ant to wake, but neither the dog nor the man made a peep. Curious, she walked around the corner.

Ant was lying across the couch, with his elbows propped up and a phone in his hands. The space between his cell and the blanket strewn across his hips housed a black Lab.

Lily couldn't help but give a little laugh at the sight.

"And here I thought no one would ever replace me in the eyes of Cook the Lab."

Cook's tail wagged in sync with Ant's laughter. He set down his phone as the dog scrambled off him and toward her.

"I hope it's okay that he's up here. I kind of patted my chest when he was coming back from using the bathroom and then it was game over."

Lily gave Cook a good scratch. She snorted.

"To be fair, he's somewhat of a clingy dog. The pat probably wasn't needed."

Ant was sitting up now. Once again he was shirtless. Lily made sure to rein her focus to his face. A task made easier considering the state of it.

"How's your—" Lily motioned to all of her face.

Ant smirked. He fingered the scab over his eyebrow.

"Again, not the worst scrapes I've gotten through the years. Hurts a little, will look cooler if it scars. If not I'm sure it'll be fine in a few days." Those dark eyes moved to Lily's cheek. She was glad for the distance between them. "What about you? Your jaw isn't bruising like I thought it might. How's the cheek?"

Lily had already examined her injuries in the mirror while getting ready. He was right, the punch she'd taken to the jaw hadn't left as much of a bruise as it could have. Didn't mean it hurt less but it was nice that the wound wasn't noticeable. The scrape on her cheek was another story. It was a kiss of red with some light scabbing. If she'd felt so inclined, she might have covered it with some foundation.

"Neither really hurt," she decided to say. "Would be cool if it scars but if not I'll be okay in a few days."

Ant wasn't distracted by her humor. He stood and crossed his arms over his chest.

"But something's bothering you," he guessed. "Something hurts. I can tell by how you're holding yourself. What is it?"

Lily sighed. She was going to have to get a better poker face for her entire body.

"My shoulder." She shrugged the one in question. It hurt. Plain and simple. "You'd think all the rain we've had would have softened the ground a little. I hit it when I first went to the ground avoiding the shovel." Ant's own body language betrayed him. He was readying to close the distance between them again. Lily didn't want that. She started to walk toward the kitchen to avoid the closeness. "I already took some meds, though. Right now I could really do with some coffee. Do you want some?"

The coffee maker was perhaps the most used appliance in the house. It was a single-cup and had been bought for the express purpose of trying to limit how much caffeine she consumed in a day. That had been a woefully unachieved goal. Lily found comfort in the smell of it, the feel of the mug in her hand, the routine. The actual taste ranked last in things she craved from the drink. Lily was searching for that constant now. She opened her cupboard and selected one of her travel mugs.

She hadn't said so, but she wasn't planning on sticking around long that morning.

Ant found a way to break the routine by way of a simple comment.

"I remember seeing your dad out on your front porch every morning with a mug like that in his hand." He was leaning against the counter, just as he had at the station.

Unbothered. Yet forever haunted. A combination that shouldn't work but did for him.

Lily felt a flash of envy. He was so easy to be with and she...had to run to the coffeepot to avoid the world.

"He always tipped his head and cup to me when I was on the way to school." Ant mimicked the motion. That flash of envy Lily had felt now turned into a smoldering ache. She hoped she hid the change. She tried to smile into the memories.

"Do you know that he made a cup every morning, came home to get a cup at lunch, and then had another one right after dinner?" Lily placed her own mug beneath the dispenser. She mirrored Ant's stance against the counter next to her. "As a kid I wondered how he fell asleep after all that caffeine. As an adult in law enforcement I wonder how he stopped at three cups a day."

Ant laughed. It wasn't as boisterous as she was finding his normal trill was.

"My cousin Shandra told me a while back that they moved, your parents," he ventured. "How are they doing?"

Lily held back that emotional switch in perfect stillness.

"Good. They moved right before I went to college. Up to a place called Beaver Creek, New York, if you can believe it." Ant's eyebrow rose high at that. "Dad lived there in his teens and fell in love with the place. Once I was out of the house for good they decided it was as good a time as any." She bit down hard on the rest of the truth—her parents had told her they were leaving before she'd actually gone to school. Most longtime locals only left because of The Flood. But not her parents. They had packed up and left their home behind because of her.

Because Lily couldn't stop obsessing over Ida.

You won't be a ghost in our home any longer, her mother had told her one morning, her father's first cup of coffee of the day brewing in the background. *If you won't try to move on by yourself, then we're just going to have to force you to take the first step.*

So they'd gone.

Then so had Lily.

Ant nodded now, unaware of the words she was keeping in. Her own coffee started to pour next to her.

"Mom tried staying for a while," he told her. "She made it a lot longer than I did, but finally moved to El Paso to be with my aunt."

"That's nice," Lily said, honest. She knew his father had passed away when Ida was a baby. That had only made the family that much closer.

Ant agreed.

"We video chat or talk on the phone at least once a week. Her latest kick has been enjoying her time as great-aunt to my cousin Phillipe's new kid. Though that happiness has turned into a very pointed kind of peer pressure." Ant laughed again. His tone had changed once more. It was lighter. "Apparently I was supposed to supply her with a grandchild years ago and I just didn't get the memo."

Lily felt heat in her belly at that. Not a lot but it was there.

"Hey, it could be worse. At least it's your mom pushing you about it and not your girlfriend."

This time the laughter came out in a boom. Ant was grinning hard when it was through.

"Was that your way of fishing to see if I'm dating anyone?" Ant asked, teasing. The heat in her belly became the heat in her face.

"No," she defended. "It was just an observation!"

Ant crossed his arms over his chest.

"I don't think so. In fact, I think Lily Howard, Detective Extraordinaire, was trying to do some snooping."

Lily snorted. She rolled her eyes and went for her cup as the sound of the coffee maker cut off.

"It was *conversation*, not snooping," she returned. "If I was snooping I would have just straight-up asked you if you had some girlfriend up in North Carolina."

Ant was still having fun, laughing behind her.

Again that envy crawled back up to say hi to her. Sometimes Ant could be so easy when she felt so defensive and stiff.

He was brandishing a small smile when she went into the walk-in pantry for Cook's food. It was still turning up the corners of his lips when he guided her out of the way and took the plastic kibble scoop from her.

"Your shoulder is hurt, Detective Howard," he said. "Let me get Cook sorted and you just worry about your coffee."

Lily hesitated for a moment. She relented in the next. Cook let out a yip of excitement the second he heard his food hit the scoop. He wasn't at all patient as he followed Ant to his bowl. If he hadn't already been a fan of the man, that would have cinched it.

Ant moved back through the kitchen and into the pantry again like it was old habit.

"I don't have one, by the way," he called out. "A girlfriend. I did but we broke up last year. What about you?"

Lily hurriedly answered before he could come back out. Not that it needed any great length of time.

"Nope. Just dating my job."

She wasn't embarrassed by her answer but she couldn't deny she was glad at the subject change when he emerged.

"Speaking of, I was thinking about last night." He took a seat opposite her at the table. His busted eyebrow and lip really did look bad in the LED lighting. "The box in the ground had to be meant for someone other than the man who buried it, right?" he asked. "Why else have nothing but a recording on repeat in there? What would be the point of doing it for yourself?"

"You think he wanted someone else to find it?" Lily couldn't deny she had thought the same before falling asleep the night before. One of many strange possibilities.

"Yeah. I mean, I would have guessed it was some kind of prank had it not been for the man wielding a shovel. That takes a bad joke and turns it into a violent affair. Makes no sense to escalate like that over something supposed to be funny."

Lily took a pull of her coffee. She was seeing the rain and the woods in her memory.

"But then why would he want someone to find the box?" she wondered aloud. "Was it a message? A threat? A weird science experiment?"

"In Kelby Creek? Who knows but here's to hoping he spills his guts when you interrogate him today."

Lily sighed.

"I'm not sure they'll let me talk to him," she admitted. "Other than a statement about being involved, it's not really my place to investigate."

Ant grunted.

"Aren't you a detective? Isn't investigating your whole thing?"

"I am but I was hired for the cold case task force. I don't even report to Detective Lovett on a normal day."

Ant gave her a raised eyebrow again.

"I knew the department was focusing on cold cases but I didn't realize there was a legit task force to do it. I just assumed it was something y'all were doing in your spare time."

It was a common misconception, especially given Dawn County's small size, but Kelby Creek wasn't like most towns. Not since Annie McHale was kidnapped and The Flood followed.

Not since Ida, for some of them at least.

"There were already a few too many cold cases in town before all of the corruption was uncovered," she said diplomatically. "After The Flood everyone wanted to make sure closed, open and dismissed cases alike were handled correctly. Including the people hired to do it. People 'above reproach' and highly motivated. That's why Kenneth Gray got the job of heading it."

"Gray. His wife's murder was a cold case for a long time, wasn't it?"

Lily nodded.

"He was also thoroughly investigated after The Flood and came up as clean as a whistle. He's become somewhat of a symbol for hunting down justice in town now, apparently. We were at lunch after I was first hired and a woman connected to a case he helped close spent the entire meal almost in tears thanking him. He goes the extra mile without being asked, which I like in a boss."

Ant's face was a mask of concentration. He seemed genuinely curious.

"Who else is on the task force?"

"Me and Kathryn Juliet. But she goes by Juliet. Do you know her? She's a few years older. Married to James Hornwell, a nice guy, but didn't take his last name."

Ant shook his head.

"Juliet sounds familiar but, well, I might just be thinking Shakespeare."

Lily hid her smile. Mostly because she'd thought the same thing upon meeting Juliet.

"She's a true local, a few generations deep." Lily sobered. "Her family decided to leave after The Flood but she stayed. Her brother was killed in a car accident in the city shortly after. They were very close. She blames The Flood for his death. She's since been very driven to see that no other traces of corruption go unpunished. She also honestly cares, which is always a good thing."

Neither one of them spoke for a moment. A weight, not unfamiliar, settled between them.

Ant was the one who broke it.

"Then there's you."

Lily took another sip of coffee.

"Then there's me."

The woman stuck in the past.

The woman still hunting for her own justice.

The woman who'd been hollowed out by guilt and anger as a girl.

The woman who had never stopped investigating a case, even as it became as cold as ice over the years.

Lily didn't say any of that, though, and when Ant didn't ask why she'd gotten the job, she knew that *he* knew the answer already.

So instead the silence came back and picked at them.

Lily wanted to do a lot of things to break it—ask him about his life, about his job, about his breakup.

Ask about why he hadn't asked her anything else concerning the lead she'd told him about Ida the night before.

But she didn't.

There were just some wounds too deep and old to ever fully heal.

And, for Lily, one was sitting across the table from her.

ANT COMBED A hand through his hair and hoped Lily Howard couldn't tell he was sitting on a truth he didn't want to be telling.

Her coffee cup was in the sink, his bag was on his back,

and they'd made their way to the garage while the rain drizzled on the world around them.

"At least the sun is rising." That was the first thing Lily had said in a few minutes. They'd just been revolving around one another. Normally, he would have spoken up but Ant was trying to tiptoe around his next plans.

He nodded. "I never could decide if rain every day was better than the musty humidity that hung out after. I guess it would be easier just to dislike both, huh?"

Lily flashed a polite smile. Then she glanced at the time on her phone again.

She was anxious to leave.

So was Ant.

"Thanks again for the place to stay," he said, fishing his keys out of his bag. "I like my car but after the all-day drive yesterday it really did feel good to sleep somewhere I actually fit comfortably."

Lily shrugged.

"Thanks for having quick reflexes during the fight. I'm certainly not going to look at a shovel the same way again."

"No problem."

Lily hit the unlock button on her key ring.

"Sorry but I should get going."

Ant held up his hands. He was already backing up.

"I wouldn't want you to miss out on getting that guy to talk."

Lily opened her door but hesitated. Her tone changed when she finally spoke but he couldn't get a beat on the emotion behind it. Maybe it was just plain ol' conversation.

"Are you staying in town or…"

There it was. Time to sidestep the truth.

"For now, yeah. I am."

Then he zipped his mouth shut.

Lily didn't ask for him to elaborate. He could already

tell her own wheels were turning for what she had to face at work.

"Good luck."

He waved bye and Lily was fast to go.

It made his next move easier.

Ant pulled out his phone and opened the Google app.

In the search bar he put only one name.

Bryant Lautner.

Chapter Seven

"The man with the shovel is Arturo Hanson. He moved into town a few years back and works at the hardware store downtown. His boss, Mr. Klein, said he's a weird fella but puts in the work and the work's always good."

Kenneth Gray was in a suit wearing a scowl. They were in the hallway outside their office while Juliet was on the phone at her desk. Lily hadn't even put her stuff down before stopping the boss. Not that he seemed to mind.

"I've been around some weird people before and none of them buried boxes with recordings of women screaming in them," Lily pointed out.

Kenneth agreed with that.

"Arturo isn't talking. He *was* cleared by the hospital last night and he's in holding."

Lily was glad for that. In holding meant he was in house, which meant she stood a better chance of getting to him for a conversation.

Kenneth seemed to pick up on that thought. He was nothing but apologetic.

"He lawyered up late last night," he interjected before her hopes could get too high. "That lawyer showed up at the crack of dawn. Arturo might be weird but his lawyer was all straight arrows according to Foster."

Lily held the lid on her emotions tightly closed.

She pushed her shoulders back. She could still feel the strain in her.

"Having a lawyer doesn't preclude me from questioning him, though. And that's what I want to do."

Kenneth was still all apologetic.

"Foster has officially taken the case on, which means you aren't assigned to it." Lily opened her mouth to object, emotions be damned, but Kenneth held up his hand to stop her. "He's agreed to keep us firmly in the loop."

Kenneth flipped his wrist over to look at his watch.

"In fact, we're meeting him in two hours for a full rundown along with the sheriff. Any and all questions, concerns and theories can be shared there. Okay?"

Lily was chomping at the metaphorical bit.

Yet she nodded.

"Okay."

Kenneth motioned to the file tucked under his arm.

"Let's get back to our cold cases and see if we can't heat one of them up until then."

He excused himself while Lily went to her desk. Juliet gave her a quick nod of greeting but never left her phone conversation. Lily did her best to block the woman out to give her some privacy. She booted up her computer, checked her emails when it came to life, and then caught herself staring blankly at the screen.

She didn't like waiting.

In fact, she hated it.

Lily grabbed her phone and went out into the heart of the department before going toward Foster Lovett's office.

The door was open but he wasn't alone inside. Deputy Sterling Costner was standing in front of his desk, his arms motioning to the detective and his voice low. His partner, Marigold Mathers, was leaning against the door in the hallway, arms crossed. She spotted Lily and kept her voice on the low side, too.

"If you want a crack at Foster, you're going to have to wait until Sterling gets it out of his system," Marigold said. "Fair warning, he just started."

Lily wasn't particularly close to anyone at the department but she knew enough about each of her colleagues to form some curiosity and make some light inquiries here and there. However, Sterling Costner's recent brush with danger and his role in bringing down a key player from The Flood, with the help of his now-wife, had been big news that needed no prying to uncover.

But why he was now hot in the face at Foster definitely was a mystery that had her piqued.

"Is this about last night?" Lily asked.

"Yeah." Marigold's expression softened. "He's been beating himself everywhere till Sunday about not finding the hole the first time. Then not staying to wait for you."

"He couldn't have known, on either front."

Marigold sighed so low that if Lily hadn't seen her do it, she wouldn't have known she'd done it at all.

"I know and I'm pretty sure *he* knows but he's still all guilt-ridden. He wants to go back out there and make sure there are no other boxes. He's worried one of them might not just have a recording of a lady screaming but the real thing." Marigold shook her head. "He also really wants to make that Arturo guy talk, but it's not our case, so here we are."

Lily sympathized. "I feel that."

Her plans to try to sway Foster to let her talk to Arturo started to fade fast. She decided to switch gears.

"Speaking about the recording, do you know where it is now?"

"Yeah." Marigold pointed down the hall. "Only because Sterling already demanded to listen to it. It should still be in the meeting room. Sheriff Bennet and Foster were listening to it earlier in there."

Lily backtracked to the meeting room the department used to conduct more convivial interviews. A somewhat new deputy to the department kindly stepped outside the door to give her some privacy.

"A pretty popular recording this morning," he commented before shutting the door behind him.

Lily had no doubt that was true.

The recorder looked odd in the fluorescent lighting. Without rain or mud across it, too. Lily slid into the chair in front of it and ignored the few notes that had been taken on the pad next to it.

If she couldn't talk to Arturo then she could follow up on some other pieces of evidence. Start her own chain of investigation before looping back up to the man in question. After the recording she'd go to the box, and after the box she'd reexamine the scene. Until she was told that there were answers, Lily was going to operate under the assumption that they were still in the questions-only stage.

And she didn't aim to be there long.

Lily put her phone on the table and hit Record. She slipped on some latex gloves and set the tape up to play from the beginning.

The screaming was instant. No wonder Deputy Benz had been quick to shut the door.

"Help!" the woman yelled. *"Help me!"*

Lily leaned forward, head tilting. There was no background sound that she could hear, no ambient noise or even static. It was a clear recording. Just a woman screaming, then, after a minute, the tape noticeably looped.

Lily scanned the notes as the second loop began. According to whoever had jotted down the remarks, the tape in its entirety lasted sixty-two minutes, cutting off during the middle of the last loop. The manufacturer of the recorder had been out of business for ten years, having only found relative success in vintage and novelty equipment before their closing. She took the brand's name, TechTon, and pressed it into her memory as another something to look into once this link in the chain was complete.

"Help! Help me!"

Lily glanced back at the recorder. She let her eyes become unfocused.

A nagging feeling rose in her stomach.

"Help! Help me!"

It clawed its way up through her.

"Help!"

Something…was right there.

"Help me!"

If she could only reach it…

"Help!"

Her adrenaline started to spike. The screams. They sounded familiar…

"Help me!"

But why? Was it from a TV show or movie?

Lily hadn't been an avid watcher of either over the years. She was usually a day late and a buck short when it came to what was trending. She also hadn't lied to Ant about her love life being her professional life. She had as little time for men as she had for Netflix.

But if the scream wasn't recorded from a movie or TV show then how would she know it?

It wasn't Ida's. Her screaming for help was a memory burned forever inside Lily's head. She could pick that sound out of ten bands battling each other for dominance. That sound was a bad laugh track in her nightmares.

Who else's scream would she know?

Who else's scream would she recognize by only a few syllables?

"Help! Help me!"

Lily sat up, ramrod straight.

She clicked the stop button on the recorder and her phone. Her gloves went into the trash on the way out of the meeting room. She was at her desk in less than thirty seconds. The internet search bar was up right after that.

Juliet, now off the phone, turned her attention to her desk mate.

Her dark eyebrows were raised high.

"What's going on, Howie?" There was clear concern in her question. It wasn't every day that Lily made a fuss. Even if it was a silent one.

"The recording, the one that we found in the box," she started. Lily's fingers were like lightning across the keyboard. She waited until she found the search results she was looking for. "I recognized the scream."

Juliet's chair scraped back.

"What do you mean you recognized the scream?" Lily knew the moment the detective saw her screen. Juliet let out a little gasp at the video she'd pulled up. "Are you serious?"

Annie McHale's ransom video was over five years old but still as captivating as the day it had been uploaded by hackers to the town's former website.

Beloved Annie was tied to a chair, hurt and yelling. It was the only visual anyone had had of her since her abduction days before it was posted.

Lily put her phone on the desktop. She pressed Play on her recording.

The second set of screams didn't sync up with Annie's video, but there was no denying they were one and the same.

"Wow. That's a cruel, weird joke." Juliet huffed. "But I guess we all knew once Annie's ransom video went viral there was no avoiding sick ploys for attention like this."

Lily shook her head. Her heartbeat was speeding up as her thoughts tumbled out ahead of it.

She placed the new nagging feeling easier this time.

"There's static in the video." Lily pressed her finger to the screen so there was no confusion.

"Yeah. There always has been. The FBI tech guys said the video camera wasn't great. Something about its battery. I can't remember."

Lily paused Annie's video but the recording on her phone kept playing.

"The recording has no static. It's as clear as day."

Juliet opened her mouth. Then shut it. They both went back to staring at Lily's phone.

"Maybe it's some new kind of audio trick to filter out the background noise?" Juliet suggested. "They could do that now."

"But why? Why go through that trouble? Why not put the original one in that went viral? Had we not found this version in a buried box, I would have thought it was a sick, easy joke to use her recording."

"But since Annie McHale was never found and *that* was found in a box buried in the woods..."

"What if it was recorded in person?"

Juliet's words were clipped. Analytical. They weren't just talking about some old case. They were talking about *the* case that was the beginning of the end for Kelby Creek. And that held a lot of weight, especially for Juliet. It also was surprisingly heavy for Lily, even though she still resented the attention it had gotten compared to Ida's case.

"You think Arturo was recording Annie McHale in person?"

"Or he might know who did."

Juliet was quiet.

Lily was already onto her next link in the chain.

WHAT ANT LACKED in terms of a badge, he more than made up for in conviction. What he also lacked in polite grace, he compensated for with quick-talking. He knew he might need both when he cut his engine in the parking lot of the Bean Dean Brewery on the north side of town and saw his old friend standing under an umbrella next to her van, a cup of coffee firmly in hand.

The descriptor of "friend" being generous, if he was being honest. The last time Ant had seen Mrs. Jane Dahls, Ida had still been a carefree sixteen-year-old safe and sound at home. Now Mrs. Jane was in her seventies. Though time didn't seem to have wiped away her like for Ant. The moment he was out of the truck, she was calling out to him.

"Mr. Perez, you sure grew another foot since the last time I laid eyes on you."

Ant cracked a smile and met the woman with a careful embrace. His former babysitter did indeed seem to be smaller than he remembered.

"I kept growing to make sure I could reach every high shelf in the grocery store that you ever needed me to reach," he returned. "Don't think I forgot about that time that I had to climb up on the shelf to grab you some wafers and almost took out the entire aisle when I fell."

Mrs. Jane was rolling her eyes when he stepped back but she was still smiling.

"I never asked you to become a monkey and scale up the thing. That was all you and those young-boy urges to climb everything." She chuckled. "Though I'll say I'll never forgot how Robert Tate Sr. nearly had a heart attack when the whole thing started wobbling. Like one shelf of cookies falling was going to bankrupt him. God rest his overdramatic soul."

Ant nodded, though he'd forgotten about the owner of the grocery store nearly losing his head over it all.

Then again, he'd forgotten a lot about his past.

There wasn't much use in remembering it. Most times it just hurt.

Which was why he'd called Mrs. Jane after all these years for a meeting.

Not only was she whip smart, she was a front-porch vigilante. She had long-standing knowledge of the town and most of its locals thanks to her skills in the art of word-of-mouth information and her being tapped into the gossip mill since the '80s.

She knew things.

She knew people.

Now Mrs. Jane proved that herself. She gave Ant a long look. Her smile folded.

"I heard about the woods last night," she said. "Must have been hard to be out there, especially with Miss Howard. How's she doing?"

Ant didn't ask how she knew about the night before—all it took was one deputy to mention it to a loved one, who then mentioned it to someone else, and eventually that someone went to Mrs. Jane—but he kept his answer vague regardless.

"She's good. Held her own. She's at work now."

Mrs. Jane nodded deep. She reached her free hand out and touched his arm.

"And what about you? How are you doing?" Her gaze went to his eyebrow, then lip. He was surprised she hadn't lead with the question.

Ant took her hand in his and squeezed before letting it go.

"Nothing I can't handle."

Mrs. Jane had never been one to leave something like that without prodding but this time she did.

"I bet," she said instead. "Is that why you called on me? The man in the woods?"

Ant shook his head.

"No, ma'am. I actually wanted to ask you about someone else. The guy I'm trying to find is named Bryant Lautner. Have you heard of him?"

Mrs. Jane chewed on that for a little bit.

She nodded, slow.

"I haven't heard the name in a while but yes. After what happened to his wife, poor man has had a whole slew of problems through the years."

Ant could feel his blood pumping harder.

"Has had?" Ant repeated. "Meaning he's still around here?"

"I mean, I haven't seen him since he moved out of his and his late wife's house, but I think he's still rattling around that workshop of his."

That had Ant's ears up.

"He has a workshop?"

Mrs. Jane snorted, rolling her eyes one more time.

"Him and his little golfing buddies used to joke that it was a way to escape their wives and have a few beers without being nagged. Once Patricia passed, the joke wasn't funny anymore. If you ask me, it never was."

"But you said he doesn't live there anymore?"

"He doesn't live at his old house but the workshop wasn't on that property. I actually don't know who owns the land it's on. I always assumed it belonged to his father."

"But you know where it is?"

Mrs. Jane looked peachy proud.

"Buy me a muffin and I'll write down the directions."

Ant didn't hesitate.

"Yes, ma'am."

Chapter Eight

Foster got a call from his wife, Millie, and was off before Lily could tell him what she thought she'd discovered. Kenneth, however, lapped up the news. He had Annie McHale's video up on the computer in the cold case task force's office and was paying rapt attention.

"I can't believe I didn't get this earlier," he said, after pausing the video and playing the recording twice. "This is a great catch, Lily."

Lily was standing next to Juliet, who seconded the sentiment.

"Especially since poor Annie yelling for help used to be a soundtrack to this town." Juliet's expression turned in on itself, propelled by grief. If Annie McHale had never been kidnapped, Juliet's brother never would have died in the city after leaving town.

It was a sore spot.

That sore spot was also what made Juliet a great detective. Just like Kenneth's late wife's murder and his pursuit of justice made him a more driven man now.

That said, Lily didn't fault either of them for missing the connection.

The only reason Lily had recognized Annie's screams was because she, at first, knew without a doubt that they hadn't been Ida's.

"I'd like to talk to him now," Lily said, sidestepping their praise. "Arturo."

Kenneth rubbed his jaw in thought.

It wasn't a thought that was going to give her a way into the investigation she'd already been side-lined from.

"If this recording is authentic, then that means Arturo either recorded Annie during her captivity in person or he knew someone who did," Kenneth underlined. "That's insanely big news. Which means we need to make sure we handle it right." He pushed back in the chair. "I need to talk to Foster and the sheriff first."

If Lily were one to show outbursts of emotion, she would have made a growling noise. Instead she shifted her hip, putting her more squarely between her boss and the door.

"Annie was five years ago," Lily said. "That box buried in the ground was yesterday. What if there are other boxes? What if one of them has an actual woman inside it?"

She could see Kenneth consider that.

She could also see he understood her frustration.

"Arturo lawyered up and, quite frankly, putting the person who helped knock him out the night before in front of him isn't going to help anyone. But let me talk to Foster. The reason this task force works is because we have clear boundaries for our cases and for current cases."

Lily nodded. She didn't grit her teeth until he was out in the hallway and out of earshot.

Juliet waited.

"He's right, you know," she said. "But just because you can't talk to Arturo right now doesn't mean you can't work him. Right?"

The adrenaline rush of finding a lead refueled and re-directed.

"You're right."

Lily was back at her computer and searching again. Juliet went to her desk and did the same. If Arturo had an original recording of Annie, then there had to be a connection between them somehow.

Somewhere.

Lily did a deep dive on the internet, scouring any and all public information on Arturo. She came up with four poorly made social media profiles. Two were public; only one had been used in the past year. Several posts complained of the weather, local politics and income tax. One was a rant about what a load of crock mechanics were based on how much they charged to fix problems he could do himself. That post had a picture attached of an old Ford without its tires. The vehicle was up on four cinder blocks.

Lily saved the picture before reexamining it.

The truck was beneath a metal overhang sitting above a cracked concrete slab. That slab was at the end of what looked like a dirt road. Grass and more dirt could be seen around it. In the background there were trees, thick and green.

Lily went back to the date on the original post.

A year and some months ago.

The location tag was off but when it came to the woods, Lily was an expert.

She scoured the rest of his public profiles and found two more pictures of the same overhang and carport. One was the same setup but the other picture was angled from the side. In it she could see the building it was attached to. It was a narrow wooden structure that was as worn as the brush around it was overgrown.

There was also a sign in the distance. More worn and weathered than the building.

"No Fishing" could just barely be made out across its front.

Directly behind it was what looked like another dirt road.

Lily took a moment and closed her eyes.

When she opened them again, she knew where she needed to go.

MRS. JANE HAD a muffin and twenty minutes later, Ant was staring at Bryant Lautner's workshop.

After leaving the café Ant had been pure speed. Every mile he ate up, every turn he whipped around and every tree he passed he felt a surge of purpose. Of energy. Of dogged hope that he was going to cinch an answer.

Finally.

Now, though, that feeling was deflating.

The workshop looked like it hadn't been touched in years.

Ant crept up to the front door, minding the windows on either side. He'd already parked his car further back in the trees and made his way up the road quickly and quietly. Thin lead or not, he wasn't taking any chances of spooking the one man he needed to question.

If it had been anyone else—if he had been there for anything else—Ant might have questioned his methods.

But it was for Ida. This could *be* Ida's abductor.

Ant felt the heat of rage rise within him. He shook his shoulders out to belay it. The first window was blocked by a curtain. The second, something wooden. He went to the door last. He knocked harder than he'd meant to knock.

Ant waited for movement but nothing happened. No back doors or windows opening and shutting, no one running off into the woods to hide from him.

No nothing.

Ant gave it another series of loud knocks.

No sounds inside. None outside, either. Only birds singing, probably happy that the rain had let up.

Ant stood there a moment.

He should leave—there obviously hadn't been someone there in a while—but he couldn't.

It was quiet but it was there. In the back of his mind.

Ida, yelling for him.

Ant sighed heavy and true.

He wasn't leaving until he'd seen the inside.

Like Mrs. Jane had described it, the building was on the smaller side. Without going in, Ant pictured one open living area, a bathroom, and maybe a separate room that acted as a bedroom or storage. The back porch had seen better days but held firm beneath his weight as he tried the back door. It didn't budge an inch.

Ant tried the windows next. One was painted shut, the other was flimsy as all get-out. He pushed on the latter until it slid all the way up. Once again, no one moved or made a sound.

So he climbed in.

If the outside hadn't been well kept, Ant would have known just by the smell inside that the workshop had been left closed up for a long while. It was stale air mixed with a dampness that pressed against him when he straightened.

The main room was more or less like he'd pictured it. Open but missing most of the furniture. There was a small kitchenette in the corner and a lone patio couch next to the front door. But to his surprise there were three doors that led off the main room. He unlocked the back door, just in case he needed to get out quick if someone came in through the front, before he went to the first one.

Ant didn't knock this time. The door opened with no problem.

A billiard table took up most of the space. It would have been out of place had it not matched the run-down vibe of the rest of the workshop. The whole thing was leaning to one corner, sloped and stained. The green felt was torn and the legs beneath were struggling to stay upright. Ant wasn't sure but he didn't think disuse alone could have put the table in such bad shape. A fight could have done the trick; so could horsing around. If Bryant and his buddies had used the workshop as an escape from their wives then there probably was a drunken mix of the two at some point.

Ant went to the second room next.

The bathroom was small and surprisingly not as dingy. It also had running water. He flipped the light switch. The lights struggled on.

Ant looked up at them, curious.

So the workshop hadn't been completely abandoned.

Ant started to go for the third door but froze at the sound of footsteps. Someone was walking up the back steps.

Ant moved inside the billiard room and grabbed a cob-web-covered pool cue off the wall in one fluid movement. He kept it low at his side, ready. He usually wasn't a man to hide but he didn't want to startle Bryant Lautner into running or shooting, if he was like most Southern property owners and carried a gun.

Ant held his breath as the back door creaked open, slow. He shouldn't have unlocked it. Now Bryant was going to know someone was inside. Ant put himself in a better stance to fight, if needed. Or run, if he decided that was the better option.

It was a mistake.

He hit a spot on the floor that creaked louder than the back door had.

Ant cussed low. There was no point pretending he wasn't there now.

"I'm just here to talk," he decided to yell out. "I'm coming out, unarmed."

He put the stick on the table, brought his hands up and entered the main room, hoping to God that Bryant Lautner didn't shoot first, ask questions later.

All his hope and he still got a gun pointed at him.

All his luck made the person aiming it a sight for sore eyes.

Lily's eyebrows were sky high. She lowered her gun.

"You're still following me?" she exclaimed. "How do you think that's a good idea?"

Ant dropped his hands.

"Following you?" He closed the gap between them. "I'm not following you."

She didn't look convinced.

"Then why are you here?"

Ant thought it was obvious. He said as much.

"The same reason you are. Bryant Lautner."

If her initial surprise at seeing him could be scaled at a ten out of ten, the look that scrunched her face now ranked at a solid thirteen.

"You aren't here because of Bryant?" he followed up.

She shook her head. "No."

Lily's body language changed for the worse. It put him even closer to the edge.

"Then why?" he asked, low.

Lily opened her mouth but no words came out.

A car door shut out front.

Both Ant's and Lily's heads turned in sync.

"Were you expecting anyone?" Ant asked.

Lily pulled up her gun. It was enough of an answer, but still she added to it.

"I wasn't even expecting you."

Chapter Nine

Lily had Ant's hand and was pulling him out the back door in a move that was the epitome of clumsy stealth. It only came after the decision that getting caught inside of a suspect's house alone, without permission, wasn't a smart move. Getting caught inside a suspect's house *with* a civilian was even less appealing.

So Ant's hand was warm in hers as the two made it out of the door and into the trees surrounding the building. He, thankfully, understood her intent. He was quiet and quick. They made it into the cover of the trees before the sound of the front door shutting echoed out to them.

Lily holstered her gun and peeked around a tree at the building.

No one was looking back. Nor were they yelling.

"I don't think anyone saw us," she breathed out. Her shoulders dragged down a little. She'd been sloppy. She wasn't happy about it.

Ant was taking cover behind a neighboring tree.

"Won't he see your car?" he asked.

"No. I parked off the main road. I'm not exactly supposed to be here."

Ant faced her. A whisper of a smirk was across his lips.

"Great minds," he said, simply. "Mine is off a ways, too. I didn't want Bryant to get spooked."

"Bryant?" Lily looked away from the house completely, shifting her attention to Ant. She didn't understand. "Bryant Lautner?"

Ant stepped back so he was securely behind the tree.

"Yeah. This was his workshop back in the day. Word was he still hangs out here." That was news to Lily. "But you're not here because of Bryant...or me?"

Lily shook her head.

"I'm here for Arturo Hanson."

They clearly weren't on the same page.

"Who's Arturo Hanson?" he asked.

"The guy with the shovel who attacked us. I found some old social media posts he made with pictures that looked like they were taken here. So I thought I'd come check the place out."

"And you didn't knock?"

Lily felt a brief flair of professional shame. She shook it off in the next second.

"There wasn't a vehicle, no lights, and I wasn't looking to be surprised. Then I saw the open window and tried the back door. And, well, then *you*." She waved her hand through the air to stop the conversation. "But we can talk about all of this later. Right now we need to go see who showed up and ask them some questions."

Ant looked skeptical. He craned his neck around the tree to see the house again. He nodded to the right.

"We can go that way, curve around and walk up to the front door. Might feel a bit hinky since neither one of us is rolling up in a car, though, but maybe that badge of yours will distract them from asking about our transportation."

He wasn't wrong. Lily used her free hand to confirm her badge was hanging on the chain outside her blazer.

"Listen, I don't want to break eye contact with this place, even for a second," she said. "If this really is Bryant's place, then this is a lead. If it's not, it's still a lead for Arturo. I'm not letting whoever just showed up get away without identifying them and asking some questions. Got it?"

Ant sense of urgency seemed to mirror hers.

"Let's hurry then."

They circled the building and kept to the trees. No one came out, no one yelled. Lily only took a small beat when they were near the front before hustling toward the front porch. She paused one more time by the car to confirm that no one was inside.

"It's running," she realized, whispering over her shoulder to Ant. "Whoever is here, they're not planning on staying long."

It was an old Cadillac and not at all in good condition. White paint chipped, everything silver rusted to some degree, and the interior wasn't faring any better. There was nothing notable in view on the seats. A quick look showed no plates. Ant beat Lily to taking a quick picture with his phone. Lily beat him to the front porch steps.

Something Ant wasn't too keen on.

He shouldered in front of Lily before she could make it to the door.

"I'm the one with the gun and badge," she whispered quickly.

Ant leaned over, eyes still on the door, and matched her volume. He was so close she could feel his breath on her cheek.

"A badge and gun don't mean a thing if someone starts shooting."

Lily was about to point out that it meant she'd start shooting back but he had his knuckles up ready to knock.

"Dawn County Sheriff's Department," she called out, beating him to the punch. "We just want to talk!"

No response.

Ant turned his head a little like Cook did when he was

trying to suss out a sound. He shook his head. Lily knocked and repeated her call again.

They waited.

Not one sound.

Ant was tensing up by the second. He put his ear to the door and then shook his head again.

"Nothing," he mouthed.

Lily pulled her gun out of its holster. She kept it at her side.

"We could go around back again," Ant offered. "We know the door is open."

Lily didn't like that idea.

Just like she wasn't a fan of the new feeling in her gut.

Something wasn't right.

Just like a woman's voice screaming from beneath the ground.

Just like that rising, burning feeling she'd felt in the woods while chasing an unknown man dragging off a girl into the dark.

Urgency, deep and powerful, came next.

True urgency.

Lily glanced at Ant. He looked so much like he had that night. Dark hair wet with creek water and rain, a hardened face trying to figure out why the world wasn't lining up the way it was supposed to, eyes as black as the night his sister was disappearing into.

Lily put her hand on the doorknob and turned. It was unlocked. They didn't have the time to wait.

The door opened with ease.

Whatever happened next, she and Ant were in it together.

THE LIGHTS WEREN'T ON.

It was the second thing Ant noticed as he and Lily went inside.

The first?

No one was home.

At least not in the main room.

Lily had her service weapon at the ready. Ant had his fists balled.

"Dawn County Sheriff's Department," she yelled out. Still nothing.

The back door was still unlocked. The window he'd climbed through was still open. The same went for the door to the bathroom that was ajar, the light on inside.

Ant nudged Lily and nodded to the pool table room.

She took the lead with notable aggression.

Ant hurried in after her.

Nothing had changed and no one else was waiting for them there.

Lily backed out. Ant grabbed the pool cue he'd wielded earlier and followed.

It might not be a gun but he could still make it hurt if he needed.

There was only one room left that neither had seen inside before. Ant did a dance around her to get to the doorknob first. Lily raised her gun. She didn't need to say a word to let him know this was it.

This was game time and she wasn't going to be the one to fumble the ball.

The second Ant had the door open, Lily took a powerful step forward.

Then she stopped as if she'd hit a brick wall.

Ant was behind her in a flash.

He was so dumbstruck he couldn't even find the right cuss to fit the situation.

The room was the same size as the one with the pool table, and just as decrepit. The paint was escaping parts of the wall, the floor had chips in it and there was a slight sag in the roof. Still it was in far better shape than what was stored within it.

The trash alone would have been alarming. There were bags and wrappers among bottles and beakers and plastic containers cluttering the floor. Batteries sat on top of a pail of kitty litter in the corner, a blender beaten to near death on a table next to it. Buckets and paper towels and rubbing alcohol containers were scattered around like clunky confetti. Ant stopped next to a spool of aluminum foil and a pile of coffee filters. Lily was slightly ahead of him, stopping again by several strainers, rubber tubing and a propane cylinder on its side. Beneath the window opposite them was a twin mattress, stripped bare, on the floor. A lone pillow without a case was at its head.

Lily lowered her gun. She covered her nose with her arm and turned to him.

"Back out of here," she said on a hurried breath. "This is a meth lab."

It should have clicked sooner but the moment she said it, everything in the room made sense.

Everything but an open box at the foot of the mattress. There was something at the very top. Something that didn't fit the rest of the room but something they'd definitely seen before.

Ant pointed to it, covering his nose and mouth with his other arm in an attempt to avoid exposure to the hazardous chemicals around them.

"One of these things is not like the other."

Lily was fast. Her gun went into her holster and she pulled a pair of blue latex gloves out of her blazer pocket. She was on the box in seconds, picking up the item on top.

"It's a recorder." Lily turned the black box this way and that between her hands. "It's identical to the one that was buried."

Ant, who had up until then thought of the workshop as something only related to Bryant Lautner, said the obvious.

"This all can't be a coincidence."

Lily didn't comment on the thought. She was peering into the box.

"This thing is filled with recorders. Maybe ten. Maybe twelve." Lily's gaze went back to the one in her hand.

"Does that one have a tape in it?" Ant asked her.

Lily answered by clicking the play button.

The screaming that echoed out of it wasn't as off-putting as it had been the night before, but that didn't mean Ant was a fan. He watched Lily visibly tense.

"It's Annie McHale again."

Ant had to pause at that.

He had sympathy for what had happened to Annie, but that didn't stop the well of resentment that lived within him at her family. At Kelby Creek. It was why he avoided talking about Annie and The Flood in general. Others could shake their heads and say *what a pity.* Ant had a harder time not comparing everything to Ida.

"What do you mean it's Annie again?" There was no point sugarcoating his voice. It was dripping in his feelings that he knew, in some small part, Lily shared.

Lily was unfazed. Her attention went back to the box.

Where it went after that, Ant wouldn't know.

A car door shut outside.

Ant didn't wait around to see what happened next.

He was out of the room and on the front porch in a blink. The mention of Annie, the possibility that Bryant Lautner was connected to Ida, and Lily showing up for the man that had nearly maimed her all had Ant raring to go.

The Cadillac reversing at an alarming speed was just the cherry on top that he needed.

"Hey!"

Ant jumped off the porch in one quick bound. The distance between him and the car was widening. He couldn't see who was driving.

"Stop!"

The car gave off a God-awful squeal. The driver swung it around so both were facing the dirt road. Ant wasn't going to stand for that. He charged ahead with every intention of catching the car when the driver had to slow down to turn. Then he could open the door and get some answers. At the very least he could get a better look at the driver's face.

It didn't take long to realize that he was actually going to do it. He could catch it. He was fast enough.

He—

He smelled smoke.

And it wasn't coming from the car.

Ant stopped in his tracks. Ice filled his veins. He spun around, abandoning his pursuit of the car and hoping with all his might that Lily had followed him out of the house. That she was sprinting only a few steps behind him.

But she wasn't.

All he saw were the budding flames that were now licking the right side of the workshop.

"Lily!"

The car behind him kicked up dirt and rocks. It became background noise to him repeating Lily's name.

Those were the last two things he heard before the workshop exploded.

Chapter Ten

The heat.

Blistering as it was, it didn't compare to the force of the explosion.

Ant went from upright and facing the house to on his back staring up at the sky within the blink of an eye. Pain was a burn in his chest; pressure was a vise on his lungs. He was coughing before he was sitting up and was pretty damn sure that something on him was broken. Cracked at the least. Bruised for certain.

Ant wasn't going to know for a while because there was no way he was going to sit there, take a break and tally up his injuries. Not when he had no idea where Lily was. He rolled onto his side and managed to push up. It took him two tries but he made it up with a wobble. He coughed all the while, trying to suck in the air that had been knocked out of him. Enough, at least, to yell.

"Lily!"

The house was a scene right out of a nightmare. Flames ate at the entire right side of the building, dark smoke rolling up high, while the left side looked like it had been simultaneously crushed and then snapped like a rubber band stretched out too far. The porch was crippled and the front door was broken in two. None of it stopped Ant. He covered his nose and mouth with an aching arm and ventured inside what used to be a building.

"Lily!"

Ant kicked away broken remnants of the structure around him, only eyeing the buckling ceiling above the living space with mild concern for himself. He made it two steps toward where the second bedroom had been before he had to stop. There was no way he was getting inside that room.

It wasn't even a room anymore.

That ice in his veins hardened into a weight that threatened to drag him all the way down.

If Lily had been in that room when it blew...

No.

He wasn't going to accept that.

Ant pulled his shirt up to his nose and surveyed the destruction in front of him. There wasn't any way he could get into the area safely. In fact, he doubted there was a way he could break through the debris without bringing down the rest of the building. But maybe if he was fast... Maybe if he dove in with his fists and muscle he could dig her out... Maybe if—

Coughing.

It was faint but it was unmistakable.

Ant spun to his left, trying to track the sound.

"Lily?"

Something shifted near the back door. It was a part of the ceiling, now on the floor. The boot that moved beneath it was like a gut punch.

"Lily," he yelled. "I'm here!"

Ant made it over and tossed the wood to the side just in time to see Lily struggling to push herself off the floor. She was on her stomach, with her weight spread between it and her elbows. The effort didn't seem to be working. At least not fast enough.

A loud cracking noise split through the flames lapping up the beams.

Ant couldn't be gentle, but he could be fast.

He moved his arm beneath Lily's waist and pulled her up against him. She started to convulse in a coughing fit. Ant felt for her but he wasn't about to stop and hang around. Holding her close, Ant ran out of the building and into the woods. He didn't even think about slowing until the trees enveloped them.

When he finally did, he still didn't let Lily go completely.

"I got you," he told her. He crouched down and tried to maneuver her onto her back with as little jostling as possible.

Good intentions but bad execution. He lost his balance and fell to the dirt with a painful thud. Lily slipped out of his hold but he was quick to wrangle her against him so she didn't hit the ground.

Her long hair, smelling of smoke, rested against his chest. Her coughing became a slow reverberation that went all the way through him. Ant kept one arm wrapped firmly around her, as if it was a safety measure against the danger that had exploded around them.

If Lily minded, she didn't say so.

Once she caught her breath, he felt her relax into him a bit.

They sat like that for a few moments before the cracking sound grew sharper, louder, echoing through the trees.

Bryant Lautner's workshop seemed to take one big collective breath before collapsing in on itself.

Ant couldn't move. He could only watch the way the

smoke became darker, reaching for the sky above them like a hand of death.

A hand that had almost taken Lily.

Ant tightened his hold ever so slightly on the woman against him.

THE FIRE DEPARTMENT couldn't save the building by the time they arrived fifteen minutes later so they focused on saving the trees instead. An ambulance hauled tail between Sheriff Bennet's truck and Detective Gray's shiny new SUV. Two deputy cruisers rounded out the caravan but Lily was sure others were spread out and blocking the road off at both ends.

The rest of the department sure as hell better be trying to find the man in the Cadillac.

"Detective Howard, I'm telling you we're going to the hospital," the EMT named Colton said after a cursory examination at the road.

Lily had one leg out of the ambulance and the other ready to walk her the rest of the way out of the back. Her attention was past them to the sheriff. Blake Bennet was huffing and puffing on her cell phone and her radio, pacing a line in the dirt. Her braid was swinging, her lips thin and angry.

"And I'm telling you I feel fine," Lily shot back at the man. She motioned to her body. It probably wasn't the most convincing move. She hadn't caught her reflection yet but by the concern in everyone's eyes, she wasn't winning any awards for being pristine.

Movement from the side of the ambulance drew her attention. Ant had his arms crossed over his chest. He eyed her like she was an errant child.

"You just got blown up by a meth lab." His words were stern, matching his body language. "And before you try to downplay that just remember that I'm the one who helped lift a piece of the ceiling off you. You're going to the hospital."

Lily was shocked at the resolve. Though not as much as she had been at the situation they'd wound up in. She'd come chasing a thin lead. She was about to leave in an ambulance.

It didn't sit right with her.

"The bulk of the explosion was in the other room and we weren't exposed long," she tried.

Ant and the EMT weren't having it. They spit some more concern and facts her way until Sheriff Bennet's gaze swung to Lily's and everything turned angry. She moved her phone to her shoulder and hollered.

"Why aren't y'all on the way to Haven? Get going!"

Lily didn't want to be toted off to the hospital. She wanted to stay and work the scene, or dig deep on the clues she'd found inside, but the sheriff's words stopped her short.

The sheriff hadn't held her position long but she was no stranger to the power of her command.

EMT Colton she could bypass. Ant she could maybe sway. Sheriff Bennet's orders? She didn't want to push her luck.

"Fine." Lily pulled her legs back in. "But I'm telling you, I'm okay."

No sooner had she said it than she was struck by breath-stealing pain as she attempted to settle on the gurney. Lily gathered up every acting skill she had to hide the pain.

It didn't work.

Ant got in behind her and sat on the bench at her side.

"Next time you say that, hide the flinch and I might believe you."

Colton banged on the window to the front seat to signal

the driver. He told the man to take it slow on the pits and dips of the aged road.

"We about lost an axle flooring it here," he explained to them. "Though I guess it was worth the risk to avoid getting stuck in the mud had it been flooding again." He made a tsking sound. "My cousin Benny is a firefighter in the county over and said they had to call in the cavalry after one of their trucks got sucked into a ditch last night. We only have the two ambulances in Dawn County so I think we better not chance it breaking down."

Lily wasn't going to comment, mainly because she didn't think it was a conversation worth having. Small talk wasn't her favorite thing, especially coupled with being in a tight space. Ant, though, seemed to really take to it.

"I worked on towing a fire truck once back at my last job working for a mechanic," he told Colton. "It was tricky business. My boss about blew a gasket after our first towing line snapped."

Lily tilted her head a little at that.

"I didn't know you worked as a mechanic. The last I heard you were tending bar in Richmond."

Ant laughed.

"The last you heard was a few years ago. It's been a hot minute since I was slinging drinks in Virginia."

A tinge of *something* pinched at Lily.

No one had expected her to keep in touch with Ant through the years and she hadn't. Only a few times had it been necessary to track him down to speak about Ida's case. She already knew her knowledge of his life as an adult was slim. Yet there she was, feeling a certain way about it.

"I wasn't much a fan of bartending, to tell you the truth," he told Colton. "I know you must see some holy horrible things at this job but when I say I saw my fair share of bloodshed and cringe-worthy injuries while dol-ing out alcohol, let me tell you I mean it."

Colton didn't challenge Ant's claim and the conversa-tion took another turn toward convivial. Lily didn't pre-tend to want to join. She instead turned inward to catalog how she was feeling. It wasn't until they took a turn into the parking lot of Haven Hospital that Lily finally circled in on what was bothering her.

The realization must not have been missed. While Colton spoke to the driver, Ant leaned in.

"If you won't tell the professional what's hurting, tell me, so I can do absolutely nothing helpful since I know more about cars and beer than humans."

His sarcasm barely concealed his concern. Lily rolled her eyes but kept the same closeness between them.

"It's not what's hurting," she said. "It's what's not sit-ting right with me."

"And what's that? Because, I'll be honest, none of what's happened since I got back to Kelby Creek has been sitting right with me."

Lily shook her head. It hurt.

She kept on.

"Let's make an assumption that whoever started the fire knew exactly where they were starting it. That they knew a meth lab filled with hazardous materials was right there, just waiting for a spark."

"An easy assumption to make," Ant added.

"And, since you told me the only person you told was Mrs. Jane and until Juliet asks if she told anyone we're going to act like she didn't, we didn't tell anyone when and where we were going, let's assume that no one knew we were out there." She didn't mention the fact that she and Ant had both hidden their cars from view, though that was definitely a point in the No One Knew They Were There column.

"All right."

"That means someone meant to destroy that house and they meant to do it while it was empty. Why?"

Ant's brow furrowed. This close to him, Lily let her eyes trace his face, follow the smears of dirt and sweat across his skin. She felt relief at the distance he'd managed to put between the workshop and himself before the explosion. It had been his yell for her that had made her drop the recorder and bolt from the room. Had she not tripped, she would have made it out of the building safely and not needed this trip to the hospital.

"Well, from what I heard you tell Detective Gray, it was a textbook meth lab in there," Ant supplied. "Maybe a competitor wanted to end its production? Maybe it was Bryant's *or* Arturo's and they wanted someone to cover it up?"

Lily snapped her fingers.

"That's another thing." She lowered her voice even more. "It was textbook. Yet the rest of the house didn't smell like anything other than mildew. Why was there no spillover into the rest of the house?"

Lily quieted as the ambulance came to a stop. The EMT opened the back doors and hopped out. He was waving at someone inside the hospital.

Ant's attention was still squarely on Lily.

"You don't think it was real. The meth lab."

Lily shrugged through her pain.

"The recorders are the only thing in that house that made sense to me. They connect us back to the box in the ground and Arturo, both of which sent me there in the first place." Colton was talking to a nurse who'd come out. Lily side-eyed them to make sure they weren't listening. Ant came in so close that Lily could feel his warmth against her cheek. "If we can't get answers from the box, that workshop, or Arturo, then maybe the recording itself is where we look now."

"Annie McHale screaming." He sucked on his teeth a second. "That's a case worked to death. Are you looking to ask the FBI agents who investigated or go local? Because you and I both know neither are going to give you much. I'm sure they've lost count of how many tips, leads and conspiracy theories they've gotten over the years."

Lily knew that was true.

She also knew something Ant didn't.

"Not every McHale left town after the investigation was over. I know someone who stayed."

Chapter Eleven

Any and all investigative routes Lily had been itching to take were blocked by the simple fact that she was worse off than she'd pretended to be.

Where her ribs weren't bruised, they were broken. She had a concussion that brought on a headache that had made her sick. There was a nasty cut along the back of her thigh from falling debris and bruising along the front of her from being thrown to the ground.

By the time she got into an examination room at the hospital she'd gone from telling everyone she was fine to asking for pain meds.

Ant didn't like it. He didn't like it at all.

When the doctor insisted she get into a hospital gown and right into a bed, he was a mass of constantly moving anxiousness. He hovered, he insisted, he was eventually told to leave. He would, though only after she spoke to him, before the meds took over.

"They want me to stay the night but I don't have anyone to watch Cook," Lily told him when they finally were alone. Ant could tell she was trying not to move too much. The sight ate at him.

"I can see to him," he said. "We already know he's a fan of me."

Lily gave him a brief smile. She let her head rest back

against the pillow. Ant didn't want to get too close, even though he'd changed out of his contaminated clothing into scrubs the hospital had given him.

Yet it was a hard personal ask. Every time he looked at her, he wanted to do the opposite.

He wanted to hold her again like he'd done in the woods.

He wanted to protect her.

"Juliet is going out there to get a file from my office," Lily added, becoming more quiet on every syllable. "She won't mind giving you a ride."

"I'll make sure everything is good," he promised, forgoing reaching for her hand. "Don't you worry."

Lily's eyes closed but Ant stayed a moment longer.

She'd been blown up the day after she'd been attacked.

Leaving her didn't feel right.

The rhythmic beep of the monitor next to the bed was steady.

Lily was okay for now.

But he'd thought she was okay that morning when he'd left.

A nurse came in then and shooed him into the hall with reassurances that Lily just needed to rest. Once he stepped out, Detective Juliet approached him. She'd obviously heard the nurse's comment.

"I'd sleep for a week straight after all of that, truth be told." She eyed him critically. "I don't know how you're not laid up, too."

Ant shrugged off the concern.

"She took the brunt of it, believe me. All I needed was an ibuprofen."

"Tough guy." She grinned. "No wonder Howie's been hanging with you."

The detective told him to call her Juliet and, as Lily had said, had no issue with letting him tag along to her house.

Their conversation on the ride over was surprisingly bland, though. Ant wasn't sure why she wasn't bringing up the workshop, Lautner or Arturo, but he wasn't going to be the one to do so.

If he was being honest, the idea of discussing the case with a woman who wasn't Lily felt wrong somehow.

He did, however, decide that he liked Juliet. She was easygoing until it was time to focus. The second they walked into Lily's house she met Cook with a whole heap of scratches before making a game plan.

"I'll meet you here when I'm done. It shouldn't be long. Well, unless she doesn't have any sort of ordering system to her files then I might be a bit." She sighed but it didn't feel accusatory. "Bless her, Howie's good, but sometimes she's too good."

Ant liked the compliment. He wasn't sure Lily would. Neither was he sure about the nickname.

"I've heard her called a lot of things but I don't think I've heard Howie."

Juliet laughed freely. She pointed at Cook, still bouncing between them.

"I'm a firm believer that Cook and Howie has a great *Turner & Hooch* ring to it." She spread her hands out in the air between them like she was reading a banner. She adopted an announcer-style voice. "Cook and Howie, service dog and dogged detective fighting injustice while trying to navigate the small town niceties…that and Mrs. Belview's constant complaints about the neighborhood kids walking on her grass."

She was grinning. It was definitely a bit she'd done before. She looked at him for a reaction but his focus had shifted.

"I didn't realize Cook was a service dog with the department." Cook nudged his hand, picking up on his name. "I guess that's why he held his own in a fight."

"Oh, no, I *wish* he was with our department. I've been told Kelby Creek is looking to build us a K-9 unit next but I've been holding my breath with that news for two years." The next part came out so effortlessly that Ant guessed Juliet probably hadn't even realized she was sharing it. Or had assumed that Ant was a lot closer with Lily than he was. "Cook was a PTSD service dog in North Carolina. Lily got him just as the funding to the program was cut. She petitioned to keep him and now he's the adorable leading man in the duo that is Cook and Howie." Juliet swooped her hand down to give the dog a few more pets.

Then all the jovial easiness from the detective became focused. Before Ant could collect his thoughts, she was clouding them up again.

"I know she was concerned about him for the night but did she ask you to pack a bag for her? If she's staying at the hospital, she'll probably need one."

Lily hadn't asked. She hadn't asked for anything for herself since they'd arrived at Haven Hospital. Her concern had landed on him and Cook only.

"Yeah, she did," he lied. "I'm running up there now."

Juliet led the way until they went in opposite directions at the top of the stairs. Cook followed Ant and looked up at him once they were both inside the bedroom.

"PTSD, huh?" Ant patted the dog's head. "I didn't realize she was having issues."

The second he whispered it to Cook, Ant felt shame wallop him.

He was the brother who'd lost his sister. He'd been attacked, left for dead and then left searching for years. Ant didn't settle. He didn't form long-standing relationships. He didn't even stay in the same place for more than six months.

He had trauma.

He had nightmares.

He hadn't thought about Lily in the same light.

She had drive, determination and a career she'd been cultivating since leaving town. Sure, Ant knew there had to be scars there. Emotional, mental.

Yet, there he was in her bedroom, for the first time realizing he hadn't wondered about Lily's suffering.

He was the brother who had lost his sister. She was the girl who had run into the darkness ahead of him.

He'd been attacked. She'd fought, too.

He'd been left for dead in the creek water. She'd been the one to pull him out.

He'd been the one screaming out for Ida in the rain. She'd been the one that spent years in law enforcement... only to come right back with training, skills and a life that had been forever changed by a night in the woods.

Of course, she wouldn't have just gotten over that.

Who would?

Who could?

Ant wanted to talk to Lily, right then and there, and apologize.

He was sorry he hadn't kept in touch. He was sorry he hadn't been there for her. He was sorry that, even now, she might be in the same boat as him.

Lily Howard might have spent the past fourteen years seeing the same ghosts, and all he'd done about it was a big fat nothing.

Cook's body weight thudded against his leg. On reflex, Ant reached out to stroke his fur.

"Don't worry," he told the dog. "I'm not leaving her alone again."

THE WAY TO hell was paved with good intentions.

And Lily sure had had good intentions two days before.

"This is ridiculous," she said now, shooing away the reaching hands of someone else with good intentions. "I'm a little beat-up but I can get out of the car without your help. Thanks."

She knew her tone was flat—she *felt* flat—but Lily wasn't going to apologize.

She was grumpy, if she was being honest. Grumpy, hungry and in need of four walls around her that weren't lined with beeping machines.

Her helper rolled his eyes. He waved his hand, unperturbed.

"Just take my hand, Oscar the Grouch."

Lily gave Ant a look she hoped hurt, just a little. He'd been an orbiting planet to her sun for the past two days. She hadn't asked for the attention but she'd more than received it. When Ant wasn't at her home taking care of Cook, he was in her hospital room offering up theories on Arturo and the box, telling her stories of his life over the past fourteen years, or simply just sitting there, his face behind his phone.

It had driven Lily crazy.

She'd gone from a relatively solitary life to one where she hadn't been alone in days.

All thanks to one little explosion.

Lily let out a sigh. She stood tall after it.

The wrap on her ribs was tight; the dull pain of healing bruises made her stiff. She smiled at her house.

"Look how beautiful this *not*-hospital is. It should be on a postcard."

Ant laughed and let her go. A second later he was back with her bag in one hand and the other held out to her.

Lily wasn't having it.

"You've seen me walk on my own," she said. "I can manage it here."

"You also had to stay an extra day in the hospital because managing it alone wasn't something you should have been doing."

Lily grumbled beneath her breath.

"I'm sorry, I didn't catch that," Ant teased.

"I said, I only stayed to keep you and Juliet off my case. I don't need help now." She held her head high.

Ant didn't laugh again, or roll his eyes, but she thought he might be struggling to not smile. Regardless, she set out to keep her word. The walk to the garage door was a slow one, but one she managed with—dare she think it—grace.

That grace all but left when she laid eyes on Cook.

The dog was normally well-behaved but this was the longest they'd gone without seeing each other. Both parties got a little sloppy with their hellos. Cook almost toppled Lily over and Lily almost let him. It was only Ant who remained upright and strong. He put a hand between them to calm them both down and redirect them to the couch. Lily didn't realize until she was settled on a cushion that she was near tears.

Ant, thankfully, had excused himself upstairs with her bag.

Lily took the moment alone to reassure her best friend.

"I really am okay," she whispered to Cook. "Just a few bumps and bruises."

Cook lapped at her face. He'd barely settled by the time Ant had come back down.

"Bag is up, my car and your car are outside, Cook has been fed, walked and is mud-free, and *now* I'm hungry. You and your folks used to eat at Crisp's Kitchen a lot, right? Want me to order some lunch from there?"

Lily had been trying to keep her emotions off her face

for as long as she could remember. It was habit. Necessary for her job, practical for her personal life. But during the past four days it had been more of an exercise than second nature. An exercise she found easier to fail in Ant's presence.

As he listed all the ways he was helping her, and still wanted to help her, Lily was caught between a myriad of emotions.

Ant was taking care of her.

She hadn't been taken care of in a long while.

Not since Ida was taken.

Lily's stomach betrayed her need to try to put distance between her confusion, gratefulness and long-planted guilt. It growled so loudly that Cook's ears perked up.

"I guess that would probably be a good idea," she relented.

Ant was pleased and stepped into the kitchen to place their order with a smile on his face and an almost-bounce to his step.

How long was he going to be with her?

How long was he going to stay in town?

Two questions that had stood tall in her mind over the past few days.

It didn't help that her professional questions weren't getting answered, either.

The workshop had indeed been a spot that Bryant Lautner had frequented, but the man himself was hard to find. Juliet and Kenneth had been searching through the internet, the town and local word-of-mouth. Last Lily had heard no one had been able to find out who owned the land Bryant's workshop was on. Or had been on. The lab within it had done a great job of destroying the rest of the house when everything went up in flames.

Everything, including the box of recorders.

Arturo had been questioned about them, about the workshop and his corresponding social media posts that had led Lily to investigate the property, but he'd clammed up quickly. Now he was in the county jail for assault and waiting for a trial. His bail had been set but not paid.

The man and the Cadillac outside the workshop?

Gone in the wind, though an all-points bulletin had been released to the public. She wasn't putting much stock in that panning out. The meth lab explosion had made the news quickly. If the man who'd started the fire had even one brain cell, he'd dumped the car right away.

It all ate at Lily.

She wasn't the only one.

Kenneth had visited her the day before and given his two cents on Arturo, the box in the ground, and the workshop's connection to Bryant.

"Kelby Creek might be small, but her confusing, complicated mysteries are mighty." He'd taken a moment to look down at his wedding band. "But we're patient and that counts for something."

Lily hadn't corrected him then.

Sometimes she was patient, but only because she'd had to be.

Right now, she didn't want to be patient.

Right now, she wanted answers.

Right now she—

"Hey, Lily?"

Ant's voice carried in from the kitchen. Less than a second later and Cook was up, alert.

She turned her head so quickly to the front of the house that the movement brought a searing pain. Lily clenched her teeth then spoke through them.

"Yeah?"

Ant came into view but only to walk to the front window. He looked almost comical as he spied through the curtains.

"Were you expecting any company?"

Cook joined him.

Lily could hear footsteps coming up the front porch stairs.

"No. I wasn't even expecting you to still be here," she said honestly.

Ant stood tall and gave her a look she couldn't decipher. "Well then, you're definitely in for a surprise."

Chapter Twelve

"Coulrophobia."

Lily was in the kitchen, a newly poured cup of coffee in her hand. Ant was a breath away from her, head bent down so the new arrival in the living room couldn't hear them.

"Coulrophobia," he repeated back.

Lily nodded.

"That's what it's called—the phobia of clowns. A girl I knew in the academy had it. Broke down into a fit when someone brought in their bobblehead of Pennywise from Stephen King's *It*. She couldn't function until it was out of the building."

They both looked at the hallway separating them from the living room.

"Well it's a dang good thing we're not suffering from it, too."

Lily agreed.

"It would make questioning her less than ideal, that's for sure."

Lily handed Ant the coffee and grabbed her detective's notepad from the counter. Hurt or not, it didn't matter. Ant watched as Lily went from off the clock and wounded to ready-for-anything detective. That anything just so happened to be a young woman sitting on her couch in full clown makeup and costume.

"I'm so sorry again for the way I look," the young woman said as soon as they rounded the corner. "We have a show tonight at the fair and dress rehearsal is in an hour. I would have come over before costume and makeup but, uh, I wasn't even sure I was going to come until I was in the car."

Ant handed her the coffee.

The young woman took the cup and smiled shakily. Lily let her take a sip. She hadn't asked a question yet. Just invited the woman in when she'd told them she had to talk.

Lily instead looked at Ant, then motioned to the love seat.

At the nonverbal cue he pushed the love seat across the hardwood floor. It went from being next to the couch to across from it. Lily could now sit down opposite the woman, which she did. Ant took the seat next to Lily. He wasn't even sure the young woman registered either.

When she was done with her drink all she did was look at them for a moment before the rest of her words came out in a tumble.

It turned out Lily didn't have to ask any questions at all to get some answers. Maybe that's why she'd offered the coffee. She was simply waiting for the woman to find her ground.

"I'm—I'm Winnie. Uh, Winnie Johnson. I, um, I actually live in the neighborhood." She pointed over her shoulder. Her puffy, striped sleeves shifted. "On Kellogg Street, the house with the dark blue door in the middle of the block."

Lily nodded. "I've seen it. It's a nice door."

Her voice had changed. It had gone from annoyed at him, to flat when inviting Winnie in, and now it was soft. Not quiet, just soft. It seemed to encourage Winnie.

"Yeah, thanks." She laughed a little but there was nothing but nerves in it. She sobered after that. "That's how I knew where to come to see you, Miss Howard. Oh, sorry, Detective Howard."

"Lily's fine. And this is my friend Anthony."

Ant hadn't expected an introduction but he outstretched his hand and shook Winnie's with a smile.

The wobble in the woman's voice returned as she continued.

"I saw you, uh, when you moved in and Mrs. Claudine told me about you. That you were a detective. Me and my friend Kris—Kristine Cho—were curious and looked you up and found a few articles online about some cases you were on in Huntsville. The one where you were stabbed when you found that man trying to bury that jogger's body."

Ant tried to keep his cool at that.

He failed.

"You were stabbed?"

Lily didn't break composure. She nodded, all nonchalant.

"A man was stalking another woman when a jogger caught him by surprise. He was under the influence of some pretty intense narcotics and killed her. I responded to a call about screaming and found him trying to bury her in a shallow grave. Now he's in prison for life and I have a tiny scar. Both better outcomes than the woman's."

Ant knew his mouth was hanging open but he didn't comment again. Winnie kept on.

"Well, Kris just thought that was awesome. I mean, not the murder part, but how you manhandled this guy who was twice your size and drugged up. You see, we're in college. We go to the community college up the road and we've been trying to figure out what's next." Winnie laughed; it was self-deprecating. She waved her hand over her costume. "Clearly signing up to be a clown with the theater club wasn't what I imagined but well, it doesn't matter."

Winnie put her mug on the coffee table between them. Her hand shook.

"The reason why I'm here is because as far as I can tell, you're great at your job and you care and…well, you weren't here for The Flood. Which hopefully means you're not corrupt. I mean, I know there are others in the sheriff's department who are new and have come back to town to try and fix this place but a lot of us are still a bit weirded out by everything and—"

Lily reached out. Her hand rested on top of Winnie's forearm.

"Take a deep breath," she instructed. "In through the nose, out through the mouth."

Ant watched as both women did it together. Winnie's shoulders relaxed just enough to show that it had an effect.

She nodded when she was done.

"Now, tell me why you wanted to talk to me," Lily coaxed, her voice still as soft as a feather. A feather that weighed the same as a brick.

Winnie took another breath. Her entire demeanor changed.

"Kris left the fairgrounds early last night and now I can't find her." Winnie pulled her phone from her jumper's pocket. She unlocked it and held the screen up so they could see the picture. It was of Winnie and another young woman, their faces pressed together smiling while lights twinkled behind them. "It was the only night we could go without working so we went with a few people. But Kris left early. We drove there in my car because Monday night she got hers stuck in some mud out on Old Cherry Street and I kind of broke her bumper trying to tow her out. So when one of our friends saw her leave the fair early with someone, I didn't think much of it."

Ant had gone straight as an arrow. And it wasn't because the fair was the last thing he wanted to think about since once he thought about the fairgrounds, he thought about the woods behind it, and when he thought about the woods behind it, he thought about the creek. About the man. About Ida. He was sure Lily felt the same. Though she was much better at controlling her reaction.

She hadn't moved a muscle and when she spoke, her words sounded clear as day.

"You think she was taken from the fairgrounds against her will?"

Winnie shook her head.

"Our friend said she got into the passenger's seat without any issue but, well, one of the reasons I didn't go to the department with this is because Kris has had this secret boyfriend for a few months now." Winnie squirmed a little in her seat. "I mean she tells me everything but she gets all weird about talking about him so I... Well, I just kind of assumed he's married. So if I'm overreacting, and she just left with him and forgot her phone charger or something, and then I went to the department..."

"You're afraid you'd expose the affair," Lily finished.

Winnie nodded.

"I know that's not right but I wouldn't want to do that to Kris, especially since I don't even know that it *is* a married man." She put her phone back and gave one quick nod, seemingly to herself. Ant was surprised to hear her voice stronger than it had been since she arrived. "But I didn't want to *under*react either, not after what happened to you out at the meth lab."

Lily shared a quick look with Ant. The explosion had made the local paper and television news but he didn't get the connection between Winnie's friend and what had happened to them. Neither did Lily.

"What do you mean after what happened to us?" she asked. "Is Kris involved in drugs?"

Winnie was quick to shake her head.

"No, but my boyfriend told me this morning that whoever started the fire drove away in an old busted-up Cadillac." Winnie put her hands up quick in defense. "Uh, I'm dating Colton Dean. He's the EMT that drove y'all to the hospital. I swear he doesn't normally tell people stuff like that but, well, I kind of brought it up first."

Ant could tell Lily didn't like the breach of privacy. He could also tell she had already moved on when she spoke again.

"What about it?"

Winnie took on a pained expression.

Even through the white and red paint across her face, Ant could feel it.

Winnie didn't want her worry to be validated. She didn't want her fear to be real. She didn't want to believe something she already had started to believe.

Ant knew that feeling.

He knew that pain.

He felt it all over again when Winnie gave them their connection.

"The car that Kris left in last night was a Cadillac, busted up and old."

Winnie tried to smile. She wanted to be wrong. She wanted her gut feeling to be an overreaction. A girl crying wolf.

But Lily didn't jump in to reassure her that she had nothing to worry about.

That it was just a coincidence.

So Ant didn't see it as his place to lie, either.

LILY WAS OUT on her front porch directing an orchestra of law enforcement from the comfort of a dining room chair and her cell phone. Ant had brought it out when she'd insisted he stay inside and keep Winnie company.

"If she's comfortable with dogs, let Cook back in," Lily had told him, Kenneth's line already ringing in her ear. "He'll help her as long as you're friendly with her."

Ant hadn't questioned a thing.

Then Lily was bouncing between calls.

The first was with Kenneth and, after him initially reminding her that she was off duty for recovery, he paid rapt attention to what she had to say. A missing person was never a happy thing; a missing woman in Kelby Creek had become a lot more common than it should have been.

"She hasn't been missing an entire day yet," he pointed out, playing the devil's advocate. Lily knew it was necessary but she couldn't hold back the sharpness in her words when she replied.

"A twenty-year-old woman in a secret relationship gets into a car that matches the description of one driven by a person who set fire to a meth lab that has ties to both Arturo and Bryant. One of whom is in jail for assault on an officer after finding a buried box with a recording of a potential original tape of Annie McHale screaming during her ransom video. The other, a man I've been trying to find to question about the abduction of a sixteen year-old girl, fourteen years ago. I don't know about you but those sentences are so thick with suspicion I almost couldn't get them out."

"I'm not questioning how suspicious this all looks. I'm simply reminding you that, as you yourself just said, Arturo is in custody," Kenneth returned. "He's been there since Monday night. Kris entered the Cadillac yesterday,

Wednesday night. We can work with theories but we need to also work with what we really have too."

Lily was hot under her metaphorical collar.

And she hadn't realized it until now.

Her emotions were twisting around her words, balling her hands into fists, clenching her teeth when she wasn't speaking.

She followed her own advice and took a quick but deep breath.

Throw the switch back to Off, she told herself. *Do what you're good at.*

"Well, with what we have I'd have Juliet keep looking for Bryant Lautner, you can keep looking into the recording and its connection to Annie McHale, and Foster can keep trying to find that car and go through the current narcotics scene in Kelby Creek for more information on the meth lab and suppliers who might know who was using it. I'd put Detective Reiner on Kristine Cho since he has a knack for finding people. Best case is she's with a married man and lost track of time."

"And what about you?" he asked.

Lily glanced at Winnie's car parked at the curb.

She pictured her blue door several streets away.

"I'm off duty, remember?"

Kenneth gave her the kindness of not prodding further and promised to keep her updated if and when they found something.

He also told her to stay safe.

Lily stood, careful of her injuries.

The ground had finally dried from Tuesday night's rain. Too bad for it that another storm was coming.

Too bad for whoever was in that Cadillac that Lily was coming, too.

Chapter Thirteen

It took some time but Ant and Lily finally convinced Winnie to go to the fairgrounds for her dress rehearsal.

They weren't certain that Kristine Cho was in danger, and even if she were, Winnie stressing over it wasn't going to help anyone.

So she'd gone and left them to do some investigating.

Ant blew out a low whistle when he and Lily stepped into Winnie and Kris's living room.

"How exactly do two twenty-year-old community college students get a place like this?" he asked. "If they sold it they could make a fortune."

Lily didn't laugh but she did point toward the fireplace's mantel.

"The secret for them is Winnie's parents. They're the owners."

Cole Reiner, a detective working with Foster, had given Lily a quick rundown on Winnie's parents before they'd left her house. It's how she knew they were into real estate and had gotten lucky with the stock market before leaving Kelby Creek a year ago. Kristine, on the other hand, had lost her parents in a car accident when she was seventeen. She had no other family. Just a best friend who was extremely worried.

Ant walked up to the fireplace and went over the pictures.

"Having parents who own more than one house isn't something you can market, I guess." He ducked his head around the corner to the stairs. "This place has almost the same layout as yours."

It was the exact same layout but decorated wholly differently. Where Lily lacked framed photos, fun little knick-knacks and general color, Winnie and Kris had gone the extra mile. It gave the house a homey feeling, all warm and inviting.

That was why it looked different.

Winnie and Kris had a home that they truly lived in.

Lily stayed in a house.

"Winnie said Kris's room is on the right," she said. "Let's see if we can find something."

Lily took the lead but it was slow. She had a fresh painkiller in her but was still feeling stiff.

"I'm fine," she muttered over her shoulder, knowing that her every move was being monitored by the man behind her. "You can stop breathing on me."

Ant snorted.

"Maybe I'm just impatient," he said. "You're walking like this guy named Phil I met in Vegas when I was working at a club. He did this slow strut to let the ladies know he was single. Bless whoever's heart got stuck behind him."

Lily glazed over the Phil comment and went right for another surprise from Ant.

"You worked at a club in Vegas?"

"Yes, ma'am. One with a pool if you'd believe it. Everyone in swimsuits getting toasted."

Lily really wasn't liking the stairs. The discomfort didn't compare to her curiosity.

"You bartended at a pool club. In Vegas. Wearing a swimsuit."

"I was actually security. Bartending didn't happen until I was in Virginia."

Lily reached the landing. Ant was at her elbow. He didn't stay there long.

"Don't worry." He stepped around her to open the door and threw a grin her way. "I promise I still look great in a swimsuit."

Heat, true and fast, flourished in Lily's stomach. She didn't know how to handle it. Though she didn't have to struggle with the feeling long.

Kristine Cho's room wasn't an office. There wasn't a well-used whiteboard on one wall, several boxes with scrawled-on names on the floor, and there wasn't a desk in the middle where the young woman pored over old notes trying to find something that might not exist.

No, like with the floor beneath her room, Kris had taken the space and made it home. Although it wasn't all vibrant colors and warm sunshine.

The walls were a deep burgundy; the bedroom furniture was made of heavy oak and a little too big for the space. The throw across the bed had a kaleidoscope pattern but the colors were all deep shades. Framed pictures took up the top of the dresser beneath her window.

Lily went over to the pictures and traced each with her eyes before speaking.

"When Kristine's parents were killed she stayed with her uncle until she was eighteen, then moved in with Winnie soon after graduation." Lily motioned to the expensive bed frame. "If I had to guess, this furniture belonged to her parents."

Lily pointed back to the pictures on the dresser.

"And this is the spot I'm guessing that she reserves for pictures of only them." There were a few pictures taped to the wall over her nightstand, held up by colorful tape.

Another few were over a small vanity set up along the wall next to the closet. "Anywhere else is fair game for pictures after they passed. Not this spot, though. I think this probably acts as a shrine of sorts."

Lily touched the top of the dresser lightly.

"Mom had a spot like that for Ida." Ant was bent down inspecting one of the pictures taped to the wall. "It was this little accent table thing in the living room and it was covered in pictures of her, like you'd see at a memorial service. She cleaned it twice a week and never put anything else on there. When she moved, it was the last thing she packed."

Lily's heart pulled a little. She tried to stay focused.

"I don't know who Kristine Cho was before her parents passed but I definitely think this is the room of someone trying to feel connected to her family. I'd bet all my paychecks that she even had this color wall in her childhood home." Lily wondered if Ant had kept his own ties to Ida. Did he have pictures of her on his walls at his apartment? Had he taken any of her childhood things with him as he moved around? Lily didn't ask. But she found she wanted to. The new urge to want to know more about him, to really know and not keep loose tabs on him, was surprising. "There's nothing wrong with trying to stay connected," she added on. "But it might help point us in the right direction of her secret romance."

Ant opened the vanity drawer.

"You think she might be dating someone who reminds her of her parents? That's a really weird offshoot of daddy issues, don't you think?"

"More like she could be craving stability, a sense of being taken care of," she answered. "One day she was just a teenager probably thinking about boys and school and her future. Then the next all she had was their furniture. I think that might make anyone want something in their life they can count on. Someone who makes them feel taken care of. Whether it's subconscious or not."

"So, probably not twenty-year-old boys," Ant concluded.

"Probably not."

Lily opened the young woman's closet.

Kristine's clothes were less somber than her room but not by much. She liked bodysuits, blouses that were in part sheer, and a few T-shirts that seemed to have sentimental value. There were a few summer dresses with floral patterns and next to those were fancier cuts and material. Lily ran her hand across a slinky black number with sequins. High heels sat beneath it in a clear plastic container

Lily knew her pain meds were finally working when bending down to get the box only felt stiff, not painful. She thought Ant was about to scold her for the move but turned to see him holding his own discovery.

It was a ring with a diamond so glaring that it stunned her to silence for a moment.

Though the fact that Ant was holding it out to her might have been the real reason she'd gone quiet.

And a little fluttery.

Only for the moment, though.

"I'm no expert on expensive, shiny things but if this isn't a fake I'm guessing it's more than two months of any paycheck I've ever gotten. Something I'd probably be showing off, not shoving into the back of a drawer."

Lily held up the plastic shoebox.

"These are Louboutin heels. They're also up there in price."

"Could the ring have belonged to her parents?" Ant asked. "And the shoes something she bought herself with their life insurance money?"

"It's possible. Let's keep looking."

She put the container on the bed and went back to the closet. Ant continued his search through the vanity. It wasn't long before he found a pair of diamond earrings in the second drawer and put them on the bed. Lily's search turned up two slinky lingerie numbers in the dresser. They looked new but she didn't pull them out for display. They were already invading her privacy. Even if Winnie had asked them to do it.

Lily went to the only place she hadn't yet searched on her side of the room. The nightstand had two drawers and matched the one on the other side of the bed. Ant's search timed perfectly with Lily's. They shared a look as they stood in front of their respective pieces of furniture.

That fluttery feeling in Lily's stomach started up again.

She wasn't used to having a partner. Someone to be with instead of alone in her head. Someone who had no issues with being opposite her.

Someone who met her eye and held her after the world had exploded around her.

It was a strange feeling and one that surprised her again.

Lily tried to push it away but found it was as stubborn as the man who had put it there without knowing it.

But now wasn't the time to focus on her.

Both returned their gazes downward but Ant broke the silence they'd fallen into.

"Do you think what happened to us, what happened with Ida, really did affect us?"

The question was so broad and yet, at the same time, so direct that Lily didn't know how to answer. He must have sensed it.

"I mean with relationships, dating," he clarified. "I know I haven't been the best boyfriend in the past. I haven't really been a boyfriend all that much. The last woman I dated was a while ago and she told me I was 'commitment issues wrapped in denim.'" He chuckled. "Made me wonder about how many pairs of jeans I had then." A blink later his tone downshifted into somber. "Makes me wonder now if I've been a rolling stone all these years not because I couldn't find the right woman but because I never found Ida. Or maybe it's me I never quite found. I guess it can be hard to find yourself when you spend all of your years looking for someone else, huh?"

Lily's hands were hovering over one of the two open drawers in the nightstand.

Where had that come from?

How had they gone from searching a young woman's room to talking about this?

It was such a deep dissection made in such a casual way

How was she supposed to respond?

How did she *want* to respond?

Had Ida's kidnapping taken a happy, mentally healthy young Lily and thrust her harshly into a world she neither trusted nor related to anymore—not unless she had a case in one hand and a tragedy in the other?

Had she simply gone through the motions of dating because it was expected?

Had Lily's decision to save Ant instead of Ida become a cloud above her head that always started to rain whenever she felt even a little bit happy, reminding her that Ida would never be able to do what she was doing?

Lily didn't know.

But, if she did, would she admit it to Ant of all people?

The silence became loud. It was only by training alone that the part of her brain that wasn't panicking was still looking for clues.

Lily's vision focused past her jumbling thoughts and finally onto the contents of the drawer.

There was something there that felt out of place.

"'Finnigan's at sunset.'"

"Come again?"

Lily held up the paper.

"It's a note," she answered. "Written on a torn-off corner of paper. It says 'Finnigan's at sunset.'"

The writing was in black ink. It was jagged. As if the writer had been in a rush or impatient. It could have been anything, it could have been nothing, but the hearts that had been drawn around the phrase were in pink highlighter and the kiss print in the corner was made from lipstick, a deep red.

"Is there anything you've seen in here that has Kristine's handwriting?" Lily asked. "Something we can compare this to?"

Ant was quick.

"Actually, yes. The Polaroids taped to the wall have names or captions written on the bottom."

They went to the other side of the room where Lily held up the note between two of the pictures. One caption read the month and year the picture was taken, the other read "Spring Break" with a heart and a sun drawing on either side.

"Not the same handwriting," Lily concluded.

Ant pointed to the drawings.

"But the hearts match up."

Lily placed the paper on the bed with the other items they'd collected.

"Extremely fancy shoes, an expensive ring, diamond earrings, new lingerie sets, and a note covered in someone else's handwriting but Kristine's heart doodles and probably lip print." Lily put her hands on her hips. "Without truly knowing Kristine I can't tell if she's dug in deep with the mantra of 'treat yourself' or these are gifts from a man neither one of them want anyone else to know about."

They shared another silence. Lily was getting frustrated. She stepped away from the items and focused on the note.

"'Finnigan's at sunset,'" she read again. "Is this a meeting place for the future or something that already happened?"

"It would have to have been in the last three days if it already happened."

Lily looked up at Ant, one eyebrow raised.

"You know what Finnigan's is?"

Ant's grin was sly.

"Only because Monica Glenn gave me my first kiss there." Lily wasn't amused, Ant explained. "It's the fair. Or part of it. Finnigan's Fun House."

"And the fair has only been open for three days," she realized.

"Yep. Well—" Ant checked the time on his phone "—technically two. I saw a flyer at the café. Tonight is armband night so they're not opening until five. We've got a few hours."

Lily went back to the note.

It, like the rest of the items in the room, just felt wrong.

The innocence of the doodled hearts and lip print didn't match with the expensive, more adult items.

And, maybe, that could have been Kristine's normal. She was a young woman who liked to doodle and then buy nice things.

But the fact was that Kristine Cho was also missing.

All together, none of it felt right.

"So, what's the plan, boss?" Ant's voice caught her off guard. He sounded excited. Enthused. Ready.

And there it was again.

That feeling of having someone with her. Someone close.

That feeling ran straight into the absolute fact that the

man was also pure handsome. Being with him day in and day out had shown that not even the Off switch in her could deny that.

Lily shouldn't have felt heat at his words and attention, shouldn't have had to bite down on how it also made her feel more than what had been there before, but she did.

And she wanted to keep feeling it.

"Well, Ant Perez, it looks like we're going to the fair tonight."

He THREW THE CHAIR.

He didn't kick it. He didn't push it. He didn't dramatically tip it.

He threw it across the room so hard that it shattered the display case against the opposite wall.

Trophies and awards broke, shifted and fell over at the disruption.

He didn't care.

"Human error," he roared at the bespectacled man in the linen suit on the other side of his desk. "That's what this comes down to. Human error!"

He yelled again, a string of curses that made the other man flinch. Not that he wasn't already flinching without the less-than-polite words. He knew he'd messed up. He knew he'd collected consequences.

He knew that one more mistake would be the difference between his life and a less-than-ideal death.

Because, while he was great at his job on any other day of the week, his partner was the king of doling out consequences.

Consequences that came when the yelling finally stopped.

"Do you know how unobservant most people really are?" his partner asked, all volume and heat. "How gullible they are? How many actually look right and left before crossing the road?" He shook his head. "It takes so little to actually do a lot in this town and still you managed to get someone who messed that up."

Glass from the display cabinet crunched under the man's feet as he strode to the desk, seeming to stem his tirade. He sighed heavily and leaned over onto his desk, the tips of his fingers turning white at the pressure he was using against it.

"Idiots, pure idiots, have spent the last several years getting caught in the name of some kind of cartoon-worthy justice," he said, notably calmer. Though his quiet words managed to be worse than if he were yelling. "We are not idiots and I don't believe in justice. Fix your issues or I'll fix mine."

Though he wanted to shrink back, the man behind the desk maintained eye contact with his partner.

They both knew that the "mine" he was referring to was him.

"It'll get done," he assured him. "Then we can go underground for a while until this blows over. Just give me some time."

His partner was back to rage.

He struck his fist down hard.

"You had days. You had thousands of minutes, hundreds of opportunities, you had years, if we want to get technical. But what happened? *One* thing went wrong and then everything went wrong. Fix it. Or so help me, I'll burn you all."

He didn't say anything else and the man in the linen suit wasn't staying to chance it.

He left the room and didn't let out a shaky breath until he was outside.

He scurried through the parking lot toward his car, not caring that the dirt was no doubt staining his beige shoes.

His partner was wrong.
Their original problem hadn't been just one thing.
It had been two.
Detective Howard was back.
And she wasn't alone.

Chapter Fourteen

Cook was sitting at his side, the picture of patience. Ant finished washing the dishes in the sink with a laugh.

"I already snuck you some of my Crisp's chicken," he told the pooch. "I'm not about to let you lick the plate."

Cook didn't seem to appreciate that but stayed his course. He didn't even move when Lily appeared at the kitchen doorway with an exasperated sigh.

"Well, like I thought might be the case, no one at the sheriff's department was too happy with us poking around Winnie's house. They keep saying I need to rest and I keep saying they need to calm down because I have grade A painkillers and we don't have any idea what Kristine Cho is involved in because no one can seem to find her." Lily went from a sigh to a huff. She stayed in the doorway looking every bit as annoyed as she did focused.

She also looked like a woman in need of resting.

Painkillers or not, there was a tilt to her. A way she was cradling herself to offset her bruised and injured body. It was subtle but it was there.

But Ant wasn't going to join the chorus of people telling her to just sit it all out.

"But you told them what we found, right?" he asked, toweling off his hands. "You said that Cole guy was the one assigned to look for Kristine?"

Lily nodded. "I updated him first then called Kenneth, who looped in Foster."

"What about what they're doing? Anything on the land the workshop's on? The recorders?" Ant surprised himself. In all the commotion he'd forgotten to follow up with what she'd said in the ambulance. "And what about talking to the only McHale still in Kelby Creek?"

It had been the plan for Lily to talk to Darren McHale, Annie's uncle, about the recording and Arturo to see if there was any crossover, but then Lily had gone from a woman obsessed with finding the truth to a woman in need of medical help. Still, Ant couldn't believe he'd forgotten it. He'd just been so concerned about Lily.

That should have meant something to him but Ant didn't have the time to deep dive back into himself again. He'd already done that at Winnie's house, even talking about his past relationships, and *that* had been an unfiltered thought he wouldn't have normally shared otherwise.

Still, he would have been lying if he said he hadn't been hoping that Lily would open up about her past relationships. She might have been surprised at some of his former occupations, but he'd realized when she spoke about the man who had stabbed her in Huntsville that Ant knew even less about her life since he left Kelby Creek. And not just the trauma that might be lurking there.

He reined in those errant thoughts when Lily stepped farther into the room. "The job of questioning Darren McHale was scooped up by the sheriff. She spoke with him yesterday." Lily flashed a quick smile. "Apparently he's one of the main reasons the fair came back this year. He flashed some money incentives around and has been pretty involved. So involved that Sheriff Blake had to walk and talk with him when he was inspecting the place. She said somehow they wound up talking on the Ferris wheel."

Ant didn't know the new sheriff, not by reputation and not by name, but Lily must have liked her. There was no animosity in her words.

And there was the smile.

It was small but beautiful.

"As for all other leads, no one has been having luck," she continued. "Bryant Lautner was seen at Rosewater Inn a few weeks ago but after that he seems to have vanished. Arturo Hanson still won't talk and his lawyer isn't helping. Everything we were asking this morning is still unanswered. That isn't even counting our new questions."

Ant finished drying his hands with the towel and leaned against the counter. Cook seemed to have guessed that no more food was coming his way. He retreated to the other room.

"Kristine Cho, you mean," he said.

Lily nodded.

"I hope she doesn't fit into any of this but, if she does, I'm not sure how." Frustration, clear and pointed, came through. It took the woman's frown and deepened it. "If the driver of the Cadillac is her mystery man and that mystery man is the one who set fire to the workshop, it's still not fitting for me. And our only connections between Arturo and Bryant are the recorders and the workshop."

"And don't forget Bryant has a small connection to what happened to Ida."

Lily met his eye.

"That small connection is a man coughing," she reminded him.

Ant was unmoved.

"And what's that phrase? 'The devil is in the details.'"

She didn't fight him on that. She didn't carry the line of conversation any further, either.

"We need answers," she concluded instead. "And I can't

get them sitting here, waiting mindlessly." At the last word she reached up and touched a spot on her stomach. Her rib, more precisely.

He wondered if it was bothering her now.

He wondered if she would admit it if it was.

"Okay, well, maybe we don't wait around mindlessly." Ant pushed off the counter. "I may not have any degrees or a badge but I'm an expert at finding my way to a distraction."

Lily let out a noise of surprise as Ant took her hand and pulled her to the stairs. Cook appeared with an excited bark. Both followed him up. He didn't let go of Lily until they were in front of her bed.

It wasn't until they were standing there that Ant realized how promising distraction and then running a woman up to a bed probably looked.

One glance at Lily and it was clear that she'd reached the wrong impression. Her face was aflame. Red as a kiss.

She was a sight to behold.

A heat he hadn't felt in a long time ignited in Ant.

Maybe him running her to a bedroom wasn't all innocent intentions.

"I figured this would be easier on a flat but comfortable surface," he tried lamely to explain. Lily's eyes widened and Ant let out a nervous laugh. "What I mean to say is there's an exercise of sorts that works good for clearing the mind for a little while."

Lily's eyebrows went up so high it had to have hurt a little.

"I'm not doing myself any favors here, am I?" He motioned to the bed. It was impeccably made. He patted the spot on the left before walking around to the right. He made a show of taking off his shoes. "We're going to be witches for a bit."

Lily's deep crimson shade didn't get any deeper, and her sky-high eyebrows lowered. Her curiosity was easier to see now.

"Witches?"

Ant sat on the bed and then stretched out on his back. He stared up at the ceiling and put his hands on either side of his body, palms open to his sides.

"Do the same thing I'm doing and I'll walk you through it."

Ant wasn't looking at her but he just knew Lily was hesitating. What he didn't know was if she would actually follow his lead.

Yet, after a moment, the bed sunk in a little next to him.

"Please tell me this isn't a pickup line," she said, adjusting herself. "Then please tell me if it is that it hasn't actually worked on anyone."

Ant laughed. It vibrated the bed.

"It's not a pickup line," he assured her. "It's not even a witch thing, I don't think." He paused. Smiling at the memory he was about to let her in on was easy. Feeling the weight of the reality that followed it was not.

"When Ida was thirteen she watched some teen movie about witches," he started, his eyes fixed on the ceiling above them. "I never watched it and couldn't even tell you what it was called. All I remember was that Ida and her little friends were obsessed, especially with some trick the teenagers in the movie did. 'It's called moving your power, Ant. Very serious stuff.'" Ant snorted. "She made me do it with her after everyone went home and, well, it just kind of became a thing we randomly did. I'd be in my room playing video games and she'd fling the door open and tell me it was time to be witches. Something, I have to point out, my mother wasn't a fan of. It wasn't until she did it once with us that she realized it was basically meditation. Meditation with a lot of talking."

He'd done this routine through the years whenever that ache in his chest became too much to bear. No matter where he was, he'd find a place to lie down and go through the motions while hearing Ida's voice walking him through it.

Such a silly little thing had become a tool for him to calm down.

He'd never told anyone about it, definitely never shown them how to do it before.

"Ready?" he asked.

Lily nodded. He felt it through the bed beneath them.

"Ready."

Ant took a deep breath and let it out. Then he paraphrased his little sister.

"Power comes from the earth and your feet hit it first. So let's focus on our toes and make them tingle."

"Make them tingle?"

"With your mind, Lily," he said, all dramatic. "With your mind."

Ant felt the bed move a little as she laughed quietly.

"Oh, yeah. Sorry."

"It's okay," he said, adopting a deeper voice to really sell it. "I'll give you a moment to feel the tingle."

Ida had started to wiggle her toes at that point so Ant did that now. He tried to keep his smile in check when he noticed Lily doing the same.

"Now that we're tingling it's time to move that power from our toes to our heels and then spring it up to our knees," he continued. "Knees keep our legs together so it makes sense that they need to fill up. Let them fill up now, like bone bowls."

Lily let out a bite of laughter.

"Bone bowls?"

Ant *shh*ed her, trying to stay focused.

"Are those bowls filled? Good. Now it's time to pull that power to your belly. This is where the fun begins."

Lily followed his instruction. Ant continued on.

"Now we're going to close our eyes and make some decisions."

In the dark now, what had been fun and nostalgic was changing to a solemnness that weighted him down.

So he took the next part seriously.

"Take another deep breath and move that power to your heart. Really feel it. Really imagine that and nothing else. Then it's dealer's choice. You can move it to your arms next or go right on up to your head."

Ant felt Lily breathe in and out.

He tried to clear his thoughts, focus on his body—how he felt, how the bed felt beneath him, the AC vent blowing close enough that it brushed against his arm—but he couldn't.

"I never understood why the heart didn't get more time," he said after a moment. "We focused on knees but not the heart? Didn't seem that great of a plan." Ant's focus became full-fledged feeling. He missed his sister and had no way to fix that. Not even a witch's trick.

"One of the last times we did this together, I finally asked Ida why we didn't want the power there longer," he continued. "She told me that hearts are notorious for breaking. So why would you put all of your power there when you can put it somewhere more useful? I remember thinking how cynical that sounded from a sixteen-year-old who wasn't even dating anyone. Now, though, I guess I can see that logic."

Ant kept his eyes closed.

This was supposed to be a distraction, not a run and jump off the cliff into the past.

Ant was about to apologize and conclude their awkward meditation session but Lily spoke with notable vibrato.

"I went hands next because I use my brain all the time at work. I think they can definitely stand to get some more power in them. Where do you go next?"

Ant laughed, but even to his own ears the sound was strained.

"Head," he said. "I'm more of the opposite. I use my hands more than I ever use my brain."

Lily took Ant's right hand in hers.

"I'll let you borrow some of mine then."

She squeezed but didn't let go.

Ant didn't know how to react. Lily was a guarded woman. He hadn't expected her to reach out to him in any sense of the word. Not when he was the one who was trying to help clear her mind.

"So how do we finish?" Lily followed up. "What comes next?"

Almost all of Ant's focus was on their hands. The warmth and softness of hers.

For a moment he forgot the last step in Ida's exercise.

He cleared his throat.

"Fill the spots you haven't and then when that's done, don't say a word and inch it back through your body again. As Ida always said, 'A powerful body helps center a busy mind.'"

It sounded ridiculous.

Ant would have given anything to hear Ida try to convince him otherwise.

Lily kept his hand and Ant didn't let up his grip. Both grew quiet for a few minutes. He wasn't sure if the woman was actually imagining power going through her or if she was humoring him.

Either way, he gave her the privacy.

When Lily broke the silence, he gave her all of his attention.

"Did you know that after my twenty-third birthday I was dead set on joining the FBI?"

It was easy to be honest.

"No, I didn't know that," he answered. "That's impressive."

Lily shrugged.

"I just wanted to do more and everyone feels a certain way when they hear 'FBI' so I started the process of joining," she said. "I was excited and enjoyed it until I met another recruit named Grace. People at my last department used to say I was so quiet and brooding that I sunk the world around me, but Grace? She...was broken." Lily sighed. Ant held back his sudden anger at Lily's former colleagues.

"Grace's parents were attacked in an awful home invasion when she was twelve," she continued. "Grace was just small enough to hide in the dryer while her parents were tied up in the next room. The men killed her mother a few minutes later. Grace said she heard her scream but it was Grace's father's yelling for his wife that she'd never forget. It's what pulled her from her hiding space. She went to where she knew her father kept his gun, took it, snuck into the living room, crawled past her mom's body and then killed one of the men right then and there. The other man was so freaked out, he fled. Grace untied her father and the other man never came back."

Lily let out a low breath.

"The man who got away was the one who'd pulled the trigger on her mother and for years it drove Grace crazy.

She looked for him everywhere, in everything. Nothing else mattered. Just finding him. It got so bad that Grace's father eventually moved them across the country until she went to college. Some little town in Maine where everyone knew everyone and no surprises ever happened.

"When I met Grace, she admitted that she'd probably never stop looking," Lily continued. "Even if she wanted to move on, she'd always be on the lookout for that man. One eye forever open. And I... Well, I felt that. But not as much as I felt it when she introduced me to her fiancé"

Ant chanced a look over at Lily. Her eyes were open but she was staring up. He could see her brow drawn, her lips downturned. She looked confused.

"Despite everything she had been through, despite her trauma and inability to let go, she managed to keep living. She managed to stay human."

Lily turned her head so she could meet his gaze.

"You asked me earlier if I thought what happened to Ida really affected us and our relationships," she said. "Before Grace I would have said yes. I would have said that I've been so focused on righting my wrong with Ida that I haven't had room for anything else. But then what about Grace? Have I been going through life using what happened as an excuse because it's easier?"

Ant wasn't sure she was looking for an answer so he didn't respond.

Lily didn't need him to.

She finished her story.

"That's when I realized that I wasn't ready to be Grace. And I, well, I didn't want to. All I wanted was to fix something. To undo my mistakes by helping others. And what better place to be when you want to fix mistakes and help others than Kelby Creek?"

"That's why you came back," Ant realized.

Lily nodded.

"If I can't find a way to live, I might as well be useful to those who can." She laughed a little; it wasn't all humor. "And I know that sounds dramatic but—"

Ant wasn't on any grade A painkillers for his bruised ribs. He could still feel the dull throb in them, in the bruises he had from the fight with Arturo and the explosion at the workshop. He also hadn't gotten a lot of sleep in the past few days and he'd be lying if he said he didn't feel that weighing him down a little.

Yet Ant felt nothing but ease as he moved across the bed and kissed Lily Howard right on the lips.

No pain.

None at all.

Chapter Fifteen

Life was strange.

One second you were moving power to your fingertips, the next you were kissing the one man in the entire world you never thought you'd kiss.

And enjoying it.

Lily's eyes fluttered as Ant ran his fingers along her jaw, pausing at her chin.

His lips felt like his hand in hers.

A little calloused but there was strength there and, like with the man himself, a surprising softness.

Ant wasn't just kissing her, he was caressing her with that kiss.

He was gentle.

He broke the kiss with the same carefulness.

Lily didn't want to open her eyes but she did.

Ant had propped himself up, which meant all Lily had to do to initiate another kiss was lean forward. An easy feat.

Instead, she couldn't help but fall to her insecurities.

"Why did you do that?" she asked, her voice breaking a little.

The kiss hadn't been long but it had been effective. Her entire body was still consumed by heat and nerves.

"Because you're not some ghost, Lily Howard." His

hand found her check. His thumb rubbed a small circle, eliciting goose bumps across her arms. "You might be haunted but you're still alive. I know because you make me—"

Lily's phone blared to life in her jeans pocket. It took their intimate moment and shattered it with a gasp from her.

Ant dropped his hand and whatever he was about to say. "I think you have a call to answer."

Lily sat up. She was hot. She was anxious. She wanted Ant to finish his sentence.

What she *did* was answer the phone.

"Hello?"

There was immediate silence. Lily pulled the phone away to make sure the call hadn't dropped. Then she heard a voice come through.

"Hi, is this Detective Lillian Howard?"

It was a man. He didn't sound familiar.

"Yes, this is she. May I ask who's calling?"

Ant sat up next to her. His eyebrow went high in question.

"I actually have information that I think you should know. It's about Arturo Hanson."

Lily shared a look with Ant. He motioned to his ears. He couldn't hear what the man had said. She held up her finger so he'd give her a minute.

"What kind of information?" She was careful not to sound too eager.

The man on the other end of the line was moving. There was a slight rustling sound coming through.

"I'd rather have this conversation in person. I feel like it would be safer to talk that way."

Lily struggled out of bed. Ant followed with more grace. "Are you saying you're currently in danger?"

"No," the man said quickly. "I—I'd just rather do this face-to-face. It's hard to trust someone over the phone. Can we meet? In a half hour or so?"

Lily gave the phone an incredulous look. She kept her tone even.

"You haven't even told me your name."

The man hesitated.

"I…want to remain anonymous."

"I hate to break it to you, but the second I see you in person, that anonymity goes out the window," she pointed out.

The man didn't skip a beat.

"And when we're face-to-face you're going to realize why I want to remain anonymous for as long as I can." Impatience was clear in his tone. "Now, if you want to know about Arturo, meet me at Henderson Farm in a half hour."

Lily did a quick mental calculation.

"Next to the fairgrounds?"

"Yes, and Detective, come alone or it's no deal."

Red flags went from peeking out of the ground to up and at attention en masse.

"You won't tell me your name, you want me to meet you at an out-of-the-way location and you want me to come alone. I don't think that's—"

"And you want to know what Arturo wanted to do with that box," he interrupted. "Come alone or don't expect me to talk."

The phone call ended.

Lily pulled the cell away to look at the number.

It was blocked.

"What's going on?" Ant asked. "Who was that?"

Lily checked the time. It was two fifteen. Henderson Farm was twenty minutes out, not even technically a part of Dawn County, though it shared a plot of land with the fair.

"Lily."

Ant's voice grabbed her focus.

"Some man wants to meet me at Henderson Farm to give me information on Arturo. Just me. And he wants to stay anonymous until then."

Lily already knew Ant was going to be against the plan. What she didn't know was how much. He was off the bed in a flash, shaking his head.

"You're not thinking about doing that, are you?"

When Lily didn't instantly say no, his stance grew rigid.

"You know how in the movies when we know there's a trap set up for our heroes and we yell at the screen to not be that stupid? But then they're stupid anyway? This is one of those situations, Lily."

Lily matched his stance, getting out of bed, though a little bit slower.

"Are you calling me stupid?"

Ant blew out a frustrated breath.

"No. Lily, I—"

"Because the last time someone wanted to talk to just me, it worked out," she interrupted. "We wouldn't even know Kristine Cho was missing if not."

"Yeah but Winnie didn't give you a time, place and set of rules. She just showed up."

He had a point, but he was making it in a way that rubbed Lily wrong.

"You're acting like I've never been in a dangerous situation before," Lily said.

Ant put his hands on his hips in a move that showed nothing but exasperation.

"My God, you're really going to go out there alone, aren't you?"

"What if this guy just wants to remain anonymous and

really does know something about Arturo?" she shot back. "I'll take my chances if that's the good outcome."

Ant's voice raised higher.

"And what about any other outcome? What if this guy is the guy we're looking for and he makes you disappear, too? You do remember the last two times you went somewhere alone, right? You were attacked and then *blown up.*" He shook his head. *"No way, no way,* you're going alone. We go together."

Lily knew on some level that Ant was right. That going alone was foolish and everything about the situation sounded suspicious. Yet she couldn't stop the anger that inflamed her. For so many reasons and none of them Ant's fault.

But there he was.

Her only target.

"What *we,* Ant?" she yelled. "There is no *we*! I'm the detective, I'm the one whose job this is. Just because you follow me everywhere doesn't mean you belong here. This is my case and I can't keep entertaining you because I feel bad for you!"

All of Lily's guilt and anger and frustration melded together in another wave of true urgency. She hadn't meant to say exactly what she'd said but she was glad to see it had worked.

Ant's face went from angry to impassive in a flash. As if her words had wiped his expression clean.

Lily's chest rose and fell in fast breaths. Her heart rate was running a marathon.

Ant, however, looked calm.

He rolled his shoulders back and nodded.

"Fine," he said. "Then I'll leave."

He left the room without another word. Lily followed him but stopped at the top of the stairs.

Her heart hurt.

Her head told her to let him go.

She'd already caused him the pain of losing a sister. What was a little more?

Ant stopped at the first-floor landing. He turned around and met her stare.

His kiss already felt like a lifetime ago.

"Being desperate for answers isn't a good reason to get killed, Lily. Promise me you'll at least tell someone at the department where you're going."

Lily thought of the dresser covered in pictures of Kristine Cho and her parents. The somber room and the too big furniture.

She thought of the box. She thought of Arturo and his recorder. She thought of the workshop. She thought of the Cadillac.

They had no answers.

If there was even a chance that she could get one, wasn't the risk worth it?

"I'll call the sheriff," she said.

It was a lie.

But Ant took it with him as he left.

HALF AN HOUR LATER, on the dot, Lily was parking her car at the end of the drive for Henderson Farm. A minute after that she was standing next to her door and rubbing her finger along the scar on her side.

Winnie and Kristine's favorite story of Lily's takedown of Jeffrey Becker wasn't one she liked to talk about. Finding him trying to bury the body of a woman who had had an entire life ahead of her wasn't a good memory. Neither was the fight to get him into custody. Hence the scar that was rigid beneath her finger.

What most people didn't know was that Lily had to make a choice that night.

She'd been the first to arrive and was told to wait for backup. She hadn't. Instead Lily had hurried into the dark in hopes of saving whoever was in distress.

The victim was already gone but Lily had been able to make her killer pay. Had she waited, that might not have been the case.

But then Arturo would have killed you with a shovel.

The voice in her head made Lily sigh into the cool afternoon air.

She'd gone alone to the woods and had only walked away because of Ant's interference.

There was no way to know what was the right choice until it was too late to change it.

Lily shook her shoulders back. She checked her service weapon at her hip, pulled her detective's badge out and made sure her phone was in her blazer pocket. She strode forward, hoping that Ant was wrong.

Henderson Farm used to be a dairy farm back in the early 2000s. Owned and operated by the Henderson family of six, its first building at the front of the land was their old home. Two stories, wraparound porch and faded red paint. Past the house were dirt roads that led to the barn and the old stalls. Lily had visited them on a field trip in middle school.

The Henderson patriarch had suffered an accident on the land that had put the family into financial ruin. That was until the McHale family had stepped in. They'd bought the land and whatever the price it had been enough for the Hendersons to leave Kelby Creek for a different life. Since the Hendersons had been well-liked, it had helped the town fall even more in love with the McHales.

Lily wondered if they would have finally made something of the farm if Annie had never been taken.

Now it looked beat-up and forgotten.

The perfect place to trap an unsuspecting victim.

Too bad Lily wasn't about that.

She pulled her service weapon out and held it low at her hip. Instead of going up to the front door, she walked around to the back, following the drive.

Nothing and no one made a sound.

There was, however, a vehicle parked by the back porch.

A white Cadillac in need of some upkeep. No tags.

Lily's adrenaline spiked.

She touched the back of the trunk. She couldn't see anyone through the back windshield. She walked around to the driver's side, not putting her back to the house. Last time she'd looked inside the Cadillac there hadn't been anything of note.

That wasn't the case now.

On the floorboard of the passenger seat Lily could see a few scattered pens. They were hollowed out. She spied a razor blade, too.

Both were common in meth use.

Lily heard Ant's anger in her head. His concern.

This wasn't just some source she was meeting.

This was the driver of the Cadillac.

The one who caused the explosion.

The one who'd almost killed her.

She put her gun in her holster long enough to pull out her phone. She cued up Kenneth's number.

It was only lucky that she hit Call just as the man walked out onto the back porch.

He had no holster but his gun was aimed squarely at her.

"Detective Howard?" he asked. "Did you come alone?"

Lily wasn't sure if Kenneth had picked up. She dropped

her phone at the same time she replied so the man wouldn't hear it hit the dirt.

"Yes, I came alone." She spoke slowly and loudly. "Henderson Farm, by myself. I even got here in half an hour. I listened to your requests because I want to know what you know about Arturo Hanson. But why do you have a gun on me?"

Lily didn't recognize the man. Not even a little.

He was older, maybe late forties. A perfect tan, sculpted facial hair and a bald head that had a shine to it. He was dressed in business casual—a polo and khakis. Lily could see what looked like a Rolex on his wrist.

Whoever he was, he didn't fit with the Henderson house behind him.

Certainly not with the Cadillac.

He also didn't look comfortable with a gun, but that didn't stop him from using it as a threat.

"Walk toward me, slowly, or I'll shoot until I hit something."

Lily had already run her mental numbers. She might have had the car between her and the house but it wasn't a big car and it wasn't in the greatest of shape. She wasn't sure she could use it as cover.

And she really wanted to know who this guy was.

So Lily made another choice.

She just hoped it wasn't a bad one.

"Okay. Just don't shoot."

Lily left her phone in the dirt and walked slowly until she was in the Henderson house.

Chapter Sixteen

It was quaint, all things considered.

The back door led into the kitchen that passed through what seemed to act as an old office and then opened up to the entryway and the stairs. The furniture in each room looked maintained, albeit a bit dusty, and the walls, floors and tile were all in good shape. There was no peeling paint, no sagging ceilings, and definitely no meth labs. Just the most basic version of a house unlived in. But the lights worked. The air conditioner must have worked too because the coolness of the interior pushed into Lily's skin as she was told to walk up the stairs without making any sudden movements.

Whoever the man was, her opinion of him hadn't changed.

He was uncomfortable, not at all at ease.

There was sweat beading on his brow and no confidence in his game.

There also didn't feel like there was any experience in it.

The man hadn't asked for her phone and he hadn't asked for the gun riding on her hip. Surely, he had to know it was there.

Lily wasn't going to bring it up, regardless.

She went up the stairs at a fast clip, the man scrambling

to keep the pace. Lily ignored the pain that was pulsing in her ribs.

"The—the door straight ahead," the man said, his voice loud but not at all stable. "We can talk in there."

There were several doors before the one she was directed to go through, all of them closed.

Whether she believed the man might shoot her or not, not knowing what was in each room made her cool façade crack just a little. Last time she'd waited to open a closed door she'd ended up with singed clothes and broken ribs.

"This talk we're about to have, does it have to involve the gun?" Lily was at the door at the end of the hall. She stopped.

"I need it so you'll listen. Now go."

Relief poured through Lily at seeing a room that was neither a meth lab nor some type of torture scene. Instead it was an attic space that had been renovated into a bedroom. It was long but narrow, with the ceiling lowering on either side, and had two twin bed frames pushed up against the opposite walls. There was one window. It looked over the property behind the house, showing the high grass of a farm that hadn't been as well-kept as the main house.

The man surprised Lily by walking around her and stopping in front of the window. The gray skies emitted a natural light that framed him and his gun and cast the room in an almost eerie glow.

It also made Lily's opinion of the man change slightly. He didn't just lack the confidence and practice to do what he was doing—he also looked very much like a man who didn't want to be there.

But he was there and so was Lily. It was time they dropped their pretenses.

"I want to know who you are, if that's your Cadillac

out back and what it is that you know about Arturo Hanson," she commanded.

Lily expected the man to offer a clever little spiel, the downfall of many egotistical men up to no good, yet he surprised her.

"My name is Jacob Anderson. I know Arturo because he's been trying to stop me from distributing meth in his territory. I didn't listen. So he threatened my mistress, Kristine Cho, and even though he was caught, his partner carried the threat through. Now she's gone."

Lily threw her mental switch that kept her emotions from reacting. She took on a clinical, calm tone.

"What do you mean, she's gone? Where is Kristine?"

Jacob shook his head. His gun bobbed up and down.

"It was a mistake," he said. His eyes were not even on her but somewhere on the ceiling, as if he was recalling something. "An accident. I wasn't even supposed to be there. I—" He stopped himself and his gaze snapped back to Lily. "Arturo put the box in the ground as a bluff to show me what would happen if I didn't stop my operation, but I didn't get there before you showed up. I was enraged when I found out and wanted to send my own message by burning down his lab. I didn't know he had a partner." He let out a breath that shook. "If I had... I wouldn't have said anything. Done anything. I wouldn't have stayed."

Lily took a chance. She slid her foot forward to get her an inch closer. The small movement focused Jacob's attention.

"Who is Arturo's partner?" she asked, softening her voice to nearly a whisper. "And, Jacob, where is Kristine?"

Lily's gut started to overturn her original thought that he wouldn't use his gun. The man's eyes became wide and wild. He was degrading at an alarming pace.

"Arturo was working with Bryant Lautner." His voice

broke. His eyes were starting to tear up. Lily's read on the man fell with the drop of her stomach.

If he was this upset... What had happened to Kristine?

"I didn't know he had a partner," he repeated before Lily could say a word. "I didn't know."

Jacob brought his gun up to his head.

Lily didn't hesitate.

She pulled hers out and aimed it at the man.

"Stop," she yelled. "Please."

Jacob kept her stare, the barrel of his gun against his temple.

"Kristine is gone."

"She's not just gone, Jacob. She is somewhere no matter what happened. *Please* put the gun down and tell me."

He shook his head.

Lily dug in, hoping to play on the man's feelings for his young lover. "Think about her, think about Kristine. Think about everything she's been through. Think about how she deserves more than this. Think about Finnigan's at sunset."

Jacob's brow pulled in, like he'd heard a sound he couldn't place.

Like he was confused.

Like part of him wanted the pain to end and the other wanted to do right by the woman he loved.

A quiet settled between them.

Then, slowly, Jacob started to lower the gun.

"Thank you," Lily told him, meaning it.

Jacob shook his head again.

All at once every part of him that had felt off and broken became firm and confident. His words next had no break in them. Had no waver.

He was just a man giving her a message.

"Tell her I love her."

Lily yelled out but it was too late.

The gunshot was so loud it felt like the entire world had to have heard it.

Somehow, though, the silence that followed still managed to be louder.

THE "WELCOME TO KELBY CREEK" sign was in his rearview and the Holiday Inn's "Vacancy" was blinking in front of him when Ant thought about mud and put his Camaro in reverse.

He was still thinking about mud when Winnie answered her door ten minutes later.

She'd taken off her clown costume but some of her makeup still lingered. If Ant hadn't already seen her earlier that day, it would have given him pause. Now he was just glad she was home.

"Monday there was a big storm and you said you had to tow Kristine's car out of the mud, right?"

Winnie didn't ask any questions, just answered.

"Yeah. She wasn't too deep in so I thought I could do it," she said. "I mean, I did get her out. I just kind of broke her bumper. The car is still at Davie's Automotive."

"And she was stuck on Old Cherry Street?" Winnie nodded. "Did she tell you why she was on Old Cherry Street?"

Winnie's brows drew together in thought.

"She said she was using it as a shortcut to the fairgrounds. She left part of her costume in the theater trailer and wanted to clean it. After it took us forever to get her car out, she waited until Tuesday morning instead."

Ant could have been on to nothing or he could have finally found something useful.

"Unless there's another Old Cherry Street that I don't know about or the fairgrounds have moved, that's not a shortcut to the fair," he said. "There's really no shortcut. You just make it to the main road and boom, you're there."

Winnie's eyes widened.

"Oh my God, you're right. I—I didn't even question it."

Ant nodded. "Okay, well, thanks. I just wanted to ask."

He started to turn but Winnie caught his arm.

"Where are you going? Are you going out there?"

She let him go but he understood the look she was giving him. There was a lead. Small but there.

It was blood in the water and they were sharks hungry for the truth.

"Yeah," he said. "I'm going to see if there's anything interesting on Old Cherry Street. It's been a long time since I've actually driven it."

Winnie ducked back into the house and disappeared from view for a moment. When she reappeared she had on a rain jacket and held her keys.

"Can I come with you?"

"There's probably nothing out there," Ant tried. "It would just bother me if I didn't at least look."

"Well, I can tell you that there's nothing in here worth me doing," she replied. "I didn't even stay at dress rehearsal. After that detective that Lily sent started asking everyone questions it all became too real. I've just been sitting in the kitchen, staring at the wall ever since. I'd rather try to do something productive."

Ant sighed. Then he nodded.

"Let's go then before it decides to rain again."

Winnie locked up the house and bounded to the car. It wasn't until they were driving out of Holly Grove that she thought to ask about Lily.

"Did she find something, too? Is that why she isn't here?"

Ant bit down on a grumble.

"She's working a lead, yeah," he sidestepped. "It's more official than looking at a once-muddy road so we split up."

Winnie didn't question that. She did, however, give him a look that made Ant uncomfortable. It was as if she was seeing him differently than the last time they'd talked. Before he could ask her about it, she spoke.

"I, uh, I looked you up earlier," she said. "I mean I knew about Lily's career record and even found the story about her fighting a kidnapper here in Kelby Creek when she was seventeen, but I didn't realize— I didn't put it together when I first met you that it was your sister. The girl who was kidnapped. And, well, that you two tried to stop her abductor. I—I can't even imagine."

Ant gave a stiff nod.

"It's not something we like to talk about."

"I don't blame you, but I — Well, I just thought that it was kind of nice that the two of you—you and Lily—are still fighting crime together. Or, I guess, still trying to help others together." He saw her shrug out of his periphery. "Y'all stuck together. Y'all must be close."

Ant kept driving, going through the last light they'd pass before the roads started branching off and asphalt turned to dirt.

He didn't know what to say.

He didn't want to lie.

He didn't know what the truth was.

"Lily is the only woman who's ever made me nervous and I can't say I know why." Ant surprised himself with that. "I've spent the last fourteen years knowing other women, trying at relationships, and feeling, and not feeling, all sorts of things. But one look at Lily? I get all jumpy inside. It's not just jumpy, either. She frustrates me like no one else but I'm proud to know her, more than I'm proud of even myself. She's spent over a decade trying to solve everyone's issues and I bet she thinks working on herself is a luxury. Something she can't do until all the cars have left the lot and the lights have been switched off," Ant grumbled. "The fact is that being with her should feel like losing Ida all over again but it doesn't."

Their fight had affected him more than any one thing had since he'd left Kelby Creek as a young adult. A little while ago he'd packed up and left, stung at her words. At the feeling behind them.

At the fact that she had been right.

He had shown up and then hadn't left.

She had never asked him to stay.

Ant gripped the steering wheel.

Then he let that grip loosen.

He sighed.

"You had it right. Being with Lily feels nice...and I don't think I've ever actually told her that."

There it was.

How he was feeling boiled down into a conversation with a woman he barely knew on the way to look at mud.

He gave Winnie a quick look.

"Sorry," he told her. "I guess I need to get better at communicating."

Winnie was smiling.

"No problem," she said. "If it makes you feel better, when Colton first told me he loved me it was during a fight about him eating my leftovers out of the fridge. Sometimes you just don't know how you feel until you accidentally say it."

Ant was about to point out he hadn't said anything about love but the road sign for Old Cherry Street came into view.

Winnie's smile dropped. They were nothing but focused driving down the old road. Winnie was quiet until she pointed out the tire marks that were still there.

"That's from me," she said. "I pulled up next to her because I was afraid to get on the shoulder behind her. I don't have the best nighttime vision and didn't want to chance us both getting stuck."

Ant pulled over and threw on his flashers. They got out into the falling chill of the day.

"She was stopped on the side of the road?" Ant walked over to the tracks. Old Cherry Street was a dirt road in the trees for half of its expanse. The other half had grass fields if he was remembering correctly. There weren't even streetlights along the four-mile drive.

"Yeah," Winnie answered but that answer turned into an uncertain statement. "But why was she stopped here at all? Why did she pull to the side of the road?"

Ant's thoughts exactly.

There was no real reason to take Old Cherry Street as a shortcut to the fairgrounds. There was even less reason to stop on it.

Winnie let out a small yell of frustration.

She had her hands in her hair.

"How could I not ask about any of this?" she cried out. "Why didn't I question it? I just came out here, *laughed* at the fact that she got stuck, and then joked about it when we got home. How oblivious can one person be?"

"This could still be nothing," he reminded her. "And even if it isn't, this isn't your fault."

Winnie didn't look so sure.

She turned to stare down the road ahead.

"I've lived in Kelby Creek all my life and I don't even know what's at the other end of this dumb street! But how could I not realize that it definitely wasn't the fair?"

Ant went over to the young woman. He tried to be soothing.

"The only thing in that direction of town are two neighborhoods that you wouldn't visit unless you're flush with cash."

Winnie gave him a questioning look.

"The country club, the Justine Park subdivision, and the McHale mansion are that way. Old Cherry connects to the nicely paved street that never has potholes that loops in front of all three." Ant stopped himself. Winnie picked up the thought.

"Somewhere a married man with money who was having an affair might live."

Ant looked at Old Cherry differently now.

"She could have been meeting him here," he said. "Halfway between your place and his."

They both chewed on that for a minute. Before Ant could decide what to do next, his phone rang in his pocket.

He pulled it out. The ID read Unknown.

He'd hoped it was Lily.

"Hello?"

"Hey, Anthony? This is Kathryn Juliet. Are you still in town?"

Ant might have trouble with sharing his feelings but right then and there he knew he felt nothing but pure worry.

"I am. What's wrong?"

The detective's voice lowered to a whisper. It set him even further on edge.

"We need to talk."

Chapter Seventeen

Cook was leaning heavy against her. He'd already nudged her hand several times. He was a weight, a pressure, an attempted comfort. Now he was trying his best to take the pain from his human and change it into something else. Something happier.

Something less *numb*.

Lily stared at the tabletop and the holster resting there. Her detective's badge was next to it.

Her phone was by her hand. No one had called her. They didn't need to since she'd left the department.

Jacob Anderson was dead. Bryant Lautner was still in the wind. The Henderson Farm had law all over it. The search for Kristine Cho did, too.

All Lily had was an awful feeling in her gut, literal blood on her arm and three words on repeat in her head.

Kristine is gone.

Lily balled her hand on the table.

Cook whined.

She didn't know Kristine, hadn't even heard the name until that morning, but all of her ached for the woman. After losing her parents she had deserved a lifetime of better and what had she gotten instead? Used as a pawn between two drug dealers.

Lily hated it.

She hated all of it.

Cook shifted against her leg. Lily thought it was his training trying to sway her to a lighter place but he was looking toward the front of the house.

That's when she heard the car door shut.

Lily sighed and dragged herself up and out of the chair. Despite telling him to leave, she knew it would be Ant stopping by. Juliet had at least given her a heads-up that she'd called him.

"You need a friend," she'd told her. "He seems to be a good one."

Lily hadn't corrected the woman then—hadn't told her that all Ant was, was a man who had gone through a trauma with her and then gotten pulled into another—but she fully intended to let Ant off the hook now.

If he wanted to stay in town until Bryant Lautner was found for Kristine's sake and then the questioning of his connection to Ida's abduction?

That was fine.

If he wanted to stay in town because he thought she needed protecting? That she needed his help? His concern?

No.

She'd kindly turn him around and remind him that she'd made it fourteen years without needing someone. She could make it through this.

Lily gave Cook a pat and was at the door just as a knock sounded.

She opened it wide and, sure enough, there he was.

Anthony Perez.

Dark hair.

Dark eyes.

Once a boy in her lap, the creek behind them.

Lily opened her mouth to tell him to go. To tell him she was fine. To tell him something.

Yet the words never came.

One look at Ant and Lily did something she hadn't done before.

She let go.

A sob was the first thing to tear itself out of her. The tears came next. In between the two there was Ant.

He pulled her into his chest without a word. When Lily went limp against him, he scooped her up gently, lifting her off the ground and stepping inside the house.

She didn't hear the door shut behind them. She didn't notice the stairs passing beneath them. She didn't even register the water turning on in the shower until the water was hitting her.

Hitting both of them.

Lily watched between her sobs as blood and mud swirled down the drain.

She felt the washcloth on her arm and then on her face.

Jacob Anderson's blood.

Lily lost it after that. Truly and completely.

That numb feeling had exploded into anger, regret, pain.

From witnessing what she had, to Kristine Cho's fate, to the pain of her injuries, and all the way to hearing Ida scream for the first time.

It all was too much.

And Ant somehow knew that.

He took over completely, drying her off, helping her change and then placing her right into bed.

"You're going to be okay," he told her, pulling the covers up over her.

He stepped back. Lily wasn't sure if he was just giving her space or if he meant to leave, but she didn't like either option.

She grabbed his hand.

Not only had Lily finally let go, she had another surprising first.

She asked someone to stay.

"Don't leave."

Her words were broken and cracked, filled with tears and, at the same time, drained of them. She knew she didn't look much better. She understood it wasn't just the outside of her that was showing how vulnerable she was.

If he left? If Ant walked out of the room?

It would be okay.

It would—

Ant walked around to the other side of the bed and slipped beneath the covers. His arm, unbelievably warm, wrapped around her shivering body. He pulled her against his chest.

Lily felt his heartbeat pulse through her.

Then she cried herself to sleep.

SOMEONE'S PHONE WAS VIBRATING.

Ant pictured his cell phone on his nightstand and tried to flip over and slap at it. Something kept him from doing it. A few seconds passed before he realized that something was a woman.

Lily.

They were in her bed.

That was her phone vibrating on her nightstand.

She stirred, still pinned to him by his arm around her waist. Ant lifted it up just as her movements became more coordinated. She threw her legs over the bed and made a noise that let him know she'd hurt herself. Ant didn't say anything, though. Lily cleared her throat, answered the phone and then crept to the bathroom to talk.

She hadn't realized Ant was awake.

He hadn't realized when Juliet had called him the second time to tell him that Lily was home that he'd be in her bed later.

Ant rolled onto his back. The room was dark. No sunlight or afternoon glow filtered in between the curtains. Based on how he felt, he guessed they'd been asleep for a few hours at least. He hadn't known how much he needed it until Lily's breathing had evened out against him. After that? Her momentary peace had been a lullaby that had taken him under quick.

And kept him under apparently.

He stretched and wondered if he should get up.

He toyed with the decision until he heard water running in the bathroom sink. Shortly after, Lily was back in the bedroom. She put her phone back on the nightstand and slid carefully back beneath the sheets.

She was quiet a moment.

Then she whispered into the darkness.

"Are you awake?"

He nodded then realized she couldn't see him.

"I am."

"Oh. Sorry," she said. "That was Kenneth."

Ant sat up a little.

"Is everything okay?"

The bed moved as Lily shifted her weight. A second later the lamp on her nightstand came on. It wasn't bright but it still made Ant blink a few times. It also showed him Lily's very swollen eyes.

He wanted to reach out but, considering they'd just woken tangled up together, he didn't want to keep crowding her.

"He wanted to update me on what they'd found since I left. Wait, how much did Juliet tell you about what happened?"

There was no reason to lie.

"Everything you told her when she and Kenneth showed up at the farm."

"Everything?"

He nodded.

"She said if you trust me, she trusts me. Plus, she figured you'd tell me anyway."

Juliet had also said she wanted him to be prepared when he saw Lily again. She'd been too quiet at the farm, too quiet at the department. It had worried Juliet. Ant refrained from telling her all of that, though.

Lily let out a small sigh.

"Then you know Jacob Anderson admitted to being Kristine's boyfriend." He nodded. "And that he admitted to fighting with Arturo." He nodded again.

"Yeah, and that Bryant Lautner was Arturo's partner and that, best as anyone can guess, he's the one who took Kristine from Jacob at some point after they left the fair together last night."

Lily looked surprised.

"She really did tell you everything." She shook her head to get back on track. "They're still looking for Kris and Bryant but Foster went to Jacob Anderson's house and they found evidence to support the affair, including receipts for all of the things in her room that were expensive like the earrings, shoes, and lingerie. I think he said something about pictures of Kris on Jacob's computer too. His wife had no idea about the relationship or the drug dealing. They were high school sweethearts and she said he didn't even smoke cigarettes."

"It's never the people you suspect, I guess," Ant said.

Lily agreed with that.

"Apparently news of what happened made it to Arturo," she continued. "He requested a meeting with Sheriff Blake and a few minutes ago confirmed everything Jacob told me. He's been feuding with Jacob over territory and after he caught him and Kris together, he decided to try and use her against him. He never counted on a hunter finding the hole or us finding the box. He also never counted on being taken into custody. After that he guessed Bryant escalated."

Lily's face fell.

"It's not your fault that Bryant went after Kris," Ant jumped in. "I know that's what you're thinking but Arturo is the one who attacked us. You did your job. None of what happened next was your fault."

Ant wasn't sure if his reasoning landed. He wasn't the only one who had tried it.

"Kenneth said the same thing," she admitted. "He also told me, in not so many words, to not leave this house unless it was an emergency *but* that he'd let me know if anything happened."

Lily let out another sigh. This time she sank back into her pillow.

"Normally, I would have laughed at the order to stay home. But, I guess, having a breakdown puts things into perspective."

Ant rolled onto his back and joined her in staring at the ceiling, just as they had done earlier.

It was amazing how much had changed since then.

"Speaking of which, thank you," Lily added. "I didn't expect to lose it like that."

Ant shrugged.

"I don't think anyone ever does."

They shared a companionable silence.

But then things started to change.

Ant was in his briefs. Only his briefs. He'd taken off his wet clothes after the shower but hadn't had the chance to get dry ones from his backpack. Not when a wet and shivering Lily had needed him. He'd made fast work of dressing her in the first nightshirt and panties he'd found in her dresser.

Had he seen her naked?

Yes.

Had it been anything other than technical work?

No.

Now? Now Lily wasn't crying. She wasn't shivering. She didn't have blood on her from a dead man.

She was next to him, breathing easier, and he could still feel her warmth against him.

Ant went from feelings of being protective to feelings that ran more carnal.

It wasn't the time.

Yet he turned his head to face her all the same.

Lily was already looking at him.

Even in the dim light her eyes still managed to pull all of him in.

His gaze traveled to her lips as she spoke.

"When we were being witches, you told me that I wasn't some ghost. That I was alive because I made you...something. You never finished." She tilted her head a little against the pillow. "What were you going to say?"

Ant didn't pretend that he couldn't remember.

"I know you're alive because you make *me* feel alive when I'm with you."

It was the truth.

Just as he'd told Winnie in his accidental confession.

The past week had felt wholly different than the past fourteen years.

The only difference?

Lillian Howard.

She shook her head. Her hair shifted and trailed down the pillow at the movement.

"You only feel alive with me because you feel some misplaced obligation to me." Her voice was soft but strained. "Because I saved you from the creek. But, Anthony, I *need* you to remember what happened. I *need* you to remember that I'm the reason Ida was taken. I'm the reason she's gone."

It wasn't like earlier. The tears that came were few. They slid, one by one, down Lily's cheeks.

It wasn't a chaotic burst of emotion. It wasn't a bottle finally uncorked.

It was long-standing pain.

It was something that Lily had been living with since that night in the woods

And, once again, Ant hadn't seen it until now.

"Oh, Lily." He reached out and cradled her face in his hand. "You didn't choose me over Ida. There was no choice at all. You saved the only person you could."

He pushed up on his elbow so he was looking down at her. Ant wanted to make sure she saw his sincerity. He smiled. "I have *never* blamed you for not going after Ida and I'm so sorry I didn't tell you that then. It just never crossed my mind that you would blame yourself because I, well, I don't. Not once. Not ever."

Ant ran a strand of her hair behind her ear.

"We shouldn't have had to live that night and I know it's changed us from whatever we might've been, but I can't help but be grateful for where it's led us. Where it's led me." Ant tipped Lily's chin up with his fingers. She let him kiss her softly. Then he was back to staring down at her. "But I'm not the only one who lived through it. I didn't have to save a boy. I didn't have to see a girl being pulled away into the darkness and think that I was the reason behind it. So, if being with me is too hard, tell me. I'll leave.

Just know that, no matter what, I was truly happy here. With you. And not because of some misplaced obligation."

Ant released his hold on her. He meant every word he'd said.

It was selfish to want to be with Lily. He saw that now. Just because he felt alive around her didn't mean she was feeling the same.

He'd leave.

Lily didn't say anything for a moment.

When she did speak, it was on the tail of a deep exhale.

And it was just one word.

"Stay."

Chapter Eighteen

It was Lily's turn to show Ant just how much she'd been fighting against him until now.

The moment he smiled at her admission that she wanted him to stay, it was all over for her.

Lily wrapped her arm around his back and laced her fingers into his hair. She pulled his head down and let his kiss devour her.

There was no pulling away now.

No ill-timed phone calls or heartbreaking worries.

Ant didn't blame her for saving him and not running after Ida.

He had never blamed her.

And Lily believed him.

Ant dropped his hand to her waist. It trailed up her side beneath her shirt. Lily moved up against him. His chest was hard, unmovable.

Just what she wanted.

As their kiss turned deep, Lily pulled him on top of her. A second later she remembered her ribs might not like that. Thankfully, Ant had already thought ahead. He made a cage around her, keeping his weight off her upper body.

His lower half, however, was right where it needed to be. Lily wrapped her legs around him to straddle the hardness of his pleasure.

She moaned against his lips.

When Ant pulled back, she almost groaned in anger.

"I don't want to hurt you," he breathed out, ragged. "Tell me if you want me to stop."

But Lily merely pulled him back down to her.

That was the golden ticket for the rest of the ride. Ant didn't stop them again, he didn't ask if she was okay, and when Lily yelled out later he didn't hesitate, thinking he'd hurt her.

Instead the two of them found a rhythm, a pulse, an understanding.

A connection that didn't include a creek or rain or darkness.

It was something completely new, something only for the two of them.

And, when their breathing calmed and their bodies relaxed, Lily knew she didn't want whatever they had just become to end.

It had been a long, long time since she'd gone to bed with a smile on her face.

But she did that night, even as worries of the future tried to claw their way in.

It was Friday at noon and the sun felt like only a memory. Lily was in the backyard before the inevitable rain, with Cook and Sheriff Bennet.

Neither woman was wearing her usual uniform but they were together to talk about work. That much was made clear when the sheriff called to ask for a moment. Now was that moment and Lily looked across her patio set with an anxiousness she felt to her bones.

"You know, when I first was elected to this job, to this town, I knew it would be a ride," the sheriff started after they'd exhausted all the niceties in Southern greetings. "I was even told after the fact to watch out because you could be clear sailin' on a Monday and then have the world flip three different ways by Friday. That's just how this town has become since The Flood. I guess I thought everyone was being overdramatic." She sighed, drank some of the coffee that Lily had prepared for them and slid right into what she really wanted to talk about.

"We found Bryant Lautner this morning." Lily sat straighter. Her ribs complained at the move. The sheriff raised her hand in a "stop" motion. "It was my call not to loop you in until now but I wanted to come over and tell you what we learned face-to-face because you earned that much."

Lily tried to keep her emotions in check.

"Okay."

Sheriff Bennet nodded then got to it.

"He didn't say much in the beginning. He denied taking Kristine and he stuck to silence when we asked where he had been prior to us picking him up." The sheriff readjusted her matter-of-fact tone to what Lily might describe as a warmer approach. "The first answer we got was to his whereabouts fourteen years ago, the day that Ida Perez went missing."

Lily felt her eyes widen in surprise.

The sheriff continued.

"Gray told me about the lead you were chasing with Bryant before all of this mess came to light, said that was why Anthony was here too most likely. He said you should have been the one asking but if you weren't there, he wasn't leaving until he at least did." She snorted. "Detective Lovett also pointed out how it could be relevant, and who am I to fight that?"

Lily was touched. Kenneth had fought for her. Foster, too.

That meant something to her. She'd have to tell them later. "What did Bryant say?"

The sheriff's warmth became something more clinical. Lily knew it wasn't the news she wanted to hear even before she said it.

"He knew exactly where he was because he was on the way to his mother's funeral. The funeral home hasn't changed in over three decades so it wasn't too hard to confirm. I did it myself, actually. Pulled the old director out of bed and we looked into his files. Bryant was seen by several witnesses at the funeral that afternoon, the memorial at his mother's house after and the bar that night. Deputy Costner even took it a step further and found an old girlfriend of Bryant's who said he spent the next day passed out and then hung over."

Lily sighed.

"Which means Bryant Lautner didn't abduct Ida."

The sheriff shook her head.

"Not unless he could be in two places at once, no."

Lily sat with that for a minute. She didn't know what to feel so she did what she always did. Focused on the case at hand.

"Bryant didn't say anything else?" Lily asked. "About Kristine?"

"If cussing counts, yes. If not, no. For a man who's already been outed by his partner and the man he was threatening, he seems to think his silence is going to be the key to get out. After talk of Ida, he doubled down on the nothing he was giving. But we'll see how long that lasts. I've found during my time on the job that men are the ones who really love to talk."

"Let's hope for Kristine's sake he does it sooner rather than later."

Sheriff Bennet agreed with that. She'd already told Lily

that the search for Kristine had been expanded. Police from the city, reserve deputies and volunteers had been activated.

It was a familiar feeling for the town.

Something the sheriff noted.

"I wonder if the fair will ever come back to Kelby Creek now," she wondered aloud. "After everything Darren McHale must have done to convince them to come back too, only to have Jacob, his own assistant, turn out to be a son of a gun."

That was news to Lily.

"Jacob Anderson worked for Darren McHale?"

"Yep. Apparently he's had the gig for upward of five years."

Lily let out a cuss. The sheriff didn't seem to mind.

"Why does someone working for a McHale try his hand at getting into the meth business? That's like winning the lottery and then trying to start up a counterfeit money ring."

"Oh, no. Jacob was broke," the sheriff corrected. "I mean, no savings, credit cards maxed, in debt up to his eyeballs." When Lily gave her a questioning look she explained. "His wife, Gwen, told us they had gone through two failed IVF rounds in the last two years. Insurance didn't cover either and they had to pay out-of-pocket." She shook her head, disgusted. "Can you imagine going through all that only to find out that your husband of ten years was seeing a twenty-year-old?"

Lily couldn't.

"Some people make decisions that keep me up at night," she said. "I can't imagine how their loved ones feel."

The sheriff agreed and stood with a stretch. She thanked Lily for the coffee and said it was time to go.

"You earned the update," she told Lily at the front door.

"But you've also earned the rest. I don't expect to talk to you until next week, okay?"

Lily nodded.

"Okay."

Sheriff Bennet walked out to her truck just as the sound of footfalls came down the stairs behind Lily.

"I was going to come out earlier but I figured you might not want a dripping-wet man in a towel to come say hi to your boss. So I decided to stay out of sight for a bit."

Ant was grinning. It made Lily's stomach fluttery again, a feeling she was starting to equate with the man.

"I'm sure Sheriff Bennet would have had a fun time with that."

They went to the kitchen together where Lily brewed him a cup of coffee. He'd had a later start to the day after finally getting some good sleep, only waking up after Lily had finished with her own shower and dressed.

Ant took the cup but didn't waste any time with his curiosity.

"Was the sheriff's visit a good one or a bad one?"

Lily led him to the dining room table. She was hesitant to answer but didn't realize why right away.

"Kristine is still missing but they found Bryant Lautner."

Ant sat up straight in his chair.

It dawned on Lily then that a part of her didn't want to tell Ant what she'd learned. That Bryant hadn't been involved in Ida's kidnapping. That her small lead that had brought him to town, to her, was now gone.

It made guilt well up in Lily.

She shouldn't have wanted to tell him because it meant that what had happened to Ida was still as unsolved as it had been fourteen years ago.

Yet the main worry she felt now was that he would leave.

Sure, they'd had a great night, but nothing between them had been set in stone.

Ant still had an apartment and life in North Carolina.

She had a life in Kelby Creek.

Neither had even broached the subject of their individual futures, never mind one that might have them together.

But she wasn't about to keep the truth from the man.

So Lily told him exactly what the sheriff had told her.

"I guess it *was* a coincidence, in a roundabout way," she added on when she was finished. "Looking into someone from an old lead at the same time they're involved in an active case. I can't say that's happened to me before."

Ant didn't say anything for a moment.

Lily let him have his thoughts.

When he met her eyes again, Lily felt heat rise in her. Something she was also starting to equate with the man.

"So, what happens next?"

Like in Kristine Cho's bedroom, it was another broad question.

This time, Lily had some answers.

"Everyone in the department is focused on looking for Kristine and trying to figure out the missing pieces between Arturo, Jacob and Bryant. Everything we've learned since finding the buried box has been passed over to Kenneth and Foster while they work together. On that front, we wait." Lily didn't like waiting; she didn't like admitting that that was the smartest play for her. It felt like giving up, even though she knew it wasn't. "As for Ida...we keep looking."

Ant nodded deep.

"I'm good with that."

He didn't ask about what that meant for him and Lily and she didn't bring it up. He did, however, have a more immediate plan.

"If you're feeling up to it, I thought we could go pay Winnie a visit," he added on. "When I dropped her off last night she seemed so...lost. I know we can't do more for her with Kris than is already being done but maybe we could keep her company for a little bit? Order in some Crisp's?"

The heat she'd been feeling around Ant became a nice warmth.

"I think that's a great idea."

They finished their coffees, grabbed their things and decided Cook should ride along. According to Ant his presence had seemed to help the young woman the other day.

Lily paused by the gun safe in her closet when grabbing her blazer.

It was over.

She was off the clock.

She didn't need her handgun.

Lily felt that helplessness she'd been staving off since finding out Kristine was missing. The same vulnerability that had made a home in her after Ida had been taken. She hesitated a beat longer before making a decision.

She shut the closet door. Then they piled into her car and drove a few streets down to Winnie's.

Lily wondered if she'd have guests, perhaps her parents or her boyfriend, after everything that had happened.

But there was no car in the drive at all.

The front door, however, was ajar.

Lily and Ant shared a look. She let him take the lead into the home.

"Winnie?" he called out. "It's Ant and Lily."

No one answered and, as far as Lily could tell, nothing was disturbed.

Wordlessly they went to the second floor and split to explore in opposite directions.

Ant went to Winnie's room, Lily to Kris's.

Once again, nothing look disturbed.

She went to the closet, opened it and saw the expensive shoes in a box. She went to the dresser, found the lingerie. The note, however, wasn't in the nightstand. Neither was the diamond ring in the vanity.

Ant filled the doorway with his broad frame. His face was solemn.

"She's not in her room. But this was on the floor next to her bed."

He held out a small piece of paper.

Compact handwriting spelled out a simple name.

"'Finnigan's,'" she read out. "Finnigan's Fun House?"

Ant wasn't pleased.

"It looks like it might be time to finally go to the fair."

Chapter Nineteen

"We've never seen the handwriting on that note before," Lily pointed out from the driver's seat. "For all we know it could be Winnie's."

She said the words and Ant heard the anxiety in them.

"The front door was left open and the number she gave us is going to voice mail," Ant returned.

Lily shifted in her seat. They were almost to the fair-grounds.

"We're also on edge," she continued. "That has to be noted."

Ant confirmed. "Definitely noted."

The rain hadn't come yet but the sky was a dark blanket of warning. The local radio station had already issued an alert for a storm expected to be on the bad side of awful. They'd even been put in a tornado watch, though that was more normal than not.

What wasn't normal was Winnie's front door being open and a note that matched one her missing roommate had been given. At least, the location.

"You said your guys looked into Finnigan's Fun House after we found Kristine's note, right?"

Lily nodded. "They even talked to the operator and he said he saw nothing out of the ordinary. He didn't recognize Kristine's picture, either."

"Then again, a lot of people go to the fair. He could be mistaken."

"True." Lily let out a long sigh. She turned them onto the dirt road that led to the parking lot in the distance.

The woods began behind that.

Normally he wouldn't talk about those woods but after the night he'd spent with Lily—after the feelings he'd shared—he didn't feel the need to censor himself.

"I hate being this close to them." His words had turned bitter.

Lily didn't need him to explain.

"Me too."

Kelby Creek might have been a small town but the fairgrounds looked like they went on forever. That included the makeshift lot, mowed down and covered in dirt, that ran the length of the main fairway behind the ticket stands. There were only a few cars in the lot where there were usually hundreds. Lily parked in the row closest to the entrance.

"I saw a post online that said today's opening was delayed for the weather but some staff and maintenance workers were asked to come in still." She shut off the engine. Cook sat up in the back seat. Ant pointed to one of the cars near them.

"That's Winnie's car," he said.

"Maybe she's here working on the clown routine." It was a statement but Lily didn't sound like she believed it. "But it can't hurt to go in and check. Come on."

They got out of the car, Cook leashed to Ant's hand, and walked fast to the ticket booth. There was a lone worker behind the Plexiglas window. He looked fresh out of high school. He also looked fresh out of patience.

"Fair's closed until the storm front passes through," he said with clear annoyance in his voice.

Lily matched his volume but put authority in her every word.

"I'm Detective Howard with the Dawn County Sheriff's Department. Have you seen this woman?" Lily pulled out her phone and in the process flashed her holstered gun and badge.

Ant hadn't realized she'd brought either with her when they'd gone to Winnie's.

He was glad for it now.

The boy sat up and dropped his phone. A game danced on the screen but his focus was all Lily.

She tapped Winnie's face in the picture they had of her and Kristine.

The boy nodded quickly.

"Yeah, she's inside. Came in a few minutes ago with some guy."

"I thought you said the fair was closed?" Lily asked.

The boy went red in the face. He got all squirmy.

"He, uh, paid me to give him a few minutes."

"And what did he look like?" Ant could feel Lily vibrating with the need to go. To do something. Cook's tail thumped him in the leg, the dog no doubt picking up on their readiness.

The boy looked perplexed by the question.

"Uh, I don't know. Older? He gave me a hundred so I figured it was a good cause. Plus his lady looked upset so I thought why not since this place probably isn't opening until right before closing time anyway."

Lily turned to Ant.

"Older, has money to spend, Finnigan's?" Before he could comment back Lily was barking at the boy, "We're going in."

He didn't try to stop them but did call out when Lily hustled through the gate.

She didn't listen.

"Jacob and his wife were broke, doing IVF for at least two years, and married ten," she hurriedly said, matching her stride that had her, Ant and Cook making quick work of the lit-up thoroughfare. "Then suddenly he's dishing out expensive things, trying to be a meth supplier and seeing a twenty-year-old? And *then* after all of that he admits to it, says Kris is gone, and tells me to tell 'her' that he loves her. If he knew Kristine was gone, was he talking about his wife?"

"You don't think Jacob was who Kristine was having an affair with?"

"Do you? I mean, either Jacob was that good at hiding who he really was or—"

"He took the fall for who it really was."

Lily shrugged as she walked. They were almost past the food vendors' booths.

"Or he was blackmailed? His family threatened maybe?"

"So, what, you think that Winnie could be with Kristine's real mystery guy?"

Lily gave him a slightly exasperated look.

"Weren't you the one who wanted us to bolt out here because you were worried that something was going on with Winnie?"

He wasn't going to deny it. He was going to go to the next logical question.

"If she is here with him, then does that mean she's been in on it or she's the next victim?"

"Let's find her first. I haven't been here in so long. Do you know where Finnigan's is?"

Ant did know but only because the fair hardly ever changed. The fun house, house of mirrors and horror motel were all in a line on the west side of the fair. He led the way, Cook jogging along to keep up at his side, when after passing the Tilt-A-Whirl he finally saw the two-story attraction and its bright red-and-orange sign.

"The bottom floor has your standard fun house tricks and in the back you can take the stairs up to the second floor, which has the black light room," Ant said. "There's usually an operator at the side there but it looks like—"

A woman screamed, interrupting him.

Lily was off, her gun out, within a second. Ant only made it past her because he had longer legs and no broken ribs. He bounded up the first metal stairs and jumped the gate made for the line. He was inside the first floor, running past the moving mirrors, sliding floors and rotating tunnel. Ant was grateful they were all turned off. He was also grateful the house hadn't changed since he was a teenager.

The back stairs were right where he remembered.

He took them two at a time and spun around into the main section of the second floor.

The moving parts weren't on downstairs but up here the black lights were.

Ant's surroundings were bathed in bright shades of neon.

So was the man holding Winnie in the middle of the room.

"Hey!" Ant's yell came out only a second before he had his hands on the back of the man's shirt. He yanked him away from Winnie in a move that worked every arm muscle he had.

Lily was right behind him, yelling out an identification and showing her weapon.

The man didn't fight back.

He looked confused.

So was Ant when he heard Winnie yelling, too.

"Stop! Let him go!"

THE BLACK LIGHT room turned to normal again as Winnie flipped a switch in the corner. Her eyes were swollen but it didn't look like she was currently crying.

"That's my boyfriend," she added, pointing to the man that Ant had thrown almost clear across the room.

Now with better lighting Lily recognized the EMT who'd helped her a few days ago. Colton, in street clothes, looked slightly terrified.

Ant, still huffing from adrenaline most likely, gave Winnie what Lily could only describe as a big brother tone.

"We heard you scream!"

Winnie pointed to a dip in the floor at the front of the room.

"I tripped. Colton just picked me up."

Lily lowered her weapon.

"We went by your house to check on you," she explained. "Your front door was open and a note that said 'Finnigan's' was on your floor."

If Winnie was offended at her privacy being invaded, she didn't say so. Instead she gave Colton a confused glance. Despite having just gotten himself off the floor, he looked sheepish.

"I was talking to my partner and he was going on and on about next week's schedule and I must have spaced on locking up. I'm sorry." Colton looked to Lily. "The front door latch sometimes doesn't catch."

"And the note?" Ant still sounded hot. He'd been ready to defend Winnie and have to fight for her. His fists were still at his sides.

Colton gave Winnie a confused look this time. She returned it then answered Lily.

"I don't know about a note."

Lily and Ant turned to each other, equally perplexed.

"Then why are you two here? At Finnigan's?" Lily asked.

Colton spoke up.

"After everything that's happened I wanted to try and cheer Winnie up," he said. "I knew she didn't want to be around a lot of people so I thought I'd take her to her favorite ride when no one was here. I paid the ticket guy up front for five minutes."

"You paid him one hundred dollars for five minutes?" Ant asked.

Winnie looked startled at that.

"You paid him a hundred dollars?"

Colton answered them both with a nod.

"I just wanted to give her some happiness, even if it was only for a few minutes."

Winnie melted into a smile, a look that was reflected on Colton's face.

Lily holstered her gun. They were just two people in love trying to grab on to something happy during a troubling time.

Lily understood the urge.

The impulse.

She glanced at Ant, who was already looking at her.

That heat, that flutter, both came back with a vengeance.

Lily cleared her throat.

She wasn't the only one.

Ant made little work of the space between them as a new figure entered the room.

An intimidatingly tall man, in a button-down shirt, dark jeans and loafers. He had brown hair slicked back and Cook on a leash at his side.

Lily hooked her hand around Ant's elbow to stop him from advancing on the man.

They'd already busted in on a couple's innocent fun, it would be a shame to bust up a McHale.

"Mr. McHale," Lily called out. The older man looked as startled as Ant when he finally made the connection.

He stopped in his tracks.

Darren McHale wasn't as widely popular as his older brother and sister-in-law. He had nowhere near his niece Annie's fame. The news stories, tabloids, online conspiracy theories and even locals often forgot his name. That was if they ever knew he existed at all. He had money, sure, but he'd never spent it as publicly or as charitably as his family.

The only thing of note he'd done since Annie's kidnapping and then her parents leaving town was to take up residence in their old home. The rumor was that he'd stayed in case Annie came back so that his brother and sister-in-law could leave without guilt, and grieve and heal in peace somewhere.

Lily wasn't sure if that was true but she felt pity for the man.

He ran his own lumber business, was unmarried, had had a falling-out with his son and lived in a town that mourned his niece more than it ever recognized that he was still with them.

Ant had told Lily she wasn't some ghost.

She felt like that wasn't true for Darren.

Even the smile in greeting he gave them looked off.

"I'm sorry if I scared you, I—I heard yelling." He motioned to Cook, who licked at his hand. "And then I saw this guy outside."

"That would be my bad." Ant reached out for the leash and Cook happily changed sides. "We thought Winnie was in trouble so I just ran."

Darren surveyed the room. Lily felt another blush, though this one was more professional.

"Mr. McHale, I'm Detective Howard with the sheriff's

department and this is Anthony Perez. We had cause to worry that our friend Winnie here was in danger and we came to check it out." Lily gave a little laugh. "Turns out all we did was interrupt a date and we were just figuring that out."

Darren's eyebrows scrunched together.

One of the pitfalls of not knowing much about Darren McHale was not knowing his manner. Did he think this was funny? Or was he about to raise hell?

Lily wanted to bypass finding out.

Plus, since he was there, she might as well ask him some questions that were now burning a hole in her about Jacob Anderson.

"Now that you're here though, this works out," she hurriedly tacked on. "I was actually wondering if I could ask you a few questions?"

Lily couldn't read the man's expression right away. She worried she'd crossed a line while off duty. Yet a warm enough smile spread across his lips after a moment.

"I have a few things I need to do before the storm rolls in but if you don't mind walking and talking while I do them, I don't mind, either." He looked at the other three adults. "But I'm afraid you all can't stay in the fun house. Not unattended. It's a liability issue."

Colton was the first to comply. Probably since he'd been the first to break the rules. He led the way back outside. The sky overhead seemed to have darkened even more. It felt like night.

"I have a few things to do in the back office," Darren reiterated. "I can talk to you on the way."

There was an emphasis on the word *you*. Lily picked up on it. So did Ant.

"I'll walk them out," he said, indicating Colton and Winnie. "Cook and I will stay by the car."

Lily mouthed her thanks, then turned to her new companion. "I'm ready when you are."

Darren McHale smiled again.

If Lily had known what the next hour would bring, she would have grabbed Ant's hand and never let go.

But she hadn't known.

None of them had.

Chapter Twenty

"Jacob was a good man, but isn't that how it always starts?"

Darren McHale was walking at a brisk pace but his tone was the opposite of energetic. He sounded tired. A man who knew of tragedy. A man who knew that anyone could become a monster.

"I originally hired him as my assistant because of his attention to detail, his drive to get the job done and, to be frank, his utter disinterest in gossip," Darren continued. "Spreading it, listening to it, trying to find more to add to it. As you can probably guess, that's a quality I've come to deeply appreciate, especially after what happened with my niece."

Lily hadn't expected him to mention Annie McHale at all. She decided to show him that she wasn't here for anything other than what he knew about their current case.

"So you had no idea, no suspicion of him?" she asked. "He wasn't acting odd or changing up his work habits?"

Darren shook his head. They walked past the teacups that she'd almost thrown up on while riding with her father when she was a kid. It felt like an odd juxtaposition to their situation now.

"No. I had no idea," he answered. "Whatever stress or concern I felt from him I counted it toward his and Gwen's attempts to get pregnant. When Sheriff Bennet visited me last night I had to ask her three times if she was sure it was him."

Lily didn't mean to but she imagined Jacob's last moments with a stomach-turning vividness.

"It was Jacob all right."

Darren slowed a little.

"I heard what you went through with him. I truly am sorry. That had to be hard, especially with what you've already been through."

They turned by the Ferris wheel while a crack of thunder sounded in the distance. The entire fair was lit up around them but absent of any workers or staff. A ghost town for two haunted souls.

Lily hoped the rain would hold off while her haunted self finished her impromptu interview.

"The last week definitely hasn't been the best," she concluded. "I'm still standing though and I'm grateful for that."

Darren smiled.

"While I agree your week has probably been a little wild compared to what it is normally, I was referring to what happened when you were a teen."

They slowed and turned off to follow a gravel path to the back office. The building was half office, half warehouse. It was the only structure that was permanent on the fairgrounds, even when the fair wasn't in town. She'd been in there once before.

Lily gave him a questioning look.

"When I was a teen?" She knew he meant what happened to Ida, but still, she wanted him to clarify. Once she'd become an adult Lily could count on one hand how many people had mentioned what happened to her back then.

"The abduction of Miss Ida Perez," he confirmed.

Lily kept her question on her face.

He gave her another apologetic look.

"When your niece's abduction makes national news and is still unsolved, you become familiar with all the unsolved abductions in the area," he explained. "Though, to be honest, I remember Miss Perez's case from the news. It's also a memory that sticks considering my son Parker and I had our falling-out a few weeks later. He's always been against this town. One of his former classmates being taken was just the excuse he needed to finally leave."

He opened the side door with one of his keys. It led into the warehouse portion of the building. The space was expansive, cold, and partially filled with boxes, tools and miscellaneous parts from rides and attractions. He waved his hand to the opposite side of the room where the offices were.

Lily had already known that he and his son were estranged but she hadn't known the reason Parker had left.

"I had no idea he left because of what happened to Ida."

Darren let out a tired laugh.

"That and my overbearing parenting apparently," he said. "His mother, rest her soul, was the one with the soft touch and kind words. According to him, I was wanting in that area. I'm not sure I blame him for leaving, though. We both know that this town takes more than it ever gives."

Lily knew he was right. He kept on to drive his point home.

"Ida should have had a full, happy life. Just as sweet Annie, Kristine and Claudia should have had. The same for Jacob and his wife."

Lily ran names in her memory.

"Claudia?"

Darren slowed. It put them halfway through the warehouse. Another crack of thunder sounded. This time it was closer.

"A young woman who was taken from the next county around the same time Miss Perez was."

Lily shook her head.

"I don't remember hearing about that one." Lily knew she wasn't an expert in many things but one investigation she knew inside and out was Ida's. There had been no abduction in the entire state of Alabama for two weeks before and after Ida's. The next person to be taken was a child in north Alabama by his father, later returned safely to his mother. There was no Claudia.

Darren looked thoughtful.

"I suppose I'm misremembering, then." He sighed. "Sometimes it's hard to keep all of Kelby Creek's tragedies in line."

Lily would have normally given that to him but a nagging feeling had been woken up within her. She didn't know why but that brought her right back to Bryant Lautner.

"Speaking of tragedies, what do you know about Bryant Lautner?" she asked. "He's around your age and Kelby Creek's so small. You must have known him when you were younger?"

Darren shook his head.

They were almost to the door now.

"The only thing I really remember about that man when we were younger was this awful flu he gave me when he was setting up his mother's memorial service with my sister-in-law's help," he said. "It was so rough I coughed up blood at one point. It was probably the worst I've ever felt."

Lily didn't realize it but she'd already stopped walking.

The switch she normally threw to keep her emotions out of the equation had just been yanked off the wall.

There was no way.

No way she'd heard him right.

He couldn't have been...

Was he?

Lily's mind filled to the brim with questions.

Yet, she focused on the memory from the woods.

The sound of a man coughing.

After all of these years, after everything she'd gone through to get to the moment of being with the man in the woods...

Was she finally there?

One look back at Darren and whatever emotion was on her face was enough to stop him in his tracks.

She knew then.

And he knew that she knew.

For a second, all they did was stare at one another.

In the next, he sighed again.

"You know, I always wondered if you heard me coughing that night." He shrugged. "I guess now I know."

Lily pulled her gun out and shot just as Darren sidestepped.

He yelled out in pain as the bullet grazed his arm but it didn't stop him from launching himself at her.

Adrenaline hadn't yet poured through her and pushed out the pain in her rib cage. She tried to avoid the force of his body weight but all she did was catch it with the left side of her body instead of head-on.

They both went down.

The air was knocked clear from Lily's lungs but Darren wasn't faring much better. Blood from his arm dripped onto her as Lily tried to bring up her gun. Darren huffed and puffed trying to straddle her but moved his attention to her weapon. He managed to use one hand to slam her wrist against the concrete floor. Lily knew her gun was coming loose so she did the only thing she could.

She flung it away from both of them then yanked her knee up to his groin.

Darren yelled out as Lily bucked him off.

The second his weight was off her, she scrambled toward her gun.

As she grabbed it she was already imagining shooting the man in the leg to disable him.

However, he said the only thing in the world that would stop her.

"Put the gun down or she dies!"

Lily spun around and froze her trigger finger.

There was a good amount of distance between them now but Lily could see his face clearly.

"Who?" Lily yelled. Her voice was hoarse. The hit to the floor had been harder than she'd thought.

Darren had his hands up. His answer was too strong. Too confident.

"Kristine Cho is in a box somewhere in this town, suffocating because you showed up here. Because you interrupted me."

Lily shook her gun.

"I don't believe you."

Darren pointed to the door they'd been about to walk through. Next to it was a shovel.

"I was about to go get her since she's been in that box since last night. Bryant was supposed to get her but he never showed."

Lily had some decisions to make.

The first was to believe him or not.

"Why?"

"Because that's where we keep them until we move them." Lily's stomach plummeted.

"Them?"

"The girls," he yelled back. "And *that* girl is going to die if you don't put down your gun." Lily hesitated. But only for a moment.

She had no choice but to believe him.

"Where is she?"

"Put the gun and your phone down and I'll tell you. If she's not already out of air, you can save her."

Lily knew her next decision was the most crucial.

It could be the difference between her life and Kristine's.

It could be the difference between catching Darren McHale or letting him use his money to disappear.

There was no way to know until she decided.

So Lily chose Kristine, hoping he wasn't lying.

But she wasn't about to give in to him fully.

She took the clip out of her gun and put it in her pocket. She threw the rest of the gun across the floor toward the door they'd come in. Her phone went next.

Then she aimed her righteous anger at Darren McHale. "Tell me where she is!"

If the urgency hadn't been so great, she might have closed the distance between them and slugged him at how he flashed a quick smile.

"The last place you and Anthony Perez would ever look."

Lily's veins were now completely flooded with adrenaline.

She knew where Kristine was.

And Darren knew that.

"I'd be running if I were you," he warned.

Lily didn't stop to think her next move through.

She ran to the door and grabbed the shovel.

Then she was outside, opening the back gate and running into the woods with an awful sense of déjà vu.

ANT WATCHED COLTON and Winnie drive off. He'd apologized again for messing up their date, then he'd given the EMT a piece of his mind about making sure to lock his girlfriend's doors.

After that he'd leaned against Lily's car with Cook at his side.

He was mulling over what Lily had said about Jacob not being Kristine's secret boyfriend when he heard the gunshot.

Cook barked, just as Ant took off.

"Call the cops!" he yelled to the boy in the ticket stand.

Ant made fast work of running through the thoroughfare and even faster work of finding the office at the back of the fairgrounds. He heard nothing on the way to the building. Only his footfalls and Cook's panting as he followed.

He wasn't sure if that was a good thing or not.

The door closest to him was open.

"Lily!"

His voice echoed through the warehouse.

He stopped when he saw her gun on the floor ahead of him. Her phone next to it.

Ant grabbed the gun and redirected his attention to the opposite side of the room. He saw another door, open and streaked with blood.

He didn't wait around.

Ant ran full tilt toward and through it.

He was in an office. He scanned the room and his eyes lit on a back door that had blood smeared across the handle.

Ant pushed out into the darkness just in time to see a man go into the tree line in the distance.

It was without a doubt Darren McHale.

The shotgun he was holding was also unmistakable.

Ant didn't yell for Lily this time.

If Lily was being chased and without a weapon, she was going somewhere she knew better than her attacker.

Ant tried to make as little noise as he could running into the woods. Cook was still with him, running hard, about ten to twelve feet behind Darren. If the dog could ambush the man, Ant could save Lily.

A plan made harder by the fact that the gun in his hand didn't have a clip.

Still, he could use it as a blunt object. If not, he'd make sure his fists would do the trick.

Thunder boomed overhead.

Ant could barely see between the trees.

He moved fast despite his vision.

His childhood home was on the other side of the woods. Somewhere between him and it was the creek. Between it and him was Lily, unarmed and possibly hurt. Between her and Ant was a man with a shotgun.

A nearly overwhelming sense of helplessness rammed into Ant's chest.

The last time he'd been in these woods, he'd lost someone he loved.

He refused to do that again.

Chapter Twenty-One

The rain started falling just as Lily heard the creek in the distance. Before that she'd heard someone behind her.

Darren McHale had let her go knowing his secret.

There was no doubt in her mind that he would follow her into the woods and try to keep that secret from ever leaving it.

Yet Lily had believed him about Kristine so she'd done the only two things she could in the situation.

She'd run as fast as she'd ever run and then thrown herself behind a tree to hide.

She had to figure Darren had a weapon. One he would use on Lily fast once he caught her.

So she held her breath and planned to catch him first. She hadn't strayed from running the most direct path to the creek and neither had Darren. It was almost too easy to pinpoint where he was going to be.

Lily jumped out, bent low and swung the shovel like all of Wrigley Field was watching her.

She was right on the money.

The metal part of the shovel connected with Darren's legs. His momentum and sheer size sent Lily to her backside just as he yelled out and fell a few feet from her.

Lily was also right about the man having a weapon. She spied the shotgun as it flew from his hands.

Lily struggled to stand, tightening her grip on the shovel, as Darren rolled around in the dirt, feeling for the gun.

He found it but Lily was quicker with the shovel. She swung it like a golf club.

The metal head connected with a sickening thud beneath Darren's chin.

He dropped his gun, then the rest of his body went limp, falling to the dirt in a heap.

Lily was breathing hard. Adrenaline had her heart beating so fast it felt like it was about to tear out of her body.

She couldn't imagine how Kristine felt.

Lily bent down, grabbed the shotgun and ran with it and the shovel past the unconscious man.

The sound of the creek grew louder.

The trees started to thin into a clearing.

The clearing...

Lily slowed, but only for a moment.

She was standing where Darren had been all those years ago. She looked over to the water.

Where Ant had been.

Then she looked at the expanse of ground beyond the water.

Where she had been when she'd had to decide whether to save Ant or Ida.

Lily had been at that spot, at that creek, in the same woods, for years.

With startling clarity she realized she had never left.

She'd been trapped in this spot in Kelby Creek since she was seventeen.

Ant was wrong.

She was a ghost and *this* was where she haunted.

You know this place, she told herself. *You know what's different.*

Lily took the smallest of breaths.

With her eyes she traced the ground again, the water, the trees the deputies' flashlight beams had bounced across when they'd hurried out to them.

Lily stopped.

One of the trees was gone. The one with the knot that used to be as big as her hand.

The dirt where it should have been was disturbed.

Lily splashed across the water. She dropped the shotgun when she reached the fresh dirt and sank the shovel into the earth. The dirt she brought back she tossed over her shoulder. On the second stab into the ground, she hit something hard.

It timed poorly with someone crashing through the trees behind her.

Lily spun around. She must have been hurting more than she thought, because she lost her balance and hit the ground.

It was only good fortune that the man who appeared wasn't Darren McHale.

"Lily!"

Ant made it across the water without stopping. Cook was on his heels.

She could have cried, if there'd been time.

Instead, she got back up and pointed her shovel back down at the hole.

"Kristine is inside!"

Ant didn't need more of an explanation.

He took the shovel and drove it deep into the ground. He hit the top of the box and readjusted his aim. Dirt flew over his shoulder, and Lily dropped to her knees to help dig with her hands.

"It was Darren," Lily cried out. Tears of anger and exhaustion and pain were starting to burn her eyes. "Ant, he was there that night. He took Ida."

Ant didn't pause.

He didn't stop.

He kept digging.

The top of the box was fully uncovered within seconds. Ant started to move the dirt to get to the side just as they had the first night he came to town.

This time there was no recording of Annie McHale.

There was, however, a voice.

It was faint.

It was Kristine.

As Lily yelled out to her, urging her to hold on, she barely heard the splashing behind them.

Ant shouted for Lily's attention but not in time.

Darren lunged at her.

Ant managed to push her out of the way of the man but Lily still felt like a fool for not keeping the shotgun in her hands.

Terror consumed her as Darren took it back into his.

Ant was quicker with his reflexes. Just as he'd done at Bryant Lautner's workshop he ran Lily into the trees, this time dragging her.

She looked over her shoulder to see Darren cock the gun.

Ant used his strength to sling her along with him behind one of the trees. Shotgun pellets bit into the bark on the other side.

Ant wasn't done moving. He handed something to Lily so fast it took her a beat to figure out it was her gun.

She might have dropped the ball with the shotgun but at least she'd kept her clip.

Darren shot again. With his arms and body Ant made a cage around her but gave her the space she needed to load the gun.

In one fluid movement, he pulled back and Lily rolled to the side, her gun up and ready.

She couldn't see Darren all that well but he must have seen her enough to know that running for cover might be the best idea.

She caught the barest hint of movement and swung her weapon to the side, and fired.

Darren yelled out and she saw him then as he grasped his leg. She'd wounded him. He retreated across the creek. Lily tried to get another shot off but her aim wasn't there.

Ant pulled her to him. She met his eyes.

The world around them became fourteen years younger.

Ant's hair was dark and wet against his face. His eyes matched the sky, stormy and fierce. He was determined.

This time, though, he was Lily.

Seventeen, terrified, long hair tangled from the rain.

At a crossroad.

Two choices and one decision to make that could change everything.

He could save the person who needed rescuing or he could go after Ida's kidnapper.

In that moment, Lily understood that in between the softness of her sheets back home Ant had been right all along.

"There is no choice," she said. "Save the one you can."

As Ant picked up the shovel, Lily turned and ran. Ant didn't stop her.

She ran across the dirt and through the creek water, pushing past every inch of pain. Darren hadn't expected her to fight back. He hadn't expected her at all. That was more than apparent as she spotted him doubling back toward the fair. He had no plan.

And he had terrible aim.

He spun around and shot off to the side of her once. Then tried again.

That shot had Lily move for cover.

She didn't stay there long.

Lily stepped out and fired her weapon again.

Darren yelled out.

This time, he fell.

Lily was on him in a second. She picked up his discarded shotgun and trained both weapons on him.

He was in bad shape, slumped on his side.

He met her gaze and coughed through a laugh.

"They—they'll never believe you. I'm—I'm a McHale."

Lily shook her head.

"The only reason you got away from us the first time was because we were kids," she bit out. "We're not kids anymore."

Lily holstered her gun. She took the butt of the shotgun and brought it down on the man's head.

This time when he went limp, she knew he wouldn't be getting up anytime soon.

She turned and ran back to the creek.

The shovel was next to Ant. So was a piece of the box. In his arms was a young woman. Lily dropped next to them both to help pull her all the way out.

Ant held Kristine Cho as she looked up at Lily.

"Hi, Kris, we've been looking for you."

Kristine's voice was weak. "I'm glad you found me."

Lily reached out and touched Ant's shoulder.

She gave it a squeeze.

He met her eye and she knew that he knew.

Ant let out a long breath.

And just like that the ghost that haunted the woods moved on.

Two days later

THE FAIR LEFT.

The media, however, still swarmed.

Darren McHale, a part of the most beloved family in Kelby Creek, had turned out to be a devil in sheep's clothing. A villain none of them had seen coming. A monster.

No one knew yet what Darren's plan had been or the level of his involvement but by his own admission, he'd been the one to take Ida.

He'd been the man in the woods.

Ant wanted answers now that the authorities had him in custody.

But a lot of things had to happen first.

Darren had to have several surgeries, for starters. He'd had two bullet wounds, a graze, a busted knee and a broken jaw. All of which were from Lily. Something that made Ant insanely proud.

It had made Lily feel a certain type of way, too.

Later that night in her bed, she'd told Ant that it had felt vindicating to finally catch him.

He'd agreed because it was true.

Still, a part of him hurt for Ida.

What had happened to his sister?

It was a question that didn't get answered right away.

After that they'd had to wait a day for Kristine to recover enough to talk. She'd been dehydrated and close to suffocating. The doctors guessed another few minutes and she wouldn't have made it out alive. When she was able, she asked for Lily and Ant to come into her room. She was weak but she grabbed their hands and held on to them. They all stood that way for a minute before giving her space to rest.

Then Ant put on a nice shirt and jeans, helped Lily do

the same since her ribs were still bruised and broken, and they headed to the department to get some clarity on everything that happened. No one batted an eye when Cook came in with them.

The dog sat down between Lily and Ant as they settled into the conference room. Detective Gray was the only one currently inside.

"Sorry we've been a bit quiet on our side of things over the last day or so," he told them. "We've had a lot of new discoveries, and piecing together all of it has been a not-so-small task."

Lily gave the man a questioning look.

Ant voiced it.

"Does that mean we know what all happened now?"

Kenneth nodded.

"Thanks to you two, Bryant striking a deal to talk, Kristine Cho's account of what happened, and a few other sources, we do." He referred to his notes only once before continuing.

"Fourteen years ago Bryant and Darren struck up a friendship after Darren's wife passed from cancer. Bryant's mother was also fighting it and was running out of money fast for the treatment. When he approached Darren about borrowing some, Darren revealed that he wasn't exactly as wealthy as his brother. So they asked for money from Annie's parents and were turned down. Bryant's mother passed shortly after anyway but Darren and his friendship stuck. Instead of moving on, they became angry. Bitter. Bryant said that Darren equated all of his problems to not having enough money and spoke to his brother about it. He was given a handout to start his own business but he blew the money. When he needed more, he was cut off. So he and Bryant met a man who gave them a different suggestion for bringing in the big bucks."

Kenneth gave Ant a quick look. One that let Ant know he wasn't going to like what was said next.

Lily's hand found his under the table before Kenneth continued.

"They got into human trafficking and hid behind the McHale brand of fame to do it in relative secret." Ant gritted his teeth. Lily squeezed his hand. "We can't tell if they were good at it or bad. There's some information we're still getting to let us know which. But they did appear to stop for several years and we think we know why."

Kenneth slid a picture across the table.

It was a McHale family Christmas card. Ant recognized some of them but not the young man Kenneth pointed to.

"That's Parker McHale," Kenneth explained.

"Darren's son?" Lily asked.

Kenneth nodded.

"He left the family home when he was younger and has stayed out of the spotlight since. The only time he surfaced was when the FBI deep dove into the family after Annie went missing. He was, at the time, living in Tennessee on a ranch with his partner and their child. Soon after that they moved again, back off everyone's radar. We're still waiting to talk to him now."

"But what does this have to do with Ida?" Ant couldn't help but ask. "And Kristine? Was he in on it with his dad?"

Kenneth shook his head.

"We've been led to believe that he actually fled town because he knew what his father was capable of."

Kenneth shifted in his chair and Ant detected a change in his demeanor. He looked Ant right in the eye, resolute and solemn.

"From what we've been told, Ida and Parker were secretly dating at the time of her abduction and the *reason* she was taken was because she overheard Darren and Bryant planning another attempt. They found out and before she could tell anyone, she was taken."

Ant shook his head. He couldn't focus on the secret relationship because his mind went right back to the day of Ida's abduction.

"That's why she was so upset," he realized. "We were out in the yard... She'd just gotten home and I was trying to get her to tell me what was wrong. But she never did because...that's when she was taken."

Kenneth nodded.

"Bryant said Darren panicked and grabbed her."

Ant was seeing red.

"Did he say what he did to her?" He could barely get the question out.

"No. Neither man did."

Ant wanted to leave then. To go outside and yell. Yet Lily's hand had him stay.

Ida wasn't the only young woman in the story.

Kenneth seemed to realize this was his only opening to finish.

"After Ida's abduction they finished their planned job with Claudia Rikton. She was pronounced a runaway back then but now the FBI is looking into one of the names Bryant provided that he and Darren sold her to. After Claudia, though, they both stopped. They had a substantial amount of money from their trafficking. But it ran out recently. They were starting back up and trying to come up with a different plan to move women."

"By putting them in boxes," Lily guessed.

He nodded.

"They put boxes in several locations with the recorders and were testing out if they could remove them without arousing suspicion, even if the women made a fuss.

That's what Arturo was hired for and what he was doing when he was interrupted by you two."

"So the meth lab and Jacob having an affair with Kristine was just them trying to cover it all up?" Lily asked.

Kenneth nodded again.

"Arturo wasn't supposed to get caught so when he did, Bryant said Darren became enraged, threatening to kill Bryant if he didn't figure out how to fix it. Apparently neither man accounted for you two. Since we've had a few meth labs pop up here and there, Bryant thought making Arturo's hideout look like one so when he burned the evidence no one would think anything other than a lab explosion. They also didn't account for Kristine getting suspicious of her secret boyfriend."

Darren McHale.

That had been a shock among shocks when Kris had admitted to them that it was the McHale she'd been seeing. Jacob Anderson had taken the fall for it, even going as far to help plant the evidence against him.

"Kristine confronted Darren after he lied about where he'd been during the meth lab fire and he decided to use her as the first test for their new box trick," Kenneth continued. "Since you two were back, he used the spot he'd created out there."

Lily was disgusted.

"Because it was the last place we would look. He told me that."

Ant grumbled. His anger was escalating once again.

"What about Jacob?" Lily followed up. "Why did he agree to take the fall?"

Kenneth was somber when he replied.

"He walked in on Bryant making the recordings off of Darren's computer one day when he was working. Jacob immediately went to Darren to let him know Bryant was messing around on his computer, thinking he was doing the right thing."

"'I didn't know he had a partner,'" Lily said. "That's what Jacob kept saying. He wasn't talking about Arturo and Bryant. He was talking about Bryant and Darren."

"Bryant said that Darren and Jacob had a long talk but he didn't know how Jacob was threatened to take the fall. He guessed it was something that involved his wife, Gwen. Something that spooked him enough to fully commit to Darren's orders."

"It must have been a terrifying threat for him to take his life," Ant added. "One he believed Darren would carry out if he didn't follow the plan."

Kenneth was fast with a response they all knew to be true.

"We're still trying to figure out what that threat was but only Darren and Jacob knew. The name McHale carries a lot of weight in this town. Apparently that weight can be used for awful things."

They all quieted at that.

Lily broke the silence after a moment.

"Then there's the whole question of why Darren McHale had a potentially clear recording of Annie's video on his computer," Kenneth continued. "That's currently unsolved at the moment but something we're looking into. It might just take some time."

Lily nodded, so did Ant.

"So that answers all of my questions but one," she said.

Kenneth's eyebrow raised.

"What is that?"

Lily leaned forward.

"How do you know so much about what Parker McHale did if you haven't actually talked to him yet?"

Kenneth didn't answer at first. He stood, and Ant could have sworn he saw a small smile pass over the man's lips.

"Because his partner and their child came forward as soon as the news went out that Darren McHale had been caught."

Kenneth went to the door. He opened it and stepped aside.

After a moment a preteen boy came in, tall and dark-haired. He looked familiar but Ant couldn't place him.

When his mother walked in, Ant had no trouble at all recognizing her.

Ida was older but the moment she said his name all he saw was the sixteen-year-old girl he'd been missing for fourteen years.

Epilogue

Six months later

"Listen, I know it's too soon but maybe we can just take a gander at some dresses tomorrow?"

Winnie was giving her a look that Lily had come to understand meant that Winnie had already planned their shopping expedition. Beside her, Colton wore an expression that told Lily it was a lost cause to fight his girlfriend. Still, Lily was trying to be practical.

"Winnie, we're in the middle of my engagement party. For an engagement that happened less than two days ago. Maybe we should hold off on wedding dress shopping for at least a week?"

Winnie made an exasperated sound. She threw up her hands, turned to Kristine across the decorated backyard and shook her head.

Kris was dramatic with her disappointment. It made her date laugh.

"Fine. I'll let you catch your breath, I guess," Winnie said. She lowered her voice. "But you better believe I'm not the only one who's going to pressure you tonight." She nodded, not so inconspicuously, to the patio. "You best believe those two are coming for you next."

Lily looked over to see that Kristine hadn't been the

only one watching them. Ida and Juliet pretended, at least, to be disinterested in her.

Ida's big brother, however, feigned no such thing.

He entered the conversation by picking Lily up and spinning her into a kiss.

When her feet were on the ground again, he excused them both.

"They bothering you about the wedding already?" he asked, laughing before she could answer.

"Yes! Wedding dress shopping tomorrow, never mind that I have work."

Ant laughed again.

"You can't blame them. After the wedding you pulled off for Ida and Parker, everyone wants to return the favor."

Even after six months, the way Ant said Ida's name still made Lily's heart melt a little. The two syllables were filled with love and a gratefulness that she felt in her bones. Knowing that Ida's kidnapper was in prison for life was nothing compared to the feeling of seeing her alive and happy.

Though that had taken some time on both their parts.

True, Ant had been beside himself at seeing his sister after fourteen years. Those fourteen years of her staying in hiding had hit him hard. Especially when they found out that the day after Ida had been taken, she'd been freed.

"I was in Hunstville, in a trunk, and then suddenly Parker was there," she'd explained to them. "He figured out where his father's partner was and managed to help me escape. We hid, wanting to make sure we had enough to take Darren down. But then we found out I was pregnant with Beau and, well, Parker knew about all the corruption already running through the town. So we decided to hide for a while." Ida had cried then as she'd looked at

Ant. "I almost reached out to you a dozen times but I was so worried that they'd find a way to hurt Beau. And then, you moved and I almost reached out but The Flood happened and we didn't know who to trust."

Ida had been all-out sobbing then.

"Then we saw the news that Darren had been caught and I—I just knew in my bones that you were the one who'd done it."

In the darkness of their bedroom, Ant had admitted to Lily one night that while he would have made a different decision, he couldn't fault Ida and Parker for theirs.

"Being a McHale carries a certain weight with locals." He'd paraphrased Kenneth. "I guess that goes double for fear."

He wasn't wrong. Parker's reemergence and his father's arrest had brought the McHales right back into the spotlight.

And, for the first time, not as the victims.

But that was a whole new set of questions for another time.

Right now Lily was making sure to be in the moment with the man she loved and the man who loved her back enough to ask her to marry him. It had happened late one night while they were trying to be witches on her bed.

"Close your eyes," he'd said. "Now move that power from your belly to your hands, since we all know your head doesn't need it."

Lily had laughed but followed directions.

"I'd watch out if I were you," she'd responded. "If my hands get too much power they might just smack that cute mouth of yours."

"Then it's probably not a good idea to give them any more power, huh?"

She'd felt the bed move a second before she felt the ring on her finger.

When she'd opened her eyes, he'd told her to lie back down.

"Now, we're going to close our eyes and make some decisions," he'd said, repeating his words from the first time they'd done the exercise.

She hadn't said it then but there was never really any choice to make at all.

It had always been Ant.

Instead, in the moment, she'd just said yes.

Now they were surrounded by loved ones and celebrating each other after what had been a long fourteen years.

"You know, once Mom finishes moving in down the road and your parents head back here—not to mention Ida, Parker and Beau in the same neighborhood *and* Winnie and Kristine too—we're probably never going to be alone again."

Ant wrapped his arms around her and kissed her neck.

They both looked out at the party of people. Family, friends and colleagues.

He was right.

Lily relaxed against him.

Before Ant came back to town, Lily would have hated the thought.

Now, though, everything was different.

Now she didn't want to be alone anymore.

"Sounds good to me."

* * * * *

UNDERCOVER COLTON

ADDISON FOX

For our wonderful Colton readers who come back to our stories month after month. Your support and enjoyment of our books mean more than we can say. Thank you!

Chapter One

He really was a bastard.

Not in the illegitimate use of the word, Dominic Colton reflected, but in every other way that counted.

And it all centered on the woman who sat opposite him.

If the circumstances were different, he'd give in to the inconvenient feelings roiling in his chest. Her long flowing red hair, strong shoulders and sculpted arms, and a figure-hugging midnight blue dress had his mouth watering far more effectively than the lasagna on the plate before him. But it was the intelligence he saw in her rich hazel eyes, reflecting in the candlelight between them, that had really done him in.

Samantha Evans was quite a woman.

Their oh-so-convenient meeting, on a construction site where he worked the crew while she supervised the landscaping, had been the perfect cover. To her, he was Dom Conner, a hardworking contractor working his way up to owning his own construction company. He'd worked some construction in college and had enough basic knowledge of how the job operated. The backstory he'd built up for himself had sung well beneath the subtle attraction humming between them.

In reality, he was Dominic Colton, FBI agent in the International Corruption Unit, based out of Denver. He and his team had been following a series of leads that started with a disgraced senator on the take to overlook drug smuggling and had ultimately led him here: to Blue Larkspur, Colorado.

It felt a million miles away from his condo downtown, but he'd settled in well these past few weeks, his chameleon personality easily fitting in. His knowledge of the area, being born and raised here, hadn't hurt, either.

He'd always taken pride in that skill, he considered as he took in the lovely woman sitting across from him. His simple ease in fitting in no matter where he was. Whether it was due to coming from a large family or, even more specifically, being a triplet inside that large family, Dom didn't know. All he did know was that it had made him a strong asset to the Bureau and was a key requirement for his job.

So why did he feel like a wolf in sheep's clothing tonight?

Sami Evans had no idea what had brought Dom into her life. It wasn't a simple, happy accident like their first brunch date suggested, the two of them randomly meeting on a jobsite. Rather it was a carefully calculated attempt to get close to her and get underneath what she knew and how long she'd known it.

Because she might not know he was Dom Colton, son of disgraced and deceased judge Ben Colton of Lark's County. But he knew damn well who *she* was: The daughter of Mike "Lone Wolf" Evans, the current head of the Warlords motorcycle club.

Her father ran the Colorado branch of the international MC gang, believed for years to have been dormant. Only things seemed to have cropped back up, both in Europe as well as in select locations in the western part of the United States. Dom and his team had been keeping a close eye on these developments but when news of the gang settling here in Colorado became more rampant, drug traffic increasing in their wake, the FBI put Dom undercover.

Lone Wolf's daughter sat at the heart of his mission.

What did Sami Evans know?

And why did the first woman who'd infiltrated his senses with all the finesse of a sledgehammer have to be the one at the heart of his investigation?

You're in over your head, Sami-girl.

That thought had whispered through her mind over and over today and well into this evening as she'd considered her date with Dom Conner. The man made her mouth water and that was no small feat, seeing as how she spent the majority of her days around muscles and testosterone.

If she were honest with herself, she'd long believed herself immune. She had a good, thriving landscaping business. It kept her outdoors, happy and productive, and had been profitable enough she'd bought a house the prior year.

The life she'd imagined for herself was finally coming true and she didn't need anyone's interference or the sudden input of a man to get in the way of those things.

Hadn't she seen her mother live that life?

Worse, Sami thought as she reached for her drink,

a light shudder skating the length of her spine, hadn't her mother paid for that choice with her life.

"Everything okay?" Dom asked, his dark blue eyes serious from across the table.

And totally focused on her.

She took a moment to swallow her wine, trying to find some equilibrium in that fortifying sip. The gloomy thoughts that surrounded her memories of her mother never failed to ruin her mood. But she'd believed herself to have a handle on them.

So why were they cropping up on the best date she'd had in years?

Dom Conner.

Had she ever met a man who was so totally focused on her? Engaged and interested in what she had to say and, by extension, interested in *her*?

Sure, she'd had relationships. Although she avoided dating men from the jobsites she was on, she did go out from time to time. There was that junior professor from the university one of her friends had introduced her to. She and Sean had dated a few months. They'd hit it off well and enjoyed each other's company, but nothing had ever really sparked.

Without that sparkling tingle, she'd let things fizzle out.

Same with Jason, the accountant who had a small office in downtown Blue Larkspur, and Shane, the mechanic she knew from high school and had gotten reacquainted with one night while out at The Corner Pocket, the local bar in town she favored.

Nice guys, she thought. More, they were good guys, every one of them. Yet somewhere in the process of getting-to-know-you, something fizzled out.

Was it her?

She'd often wondered if growing up under the watchful and, she now knew, criminal, eye of Mike Evans had tainted her somehow. Was she unworthy of something good? Of a solid, mutually satisfying relationship?

Since Dom was still staring at her, Sami surfaced from the morose direction of her thoughts. "Good. I'm good."

"You sure?" Dom kept his question casual as he reached for his own glass of wine but she didn't miss the careful look that had settled into his smile.

Like someone trying to soothe and calm a wild animal.

"I am. I just got distracted for a moment. Woolgathering, my mother used to call it."

"Care to tell me about it?"

"Will you run screaming if I confessed this is the best date I've been on—" she hesitated, nearly tripping over the words *oh about ever*, and instead opted for, "in a long time."

"Will you run screaming or think I'm handing you a line if I tell you the same?"

"No."

"Then same." His smile broadened, which was doing something to her stomach.

That expression remained, directed at her as their waiter cleared their plates with swift efficiency. It was a nice grin, she admitted to herself. Confident, yet warm, with white even teeth and the lightest dent of a dimple in his left cheek. It was a smile that said he was enjoying himself and, in that knowledge, she had to admit the same.

And what was she doing sitting here, thinking about her messed up family when she should be focused on the six feet of *interested* hotness across the table?

While she might consider herself immune to muscles and testosterone, she'd had a damned difficult time ignoring either on Dom. The man was sculpted like a Greek god, she knew, remembering the way he looked on the Traverson job. A week ago, they'd had a particularly hot spring afternoon and she'd seen him shirtless, laying a section of roof. She'd been helpless to do anything but stand there, her shovel in hand and a pile of mulch at her feet, and just stare up at him walking that roof with the nimbleness of a cat.

It had only been the lightning quick joke of her own foreman, Steve, that had gotten her moving. His whispered, "Ogle much, Boss?" as he handed her a bottle of water before moving on had pulled her out of her reverie and, with hasty movements, she'd focused back on her mulch.

After, of course, downing the entire bottle of water.

Goodness, she was only human. And Dom's muscles were something rather spectacular. And, if she were fair, the last time she'd had sex had been with Shane and that was nearly two years ago.

Two very long years, she suddenly realized as she caught sight of Dom's warm smile once more.

"And here I go again." She determinedly pulled herself back to the present. "This is a great place. I've been wanting to come here but haven't had the chance. The food's really good."

A further sign that Blue Larkspur was a quietly growing city. Her business had seen the benefits as well, building solid and steady for the past several years. It had been enough to buy her own home and to add staff each season to take on more work. She'd further branched out into some interior landscape work as well as holiday decorations, those expansions ensuring she and her staff had work through the winter months.

All in all, it was good to be busy. And it was a dream come true to be in a place where she could do what she loved.

"Food's good," Dom agreed before lowering his voice. "The company's even better."

She blushed, the eternal curse of the fair-skinned redhead, but couldn't deny how good his words felt. Or how nice it was to be out on a date with an appreciative and attractive man sitting opposite her.

It might have been two depressing years since she'd had sex, but in the ensuing twenty-four months she'd been in a total dating slump, too. Two lukewarm first dates and a third about six months ago had firmly put her in her current emotional desert.

And using her career and getting her business up, running and thriving was fast becoming an old excuse even she was sick of.

What would be the harm in taking their date further? Dating slump aside, he was the most interesting man she'd ever met. And he had a way about him that was attentive and charming without veering into leering or lecherous.

Men wanted sex. And, as she well knew, women did, too. But a flashing neon sign that suggested a date was simply a required social nicety to get to the main event had always turned her off. Because no matter how great the sex, eventually you had to get out of bed. And she'd always appreciated spending time with someone who could effectively keep her attention in both places.

"Do you want dessert?"

Dom's question—genuinely innocent as he tapped the small menu their waiter had discreetly laid down a short while ago—pulled Sami from her increasingly heated thoughts.

A question that gave her a rather specific opportunity.

"Would you like anything?" she asked, already weighing what she was about to do.

"I could share something."

"I might have just the thing, then." She toyed with the stem of her wine glass, but never broke eye contact. "Maybe we skip dessert here and head back to my place for coffee instead."

ANY NUMBER OF warning signs went off in Dom's head as he followed behind Sami's car toward her home. He'd spent enough of his adult dating life to know that an invitation for coffee usually wasn't one. Nor was the suggestion to come directly to his date's home for said coffee at all about sharing a hit of caffeine before the date ended.

It was about sex.

Only about sex.

And he was a lying jerk, job or no job, if he even considered taking any hint of what she was offering.

But damn, the woman intrigued him. She was bright and warm, beautiful and effervescent, in a way that made him feel better just being in her company.

Yet here he was, following her through the familiar streets of Blue Larkspur, pretending he had no idea where she lived even though he knew, down to the floor plans, the layout of her home.

He'd wanted to pick her up for their evening out but she'd had a late job and suggested she'd just clean up quickly at a friend's house and then meet him. Whether true or not, he'd accepted the reason as her right to handle their date as she saw fit. As a man who worked in law enforcement and had five sisters, he knew a woman couldn't be too careful. He'd admired Sami's focus on her own plans and keeping control of the situation.

Even if the lightest whisper had drifted through his mind that she might be hiding something at home.

Only she'd turned the tables on him once more. Forget the blinding attraction that was rapidly messing with his common sense and basic human decency. She'd invited him home with a rather unmistakable invitation to come over…and likely stay.

Which meant there was no chance he'd find any hint of Lone Wolf Evans's nefarious deeds hidden in the nooks and crannies of her place.

A list of Dad's upcoming planned jobs tacked to the fridge with a magnet? Not bloody likely.

Only now, he had to find a way to tamp down on the attraction that was already messing with his focus and let her down easy.

Because damn it, he *was* attracted to her. More than he'd expected and far more than he should be. He'd never been a man who used his job as an excuse, and he wasn't about to start now. The job was his life, and he was honor bound to execute his duties, but that didn't mean he used people as collateral damage in the process.

Yet he knew, way down deep, that if he slept with Sami Evans, she'd most surely be collateral damage.

He couldn't tell her who he was or why he was there. And even if his instincts were right that she had no knowledge of her father's crimes, *he* did and that was all that mattered.

The Internal Corruption Unit had been watching Mike Evans for a while. By the time Dom was fully briefed, the situation had grown more suspicious by the day. The Warlords, believed dormant since the ICU had worked with Interpol five years before to take them down, had seemingly risen from the dead. An international gang that was causing considerable issues with the drug trade—and its flow—across Europe was gaining a stronghold here in the US as well.

Lone Wolf Evans had been rumored to be a part of several violent acts by the Warlords over the past three months, but the motorcycle club hadn't done anything concrete enough to get caught. Their low-level underlings had managed to escape any verifiable charges, too, no matter how hard the ICU tried to make some things stick.

Drug trafficking. Nope.

Running numbers. Dead end there, too.

Even a possible arson rap had been impossible to lay down, the crime committed against another known drug runner in the region.

Not that Dom minded the MC doing the government's work for them, but they hadn't simply eradicated their competition. He knew damn well they'd cleaned out any sellable drug caches before setting the fire.

They were careful. Controlled. And clearly capable of handling anything that got in their way.

Which brought him right back to tonight. What did Mike's daughter know?

She doesn't know anything.

That thought had tantalized Dom on their first date, growing louder as their second date meandered through any number of conversational topics. Even with his misgivings about what she might be hiding in her home, he was more and more convinced Sami Evans didn't know anything.

He'd probed a bit on her family. Those casual discussions when you shared information of your own before asking for the same from your date. He never spoke of his own family, his feelings about Ben Colton determinedly off-limits to *everyone*, but he'd built a pretty solid backstory as Dom Conner that would stick if questioned. Raised by a single mother, she'd given him a good heart and determination in spades, even if he'd stumbled a bit as a headstrong teenager. Stumbles that had resulted in the lion tattoo on his forearm, one fang showing as the sign that he'd completed his initiation ritual.

It had been an idea that had stuck in his early days on the ICU and while he didn't love wearing a permanent mark that could identify him, the tattoo had come in handy on undercover work. With an easily whipped up story about gang initiation, he'd used the lion to his advantage on more than a few occasions.

And if his fellow triplets, Ezra and Oliver, liked to rib him about it, well, he could live with that. He'd grown attached to his tattoo over the years.

That lion also enhanced the fictional story of his redemption. How he was now focused on making his own way in the world and even more determined to make his devoted mother proud. And, as the universe's reward for all her self-sacrifice in raising him, she'd found the love of her life in the form of a stepfather Dom loved and respected.

It worked because there was enough pathos in his made-up early days to engender trust in someone who'd experienced the same, and enough of a happy ending to calm anyone nervous who hadn't. While his little story was all further reinforcement of his earlier thoughts that he really was a bastard of the first water, his made-up family history got the job done.

And yeah, *technically*, the underlying details weren't a lie. His father *was* out of the picture and his mother had become a single parent the year Dom turned sixteen, betrayed by a man she'd believed she knew. There was no beloved stepfather but that was only because he'd heard from his siblings that their mother diligently refused to give into her growing feelings for police chief Theodore Lawson.

But the story beats were all wrong.

Because Dom Colton's father had lived a double life for years, dying in a car accident on a snowy road shortly after his crimes came to life. Dom and his eleven siblings had all been forced to live with the grief of losing someone they loved and then the added anguish of learning that man wasn't someone they'd truly known.

A county judge who'd worked the system to his corrupt advantage, taking bribes and kickbacks from the owners of both private prisons and juvenile detention centers to sentence more adults and kids to their facilities. His unceremonious removal from the bench had been the state's recourse.

Dom and his siblings had been determined to right the wrongs for those who'd been imprisoned by their father's greed—and anyone else falsely put into jail.

It had been an odd coincidence, as Dom had gotten deeper in on this case, that his father's crimes had reflected a near mirror image of his work. Ronald Spence, one of the last men his father had put in jail, had come to the Coltons' Truth Foundation seeking a review of his case. Although there were significant reasons to believe the man had been involved in the drugs moving through the state and on even farther west, his siblings, Caleb and Morgan, had ultimately gotten the man justice when it was discovered Clay Houseman had perpetrated the crimes.

But it was also further proof of how much moved in the shadows—and how little of it law enforcement could keep a handle on.

So no, the family history he'd shared with Sami wasn't true. His truth was far worse. A blight on the name of Colton they'd spent the ensuing decades trying to redeem. It was intimately tied to his determination to do his job with decency and honor. And because of that maniacal focus his entire adult life, he was now going to need to find a way to leave her after their shared cup of coffee.

Because his made-up story—of a single mother and devoted stepfather—meant he couldn't sleep with her, no matter how badly he wanted her.

No matter how badly the words burned the tip of his tongue to tell her the truth.

Chapter Two

Sami tamped down on her nerves as she stepped from the car inside her garage. Dom had followed behind her from the restaurant and she'd driven carefully through the now-darkened streets of Blue Larkspur so that he couldn't inadvertently get lost or stuck waiting for a stoplight to turn green.

He'd kept up, though. She'd given a basic indication of where they were going and she'd seen his blinker go on several times behind her, anticipation already humming in her veins at all the wonderful possibilities for the evening.

She thought she might chicken out on the drive home, reconsidering her decision at dinner to invite him over as hasty and ill-thought-out. A sort of great-second-date euphoria. Only here, now, staring at him as he stepped from his own car, parked in her driveway, all she could think was that this was exactly right. *All the way right*, her blood practically hummed, like a chorus in her veins.

She wanted this man. And while she wasn't someone who made decisions to sleep with a guy this impulsively, everything about Dom Conner seemed right. No, she amended to herself.

He *felt* right.

Dom was a great person and while she wasn't ready to picture happy-ever-after with him, she'd be remiss if she didn't admit that she could already see herself dating him. Summer picnics up in the mountains and fall walks through town had already crept into her thoughts.

Further proof she needed to keep herself firmly in line.

She wasn't a forever kind of person. Hadn't her parents' relationship proven that? Yet here she was, full of mental hearts and flowers and purple unicorns.

Why was he so damned appealing? Sure, his smile was charming and what woman wouldn't be drawn in by his warm, attentive attitude? But neither of those things were enough of a reason to already feel herself falling like this. Because one thing she knew for certain: There was no net when it came to relationships.

She was self-sufficient for a reason. So she could sleep with the guy all she wanted—she was a grown woman, for heaven's sake—but she'd do well to banish the hearts and flowers from her mental images. And that giant purple unicorn?

So not real.

"Hey there. Everything okay?" Dom stepped closer, but still stood outside the garage door. "You look like you forgot something."

Nothing but my reason, Sami mused. She'd well and truly done so. Especially if she was giving herself pep talks and thinking about sex unicorns.

Sex unicorns?

On a strangled laugh, she shook her head, then stepped closer to him, their bodies close but not touching. The early May air was cool—Colorado evenings hadn't fully warmed up yet—but she felt the heat from his body like the cozy blast from a fireplace.

"I was back to that place in my head where I talk too much."

"To yourself?" Although the question could have been skeptical, the wide smile and sexual awareness sparking in his deep blue eyes suggested he wasn't fazed by her mental musings.

"Occupational hazard, I guess. I spend a lot of time thinking as I plant flowers or plan out landscaping designs."

"I can see that would be the case."

He hadn't touched her yet but she could feel him move imperceptibly closer, that delicious heat warming her chest, at odds with the chill air whispering across her shoulders.

"I like it, even. Most of the time."

"I bet you're pretty good company." The words were low and she heard the need stamped clearly in each and every syllable.

Before she could reply—and that wasn't entirely guaranteed as her brain cells had begun a slow leak from her ears—Dom closed the rest of that narrow gap between them. His mouth settled on hers, warm and wanting, and Sami let out a small sigh as her palms sought the broad width of his shoulders.

Oh, this man was a dream. Physically perfect. She felt the hard play of muscles beneath her hands as solid and as firm as a sculpture. Only he was real. Flesh and blood, heat and desire.

And all of it was focused on her.

She leaned into the kiss, taking all he offered and

returning it back to him. His lips were as firm as the rest of him, yet as he kissed her, it was with a gentle exploration that nearly had her gasping. Especially when he took her bottom lip between his teeth, that teasing bite as tender as it was erotic. Stars exploded behind her eyes and her knees trembled, and in that moment, she knew she was exactly where she wanted to be.

With the man she wanted.

Keeping her hands in place on his shoulders, she pulled back slightly from the kiss, her gaze seeking his. Could he see the desire, marked plainly in her eyes?

How could he miss it?

"I'd like you to come inside."

"With you?"

"With me."

"Sami—" he broke off, and she saw genuine regret in his gaze before it was quickly banked.

Regret?

"I should go."

Something cold whipped in, erasing all that delicious warmth that had wrapped her up. With a deliberate step back, she dropped her hands. "I'm sorry if I misunderstood."

"No, it's not thatÁ." He reached out, settling a hand lightly on her arm. "You've misunderstood nothing."

"I thought—" she broke off, well aware of what *she* thought. But what about Dom?

"I did think along the same lines as you. And I came here, didn't I? It's just that—" He stilled on a harsh exhale. "I'd like coffee and all that comes after with you. But we don't know each other all that well and we do work together. I don't want to rush anything."

Rush anything?

If it had been any other guy, she'd have thought he was feeding her a line, but she saw genuine remorse lining his face in the overhead light from the garage.

And maybe, she saw a small whisper of truth, too. What was she doing, rushing into this? He'd been a great date—the best she'd had in a very long time. But they did work together. And they barely knew each other. And as the breeze slowly brought a bit of sense back to her through the sensual haze that had driven her actions, she had to admit the truth.

The mental images of summer picnics and fall outings was a little too much, too fast. She wasn't a woman who rushed into relationships and that included ones that were only physical. So maybe a bit of a slowdown was in order.

Even if she wasn't quite ready to send him home.

"I'd still like that cup of coffee if you're interested. I might even have a few cupcakes I bought in a moment of weakness at the grocery store this morning."

"Coffee *and* cupcakes?" His eyebrow quirked, the motion cute and remarkably warm for the seemingly momentous decision they'd just made. "How can I say no?"

"You can't."

"You're right."

Before she could say anything else, that hand that had lightly stilled her arm dropped down to take hers, linking their fingers. She glanced down, enchanted at the sweet move.

"I'm glad our evening's not over." His voice was a whisper but in it, she still heard that same swirling need that hadn't settled inside of her.

And as she glanced up from where their hands

joined, into the depths of his eyes, she couldn't hold back the smile. Coffee and cupcakes weren't sex, but it was a nice end to their evening all the same.

And holding hands with Dom Conner was even sweeter than the cupcake.

DOM SETTLED HIMSELF in a chair and considered the woman who puttered around at the kitchen counter, preparing coffee and gathering plates and utensils. Tall and confident, she moved with an easy grace that was captivating.

Alluring.

And based on the heated sense memories that still burned on his lips, proof that this job was going to be a hell of a lot harder to walk away from than he'd ever anticipated.

He shouldn't have kissed her. He'd pep-talked himself the entire drive over and had determined to act grateful for the invitation, ask her for another date to clearly express his interest and then get out of there, a cold shower in his future.

Only he'd been unable to resist the opportunity to taste her. To feel her in his arms. To torment himself, obviously, with the sexual equivalent of a medieval torture rack.

He knew undercover work. It had been a part of his career nearly from the start. He understood the importance of blending in and making just enough of an impression to be memorable yet forgettable. A warm smile. A kind word. All things that left someone feeling right in the moment yet ultimately forgetting as they moved on about their daily life.

It was a trait that served him well and he'd used it as he'd advanced through the Bureau.

So why was he having such a damned difficult time keeping himself in line around Sami?

Yes, she was beautiful. And yes, there was a deeply interesting woman that lay beneath the long red hair and pretty hazel eyes.

But he had a job to do—one that was important to shutting down a major drug node in the region—and nothing in his past had prepared him for the struggle he was facing: to keep his focus solely on that task.

He had no business losing his ability to think critically because a beautiful woman had captured his attention. If it were just the physical aspects, he could brush it off and deal with it. But he had no idea how to handle this continued conviction that she was innocent of knowing anything about Lone Wolf Evans's crimes.

Nothing in their conversation to date suggested she was innocent.

And nothing suggests she's guilty, either, his inner voice taunted him.

Sami set two mugs down on the table before turning back to the counter to grab the plates with the cupcakes she'd already settled on each. Vanilla with chocolate frosting for him and a red velvet concoction for her. Both looked decadent and sinful and, while a poor substitute for the sins he'd like to be committing with her, they weren't a horrible alternative, either.

"Coffee black," she said with a smile as she returned to the table. "An impressive feat."

"I like my caffeine as high test as possible."

"And you never worry about getting jittery walking all over a half-constructed roof like a cat?"

The question was innocent enough but he didn't miss the light twinkle in her eyes. "You noticed that?"

"Hard to miss, Mr. Conner. Especially when you're flashing abs of steel for the whole damn town to see."

He felt the dull flush creep up his neck at her teasing. He hadn't intended to be quite so memorable while on the work detail, but he was only human. The spring sun had been a lot warmer than he remembered from his days working construction in college. "I wasn't aware the crew had noticed," he added with a droll glance at her cat-who-ate-the-canary smile.

"They might have been oblivious but I don't think the neighborhood was. I saw one woman drive past three times."

"That's just—" He broke off when it was obvious she was having a good time at his expense. "Now you're making things up."

She licked a small spot of frosting off the tip of her finger, the move innocent, distracted, even. "Would I lie to you?"

Would she?

The thought caught him off guard, even as his already overheated body hitched up another few degrees at the small dart of her tongue over the frosting.

Wasn't that why he was here?

Because even if she wasn't lying to Dom Conner, affable construction guy, she could very likely be covering up for her criminal father.

Her question still hung there and Dom realized he owed her some response. "Maybe not lie. But you're certainly happy to tease me about simply trying to cool off on a hot afternoon."

Sami shrugged but the humor hadn't faded from her eyes. "I call 'em like I see 'em."

"And you think no one notices those long legs of yours?"

He knew he was playing with fire, but that teasing look of hers needed some sort of response. And since a cold shower had become his ultimate companion for the evening, he might as well enjoy himself until he got there.

"My legs?"

"Yep. You could model on those legs. Maybe you should consider taking out an insurance policy like Tina Turner."

She let out a happy bark of laughter at that one. "You're being ridiculous."

"The truth often is."

Although the smile never left her face, her voice did turn serious. "Now that's some truth, isn't it?"

Dom was about to reply when her phone went off. The cell was in the center of the table, where she'd left it before fixing the coffee and cupcakes, and their gazes hit the lit-up face at the same time.

DAD filled the screen and Dom felt the weight of the ridiculous slamming into him with all the power of an oncoming freight train.

But it was Sami's face as he glanced up at her that hit even harder.

It was his business to read people in an instant. And in that moment, all he saw glazing Sami Evans's face was terror.

Raw, stark terror.

SAMI STARED DOWN at the face of her phone, transfixed. It was only as the ringer went off for the third time that she snatched up the device, hastily standing from the table, her chair scraping over the hardwood floor. "Excuse me. I need to take this."

"Of course." Dom nodded but she didn't miss the sharpness that seemed to focus all that blue in his eyes right on her face.

Why was her father calling?

Worse, why did she still have his number in her phone? If she'd only erased his contact info, she could have easily ignored the strange number.

But she hadn't. She couldn't do it, actually.

Because no matter how much she resented him and no matter how much she still feared he was a deeply awful person, he was still her father.

And she'd never really reconciled that fact.

"Dad," Sami said on the hard exhale, "Hi."

"Hi, baby."

Something stuck hard in her throat, the intimacy of his words at odds with their actual relationship. "How are you? Is everything okay?"

"Sure it is. Why not?"

"It's sort of late."

"Oh yeah. Sure. I'm sorry. Is there a better time?"

"No, this is fine."

The conversation was inane in the extreme, but she really didn't know what to say. And on some level, resented the need to say anything at all.

Or that he had intruded on a perfectly lovely evening that had made her feel normal and *happy* for the first time in longer than she could remember.

"I've been thinking about you. And I wanted to check in and see how you're doing."

"Okay." She took a quiet breath, trying desperately to keep her breathing even through the pounding of her heart. Her father hated being contradicted under any circumstance, but when he believed himself to be benevolent that went doubly so.

"I know we haven't had the closest relationship in the past, but I've been thinking about it, and I'd like to change that."

He wanted to change their relationship?

The relationship she had spent nearly a decade trying to put behind her?

Yes, he was her father, but he was also the reason she didn't believe in love. The reason she had trouble forming normal, healthy adult bonds.

Willing to risk his wrath, she said quietly, "I think you and I do better from a distance."

"What if I want to change that?"

Because she had been bracing for anger, the softly spoken question hit her deep. "You want to change things?"

"Yeah, Sami, I do. I've been thinking, that I don't like the way we left things. In the past. And I'm back in Colorado now and I'd like to have a relationship with my daughter."

Something odd settled in her chest and she wanted to laugh at his words. Because there was no way a Friday night call could erase more than twenty-five years of bad experiences. Experiences she'd spent the past decade working so hard to move past.

But what bothered her the most was the small ball of fear that gripped her rib cage with cold fingers.

He was back in Colorado? Why?

Although they hadn't talked in five years—and she'd never asked where he'd gone when he left years ago—she'd known he was away.

Gone.

The air had somehow felt sweeter once he'd left, as if a lurking demon had taken off for parts unknown, leaving her to breathe again. It was one of the reasons she'd finally settled in Blue Larkspur, daring to hope for a future as she started her business with the small inheritance her grandmother had left her.

"I don't know what to say."

"Look, I know I've surprised you. But, Sami—"

Once more, she heard that hesitation in his voice. It was as surprising as it was concerning.

Was he in trouble?

Because the Mike Evans she knew never let anything ruffle him. He wasn't a man who took responsibility for his actions or even thought he had anything to take responsibility *for.*

Even if she knew better. Because her mother, whether directly or indirectly, had paid the price for those actions.

"Look, you don't need to decide now. But I just thought maybe, well, maybe you and I could have lunch sometime. Meet up, you know."

"Okay. Sure."

It was tentative at best, as answers went, but she didn't have any other at the moment. "Look, Dad, I'm tired, and it's been a long week at work. Why don't you let me think about it?"

"You do that. I'll give you a call in a few days."

She was about to say something, but he pressed on, beating her to an answer.

"I really do want to see you, sweetheart. I'd like the chance to talk to you. Like I said, I'll call you in a few days. Give you a chance to think about things. You have a good night, okay? Bye."

As startling as it had been to see his name on the readout of her phone, the speed with which he'd ended the call was equally startling.

Just like that, she was left staring, wondering what just happened.

Sami was still processing the conversation with her father as she walked back into the kitchen. Dom was where she had left him, sitting at the kitchen table, his coffee cup in hand.

"Everything okay?"

"Oh yeah, sure."

"Sami—" He stopped and she saw understanding lining his face as he went quiet again.

"Actually, things really aren't okay."

"You want to talk about it?"

"No. Yes." She shook her head. "That was my father. I, um, haven't talked to him in a long time."

"Is there a reason why?"

Because he's a bad person?

Because I think he's responsible for my mother's death?

Because I finally got away from him?

She discarded each comment in kind, aware none of them reflected well on her father. And equally aware they were all things that demanded far more context than a still-shaky conversation over coffee.

"We have a strained relationship. I haven't talked to

him in a long time. After I turned eighteen and I moved out. I didn't want to have anything to do with him."

Dom nodded and set his mug down on the table. "I don't want to pry, but I'm here to listen to you."

It was tempting. The simplicity in his words, and the gentle offer to simply listen.

She knew she should take it. Especially after the conversation they'd had about why they needed to re-think physical intimacy. The two of them didn't know each other well, and they did work together.

But in that moment, when she wanted to shut the rest of the world out, all she really wanted was him.

No conversation.

No questions.

No looks that were half curiosity, half sympathy.

Just physical contact.

Sami moved around the table so that she stood be-side Dom. She extended her hand and laid it on one of his broad shoulders. "I know we talked about tak-ing it slow. About not blurring the lines between work and the personal. But I really don't want you to leave."

"Sami—" He lifted one of those large capable hands and laid it over top of hers. "You had something really difficult happen tonight. And while I don't need the specifics, I know it's not right for me to stay."

She stared down into those vivid eyes, and knew, silly as it sounded, that she could get lost there.

More, she *wanted* to get lost there.

"I'm making this decision because I want to. Be-cause I would like you to stay. If you want."

The hand that lay over top of hers shifted, lifting to cup the tender skin at the back of her neck. He exerted very gentle pressure, pulling her closer to him, fitting her so that she stood between his thighs.

And as their lips met, the kitchen fell away.

The shock—and the very real fear—that she had felt at her father's phone call faded away.

And as she sunk into the kiss, planting her free hand on top of Dom's other shoulder, Sami knew she was making the perfect choice.

Chapter Three

I would like you to stay. If you want.

If he wanted?

Dom had hung by the thinnest of threads all evening, only that innate sense of right and wrong he and his siblings had been damnably adamant they wouldn't betray keeping the needs of his body in check.

But hell, he was only human.

And as he let out a hard moan in the back of his throat, he stood and pulled her fully against his chest, determined to drink his fill of this woman.

All his admonitions to himself, about the job that he had to do, the doubts that he had about her relationship with her father and even the worries about the fact that he was lying to her, faded away in the sheer magic of being with her.

"Dom," she whispered against his lips. "Why don't you come with me?"

With that sensual haze still weaving a spell around him, he took her offered hand and followed her to the bedroom. She had left a small light on beside the bed and it cast a warm glow over the room. That golden light added another layer of warmth, subtly haloing those pretty red tresses.

But when she turned to face him again, moving into his arms, Dom knew he was lost.

He bent his head to kiss her once more, that melding of lips and breath rapidly overtaking everything else.

His hands drifted to the hem of her dress, shifting the material over her hips. She stepped back slightly, giving him room to pull the garment fully over her head, and then she was bared to him in nothing more than a silky bra and matching panties.

Dom inhaled on a harsh breath, his gaze roaming over the beautiful lines of her body. Taut with muscle, this was a woman who truly used her body day in and day out. He reached out to touch her, tracing her beautiful curves with the tips of his fingers. As he did, he shifted his gaze to capture hers, pleased see the way her pupils grew wide in that captivating hazel.

"Sami." Her name burned his lips, even as desire for her coursed through him like a raging fire. "Are you sure about this?"

She smiled, and a world of temptation tilted the corners of her lips. "I can honestly say I've never been more sure about anything in my life."

Before he could say anything further, she reached behind her back and unclasped her bra, the material falling to the floor. "I want you, Dom. And I'm glad you're here tonight. With me."

Although he knew he would pay for his folly when rational thought returned, Dom wasn't strong enough to deny her. To deny this need for her that wasn't logical and certainly wasn't advisable.

But, oh, how it burned.

She reached for the buttons on his dress shirt, making quick work of the line down his chest before pushing the material off his body. The cuffs he'd rolled up earlier ensured nothing got stuck at his wrists and his shirt fell to the floor somewhere near her bra.

And then her hands were at his waist, managing the clasp of his slacks, before her clever fingers reached inside the parted material. The hands he already knew were strong from work took firm hold of his body and Dom felt the responding tug of pleasure-pain as she artfully worked his flesh.

Waves of need coursed through him, radiating from the point where their bodies connected throughout his nerve endings, his flesh heating and growing slick from the exertion.

Well aware his need for her was rapidly outpacing his ability to withstand the erotic torture of her hands, Dom stilled Sami's movements. "You're killing me here."

"That's the whole idea."

"That's big talk for a woman still wearing underwear."

She smiled against his lips. "So what are you going to do about it?"

The teasing was fun and flirty, but it couldn't hide the increasing need rapidly overtaking them both. Retrieving her hand before taking her other free one in his, Dom moved them toward the bed. Gently laying her down, he followed, fitting his body over hers. With his lips, he continued the work of his hands, trailing a path from her jaw, down over her throat and on a path to her breasts.

Sami responded as he took one nipple into his mouth, a low moan rumbling from her chest. He felt that rumble against his lips, the echo through her rib cage spurring him on as he shifted a hand to her other breast, caressing the taut peak.

"Dom." Her voice was breathy as her hands drifted to his shoulders, her fingers caressing him, her touch growing frantic as he kept up the erotic play over her breasts.

Determined to continue the ruthless assault of pleasure, he drifted a hand over her flesh to dip beneath those sexy panties she was still wearing. And was rewarded with a harsh intake of breath, matched by the tight press of her fingers into his shoulders, as he found the heated core of her.

"Dom!" His name echoed in his ears as she convulsed around him, her pleasure evident in the pulsing muscles that quivered against his palm.

He gave himself a moment, just like that, to bask in the intimacy of the pleasure between them. Even with the aching insistence of his own body spurring him on, he still gave himself that moment to simply *feel* her.

Feel what beat between them.

It was raw and exciting and, he realized as her breathing began to even out once more, that it was something he'd never experienced quite like this.

This need to savor what was happening.

Despite his desire to linger, her seeking hands over his skin and the driving needs of his own body ultimately had him shifting, drawing that small scrap of silk down her legs before he rolled to the side of the bed.

He made quick work of his slacks as his gaze drank its fill of her, shucking them and his underwear all at once. He grabbed his wallet before dropping the pile to the floor, pulling out the condom he'd hastily shoved in there earlier. Although this hadn't been his intended outcome of the evening, clearly some hidden, hopeful part of him had the foresight to be prepared.

"Is it all for me?" Sami smiled at him from where she still lay draped on the bed.

"I think it might have been a shot of hopefulness before I left the house."

She lifted up onto her knees on the bed, the hair that fell around her shoulders tousled and sexy in the golden light. "I like a man who's hopeful."

"It doesn't just look crass?"

"Do I look upset?"

As a matter of fact, she didn't look upset at all. Instead, all he saw was a clear pleasure that he'd remembered protection. Dom rejoined her on the bed, ready to make quick work of the condom when she snatched it from his hands.

"If you get to be prepared, I get to have some fun with the outcome." She smiled broadly. "All while confessing I have a brand-new box of condoms right there in that end table drawer."

"You do?"

Instead of answering, she turned the tables on him. And, oh, sweet heaven, the woman was a vixen, tearing the package open and taking her damn sweet time unrolling it over the length of him.

"Are you trying to kill me slowly?"

"Is it working?"

As she reached the end of the condom, finally ending the exquisite torture, he sought her wrists once again, tugging them over her head as he dropped the two of them back onto the bed.

"Everything seems to work with you."

Sami smiled up at him, the first hint of shyness filling her face. "Everything seems to work with you, too."

The words hit him somewhere low and deep, their truth seeping in even deeper.

Things did seem to work between them.

And wasn't it the damnedest thing?

This was a job.

And she was his mission.

But as he felt her hands reaching for his body, guiding him to her own, Dom was struck with the truth.

This was so much more.

SAMI WOKE UP to a solid wall of heat pressed along the length of her body. She wanted to curl into that heat, some still-waking sense within her recognizing safety.

It was only as that word filtered through her mind—*safety*—that Sami's eyes popped open.

Her father had called last night.

That memory was enough to douse the lovely floating haze filling her mind and had her gaze darting to the man beside her.

Dom Conner.

He'd stayed.

And they'd had sex. Amazing, toe-curling, set-the-bed-on-fire sex. All night.

It had been amazing and beautiful and was responsible for the electric hum beneath her skin that even the jarring memory of her estranged father's call couldn't erase.

Even as she had the slightest sense of ick that she was thinking about Dom and her dad in the same barrage of morning thoughts.

With a mental headshake, she disengaged herself from Dom's side, the possessive arm thrown over her waist giving her a moment of pause at how delicious it felt to wake up with him.

Get a grip, Sami girl. It was some hot sex, which you already knew it would be after three minutes in his company. It'll do you no good to get used to it.

The admonition was the last piece she needed to finally get moving and she shifted slowly so as not to disturb him. Though based on the heavy snort-slash-snore as he rolled over, she figured she had a few minutes to gather her distracted thoughts.

She reached for the silk robe that she kept perpetually draped over a small chair in the corner of her bedroom and slipped into it. As she turned to tie the sash, she gave herself one more moment to drink her fill of the man in her bed.

He really was beautiful.

A layer of stubble covered his jaw, but it couldn't hide the firm lines. Even in sleep, there was a formidable look about him that made a woman look twice. Yes, he was attractive; that was undeniable. But it was something more.

Safety.

That word drifted through her mind again, more structured and real than the way it had wisped through her thoughts as she lay in the bed.

There was something innately safe about Dom Conner.

It was an odd thought, and not one she had ever had before about a man she had dated. She couldn't say she had ever felt *un*safe, but that overwhelming sense of security had never pervaded her thoughts before.

So why now?

On a sigh, she padded from the room and headed for the kitchen. The life-giving elixir of coffee wouldn't necessarily give her the answers, but it might give her a slightly clearer mind.

And an ability to think about what she was going to do about the man she called dad.

Because while Dom felt inherently safe, her father's unexpected call was the opposite, and she couldn't deny it likely had some influence on why she was looking at Dom through rose-colored glasses.

Sami moved around the kitchen, almost on autopilot as she rinsed the pot from the night before, then started on a fresh brew. In a matter of moments, the heady scent of coffee began filling the kitchen.

When the oddest temptation gripped her to also make up a fresh batch of scones, she knew she had to stop.

Great sex *and* a guy who stayed the night was pretty fantastic. The last thing she needed to do was scare him off with baked goods.

Her gaze caught on the plates still on the table from the night before and she knew cupcakes would be a great start to the day. Making quick work of the dirty plates, she turned to the box still on the counter.

Taking out a vanilla cupcake with thick frosting, she peeled back the paper and took a bite.

Delicious.

Just like Dom.

With sugar on her tongue and the amazing night before on her mind, Sami gave herself a moment to indulge. Sex with Dom had been pretty amazing. He was a sensitive lover, and very attentive to her. In tune.

But it was more than that, she acknowledged.

Although she hadn't given him much detail about her father, he had innately sensed her upset. And he stayed. He'd even tried to use her distress as a further reason not to have sex, offering comfort and support only.

She was the one who had pressed for more.

Had needed *more*, Sami acknowledged to herself.

She had never made her parents a central point of her relationships in the past, but after dating someone for a period of time, the subject usually came up. Her dead mother. Her estranged father.

And it normally led to questions.

She still remembered Jason. She'd initially been wary of dating an accountant, thinking they had nothing in common. But she'd been wrong. In addition to attraction, they were both building small businesses and it led to a lot of shared, easy conversation. They'd been surprisingly compatible, and the relationship had moved along nicely. But about two months in, she'd opened up about her childhood.

Although Jason had listened—and she'd believed him genuinely sensitive to her past—the mention of her father's criminality had clearly done something. He'd grown increasingly distant in the weeks that followed that conversation before ultimately breaking off the relationship a few weeks later.

She could never exactly pin it on that discussion of her parents. After all, not every relationship worked out. But it had seemed suspicious to her, as she had thought about it over the years, that something that was going so well could crater so quickly after one conversation.

Especially when that conversation held the knowledge that her father was a known criminal with violent tendencies.

Because of Jason's reaction, she'd hedged with Shane, only to find that her reticence to mention her past had driven a different sort of wedge. He'd never outright accused but he'd mentioned on a few occasions that she was a woman with a past. He'd say it in a joking way, but Sami knew he felt she wasn't sharing a part of herself with him.

In the end, it had been easier to walk away than risk any real discussion of her childhood.

Which brought her right back to the subject of Dom. And, once again, her mental insistence on seeing them in a relationship.

Why did she keep doing that?

And why couldn't she, no matter how hard she inwardly admonished herself, stop hoping they could have a future?

Or a chance at one.

DOM FOUND HER that way. Standing at the counter, staring out the kitchen window with a half-eaten cupcake in her hand. Something surprising tightened in his chest as he stared at Sami Evans.

Beautiful, strong, sexy Sami.

A woman he was lying to.

The mix of guilt and self-reproach he'd managed to hold at bay throughout the night came slamming back into him with full force. The very real suspicions about both her and her father.

And the even more real investigation he was part of at the FBI's International Corruption Unit.

No amount of amazing sex could change those facts.

Even as there was something about the woman that tugged at him.

"Hey there."

She turned from the window, something dark flashing across her gaze before she quickly banked it. "Hey yourself."

"You're up early."

"I hope I didn't wake you."

"No." He shrugged and sent one more lie in what felt like an oppressive pile of them winging her way. "I work construction. I'm an early riser."

A half lie. Because even if he didn't actually work construction for a living, he was still an early riser. Always had been. And had always frustrated his triplet brothers, Oliver and Ezra, with his chipper early-morning demeanor.

When silence continued to fill the space between them, Dom went on instinct. It wasn't rational, and it likely wasn't the best choice he could make for the guilt still pounding behind his eyes, but he went with it anyway.

And moved right up into her, framing her face gently in his hands before pressing a kiss to her lips.

"Good morning."

Everything about her softened, the tension that had been so evident fading. "Hi." She glanced to the side before offering him a lopsided grin. "I just crushed my cupcake."

His gaze followed hers to the now-squished, half-eaten cupcake oozing frosting over her fingers. With deliberate movements, he lifted her hand and took some of that frosting in his mouth, his eyes never leaving hers.

It was a heady mixture, the instant sweetness on his tongue and the insistent desire that slammed through him like a hurricane, as he removed the frosting from her skin.

The moment was deeply sensual, and what had started as something sexy and silly quickly turned the tables on him.

Oh, how he wanted this woman. This insatiable feeling for her that he didn't understand yet felt so deeply within his skin.

"Would you like one?" Her voice was breathless, her gaze growing increasingly hazy with need.

"No," he said after swallowing the sweet sugar.

"You want to share mine?"

"That," Dom said, lifting her hand for another taste of frosting, "is a far better idea."

He took another bite of frosting before she turned quickly at the sink, rinsing the rest of the cupcake off her hands.

"Hey—" he protested before she turned quickly back into his arms. She wrapped herself around him, pulling him close before lifting her face to his with a smile.

"We can't get cupcake crumbs in my Egyptian cotton sheets."

"Who said anything about making it to the bedroom?" he whispered against her jaw, breathing in deep against her skin.

Before she could ask what he meant, he had her small waist in his hands and boosted her onto the counter. The increased height gave him the exact position he was looking for and he stepped between her legs.

"Why, Mr. Conner, you're so creative."

He smiled up at her now that their positions had shifted. "You have no idea."

DOM HEARD THE insistent ring of the alarm on his phone and wanted to ignore it. He and Sami had finally stumbled back up to the bedroom after a rousing round of sex in the kitchen, tangled up in each other. He'd promised that they'd get up and go to work after a quick nap.

It was Saturday, but the crew he was working with had a half day ahead of them and he was determined to show up as committed as everyone else. Especially since the weekend work had promised time and a half and it would look strange if he didn't take it.

She'd already said she wanted to get to the job site, too, to finish up a new drainage installation around the back of the house. It was a laborious task and one more sign that Sami was serious about her business.

One more sign she wasn't looking for an easy life of drug running and criminal activity like her father?

Or more of the wishful thinking he was trying to employ to ensure she couldn't possibly be involved with Lone Wolf's enterprises?

The phone continued to peal its steady alarm and he was nearly up when Sami beat him to it. She leaped out of bed with a shocking amount of energy and headed for the direction of his discarded clothes on the floor.

"That went off fast," Dom muttered, shifting into his pillow with the thought of grabbing a few more minutes—of sleep *and* the determination to quell his errant thoughts.

Willing away the questions and doubts that continued to linger, always swirling but not quite finding a place to land.

"I'm not hitting snooze, sleepyhead, so you better wake up." The ringing did stop, and he heard Sami's footsteps an instant before she lightly bopped his phone against his shoulder. "Wake up."

"I'm getting up. I swear."

Her laughter was a low rumble in her throat, but she didn't press him again and he abstractly heard her start back across the room.

Even as sleep beckoned, the strangest thought began to tug at him. Images of his clothes, balled up on the floor where he had taken them off the night before, filled his mind's eye. His wallet, where he'd pulled out the condom he'd tucked in there before leaving for their date, on top of the pile. And the heavy weight of his FBI badge, where it nestled in the folds of his wallet.

It was that last thought—his badge—that struck just as her voice erupted, ricocheting around the room. "Son of a bitch!"

The pieces came together on a hard shot of awareness as Dom sat straight up in bed.

But it was too late.

Sami stood a few steps away, his FBI badge held high in her hands.

"You're a federal agent? Dominic *Colton*."

Chapter Four

Sami stared down at the badge in her hand before her gaze shot right back to the man in her bed. Then back to the badge. Then Dom.

She'd done that at least four times already, as if the badge would somehow morph into a package of gum instead of what it really was.

Proof Dom wasn't who he said he was.

Because if he were still Dom Conner, hot construction worker and sexy lover, she wouldn't have to face the hard, cold reality that she'd let herself get carried away without really knowing the man or his intentions.

"Sami—" Dom broke off before exhaling a harsh sigh. Still naked, he got out of bed and reached for his pants. After getting dressed that far, he lifted his gaze to her. "I'll do my best to explain."

"Explain? Explain why you've been lying to me."

"Yes."

That lone word seemed to echo off the walls, final somehow.

Would he actually tell her the truth?

Would he have ever told her the truth if he hadn't gotten caught?

She supposed that line of thought wasn't overly productive. She now knew who he was, and whatever he had intended to do was moot.

Sami glanced down, realizing she was still naked, too, and crossed to her dresser. The thin tank top and shorts she dug out weren't much armor, but they were something. Without saying anything further, she slipped into the soft well-worn clothes and left the room, heading for the kitchen.

Whatever was still to come, it obviously required coffee. "All the coffee," she muttered to herself.

The pot she'd started was still hot and she poured herself a cup. In a moment of emotional generosity, she poured one for Dom, too, and handed it to him as he came into the kitchen.

"Caffeine." She pointed to the kitchen table. "Chair. Talk."

He took the cup, taking a sip with little care for the heat and crossed to the table to take a seat.

"Your father called last night."

Where he started was a surprise, but Sami nodded. "Yes, that's right."

"Your father, Mike Evans. The leader of the Warlords motorcycle club."

Her eyes widened at that. "He's not—" she stammered before continuing, "He's not a part of that any longer. He went straight."

Even as she voiced what she believed, she realized just how badly she'd been deluding herself all this time.

Dom's voice was even and steady as he spoke. "I'm afraid that's not true."

She let out a harsh sigh and took a seat opposite him. "I want to be surprised and I want to be angry, but I'm angrier at myself." She took a sip of her coffee and gathered herself. "Until last night, we haven't spoken in five years. But when we did speak last, he told me he'd given up his old life and was making a new one. That he hoped someday we could have a relationship again, but he respected my need to keep my distance."

With the information she now knew about him, she figured Dom likely knew her background, but she kept on. "I'm his only child and my mother died when I was fifteen. I left the week I turned eighteen. He was disappointed about it but he didn't hold me back."

"Any idea why? Your father's reputation isn't as a benevolent leader who allows people to escape his demands."

She considered his statement, bumping that perception up against the man she knew.

"He wasn't happy about it but I think he understood it'd be easier if I wasn't around. I never knew the full depths of his business but he knew I didn't agree with it. And he also knew I thought my mother died because of it." She shrugged. "It was likely a matter of accepting my independence or knowing that I'd eventually die, too."

"Those are awfully casual words."

"They're the truth." An image of her mother's face came to mind, that picture of how she remembered Annie Evans never failing to trip her heart. "I could never prove it, but my teenage rebellion was clear. On some level, I think he knew it was either let me go when I turned eighteen or accept his daughter's life would end the same way as his wife's."

"Do you know how your mother died?"

She glanced up at Dom and while her trust levels

weren't running particularly high, she couldn't fully dismiss the genuine question she saw there.

Was it possible the FBI didn't know about her mother's death? Or the root cause of it?

"Nothing can be proved, of course. Her legal cause of death was a heart attack. But there was no autopsy and I believe her death was caused by one of my father's enemies who'd infiltrated the organization. An overdose of drugs, stabbed in the leg when she was out on an evening walk."

"The reports were that she had a heart attack on a walking trail in Lark's County."

"It was one of her favorites. And she was in good health because she walked that path regularly."

"Did anyone see the injection site?"

"My father did. I overheard him talking to someone about it, as well as their discussion about a person named Steve. It took me a while to run it down, as I had to do my internet searches on the sly, but I finally discovered that a man named Steve was found dead on the same trail where they found my mother. Two days after she died."

"A message."

"Yep." She nodded, the pain of that time as sharp now as it had been when she was fifteen. "One that was pointedly clear."

"Did your parents have a good relationship?"

It was an unexpected tack but one that helped shift the morass of feelings that never failed to swamp her when she thought of her mother.

"Tense most often, but from time to time it could get volatile. I think he always believed he was protecting her from the seamier side of what he was involved in and she wanted him to go straight."

"So your mother was aware of his activities?"

"She—" Sami stopped, checking herself. "I don't know. I questioned it through the years but I really don't know. But I should have."

"I'm not sure that's a fair assessment."

"What do you mean? I lived in the same house. I observed the two of them. They're my parents."

"Just because they are your parents doesn't mean they don't know how to hide things."

Although she realized they didn't know each other well, there was a stark truth in Dom's words that gripped Sami in a tight fist.

"You sound like you know something about that?"

"Maybe I do."

"Then why don't you tell me, Dom? Give me just a little bit. Help me believe that you're not just using me for intel."

DOM FELT THE tables turn smoothly in front of him, a neat twist in the conversation that left him feeling open and vulnerable.

Sort of like last night.

The thought whispered through his mind, straight to the heart of the matter.

Last night had meant so much more than he could have ever expected. And despite his best intentions to keep his distance, he'd not only slept with her and stayed the night; he'd *wanted* to stay the night. Wanted that intimacy of falling asleep together and the equally intense intimacy of waking up together.

And even with the knowledge his short-sightedness

had resulted in his blown cover, he still couldn't say he'd change it.

Not one single second of it.

"I know what it is to feel betrayed by a parent, Sami."

"Why?"

In that single word, Dom felt the conversation shift. The anger she'd directed at him—all deserved—had faded a bit. And in its place, he sensed a woman who truly wanted to understand where he was coming from.

"My father was one of the most respected judges in Lark's County."

"Was?" Something flickered in her gaze before her eyes widened. "Colton is your last name. Ben Colton is your father? The disgraced judge."

"Yes. And *was*, because he passed away, and because he utterly disgraced himself on the bench."

Although it was a reality he had lived with for two decades now, Dom was amazed at how deeply that truth still cut. Razor-sharp, with an ability to go soul deep.

"I'm sorry for your loss."

He'd always hated that pity. The *I'm sorry*'s and the *you have my sympathy*'s. They were what people said to each other when faced with loss and he knew the intentions were good. But with his father's disgrace so public and his death, albeit accidental, so near to the scandal of his judgeship, those words had always felt like they were laced with acid.

Compassion and disdain simply didn't make for a matched set of emotions.

"There's nothing to be sorry for."

She stared down into her coffee before that hazel

gaze met his once more, clear and direct. "The circumstances around it don't really matter. What matters is that you lost a parent. I struggle with that, sometimes with my mom. Like whether she knew or didn't know the depth of my father's activities. It doesn't change the fact that I lost her. It doesn't change the fact that I loved her."

It was an interesting thought, and one Dom had never really considered. For all his father's faults, Ben Colton was still his father. And for the first sixteen years of his life, Dom had known a loving man who cared for him and his eleven siblings. It was only when the truth had come out, about Ben's corruption on the bench and the bribes he'd taken that funded his family's lifestyle, that Dom had been forced to change his opinion.

When it all came crashing down.

And the man he'd always put on a pedestal had shown just how little he deserved to be there.

But that truth—that hard, cold miserable reality—never changed the fact that he'd lost his illusions about his father *and* his father, all in one fell swoop.

He'd never gotten answers to his questions. Why had Ben felt that criminal activity and sentencing innocents was the answer? And why had he betrayed his legal responsibilities and loved ones like that?

The man had put money above their family, even as he deluded himself that he was doing it all *for* his family.

"Thank you."

Well aware they'd lost the plot, Dom shifted them back to the subject of Mike Evans. From all Sami had said, it sounded like she really didn't know about her dad's enterprises. But that didn't mean she hadn't observed things through the years that he could use.

"Why do you think your father reached out last night?"

"He said he wanted to talk. To see me. He could tell he caught me off guard because he said he'd call in a few days."

"Do you want to see him?"

She took a sip of her coffee, considering. "If you'd asked me that twenty-four hours ago, I'd have said no way. He and I don't have a relationship and I like it that way. But—" She tapped a finger against the handle of the mug. "But now? I don't know. I mean, if talking to him can help you in some way, then I'm willing to do it."

Help *him*?

The about-face from the angry woman in the bedroom was a surprise. But even more surprising was the fact he was even considering taking the assistance she offered.

He worked alone. He sure as hell didn't drag innocents into his jobs. And if there was the off chance that she *wasn't* so innocent, playing her part as the hurt child to the hilt, he couldn't put his mission at risk.

But...

"Why do you want to help me?"

"I owe my father nothing. And if he's up to his old habits, it's up to me to see that he is taken care of, if I have the ability to do so. His lifestyle killed my mother. It killed the man who murdered her, too. And it's taken countless others, either from his criminal lifestyle or the people who are harmed by the drugs he puts on the streets. Either way, it's on my to-try-and-do-something-about-that list."

Conviction laced her words and Dom was surprised by how readily he saw himself in her desire for action.

Hadn't he and his siblings done the same?

When it had become evident their lives had been gilded by their father's lies and bad behavior, they'd banded together and done everything in their power to right the wrongs Ben Colton had perpetrated. Ben's focus for years—putting innocent adults and children away to help put money in the pockets of private prisons and juvenile detention centers—had been the catalyst for Dom and his brothers and sisters to start the Truth Foundation years before.

Their mission was simple. They were determined to exonerate every person their father had wrongfully imprisoned and help others who had suffered the same fate from other judges.

And they'd damn near done it, too. So many people had been helped and had moved on to the lives they deserved to have as a result.

"Dom?"

Sami's question pulled him from his thoughts and he knew he owed her an answer. "How do you think you can help?"

"I don't, exactly, but I'm sure I can. He's still my father and I grew up with him. I'm sure I know things. About him and how he works."

"You haven't seen him in nearly ten years. Haven't talked to him in five. What can you possibly still know?"

"Damn it, Dom, I don't know. But I want to help."

She stood then, her nervous energy getting the better of her. He watched her as she paced, her long legs scoring a path through the kitchen as she crossed to the counter and back.

"I appreciate the desire to help, but I'm a federal agent. I can't put you in harm's way."

"My father won't hurt me."

Her clear dismissal of any other outcome was interesting. Especially considering she hadn't seen Mike Evans in nearly ten years.

"You're awfully sure of that."

"Of course I am. He's my father. And he let me walk away. In his own way, he wants what's best for me."

Regular parents had a challenging time meeting that standard always. Did she really think a career criminal was up to the task?

Was he really the person to ask that question? Dom thought with no small measure of wry censure on his own quick judgement.

He was about to make the point anyway, but something in her demeanor changed so abruptly he lost whatever argument had come to mind. Instead, all he could see was the way she nearly leaped back to the table, excitement seeming to halo her entire body.

"I have an idea."

"You're a civilian, Sami. You don't get to have ideas on this."

"But it's a great one. A really great one." She dropped into the seat, triumph filling her gaze. "You and I can pretend to be engaged."

HER WORDS HUNG THERE, hovering over the table like an ominous rain cloud.

Engaged?

Did I really just say that? No, she amended. *Did I really just offer that?*

"I can't put you in danger like that."

Of all the responses she'd expected—*have you had a break with reality?* at the top of the list—his quick and absolute pushback for her safety wasn't what she had been expecting.

And it gave her enough pause that Dom had the room to keep pressing his point.

"If what we expect is true, your father is running a major criminal outfit. He's a huge node on the drug trade in this part of the country."

"All the more reason my idea is a good one."

"Not if you get caught."

"I already told you. My father might have his flaws but he wouldn't hurt me. Besides, who can prove or disprove an engagement? I'll put on a ring and we'll tell him we're engaged. It's not like there's some sort of certificate for this. If we say we're engaged, then we are."

And now that the idea had taken root, she wasn't able to let it go.

Because you want to help? Or because the idea of being engaged to Dom isn't so bad?

Refusing to give any weight to that little voice in her brain, insistent on tossing out reams of truth, she pressed on. Because thinking of Dom through any lens that suggested long-term commitment based on trust was ridiculous.

Especially since she'd only known he was Dom *Colton* for an hour.

A fact she was still processing, both the reality of it and those little whip-quick shocks of betrayal that kept trying to sneak under her thoughts, all while she pressed him to let her participate in his work. Because no matter how much she'd wanted Dom last night, she still felt tricked that she didn't know who he was.

"You know I'm right about this."

Dom shook his head before reaching for his coffee mug, a disgusted look tightening that hard jaw even further when he realized it was empty. "I don't want to burst your bubble, but the stakes are way too high. And your father's business has grown exponentially from when you used to live under his roof."

Or so they believed.

That was Dom's real challenge, Sami knew. The FBI could have their assessments, but they'd never really know until they got someone inside.

"Do you have anyone inside who can tell you those things?"

His vivid blue eyes shuttered even further, but Sami saw a tick start in his jaw. "I can't tell you those things."

"So let's assume you don't. If you play it my way, you can get inside yourself. See for yourself and know what's going on."

"I can't put you in danger like that."

The bizarre part was that she already was in danger. If her father was up to his old tricks, then his child would always be in danger.

"You can't put this genie back in the bottle. I know what you think about my father."

"I'm not trying to put anything back."

"Sure you are. You were supposed to wine me and dine me a bit and get some intel. Too bad for you that you shoved a condom in your wallet right next to your big badass FBI badge."

"I lost myself last night. That's entirely on me."

Those words, said with such self-disgust, couldn't erase the shot of satisfaction that filled her.

He'd lost himself. Over *her*.

Since seeing that badge in his wallet, Sami had been so afraid it had just been her who'd been so carried away last night. That the attraction she'd felt so keenly had been nothing but a ruse on his part to get close to her.

That what they'd shared—sex that had been so amazing and life-affirming—had meant nothing more to him than a means to an end.

But that hadn't been the case.

Feeling far more charitable than she had since finding out who he was, Sami went for broke.

"We both lost ourselves for a while. But since we're now both thinking clearly, you have to know I'm offering you the perfect solution."

"Taking you into the inner workings of a dangerous motorcycle club, accompanied by an undercover FBI agent no less, is hardly the perfect solution. What if my cover gets blown?"

She shrugged, oddly delighted to poke at him a bit. "Clue number one there. Leave the badge at home instead of in your wallet."

"I know how to handle undercover work."

At his words, Sami knew she'd scored a solid, direct hit. And she was having far too much fun to stop now. "All evidence to the contrary."

"You can't go with me, Sami. I'll come up with something else."

She stared him dead in the eye, unwilling to back

down or back away from the frustrated ire in that liquid blue gaze. "Sorry, sweet pea, but it looks like I'm the only solution you've got."

Chapter Five

I'm the only solution you've got.

The words had played over and over in Dom's mind for the past forty-eight hours. And damn it to hell if this woman wasn't right.

Sami Evans *was* the only solution he had.

The only solution the International Corruption Unit had.

And, if he had any hope of stopping the drug trade devastating this part of Colorado and points beyond, the only solution to his problem of infiltrating the Warlords.

And double damn it if she wasn't enjoying herself, Dom thought as she tapped her finger over an acre of highly polished glass. "That's the one."

"It's too small," Dom snapped out as he stared down at the engagement ring she pointed to in the jewelry case in front of them. They'd come to the mall on a mission to get some clothes for their upcoming trip to Warlords territory. Her for a few summer dresses and him with a stop in the sporting goods store for a new sheath so he could strap a knife over his inner calf. She'd briefly toyed with buying a weapon of her own, but he hadn't missed her indecision. And while he wanted her to have protection, someone with a weapon they were hesitant to use was better off without one at all. All of which just reinforced the fact that he needed to protect her.

It was only as they'd walked the mall that he'd realized they needed a ring to pull off their little charade in front of her father.

"It's not too small, it's perfect." Sami smiled at the jeweler who'd stood a discrete distance away. Not that Dom had any illusion the man hadn't heard every word between them.

"I can buy you a bigger one, Sami."

And he could. Even if his family money had mostly vanished after the reality of his father's crimes came to life, he'd basically banked every dime he'd earned since he started working. Other than the most basic of clothes and the rent on his apartment in Denver, he had minimal living expenses. He drove a used truck, not really caring about what sort of automobile he owned. Partially because he didn't care but also because the flashier the car the more noticeable he'd be and a man in his line of work couldn't afford to be too memorable. His truck already sported a fake set of plates that were coded to whatever job and persona he was working on for the ICU.

His family loved to tease him about it, especially his triplet brother Oliver. A playboy at heart and a venture capitalist by trade, Oliver had never met a sports car he didn't love on sight or a premium bottle of wine he couldn't guzzle with gusto. He'd eased up a bit on the flash over the past few years, but his brother did love a fancy car.

As far as Dom was concerned, his brother could

have it. He was a simple man with simple tastes and he didn't need any of the finer trappings.

Hadn't that been what had actually trapped his father? The desire for a lifestyle that wasn't only beyond his means, but that was only viable by doing harm to others.

Of course, what all that frugality really meant was that, at thirty-six, Dom had a surprisingly healthy bank account.

And he was oddly offended that Sami wasn't willing to use much of it on an engagement ring.

"It's not about the size." She tapped the glass, pulling him from another round of thoughts about his father, as she kept her gaze on the ring in the case. "I like that one. I love the bezel setting because it's beautiful. And I also love that it fits with my work. I can wear that and not be worried I'll hurt the setting or lose the diamond when I'm digging in the dirt or planting bushes."

The jeweler pulled the ring from the case, gently handing it across the counter. Sami slipped it on, the white gold sliding over her slim fingers in one smooth motion. Once settled, Sami held out her hand to look at the diamond where it sparkled on her hand. "Yep. Perfect."

Oddly beguiled, he couldn't keep his gaze off her face and the way she stared at the gem as it caught the light. Her entire expression had softened into something both excited and wistful, and he couldn't deny how beautiful she looked.

Even as he knew better than to be caught up in this moment.

In any moment, really, if it was with her.

This woman was a distraction and they were in this

position because he'd gotten caught up in the moment
on Friday night and allowed it to carry him away.

But the willpower to look away escaped him.

"If that's the one you want." His words came out
on an oddly strangled whisper and the jeweler's gaze
grew knowing as he looked at Dom.

She nodded, her voice equally raspy when she spoke,
her eyes wide as she stared up at him. "It's the one."

"A beautiful choice, miss," the jeweler said before
rattling off the size of the diamond and its classifica-
tion. As Dom heard words like *impressive clarity* and
a definition called *VVS*, he figured they were on the
right track. He hadn't ever bought a diamond before
but he'd heard enough growing up with five sisters to
know that these things mattered.

Even if Sami was going to wear it when she dug
in the dirt.

Dom handed over his credit card and left Sami at
the counter so he could complete the transaction. In a
matter of minutes, they were walking back out of the
store, her sporting a ring on her left hand and him with
official papers in his pocket detailing the major purchase he'd just made.

He turned to ask her if she wanted to get some lunch
when he caught sight of her gaze. She'd lifted her hand
casually, as if to look at the department store bag she
carried. But as she did so he could see it was to get another look at the ring.

Something struck him hard and deep at that surrep-
titious glance down at her hand.

He'd never been engaged before. Had never been
in a relationship long enough or taken it to the point

where he'd wanted to get engaged, let alone even considered the notion.

Yet, here he was, buying a ring for Sami Evans and it wasn't nearly as weird as it should be. To see her so delighted with the purchase and finding ways to sneak glances where the ring rested against her flesh.

If he were honest, it even felt better than he'd have expected.

SHE NEEDED TO get a grip.

One that didn't involve holding things with her left hand so she could sneak glances at the ring on her finger.

It was the thought that kept Sami company as she waited for Dom to come back to their table with their order of burgers and fries.

The mall food court proved somewhat distracting and she watched the people scattered around. A group of teenagers, hanging out across three tables, laughing and talking, even as an elaborate courtship ritual underpinned it all. A few tables away, a harried young mother distributed child-size portions from one of the fast-food chains. And even farther down, an older couple enjoying their meal as they smiled at each other across the table.

Was that what forever looked like?

The thought pulled her up short and Sami looked away from the happy couple, her gaze unerringly finding her left hand once more.

Where a very real ring stood as a decoy for a very fake relationship.

Were they risking discovery?

She'd already insisted they have a cover should anyone they worked with see them together.

And although she'd argued with gusto for their undercover ploy as an engaged couple, over the past few days Sami had begun to question herself. She hadn't seen her father in ten years. Was he a different person? She certainly hoped she was.

Why would she assume Mike Evans hadn't changed at all in the past decade?

Whatever goodness she wanted to believe might still be inside him, the reality of his life was different. And despite his promises to her that he'd gone straight, the FBI's focus pointed to him having disregarded that promise.

Especially if an FBI agent was tailing her to find out what she knew about her father's enterprises.

An enterprise Mike Evans had spent her entire life pursuing. Sami didn't have definitive proof over her mother's death—just well-informed speculation—but she knew without question her only living parent was a criminal.

Had always known it.

He'd hidden that side of his life well from his family, building a world away from it for her and her mother in a nice home in Blue Larkspur. He'd been gone a lot, and when she was young, her mother had chalked it up to *her dad's job*.

It had struck Sami as odd at the time, but the sort of oddness a kid processed. Like she knew her life was different from her friends' but had no idea why or the deeper understanding to articulate it.

So she'd taken her mother at her word, never pressing too hard why her friends' dads didn't spend days away from home or why they didn't have bruises on their face or perpetual scrapes across their knuckles.

Whatever her father did, she'd reasoned at the time, it was for *work*.

It was only years later, when she'd gone to the reading of her grandmother's will, and gotten the small inheritance to start her business, that she'd learned more. She'd read a detailed letter her grandmother had written with the instruction not to open until her death.

The whirlwind romance between her parents. Annie's bitter disappointment once she learned about Mike's involvement in the Warlords. And the equally bitter experience her grandmother had survived when her pregnant daughter went back to her husband, determined to make a life with the man she'd married.

Was that love?

The older couple across the way stood up from the table, their movements catching Sami's eye. She continued to wonder as the man carried their tray of trash to one of the large receptacles spotted around the food court. How he made quick work of the tray before returning to his wife with a smile. And the way their hands unerringly linked, almost like magnets they stuck together so quickly, as they wended their way out of the food court.

Was that what love really looked like?

Or was it only a lucky few who ever got that sort of togetherness? That shot at forever?

"Sorry it took so long," Dom said as he settled a tray down on the table. He'd come up from the other side and she hadn't heard him because she was so engaged.

"Sami?" Dom's eyebrows drew together. "You with me?"

"Yeah. Sorry." She shook her head, covering her woolgathering by reaching for one of the wrapped burgers and a small cardboard container of fries. "This looks good."

They settled into their lunch, each taking a few bites, before her heavy thoughts got the better of her. "Do you believe in happily-ever-after?"

"No."

"You don't?" She knew her mouth dropped and was only thankful she hadn't taken a bite of food. "At all?"

"Have you ever seen anyone in your life to suggest that happily-ever-after even exists?"

"I—". She left the beginning of an argumentative response hanging there, well aware she had no understanding of that older couple's life beyond a handful of seconds of observation.

Even as she couldn't help but believe their relationship flew in the face of Dom's decided lack of optimism.

"I believe I have."

"Good for you. I've yet to see it." He frowned down at his burger before amending himself. "Or I hadn't seen it until recently. But two of my brothers and two of my sisters might be bucking the trend."

"That seems like a resounding yes, if I've ever heard one."

"Maybe." He shrugged. "Maybe not. Who knows what the future holds?"

"Maybe you'd better avoid making any toasts at their weddings."

"I didn't say they were all getting married."

"Are they?"

A small blush crept up his neck. "They look like they're heading that way. And my oldest brother, Caleb, is engaged."

"How many siblings do you have, exactly? I know you're from a big family and the Colton name is well known around Blue Larkspur, but don't know all the specifics."

As she mentioned his family, Sami realized it might be worth doing some internet diving. She knew there was some lingering scandal that his family had been a part of but it had happened when she was a kid and, well, she'd had a lot of problems of her own.

Beyond the basics of knowing there was some whiff of disgrace around them, she didn't know much more. A fact that was crystal clear when he answered her question.

"I have eleven brothers and sisters."

Whatever twisting, winding road of thoughts had been occupying her while Dom waited for lunch vanished at that news. "You're one of twelve kids?"

"Yeah."

"As in a dozen?"

His lips quirked up on one side, evidence that this was not the first time he'd endured this line of questioning. "That's typically what twelve equates to."

"As in your mother gave birth to twelve children."

Dom made a face and set his burger down. "Are you trying to make me lose my appetite? Because I was really excited to eat this double cheeseburger until you started talking about my mother experiencing childbirth."

"I'm sorry. It's just that twelve is a really big family by anyone's standards. But being pregnant twelve times is really something to digest as a woman."

"My mother wasn't pregnant that many times. Several of us are multiple births."

Suddenly captivated and curious at the idea there might be another man out there who looked exactly like the one sitting opposite her, Sami couldn't hold back the questions. Even if she had a hard time imagining anyone being just like Dom. "Are you a twin?"

"A triplet. Fraternal," he added before she could ask more.

"How many other multiples are there?"

"My oldest brother and sister, Caleb and Morgan, are twins. Then my brothers and I come next. Then come Rachel and Gideon, who arrived one at a time."

"Okay, that's seven."

"Jasper and Aubrey come next. They're twins, too."

"Wow." Sami shook her head, trying desperately as an only child to imagine what it would be like to have so many siblings. And if dealing with her father and his life choices might have been easier if she'd had a sibling to share it all with.

"And then my parents had Gavin and thought they were done."

"But that's only ten."

"Exactly. Alexa and Naomi were the double surprise that capped off our family dozen."

"That's incredible."

"It's us."

Dom said it so simply and, for him, Sami had to imagine that was true. As an outsider, she saw a huge family and a wild ride rearing children for his parents. But for him, it was the life he knew.

"Anyone else in the FBI?"

"Just me." He snatched several fries and popped them in his mouth, chewing. "But we do have a few lawyers, a social worker. One of my sisters is a US

Marshal. Jasper and Aubrey own a dude ranch. Two of my sibs even work in the entertainment and journalism businesses."

"Wow. As an only child, this is fascinating to me."

"It's just who we are. But I've lived my whole life this way, with the questions from other people once they find out how many of us there are. I'm used to the curiosity."

Yet, he'd chosen his own profession, Sami thought. Somewhere where he functioned independently and, she suspected, just as he evidently liked it. No familial interference. No one in his business. But still in an organization that functioned like a hierarchical family, which would be comfortable and familiar.

And here you go, Evans, playing armchair psychologist.

"So as an only child, I bet no one ever got the ice-cream flavor you didn't want."

"Nope." She smiled, recognizing the subject change. "I got as much Rocky Road as I wanted."

He slapped a hand over his heart. "You wound me, woman. There was never enough Rocky Road left for me. Or Moose Tracks. Or chocolate peanut butter."

"You're a chocolate man?"

"To my core."

"I'll have to remember that."

"And you?"

"I'm an equal opportunity ice-cream eater. I have yet to meet a flavor I don't like."

"Even the purple one?" He clearly searched for the flavor before snapping his fingers. "Black raspberry?"

"Mmm. One of the best."

"That's some impressive love of ice cream."

"It's a gift."

"One of many, I'm sure." Dom's gaze was warm as he said the words, his eyes direct and steady on her. "I'm looking forward finding out many more."

A FEW DAYS LATER, Dom read over the encrypted email from his boss and shot back the final plans for his infiltration of the Warlords. No plan was perfect and every agent took a risk undercover, but he was pleased with what they'd come up with.

And much as he'd been against it at first, the fake engagement angle had a lot of merit and his boss was pleased with the cover story.

A thought that kept him company as he left the small furnished house he was renting in Blue Larkspur and got in his truck to drive over to Sami's. Although he'd have preferred to stay in his apartment in Denver, the undercover op had necessitated a closer home base to Sami. The small one-story rancher in an old suburb of Blue Larkspur had fit the bill.

It would now serve a second purpose, as the Bureau had used the location to shore up his story, should anyone in the Warlords go digging into Dom Conner's background. Although it would be easy to dismiss the motorcycle club as steeped in the old ways—using guns and fists to get the work done—the Bureau knew better. They ran a sophisticated operation, with data a central part of their success.

His boss had been pleased with the shift in Dom's cover, even as the team back at the Bureau had run everything they could find on Samantha Evans. If Dom had thought they'd pulled out all the stops before he'd gone on assignment in Blue Larkspur, he hadn't anticipated the additional weight his boss could throw behind the op.

And even with all that digging, no one had come up with so much as a parking ticket. The woman was clean. Dom had known she was, but he'd been inwardly relieved that the intel proved that.

Even if it scraped at his guilt for involving her in the first place.

A useless emotion, but one he hadn't quite gotten past yet. So here they were.

After planning for a week, they were about ready. Which had left one final test before heading into Warlords territory: Pressure testing their engagement with an interested audience who would ask questions.

Lots of questions.

His sister.

He'd toyed with introducing Sami to a larger swath of his family but finally settled on a visit out to the Gemini Ranch and time with his sister, Aubrey. Although Aub would have the same level of curiosity as the rest of his family, she'd always been conscious of *the whole Colton thing*, as she often said, and the weight of their family legacy.

All in one place, they were…a lot.

For all those reasons, Aubrey made the most sense. She had the dedicated interest of a sibling, but she also knew how to modulate her interest in a way that was sweet and not too intrusive.

She'd also been through a significant experience of her own, when her boyfriend, Luke, was in hiding at Gemini Ranch. She knew how to keep a confidence when it was needed and while the temptation to tell the family about his visit would be great, he knew Aub would hold her tongue.

It was a good plan and one he'd finalized with Aubrey after Sami had reached back out to her father earlier in the week. He'd stood sentinel beside her as she'd made the call from her living room, a small script in front of her as she spoke to Mike.

Yes, she'd like to see him.

Would the following weekend work?

She'd been seeing someone. Could she bring him along?

Dom hadn't missed the hitch on the other side of the phone, or the way Sami had drawn a series of scribbles on the notepad in front of her as she spoke to her father. But despite the tense conversation, she'd held her ground. That she was a grown woman, entitled to be in a relationship. That she'd met a great guy on a work job and that they were enjoying getting to know one another. She'd even gone for broke, suggesting that Mike would like him.

The grunt through the other side of the phone had been unmistakable even without the call being on speaker, but Mike had stressed that he was looking forward to seeing them the following weekend.

That had been Tuesday. Now on Friday night, Dom knew there wasn't any way they could go back. It was time to press forward.

Dom pressed the bell on Sami's front door, catching his breath when she opened the door. She wore another vividly printed dress, and the vibrant purple and gold material swirled around her lithe frame like an invitation.

God, he wanted her.

They'd spent every day together that week, working the Traverson job so nothing looked out of place to anyone who might be observing and so they could make plans on their breaks. If anyone had noticed their time together or Sami's new ring, they'd said nothing. But with all that close proximity, it had taken everything in him not to touch her each time they were together or to take the liberty of a kiss.

But, oh, how he imagined the liberty of more.

Heated images of their night together refused to leave him, only growing more and more intense as the need for her continued to build.

But he didn't think he was welcome on that front any longer.

A situation he'd earned fair and square.

"You ready?"

Sami smiled at him, mischief lighting her hazel eyes. "You're the one that's about to brave meeting your sister."

"You're not even the tiniest bit nervous?"

"Should I be?"

"With Aubrey?" Dom smiled as he thought of his younger sister. "No, not really."

And he meant it. While he would happily introduce her to any of his siblings, Aubrey's management and ownership of Gemini Ranch was definitely an aspect of her life that kept her grounded. Her work with animals and her love of the outdoors had always given her an even-keeled outlook on life.

Add on she had also gone through finding her own romance in the past few months and he knew they would have a safe space for the evening.

"You were saying the other day that your sister is engaged?"

Dom opened the passenger side door of his truck for Sami, helping her up. "Yes. She and Luke got together a few months ago, after he hid out at the ranch."

"Hid out?"

Dom nodded. "Let me come around to my side and I'll give you the background. One you need to keep a secret."

"Of course."

It was a risk—and one that if found out would undo all the work they'd done to keep Luke safe—but she was taking several with him and Dom had sensed that giving this to her showed a bit more of his own trust in her.

As they took the roads out of her neighborhood and through Blue Larkspur toward the ranch, Dom filled her in on how scary Aubrey's experience had been as she met Luca Rossi. How Luca, an Italian journalist, had been following a major story in Italy about a criminal organization called the Camorra. Luca's exposé had put the Camorra family's crimes under the microscope and he'd been on the run, hiding first in Europe, then in Canada before finding the Gemini and coming to Colorado and ultimately changing his legal name to Luke Bishop.

"How does anyone ever truly escape that sort of family?" Sami asked, clearly caught up in the story.

"He faked his death."

It was a risk, telling her about Luca's escape. Realistically, Dom knew that. Yet, for some reason, it seemed important that she knew. Almost like a form of absolution, which made no sense at all, even as it made a weird sort of sense.

Sami's life around her dad and his gang cast a long, tall shadow over her. It was important to Dom that she understand that there were ways to get past a bad situation.

For her, she'd spent her adult life working to distance herself. But even with all that work, her father's crimes had found her—via Mike's direct, out-of-the-blue phone call and Dom's own undercover operation.

Dom wanted her to understand that, on some level, there could be a future for her. One that didn't have to have Mike Evans's crimes hanging over it.

A point he really had no business pressing. Because he could paint it any way he wanted, but nothing changed the fact that he *had* drawn her into this. He was responsible…

Damn it to hell, he mentally swore as he glanced in the rearview mirror.

"What's wrong?"

Sami's immediate ability to sense his change in demeanor was both fascinating and humbling. Was he really that transparent? Or was it just a strange connection that seemed to pulse between them, each in tune with the other in a way he had never been in his life? Even with all the connection and trust he had with Oliver and Ezra, he'd never been this transparent to anyone.

Dom glanced once more in his rearview mirror, well aware of what he was seeing. "We seem to have caught a tail."

"A what?" Her eyes widened as the truth sunk in. "Someone's following us?"

He realized that he, too, sensed what she was going to do before she did it. He laid a hand on her arm to hold her still and keep her from turning to look out the back window. "Don't look."

"But how do you know?"

"Because they're close enough to follow, far enough away to seem casual." With a deliberate flip of his blinker, Dom turned in the opposite direction from the ranch. "Let's see if the bastard can keep up."

Chapter Six

Sami kept fighting the urge to turn around— she trusted Dom implicitly on this point—but she couldn't resist keeping an eye on her passenger side mirror. The car behind them kept pace, just as Dom had said it would. Close enough to stay on them, far enough away to seem casual.

Only each time Dom turned, they turned with him.

"What are we going to do? We can't lead them to your sister's ranch."

"Oh, I'm going to lose them, don't worry about that. I just need a little runway." Dom turned to her, his smile feral. "I grew up around here, remember?"

"So did I! That doesn't mean much if they get too close. What are you going to do?"

Dom didn't say anything, just bore down on the accelerator as he took a quick turn onto the interstate that ran just outside town.

"Dom, it's all uphill here. You're never going to get far enough ahead of them."

"Watch."

Although his truck looked rather innocuous, Sami had to give Dom credit. He'd clearly had the truck enhanced because as he sped up, the vehicle moved.

As in really moved.

With what felt like minimal time to pick up speed, Dom's truck was cruising on the stretch of highway. They passed one exit, then another and she couldn't understand how he thought he'd lose their tail on a straight stretch of road.

She kept an eye on the side mirror, horrified to see the same car gaining in speed behind them, weaving between traffic the same way Dom was.

Panic slammed through her. Had her father sent those men? Because whatever part Dom might be playing right now, they had zero reason to think she was cozying up with the FBI.

But Mike did have reason to want to know more about her life.

"This is because of me."

Dom whipped the truck around a slow-moving 18-wheeler, narrowly passing a car that had been climbing speed on his left. An irate driver laid on the horn but Dom ignored it, still moving at top speed.

"This isn't because of you."

"Of course it is!" She practically screeched the words, the reality of being part of a high-speed chase slamming into her chest and stilling her breath.

"This isn't because of you. It's because of me. I've changed the equation and your father's interested in getting the upper hand."

"It's still because of me," Sami insisted.

"See that handle?" Dom pointed with his right hand to the handle above the passenger side window, his gaze never leaving the road in front of him. "Grab it tight."

"Yeah, I see it. People call it an oh, sh—" She never

got the words out because as quickly as he'd accelerated onto the highway was as fast as he slammed off. One minute they were racing down the highway and the next they were bumping over the exit ramp, dust and rocks spewing in their wake.

Dom maneuvered the truck expertly, managing to keep them on the flat road *and* finding a way to slow down all at once.

And then they were hitting the end of the exit ramp and he brought the car to a stop, following the posted signs as if he'd never broken a single traffic law.

He glanced in the rearview mirror before turning to her. "They're headed to Utah by now."

"But they'll be back. They found us. Followed us." She shook her head, still processing the reality of what had happened. "My father sent them."

"Yeah, he likely did."

Dom's voice was careful—controlled—and Sami wondered how he could remain so calm.

"That doesn't bother you?"

"I'm not happy we were followed, if that's what you mean. But it also gives me a leg up."

"How?"

"I know he's not as careful as he should be. And I also now know your father's worried about me."

"I am his only daughter."

"And you're bringing a strange man into the Warlords environment. He's on alert. I can work with that. Use it."

"Use it how?"

"That's my job to worry about. But he showed some of his hand tonight. It wasn't smart and it wasn't careful, and I thought Mike Evans was both of those things."

He turned to face the road heading back the way they came. They'd overshot their destination by about ten miles and Dom navigated a series of two-lane back roads to get them to his sister's home.

As he did so, Sami sat in silence beside him.

And wondered exactly what waited for them when they arrived at her father's house the next day.

MIKE "LONE WOLF" Evans took the call himself, listening throughout the babbled excuses and increasingly long list of mistakes.

Made in Blue Larkspur.

Chase on the highway.

Escaped off an exit ramp.

He gave his men time to dig their own grave, listening to each excuse, one more paltry than the next. And then he went in for the kill.

"You were made by a civilian in broad daylight, with my daughter in the car?"

He deliberately kept his voice low, the notes sulky, well aware the two idiots he'd sent on the job needed to lean in close to the phone to hear every word.

"It's not like that—"

"Then what's it like!" He wasn't looking for excuses. "Because from where I'm sitting, the only answer to that question was yes."

After a moment of silence, the more responsible of the two finally spoke up. "Yes, Wolf. That's what happened."

"How'd he outrun you?"

"Guy's got moves. We did nothing to draw attention

but he figured the tail in all of two minutes." The guy rushed on after dropping that news. "He's not some dumb roofer, Wolf. This one's someone we need to keep an eye on."

Mike was planning on it—wasn't that why he'd sent the two dipwads out to follow his daughter and her boyfriend, Dom Conner? But the news of the young man's skills and awareness was interesting. *And* news he could use.

"Do you want us to keep looking for them?"

"No, you've done enough. Come back to base."

"Of course."

Mike disconnected the call and sat back, his evening whiskey in hand. He'd waited a long time to have a relationship with his only child and he wasn't going to do anything to jeopardize it now. But inviting Sami back into his life was a risk. One he'd weighed and one he was willing to take.

But a risk all the same.

As adults, they had had no relationship. What he knew of her from day-to-day experience were the frustrated memories of raising a teenager. He still regretted letting her go, even as he'd known he couldn't keep her close. His work was his own and he'd long come to accept it was the only thing in the world he was good at.

But he wouldn't let it take his daughter the same way it had taken his wife.

His enemies didn't need to know he had a child. Hell, he'd only reached out now because he finally had a bit of breathing room. The Warlords had shifted their loyalties to the biggest drug supplier he'd ever met. He could make a good living, keep his profits tidy and get out of the never-ending turf wars that had taken up so much of his time as a younger man.

The supply had changed. The good stuff was brokered through a precious few and he'd stopped caring how much of that he owned. He could traffic with the best of them and had a steady stream of buyers. It had taken him nearly three decades, but Mike Evans had finally figured out what he was good at: playing the middleman.

He had access to premium grade supply and a lot of wide-open space to do his business, unseen. Add on his extensive network of buyers, cultivated over those decades, and he'd found his niche. And his life had gotten a hell of a lot safer because of it.

Which meant it was time to get Sami back.

The risks had changed. She wasn't going to end up like her mother, a victim of intergang warfare. That was, of course, assuming her new boyfriend was who he said he was.

As Lone Wolf Evans stared down at the face of his now-dark phone, the conversation with his staff replaying through his mind, he couldn't help but wonder just how innocent Dom Conner really was.

THE GEMINI RANCH spread out before them in all its one-hundred-acre glory as Dom made the turn into the property. He drove down a long, winding entrance, the view serene. Yet, even amidst all that beauty, it was evident that this was also a working ranch.

Jasper and Aubrey's dream.

He'd been careful to drive a bit, watching for another

tail, before heading to the Gemini. He had no interest in bringing his work life to his family.

Especially when they'd battled their own danger so recently.

A few of the hands were out on horseback, riding the property, and as he drove, he could see some farm equipment still moving through one of the fields.

It was spring and there was a lot of work to be done.

He'd thought to meet up with Aubrey and Luke in the main lodge, the crown jewel of the property, but Aubrey had suggested they come straight to her cabin instead. She was making dinner and suggested it might be more comfortable for Sami if they met in a place with a bit less attention. Besides, Aub had reasoned, the ranch had a large number of visitors right now and if they were in the main lodge, she'd keep getting questions from the staff.

So they were hiding out in her home tonight, she'd said with a cheeky laugh when Dom had spoken to her earlier.

For all her protests, Dom knew his sister loved her work and felt the most herself at the Gemini. But everyone was entitled to a night off, too.

Good advice, Colton. You should try taking it sometime.

Although he'd deliberately played it cool in the truck, Dom considered the high-speed chase that had escorted them out of Blue Larkspur and knew that was just the beginning of what lay ahead of him. He hadn't made up that point to Sami—Mike Evans had showed his hand with that little stunt—but it had happened anyway.

Which meant Evans was already curious about his daughter's *boyfriend*, Dom Conner.

Wait until he found out they were engaged.

Sami had deliberately kept that information separate when she spoke with her father, deciding it would be better to reveal it once they were together again. Dom hadn't totally agreed but he wanted her to have some ownership of this little show of theirs. If she wanted to hold back that detail, he'd give her the space to handle the interpersonal stuff as she saw fit.

Because the one thing she kept coming back to, over and over, was that her own dad wasn't going to hurt her.

Dom knew that magnanimous attitude didn't extend to him, but he hoped like hell Sami was right. If anything happened to her...

"This is where she lives?"

Sami stared through the windshield at the home that rose up before them. His sister and brother, despite their close bond as twins, had gone into the ranch with a clear sense of their individuality as well. They maintained separate homes on the property and divided up the various jobs, giving each areas of responsibility where they excelled.

He'd seen similar behavior in Caleb and Morgan in the way they ran their law firm, Colton & Colton. Their business was a joint effort but they'd found a way to carve out their individual paths, too.

A trick he'd never quite managed. That together-but-separate bit.

He, Oliver and Ezra, they'd each decidedly gone their own way, their lives sharing very little in common. He loved all his siblings—and the bond with his triplet brothers was undeniable—but they were still very isolated in all they did.

What it all meant about his ability to bond with others, he wasn't quite sure. A trait he hadn't had as a young man, but one he'd taken to easily after his father's betrayal and in the two decades since.

Ignoring the odd shot of remorse that coursed through him, Dom focused on answering Sami's questions. "Yep. Jasper's place is off the same road."

"It's gorgeous. It looks like something out of a TV show."

"Wait'll you get inside."

Surprised at the additional shots of nostalgia and the weird, envious thoughts of his siblings who'd managed to carve out a life together, he got out of the truck. He intended to help Sami from the high perch in the passenger seat but she'd already hopped out herself and come around the front to meet him.

But she added the real element of surprise when she slipped her hand in his and kissed his cheek.

"You ready, Colton?"

He stared down at their joined hands before lifting his gaze to meet her eyes.

They hadn't touched beyond a brush of hands or an accidental shoulder rub since their heated night together the week before. That intimate touch was electric and he felt the heat course up his arm from where their fingers met before following a more interesting path through his body.

Even more amazing, he had no idea how she knew he needed the contact.

Only she did.

Those thoughts about his siblings faded. He loved his brothers, and whether or not they had a relationship like the twins, they were their own selves.

Wishing things were different wasn't the most productive course of action. But more important, maybe they didn't need to be different.

Maybe it was okay they just *were*.

He had a bond with all his siblings—a serious stroke of good fortune he knew wasn't a given in any family, let alone a large one. Just because his relationship with Oliver and Ezra didn't look like Aub and Jasper's or Caleb and Morgan's wasn't the point. He and his triplet brothers got each other and had one another's backs. In the end, that was all that mattered.

"Dom!"

Aubrey threw open the front door of her place, her arms immediately outstretched as she pulled him close for a hug. Although no one hugged like Aubrey—with her whole heart—he was reluctant to drop Sami's hand, that small point of contact so surprising. And so welcome.

But in the face of his exuberant sister, there was nothing to be done for it. He wrapped Aubrey up, holding her tight and wondering why the moment felt as wonderful as it did ominous.

Was it those thugs on the highway?

Or was it something else?

Because no matter how he twisted and turned things in his mind, Dom felt like he was at a crossroads in his life. The thoughts about his sibling bonds, all the considerations he had about keeping Sami safe, even the very real concerns he had about her father's motives—they all roiled and cast around in his mind with the impact of a strengthening hurricane.

"Aubrey." He hugged her tightly before pulling back. "I'd like to introduce you to someone."

Aubrey's eyes twinkled behind her glasses and she gave him a quick wink before turning to Sami. "I'm Dom's sister, Aubrey. I'm thrilled to meet you."

Before Sami could even get out a hello, Aubrey was pulling her close in a tight hug. Sami shot him an amused side eye before she hugged back, adding her own replies of how happy she was to meet his sister.

As Dom watched it play out, that pointed whisper that hadn't left him since he first laid eyes on Samantha Evans piped up once more.

He was at a crossroads in his life.

He just had no idea which direction he was being pulled.

SAMI STARED AT Aubrey Colton and finally understood the meaning of the words *whirling dervish*.

From the first moment of Aubrey's ebullient greeting on the front porch to the introduction of her fiancé, Luke, to the press of appetizers, wine and conversation—all in the span of about seven and a half minutes—Sami had to admit the truth.

She was enchanted.

Dom's sister was warm and kind and the steady gleam in her eyes, as well as the easy mentions of nearly every one of their siblings, made it clear Aubrey was thrilled to be the first Colton to meet Sami. And if Aubrey was momentarily stilled by the announcement of Dom and Sami's engagement and the requisite oohing and aahing over the ring, she moved past it quickly.

She'd also given her brother a dark look when he'd sworn her to secrecy, claiming he had a big work job he needed to focus on, so it would be a few weeks until he told the rest of the family and that she needed to keep their visit to herself.

At that point Sami was half-convinced their cover was entirely blown, but Aubrey seemed to take it in stride. Especially when Luke poured more wine for everyone and then sat down close to Aubrey.

"Your engagement happened fast."

Aubrey was also direct, a trait Sami admired in spades, which made it oddly more challenging to lie. Dom saved her from having to by smoothly jumping in. "When you know, you know. Besides—" Dom leaned in to snag a cracker covered in brie "—it takes one to know one."

Luke wrapped an arm around Aubrey's shoulders, his gaze besotted and adoring as Dom's sister's. "When you know, you know."

Sami felt a momentary hitch in her chest at the obvious love and affection between the two of them. Strangely, her mind reeled back to her and Dom's trip to the mall and the older couple she'd observed in the food court.

Was this what real love looked like? Not something fake to lull a criminal out of hiding but an actual honest-to-God romance? One fueled by both passion and genuine affection and a willingness to go the distance? To commit to forever?

For all the staring and daydreaming she'd done at her left hand over the past week, had she really acknowledged just how hard this whole fake engagement would really be? To be so close to someone she was attracted to and interested in and know it was all made up?

Sure, they had chemistry. And Dom had been as in the moment and into her when they were in bed. But that wasn't a relationship. And it wasn't a promise of forever. It was a bit of fun on a Friday night between two healthy adults. Hadn't he proven that to her by how easily he'd lied about who he really was?

He'd seemed to be genuinely contrite about that and hadn't made any moves on her since she'd discovered who he really was with the discovery of his badge, which was how it should be.

Right?

Even as she asked herself that question, she knew her heart was playing traitor to her mind.

Deep down inside, she wanted him to make a move, her initial anger at being duped be damned.

"How did you two meet?" Aubrey kept Luke's hand in hers, the move easy and natural, and it dawned on Sami that she'd need to demonstrate a lot more affection toward Dom if she intended to pull this charade off to her father.

Aubrey and Luke *looked* like an engaged couple. The way they touched, their besotted stares at each other. It was easy and simple, and it telegraphed as clearly as their words how they felt about one another.

And here she and Dom sat, in two separate chairs, eating off a charcuterie board.

While it chaffed her pride a bit to only be able to touch Dom because of the show they were putting on, she also recognized that they needed to be convincing. And, if they wanted people to think they were a real couple, they needed the quiet moments when they were observed to be as impactful as the words they were telling others.

No time like the present, Sami-girl.

She set her plate down on the coffee table and reached for Dom's hand across the small space between their matched chairs. "We met on a work job."

"Work job?" Aubrey's eyebrows shot up, her smile wide. "The one that's keeping you too busy to talk about your engagement? That one?"

Sami kept her expression steady, recognizing Aubrey's inquiry made a ready test for her and Dom. Aubrey had to know her brother was a federal agent, so the announcement they worked together would raise questions for her.

Although her father had no idea what Dom's background was, any gap in their story put their fake charade at risk. They couldn't risk messing up once they were in Warlords territory. "I own my own landscaping company and Dom is working the crew renovating the same house."

For all her internal questions on how they'd keep up the charade, the regular, steady cadence of her voice gave her the additional confidence she needed to keep going. She shifted her gaze to Dom, her attention steady on him. "There was an immediate connection between us."

"It was all-consuming," Dom quickly agreed, his eyes never leaving hers.

As they sat there in his sister's living room, practicing their charade for a very interested—and highly attentive—party, Sami was once against struck by how real it all felt.

And how an increasing part of her wished the charade really were true.

Chapter Seven

Sami took a sip of her wine as her gaze followed Aubrey and Luke's retreating forms into the kitchen. She waited until they'd cleared the hallway to the kitchen before she spoke, confident she wouldn't be overheard.

"Your sister was surprised by you and me meeting on the job. And that your *job*," she emphasized the word, "was in construction."

"Yeah, she was."

"Does she know what you do?"

"She knows I'm FBI, if that's what you mean. As to the specifics?" Dom smiled but it didn't reach his eyes. "That's a hard no."

"You two are good. You communicate well without too much obvious eye contact. If I hadn't been looking for it, I'd likely have missed it."

He reached for a slice of prosciutto-wrapped melon on the charcuterie board. "You saw that."

"I could tell she was fishing without trying to be obvious. And I likely wouldn't have recognized it if I didn't know your real job."

"Then I can only return the compliment. You're good, too, because she asked how we met and you didn't miss a beat."

"I was thinking about it, and the reality is that we have to have our story straight. You were right to come here and use this as a practice run. My father's gaze will be sharp, but a sister's is, too."

Dom popped the melon in his mouth, considering. "I don't like lying to my family."

"But you didn't mind with me?"

As soon as the words were out, Sami wished she could pull them back. If she didn't want to do this, then she should have walked away. But continuing to berate him for doing his job wasn't going to put her in the best headspace for what lay ahead of them, either.

Even if a small part of her still struggled with the idea of being nothing more than a job.

"Sami. You have to know that's not true."

"Oh no?"

"I never wanted to lie to you." Dom wiped his hands on the napkin he had settled in his lap before balling the paper into a tight wad. "I recognize it's not going to seem like this from your point of view, but I didn't mean to hurt you, and I didn't want to lie to you. But there was no other way."

While she hated the reasons, she recognized that continuing to stew in her resentment over the way they'd met wasn't healthy. Worse, it put their mission at risk.

Which made her next request that much more dangerous.

"I understand there are some things you're not going to be able to tell me. But I need to ask you a favor."

"Of course."

"Don't lie to me again. If you can't tell me something, then just say that. But don't lie."

His focus on her was steady and direct, and she could feel her heart beating double time in her chest. What was it about this man? And how was he able to consume her like that, with nothing more than a gaze?

"I can do that."

She might not have any evidence that he spoke the truth, and like most things in life she was going to need to take this one on faith, but the open honesty she saw in his dark blue gaze didn't seem like something that could be faked.

"Thank you."

She had released their handhold when Aubrey and Luke left the room, recognizing they were no longer on display, which made Dom's reach for her hand an unbearably sweet gesture. She was fascinated by how his big capable palm seemed to engulf hers before their fingers linked.

"You're welcome."

Aubrey and Luke came back into the room, Luke carrying a tray of what looked like little beef Wellingtons while Aubrey carried a new bottle of wine.

Dom stared up at his sister but never let go of Sami's hand. "There's more? Sheesh, Aub, this is a feast already."

"We're celebrating. It's not every day one of my brothers gets engaged."

Dom turned to catch her gaze, his eyes bright. Sami sensed what he was telegraphing—to go with the moment—and was well aware Aubrey caught it, too.

But as she smiled back, she could only hope Aubrey interpreted Sami's wink back to Dom for what it really was.

A woman totally in the moment, even if it was fleeting.

DOM KEPT HIS gaze on the road as he navigated from Aubrey's house back to Sami's. He'd considered taking the highway but felt better staying on two-lane roads with minimal lighting. And while he wasn't expecting a return of their tail tonight, he wasn't above being too careful.

Besides, he knew the various ranches and open land between the Gemini and the more residential areas of Blue Larkspur. If he had to shake a tail, he was confident he could do it. But right now, he hoped he wouldn't have to bother because his thoughts were full of Sami.

Tonight had been a revelation.

He'd been attracted to Sami from the first moment he'd seen her. He'd had his job—and the resulting lies he had to tell to keep his cover intact—so he'd chalked his attraction up to bad timing.

Work had to come first.

Only now work was coming first, and it still put the two of them together. In even closer proximity than when he'd been trying to romance a few details out of her. And it was messing with his focus in the worst way.

Because you want her, Colton.

He wanted her and he could admit it to himself.

Even if admitting wasn't doing. A fact his body was well aware of, since the only thing he actually wanted to do was drag her into his arms and kiss her senseless.

That was even more dangerous territory than engaging with the Warlords.

"This time tomorrow night, we'll be at my father's."

Sami's comment was a strange parallel to his thoughts and Dom nodded as he made the turn into her neighborhood. "We will be. The tech team at work confirmed for me again that my digital presence is ironclad."

"You mean the persona that says you're a hot construction worker in Colorado?"

Dom knew he walked dangerous ground, but it was time to tell her what was really going on. "No, the persona that says I have a criminal record and your father can trust me as a new member of his organization."

The comment had its desired impact and Sami twisted in her seat to face him as he pulled into her driveway. Bringing the car to a stop, Dom turned to face her in kind. "It's the only way, Sami."

"To pose as a criminal?"

"An opportunistic criminal. I'm not playing this like I cozied up to you to get to your father. But I am playing it like, now that I know who he is, I might want to be a part of things for the Warlords."

"He's never going to buy that."

Her absolute expectations about her dad were an intriguing counterpoint to her willingness to take this job. She believed Mike Evans wouldn't hurt her. She'd taken, with very little prompting or convincing, his information that her father was up to his old tricks. And now she was convinced that same man was smooth enough to see through a solid FBI-created alibi.

"You need to have a little more faith in me."

"No, no. This has nothing to do with faith. This has to do with the reality of the fact that you are not a criminal."

"That's not what a quick internet search for me says."

Their conversation back at Aubrey's played through

his mind and he used that to his advantage. Pressed it, really.

"You said you want to know what's going on." He'd made that promise that he wouldn't lie. But he had, obviously, omitted these details up to now. "You said you don't want me to lie to you. This is the job, Sami. This is what I have to do."

"No, I don't want you to lie. But, Dom, you're not a criminal."

"I hate to break it to you, but my government train ing extends to a lot of different things and a lot of different personas. That's the nature of undercover work."

"And you think you can convince my father and his henchmen of this?"

"Yes, I do."

Considering the fact that she was all in, he unbuttoned his left sleeve, rolling up the cuff of his dress shirt. "See this tattoo?"

"Well sure. I noticed it right away. The lion is distinctive." He caught something flit across her face before she added a wry grin. "And to be honest, it sort of adds to your hotness. Those muscular forearms, then a beast over muscle, flexing in the sun as you work."

He felt the heat creeping up his neck and focused on what he was trying to say. "The tattoo was intentional. The design, the fang that's visible in its mouth. It's meant to signify I completed gang rituals."

"Are you serious?"

"It subtle, and the average person wouldn't know it as anything more than some misplaced male pride." He smiled at her, still easily able to remember his mother's strained words when she saw the tattoo for the first time. "But I can use it to my advantage, chalking this up to a commitment I made to criminal activity prior to coming to the Warlords."

"And the doctored FBI files, discoverable online, will seal the deal."

"Exactly."

"Were you planning this all along?"

Dom was expecting the question, but not quite the laser-like focus in her gaze. Sami missed nothing, and this line of questioning was yet another example.

"Not in the beginning. At first, I was just going to pose as your fiancé. The plan has come together over this past week as we realized there was a greater opportunity to infiltrate the Warlords."

"You think this is the right way to do it?"

"I think it's the only way."

She stared at him, searching his face. "You risk too much."

The genuine admiration in her words was a kindness, but he risked nothing compared to her. "I could say the same about you. You're the one who's risking everything. This is your father. His territory and his life that you're going back into."

"I'm not an undercover agent at risk of discovery."

"No, you're not. But this approach, created in tandem with my team back at the International Corruption Unit, will ensure that you're protected if I'm found out."

Because that was essential.

It had become increasingly clear as this op developed—as they'd worked the scenarios and weighed the pros and cons—that Sami needed to be protected at all costs.

When he had started this mission, there was the risk and the reality that she might have been aware of her father's crimes. But it had become evident as he spent more time with her that this wasn't the case. And because of it, she needed the full weight of the FBI behind her.

She needed a full alibi and protection if Dom was discovered.

Her gaze drifted away from his and onto the house. "Do you know how I got this place?"

He'd sworn he wouldn't lie to her and wasn't going to start now. "The FBI has a rather broad perspective on your life, your home included. But I'm not sure I see how it matters."

She laughed, the sound humorless as it echoed in the confines of the car. "One more thing the FBI knows about me."

He thought about saying something but anything he said would fall empty and flat. In pursuit of "Lone Wolf" Evans, the government had done its job. Apologizing wasn't going to change it.

Especially since he'd been all in.

"Why don't you tell me?"

"When I left my father's house, things were pretty bad. We had been fighting for a long time, but it all came to a head after my mother died. As I look back on it, I realize now he was dealing with his grief, too. And likely the acknowledgment that his life choices were responsible for everything that had happened to her. But I didn't know that at the time."

It sat oddly on his chest that the man he saw as an object of pursuit would grieve. That it was possible Evans could even feel that emotion. Yet, even as Dom wanted to reject the thought of Mike Evans's humanity, he also knew that ability to feel was the only thing that would possibly keep Sami safe if Dom's own cover was blown.

"What *did* you know?"

"That I needed to get out."

His heart ached for the imagined teenager in his mind. And it ached even more for the woman who sat next to him.

How had she survived it all?

Although he had been all in on this job from the very first, there was something about Sami that pulled at his heartstrings in ways he had never imagined.

And there was nothing he wouldn't do to protect her.

"How did you do it? Get out?"

"My grandmother. She was my savior in all this."

"Your dad's mother? Or your mom's?"

"You don't know that part?" Her eyebrows shot up, a quirk in the moonlight, but it wasn't enough to bring even the hint of a smile to her face. "Funny enough, my dad's mother. She loved him. Completely. But deep down inside, she knew what he was. And I suspect she knew what he was capable of."

The memory of a conversation they'd had, about their dead parents, struck Dom with blunt force. Love didn't have an expiration date. And it didn't have easy answers for navigating the brokenness in the people that you loved.

He lived with it, as did Sami. Obviously, her grandmother had, too.

"What did she do?"

"She took me in when I left my father's house, even though she was really sick at the time. And when she passed away, she left me all she had. That's how I started my business." Sami extended a hand toward the house. "How I eventually saved the money to buy my home. She gave me a future."

"She sounds like a wonderful woman."

"She was the best."

And still, Dom thought, the woman hadn't found a way to get through to her son.

One more connection with Sami, those similarities in their family situations. While his father's crimes were hidden behind the scenes, the judge's bench giving him distance, they'd ruined lives just as much as Mike Evans's more overt actions.

Ben Colton and Mike Evans lived their lives in a way that destroyed others.

It was a strange, underlying thread weaving around Dom and Sami that had somehow brought them together. And it left Dom with plenty to think about since she'd discovered who he was.

He had chosen this life, fully. Because he was called to it, yes, but also because he had a driving need to avenge his father's poor choices in life.

All his siblings shared that determination. That focus.

More, Dom acknowledged, that need.

To prove that what beat in their hearts—that what drove them all—was a belief in the power of the name Colton.

A belief that it could stand for something good.

AUBREY SNUGGLED IN CLOSE, up against Luke's chest, and stared at the empty chairs opposite them. The ones her brother had so recently sat in with his fiancée.

"It was a good night," she said, staring up into that face she held so dear.

"It was. I know I don't know him well, but your brother looks happy."

"He is." Even as she said the words, she could still picture Dom's besotted gaze as he'd stared at the pretty woman beside him. "It's a state I don't ever remember seeing him in."

"You never remember your brother being happy?"

Aubrey considered Luke's question, forcing herself to think back through the years and what had made her even say that. But as she ran through any number of memories, she knew she was right. "Laughing, yes. Telling jokes, yes. Getting into trouble with my brothers, yes. But happy? No, not really."

"That's sad to hear."

"Maybe it's just finally his turn."

Luke's gaze was adoring, but she didn't miss the slight flicker of unease before he spoke. "You think that little show tonight was real?"

Aubrey pressed on his chest as she scrambled to sit up beside him. "You think so, too!"

"Of course. It's a show. A very good one, but much acting all the same."

She loved his lingering Italian accent—how it got thicker when he was trying to say something with great care—and it touched her that he was trying to be gentle about Dom's charade without hurting her own feelings.

"I think she's part of his latest case."

"She could be."

"And I think we were the people they wanted to practice on."

The indulgent smile that had resumed once Luke realized she wasn't actually mad about his assessment fell. "Should we tell them we weren't fooled? It would do no good for him to be in jeopardy if we can help them."

"You don't think they were convincing?"

"No." Luke shook his head. "No, not that. I think they actually care for one another. That part didn't seem fake."

"No, it didn't." Aubrey reached for her wine on the coffee table, taking a sip before tapping a nail on the bowl of the glass.

"But I think they are pretending. Whether it's for his job or some other reason, they need to be careful."

"Because they'll be found out?"

"Because their emotions are much closer to the surface than either of them think."

SAMI TOOK ONE last look at herself in the full-length mirror in her bedroom and shot up a quick prayer to her grandmother for heavenly support. She'd done that a lot, after Gram had died, that desperate desire to see her business succeed and to keep a firm hold on her independence the only things driving her forward.

Forward from her grief over losing first her mother and then Gram. Forward from the life she most certainly didn't want under Mike Evans's thumb. And forward into a future that wasn't filled with answerless questions about how her dad spent his days.

What had started as prayers in those early days after her grandmother's death had shifted into little conversations, several times a day in the years since. Small communications about intense work deadlines or frustrating employees or even big jobs she wanted but wasn't sure she was ready for.

In her mind, Gram heard it all.

Which is why she'd also shared her thoughts about Dom. First, how attractive she'd found him. Then, her excitement about going out with him. And now, about the dangerous step the two of them were about to embark on.

It was scary to think about the risks they were taking—him most of all—and even if the conversations were only in her mind, it felt good to have them. To know she had a safe space to express herself.

Her life growing up had limited the number of friendships she had as a girl. Although she didn't understand it at the time, other parents were wary of her father. It had limited the number of children she played with or who invited her to birthday parties. Whether through intention or the simple outgrowth of her busy life, that hadn't changed much as an adult. She had a few friends she did things with, but no one she really confided in.

Was that a shortcoming?

Over the past few years, she'd begun to worry that it was. Yet another reason she navigated a path through life alone.

Was that why she'd developed such a growing fascination with Dom? Had she somehow needed him to be more? Or worse, had she needed him to *mean* more?

The peal of the doorbell had her shaking off the thoughts. Did the answers really matter?

Sami let that question roil around as she headed for the front door. Because whether Dom Colton meant the world to her or nothing more than the way she felt about her couch cushions, she was putting an awful lot of trust in the man to keep her safe.

A level of trust, she worried, that he hadn't really earned.

All of which faded away as she opened the front door. He stood there, early morning spring sunlight haloing his large, solid frame, and she had the fleeting thought that he just might have been sent down from Heaven by her Gram.

A thought that was even too much for a woman who held fake conversations with her beloved dead grandmother.

"Are you okay?" He stepped forward, taking her shoulders in his hands. "What happened?"

It was there—that moment—that Sami felt the atmosphere shift.

Without saying a word, he'd understood that she needed something. Some affirmation or sense that she mattered. That what was happening to her mattered.

Without checking the impulse, she moved into him, wrapping her arms around his waist before lifting her face for a kiss. If he was surprised, he didn't show it, instead responding as if they were a real couple. Two people who cared about one another.

Like that older couple in the mall. Or Aubrey and her fiancé, Luke.

Like they mattered to each other.

Sami drank him in, absorbing the delicious contact like it was air after surfacing from the deepest dive of her life. Their mouths met and merged, consuming each other in the light of a new day.

She felt it—that need for him rising up to swamp her—and marveled that, despite the challenges they faced, there was this sort of connection that beat between them.

His mouth was hot on hers, the kiss growing out of control, before he pulled back, the expression on his face one of frustration. "You sure you're okay?"

"I'm fine. Just a little—" she sought the right word before settling on the truth. "Just a little overwhelmed and maybe a little scared, too."

He nodded. "You're taking on a lot. And I know I'm asking a lot of you." His body shifted imperceptibly, as if he were going to glance over his shoulder but checked the impulse before pressing her backward. "Can I come in?"

"Sure."

She took a few more steps backward, the outside light fading as he shut the door behind them.

"Are you sure you're all right?" he asked.

"I will be. Just too much time on my hands to think about what lies ahead of us."

He'd followed her into the kitchen, but pulled lightly on her shoulder to turn her from where she stood at the sink, staring out over her small backyard.

"I will take care of you. I know that what we're facing is scary and the fact that this is your father only adds to that. But you have my word you're my first priority. And you're a priority for the FBI."

She saw the sincerity in his gaze and the raw honesty filling his deep blue eyes. But it was only as she looked there, seeking answers, that she saw something else.

A fear that matched her own.

"Something happened this morning, didn't it?"

His face slashed in hard lines and he'd banked what

was in his gaze, his features transforming before her very eyes. In place of the vulnerable man who'd stood before her, she now saw an officer of the law. A federal agent, tasked with preserving justice at all costs. It was fascinating to see and a grim reminder that this man led a life that was very different from her own.

One based on looking for—and nearly always seeing—the worst humankind could do in the world.

"Something did happen," he said. "Last night's tail was back, bright and early this morning."

"Did they follow you home last night?"

"I don't know. I don't think so but it bothers me they came back so quickly after we lost them on the highway. That they narrowed in on me like that." He took a deep breath. "And it bothers me that they're not seeing us living together. It puts us at risk. And it puts our whole story of being a couple in love at risk."

She heard what he was asking and tried desperately to stem the small leaping excitement flooding her veins. He wanted to stay here?

"You want to move in?"

"I think it's the only way. And I think we're going to need an alibi for why I didn't stay over in the event it comes up."

"I had a headache, dear?" She tapped his forehead when that grim expression refused to fade. "It's a joke, Dom."

"This isn't a joking matter."

"Maybe not, but we're going to need to find some lightness if we want to get through this. Besides," she considered their greeting when he arrived, "I just tried to suck your face off at my front door, for the entire neighborhood to see. That has to count for something."

"You're full of jokes this morning."

"We'll figure it out." With the same finger she'd used to tap on his forehead, she traced the small line between his brows, smoothing away the tension. "I'm in this with you. And I know what needs to be done. If that means you move in, then move in. You and I already spent the week refining our story of how we met and it worked like a charm last night on your sister, but if we need to practice some more, let's do it. From here on out, it's the Dom and Sami show. We're a team."

"A team."

She ran a hand over the tattoo on his forearm, reassured by the hard length of muscle beneath her palms. "It's into the lion's den, buddy. And we're all each other's got."

Chapter Eight

We're all each other's got.

Those simple words reverberated through Dom's mind as he drove the narrow winding passages up into Warlords territory. The wide-open nature of this area had always allowed Mike Evans to do his dark deeds in relative anonymity. The FBI had detailed aerial photos—which had been hard to come by after having three of their surveillance drones mysteriously fall from the sky—but they'd still managed to get something. A sense of the territory and the needed details for the rest of Dom's team back at the International Corruption Unit to ensure they had his back.

And Sami's back.

He'd spent a lot of time detailing his notes and impressions of the woman, determined to guarantee his findings on her were a clear reflection of her innocence. Sure, he'd questioned himself at first, wondering if he was a bit too besotted to be open-minded. But the past week with her had only solidified his hunch.

The FBI had never found any dirt on Sami Evans because there was none to be found.

She'd left her father's orbit as soon as she was reasonably able to and never looked back. She'd agreed, without equivocation, to help him. And that was even once she'd discovered his FBI badge in his discarded clothing after they'd slept together.

Sami had every right to behave like a woman scorned—or at least deeply misled—and she'd behaved in the exact opposite way.

She was willing to help.

Which made the fact that his head was so upside-down that much harder to settle into. It was one thing to be attracted, but the assignment had turned to protection and he needed every bit of focus he possessed.

He'd initiated this op with the sole goal of taking down the Warlords and discovering the bigger mystery of who had suddenly set them up again in grand style. Mike Evans might have a cadre of men at his command, but he wasn't the real score in all this. He was a node on a much bigger chain that the International Corruption Unit was determined to take down.

So where had Evans been for the past five years? Laying low and doing what?

Had he really gone straight, as he'd intimated to his daughter? Retired from the game? Been in isolation after being overthrown by his men?

Nothing pointed very clearly to any of those things. All that was clear was that Mike Evans had run with big dogs for years, only to vanish from the scene. And then starting around a year ago, he was back, funded by a new source and up to his old tricks.

"They're still behind us but they've kept a bit more distance today." For nearly the entire hour-long trip, Sami's gaze had returned again and again to the driver's side mirror.

"They're our escort into camp."

"And if I was coming alone?"

"It could have been the same or maybe not. I'm the new piece of the puzzle here. Your father knows how to reach you, so why send someone out to follow you, too?"

He glanced at her and didn't miss the shiver before she spoke again. "That makes an odd sort of sense. And while I'm not as adept at picking up a tail as you, I have to believe I'd have known through the years if someone was watching me. What is my father after, though?"

"I hate to break the bad news, but do you think your father has been oblivious to you for nearly a decade?"

"He's not—" Dom risked another glance away from the winding road, only to see her frown. "For what reason? I've been gone so long."

"You're still his child."

"Remember when I said I didn't want you to lie to me?"

"Yeah."

"Maybe you can keep a few of those observations to yourself."

He smiled at that, aware this was a lot for her, gentling his voice. "I'll keep that in mind."

They sat in silence for several miles, both their focus on the winding road ahead of them. It was only after they passed a small grove of aspen trees that Mike had given Sami as a landmark that Dom knew they were officially in Warlords territory.

As if to punctuate that thought, a couple of men materialized out of the trees behind them, the heavy roar of their motorcycles pulsing through Dom's truck.

"What a welcome."

Dom eyed the two keeping pace behind them in his rearview mirror. "You read my mind."

Because of the tail, Dom hadn't expected any further contact until they'd pulled into the driveway of Lone Wolf's cabin. So the double escort was not only a surprise, but a bit overkill. It might be a hidden message to Dom but it was an alarming one to send Evans's daughter after a nearly ten-year estrangement.

Was he trying to scare her off before they even got reacquainted?

It broke the pattern Dom had established in his mind and he'd learned early in his career to keep a close watch when that happened. People—criminals included—usually behaved like you expected them to.

So what had changed?

As Dom saw the black sedan that had followed them from Blue Larkspur pull up behind his truck, the answer became crystal clear. While he had zero regrets about besting Evans's tail last night, that little show had likely added to the welcoming committee.

And if he were going to make bets on it, the guys in the car weren't too happy with his antics on the highway as it had likely led to getting their asses handed to them.

Great start, Colton.

Even as he regretted the extra scrutiny, the situation couldn't be helped. And while his overt reason for shaking Lone Wolf's thugs had been to avoid leading them to the Gemini Ranch, it had served another important purpose.

The Warlords knew he was a man they shouldn't mess with.

He knew the score, knew how to lose someone following him and, more important, knew how to assess that a threat was even there.

All of which wouldn't mean a damn thing if he couldn't keep Sami safe.

It was humbling, Dom realized, to be responsible for someone in this way. He'd had assignments with assets before. He knew how to handle himself and knew how to keep them safe. It was what he'd trained for and a responsibility he'd actively chosen.

But none of them had been Sami.

Dom glanced in the rearview mirror once more, girding himself against the hulking figures looming behind his truck as he parked. Shutting off the engine, he glanced at the woman beside him. Extending his hand, he took hers, glad when she responded immediately by clasping his in return.

"We've got this."

She nodded before leaning over and pressing a quick kiss to his lips. "Totally."

SAMI TOOK HEART in those last moments with Dom before stepping out of the truck. The men who'd followed them into her father's compound remained at a distance, their stares intense as they stood sentinel around the back of Dom's truck. She considered how to play things and then opted for brazen attitude.

Their leader was her dad, after all. She might as well start testing boundaries from the very first moment.

She stared down the man closest and didn't miss the way his fingers flexed at his side. He had a gun, she had no doubt. Likely more than one. His partner, whom she'd seen beside him in the car, looked like his twin.

"Dom, honey, look at this." She pointed at the two men, pasting on a mocking smile. "Bookends."

"I see, baby."

Pleased he'd caught on to her approach, Sami turned her back on the men in blatant disregard. She moved around the front of the truck and took Dom's hand. "Let's go see my father."

He squeezed her hand lightly before letting go and wrapping an arm around her waist. The move made sense, and she locked her other arm around his waist in kind.

A united front.

And the obvious entwining of young lovers in a relationship.

All part of the act, she reminded herself, even as she reveled in the feel of his large body against hers. He was a solid wall of support.

A *sexy* solid wall of support. Her errant thoughts tripped over themselves as scorching heat ran along her skin where their bodies touched.

Further proof she needed to get it together. They were walking into the most dangerous situation she'd ever experienced, and all she could think about was the way Dom made her feel. Not a great start.

As the front door of his cabin opened, everything in Sami shifted.

This was her *father*?

Although the man standing on the porch still looked like Mike Evans, a decade's passage had done its work. The thick auburn hair she remembered had thinned, and the gray that had been visible only around his ears when she last saw him had extended all over his head.

Dom's arm was a reassuring weight around her

waist, and she used that sense of security to her advantage. "Hey, Dad."

"Samantha."

Mike moved off the porch toward them, his attention seemingly focused on her and Dom both at the same time. She sensed her father's pleasure in seeing her, but she didn't miss how closely he scrutinized the man with her.

And then they were all face-to-face.

Dom dropped his hand from around her waist, extending a hand. "Sir. I'm Dom Conner."

"I know."

Well aware there was more being communicated than simple introductions, Sami cut in smoothly "Dom Conner, please meet my father, Mike Evans."

Dom nodded, his wide legged stance easy. "It's nice to meet you, sir."

Mike said nothing at the congenial greeting, shifting all his attention to Sami. "I'm glad you're here."

"Is that why you sent out the welcoming committee?" She tilted her head in the direction of the men that still stood in the driveway but otherwise gave no indication they were there.

"I can't be too careful."

"Is that what this is?"

She hadn't intended to cause trouble within the first three minutes, but there was something about that escort through the property that still irritated her.

What if Dom hadn't been with her?

Would there still be an escort? Was this little show of dominance meant to send a message to Dom or to her?

Did it matter?

Questions upon questions and, sadly, not all that different from the type that had driven her from her family home in the first place.

How did he spend his days?

What did he know about her mother's death?

Would she ever feel safe?

The hard set of her father's jaw relaxed, and the grim line of his mouth creased up. "I'm glad you're here."

Despite the underlying reasons she was here, and the help she was willingly giving the FBI, Sami couldn't help but respond to that smile. "Thank you for having us."

"Why don't you come inside?"

"Just us?"

It was one more jab about the escort, but it hit its mark.

He lifted a hand and waved off the men still standing near Dom's truck. "I'd like for the three of us to have some time together. Some lunch, too."

"I'd like that, too."

As she heard the shuffling behind her, Sami took her first easy breath. She'd survived the escort and a reintroduction. She hadn't known if she'd want to hug him or not and was relieved the decision had been taken out of her hands.

She cared for him.

But she was wary all the same. Not just because of Dom's mission, either.

She'd spent her adult life dealing with the reality of who her father was and how he spent his days. The choices he made and the impact it had on her family, her mother most of all.

It didn't change the fact that she loved him, a larger-than-life figure.

But it left a wary confusion that she couldn't find any sense of equilibrium in. Did she hate him? No, not really. But did she love him?

That felt impossible, too.

It was the continuing confusion of her feelings that she'd lived with her entire adult life and she'd had long enough to know there wasn't an easy answer.

And, maybe, not an answer at all.

She and Dom followed Mike into the cabin. This was a new space for her father and Sami looked around, taking in the house as it spread out before her.

The home she had grown up in was much closer to Blue Larkspur, in a more traditional neighborhood. While the exterior of the cabin had looked simple and quaint, the interior was anything but. Everything was state of the art, from the alarm system visible via a panel near the front door to the small motion cameras she saw pinned in the corners of the hallway to the entertainment center that dominated the large living room.

The place had a serious set up, one more clue that while her dad might be out in the middle of nowhere, he was tapped into the very best tools and tech.

Dom had remained quiet, playing the part of the wide-eyed boyfriend, but he knew what was required of him. "Wow. This is quite a setup."

"Thank you." It was the kindest thing her father had said to Dom up until now, before Mike turned his full attention on the younger man. "Sami tells me you work construction."

"I do. I like roofing the best, but I can frame out a

house, Sheetrock the walls. Been working with an electrician who's been teaching me some things."

"A man who's not afraid to work hard."

Dom shrugged. "It's a life."

Sami pasted on a smile and shot Dom some googly eyes, willing a sort of besotted pride into her expression. If it wasn't too big a stretch, well, that was on her to worry about later. For now, they had a job to do and a very real need to convince her father the show they were putting on was 100 percent real.

"It's more than a life," Sami said, making a point to stare down at her left hand. "Dom's job is what brought us together."

"Yes, about that, Samantha." Mike started in, then stopped as he caught sight of the ring. "Are the two of you engaged?"

"We are. Dom just proposed few weeks ago." She extended her hand, showing off the ring. "I wanted to tell you in person and not on the phone."

Mike's eyes, a shade of hazel so like her own, narrowed. "How long have you been dating?"

Sami knew what he was really asking but refused to take the bait. "When you know, you know."

"How would you know anything? How long have you two even known each other?"

Whatever reams of baggage Sami carried over him, Mike's reaction was pure parental concern. His words were whip-quick, spitting out into the room like bullets, and it was enough to have Dom stepping forward.

"I'm in love with your daughter, sir. And I want to marry her."

"You barely know each other."

"How would you know that?" Sami asked.

"I—" He stopped. "I make a point to keep on top of things."

"Then you should know I haven't been happy for a very long time. Dom makes me happy."

She stared down her father, that immediate ability for the two of them to rile each other up coming back as if second nature.

Wasn't this how it always was?

Mike didn't appear convinced, but he did soften his attitude. "I invited you both here for lunch. Why don't we get to it?"

"That sounds great."

As she followed her father down the hallway to the kitchen, Sami reached for Dom's hand. It was only as his fingers linked with hers that she realized how easily she'd reached for that support.

And how effortlessly it was offered in return.

DOM CATALOGUED EACH moment of the exchange with Lone Wolf Evans, twisting and turning each syllable the man had spoken through an internal filter in his mind.

Behaving in a way that suggested dominance. Check.

Using intimidation tactics, even if subtle. Check again.

Happy to see his daughter?

It was that last one Dom kept coming back to, over and over. He hadn't missed the look of love and—relief?—that had filled Mike Evans's gaze the moment he stepped from the cabin and laid eyes on his daughter.

Had he believed she wouldn't come?

Or was it something more?

If that was the case, why was he so determined to pull the welcome routine with his thugs?

Dom considered the cabin as they walked the last few feet into the kitchen. The place was state of the art, no question about it. It matched the intel his team had gathered, from the Warlords use of satellite phones to the imagery the FBI's drones had gotten of a shed on the property believed to be the tech nerve center of the Warlords.

Evans had some set up out here, in the wilds of Colorado. Which meant he either had the wherewithal to fund tech as a key part of his organization or he had a serious benefactor who wanted Mike in communications range at all times.

For his money, Dom was betting on the latter.

The early intel they had from the Warlords' first run as a major criminal enterprise had suggested they'd tripped up a few times because they didn't have the full lay of the land or the position of their enemies. Mistakes that could have been avoided with the proper use of technology to keep their information network whole and functioning.

It was obviously a mistake the man wasn't making twice.

Even if Dom continued to puzzle over the specifics.

As of yet, the FBI hadn't cracked the compound. Aside from the aerial photos, they hadn't gotten a bead on the Warlords' communications or managed to infiltrate any of it.

Which was another gap in their ability to understand who was pulling the strings.

They all settled in at the kitchen table, lunch already spread out before them. There were various sandwiches, plated and cut, a quiche, a tossed salad and even a fruit salad.

"Wow, Dad, this is quite a spread."

"I wanted you to feel welcome in my home."

"Thank you."

They helped themselves to food and for a little while, the conversation flowed easily. Mike asked Sami about her business, and she talked about various jobs that she worked and the way landscaping changed along with the seasons.

There was an eagerness in Mike's questions as he asked her about various shrubs, or types of drainage, or even some of the lighting work she and her crew did around the holidays. It struck him that for all the intel the International Corruption Unit had on the man, this thirst for details on his daughter's life hadn't even been on their radar.

Had they been too focused on her possibly being in cahoots with Evans that they never considered the father-daughter relationship from any other angle?

Families were complicated, a fact Dom well knew. His own certainly was and that was only partially because of his father's bad decisions. Being part of such a large group of siblings added inherent drama and complexity to already intricate interpersonal dynamics. Age, the closeness between the various multiples in his family and even the individual goals each had chosen for their profession added to the complexity.

And it did make him wonder.

Mike Evans had given his daughter space for a long time. Yet, here he was, reaching out to her at the same time he'd resurrected his dominance with the Warlords, reestablishing the drug trade in the region.

Why now?

What did he want from Sami?

CALEB COLTON STARED down at the file on his desk, an uncomfortable feeling swirling in his gut. He took a sip of coffee but the brew—now cold—felt like ash coating his tongue.

Had he made a mistake?

He'd spent his adult life focused on running the Truth Foundation in tandem with Colton & Colton. Part legal calling, part personal exoneration, the organization had given him, his twin sister, Morgan, and his broader array of siblings purpose over the past decade.

The Truth Foundation's mission was to ensure justice was served and they'd been focused on the victims of their father's poor decisions on the bench since the organization's founding.

In all that time since, juggling both his legal work as well as the Foundation's mission, it had always seemed easy. And with each case the Foundation took on—and the innocence granted for victim after victim of his father's greed on the bench—Caleb had felt a wash of satisfaction and absolution.

So why couldn't he find any of that now?

"That's an awfully sour face for a blissfully engaged man." Morgan barreled into the room.

Caleb knew his twin had intended the comment as a joke, but he couldn't find any humor as he stared up at the face he knew nearly as well as his own.

"You got a minute?"

"Of course." Morgan took a seat opposite his desk, any hint of humor fading as her expression turned serious. "What's going on?"

Although he trusted their staff implicitly, that nagging in his stomach refused to abate. Caleb got up and walked over to close the door before returning to his desk. "You ever get that feeling you missed something on a case?"

"Not too often, because I hate it," Morgan said, "But yes, I know what you're talking about. That sense you missed something big."

"I think we missed something with Ronald Spence."

"What?" Morgan sat forward on her chair. "How?"

Caleb tapped the file on his desk, now thick with paperwork and notes built over the past few months. Ronald Spence, their father's last case, the final person their father had sentenced, another possible victim of his illicit decision-making on the bench, had come to the Truth Foundation, eager to have his case reviewed. Caleb had taken it on, never entirely sure if the man was innocent. Yet at the same time, there wasn't enough concrete evidence to keep him in jail anymore, after Clay Houseman had confessed to Spence's crimes. That sense of ambiguity had spurred Caleb on through the discovery phase and into the continued pressure on the DA's office to review Spence's case.

His father had made quick work of any person who came before his bench with petty crimes, using those prior poor decisions as an excuse to find guilt on larger crimes. Ben's impressive presence on the bench—and his understanding that those prior petty crimes could easily influence a jury—had been one of the core tenets of his approach to getting innocents sentenced.

Knowing that, it had all seemed open-and-shut the prior month when the DA's office arrested Clay Houseman for his long list of crimes. Crimes that included several erroneously believed to have been perpetrated by Spence.

"I've been looking at this file from Rachel." Their sister had recused herself from the Houseman case when she realized the connection to their father, but as district attorney she'd helped close-up the paperwork once Houseman was arrested and put away. "Something about Clay Houseman's arrest is bothering me."

"But Houseman was a lock." Morgan argued. "The guy did Spence's crimes. It's why Spence is out free."

It had taken a few weeks, but Caleb finally had all the motions and filings in hand from the county's prosecution of Houseman. The man had perpetrated several crimes that their father had originally attributed to Ronald Spence. The DA's office had handled the Houseman case to the letter of the law; only now Caleb wasn't so sure they'd gotten it right.

On the surface, it looked like Houseman had been guilty. He'd confessed to them, after all.

But still, Caleb wondered.

"Do you think there's some agreement between Spence and Houseman?" Morgan asked. "I wouldn't go so far as to say honor among thieves, but if the score's big enough, they could be working together."

"I just don't know." Caleb turned the file around, tapping the page that he'd read and reread about four times now. "But read this."

Morgan stood and leaned over the desk, her light blue eyes focused completely on the page of legalese. "Houseman was noted and present for the smuggling operation that was taken down a month before Spence was convicted."

"At which point Spence was already in jail."

"But that doesn't mean he didn't have a connection to the outside." His twin caught Caleb's train of thought immediately. "And if the two of them were working together, then they could be doing so now. Reinforcing the doubts we've had all along."

"Exactly." Caleb nodded, that convenient connection between the two men driving his concerns.

"We can't sit on this, Caleb. We took on the case and we need to own the consequences if Spence isn't really innocent."

"I agree."

And he did. What he hadn't been able to reconcile is whom they should go to with their suspicions. The DA's office had a person in custody with a confession. He had no doubt his sister Rachel would pursue any line of inquiry he raised, but Caleb also knew that, as shorthanded as they always were, they were going to need something real and tangible to go on.

His gut might mean something to him, but he needed something more substantial to activate any pertinent legal channels.

"Dom might have something." Morgan tapped the file once more, her gaze thoughtful. "His division of the ICU has been focused on drug-trafficking crimes in this part of Colorado. At minimum, he might be able to match up a few dates for us. See if we can't figure out where Spence was or see if that tickle in the gut is because there's something real to worry about."

"You think our little brother's going to feel particularly cooperative, knowing we possibly put one of his problems back out on the streets?"

"Better now than later. Aubrey mentioned she and Luke saw him a few days ago."

"He's in town?"

"You know how he likes to keep his professional life on lockdown but he did go to visit her. She protected his privacy and the reason for his visit but I got the sense Dom was working something."

"In this part of the state?" Caleb asked.

"So it seems. Do you think it could help us understand what's going on here?"

"I wish I knew." Caleb shook his head before dropping his gaze back to the folder and the possible incriminations inside of it. "Damn it. I thought we were doing the right thing."

She laid a hand over his, that strong, firm grip laced with support and understanding.

"We are doing the right thing. Getting justice for innocent people is always right."

Caleb looked up at his sister. "And if Spence is dirty?"

"Then we put him right back where he belongs."

Chapter Nine

Dom took a sip of his beer and considered Mike Evans across the living room. He'd deliberately worn a T-shirt for the day and knew Evans had seen the lion tattoo on his forearm, but the man hadn't said a word.

In fact, if Dom hadn't seen those hazel eyes flick over the beast when he'd reached for a sandwich at lunch, he'd have assumed the tat hadn't even registered.

Yet again, Lone Wolf Evans was a mystery. A shady figure the ICU had followed for years with minimal proof but a hell of a lot of suspicion. Now, in his company for the past few hours, Dom sensed some of the reasons why.

Evans knew how to keep his own counsel. He wasn't easily ruffled. And, probably most of all, when he chose to turn it on, the man had a congenial air that didn't hint at what he was truly capable of.

It was cold and calculating and, despite Dom's best efforts to tamp down on the train of thought, it brought to mind his own father.

Hadn't Ben Colton shown much of the same? That strange, mercurial ability to shut out the seamier side of his life when he chose to be warm, welcoming and magnanimous? Even now, twenty years later, he could still remember his father. The sheer presence of the man and how he ruled the Colton clan with a tender mix of love, affection and authority.

Ben Colton had been a *parent*. A good one. It was too bad he wasn't a very good man.

A fact he'd accepted a long time ago but which seemed more present as of the past week. Ever since Sami.

Ever since he'd been forced to acknowledge that for all his efforts to shield himself from the reality of life with a big job with a lot of authority, he wasn't nearly as well-adjusted as he'd believed.

And his father's betrayal had left him with a lot more hurt than he'd ever really acknowledged.

The Truth Foundation likely served some of that purpose for Caleb and Morgan. A vindication, of sorts, using their professional talents to make up for what had come before. But even with action—was that really addressing the problem deep down?

Did helping others with their burdens erase your own?

Because while that was beneficial to the recipient, Dom wasn't sure any amount of action could ever fully erase the way you felt. Maybe he thought that once, when he'd gone into the FBI, but after all this time he wasn't so sure.

Maybe the anger you carried just made you feel helpless and small.

All were thoughts that deserved their time and place, but likely not in the here and now.

Because Mike Evans and the thugs that lurked on the property around them were a very large problem, as was the shadowy entity helping them.

"I'm going to excuse myself for a minute. Can I get anyone anything on my way back? Another beer?" She asked the question of both Dom and her father, the light touch to his shoulder an added gesture of warmth.

"I'll pass," he said, laying a hand over hers. "Not with driving home."

Although he meant the point about the beer absolutely, he didn't miss the small beat of respect that filled Mike's gaze before the man nodded at Sami. "I'll have one more if you don't mind."

"Be back in a minute."

She left and the atmosphere shifted in the room, the air feeling even, if the actual temperature had nothing to do with it.

"You seem to be rushing things a bit with my daughter, don't you think?"

"I love her and I want to make a life with her."

"She know about that?" Mike tapped his tattooed arm.

Dom had braced for any number of comments and ways into the conversation, but he hadn't given much credence to the direct approach. Pleased there was little need to prevaricate, Dom started right in. "I am who I am. Your daughter doesn't seem to mind much."

He took the last sip of his beer before setting it on the small end table beside his chair. "I suppose she's used to what she grew up with."

"My daughter didn't grow up here."

"Sure, sure." Dom leaned forward, his forearms on his thighs. "But she's not fazed by this life. In fact, I think she'd feel good about you and I getting to know each other better. Me taking a part in the family business, as it were."

Mike only continued to stare him down, a mix of speculation and respect in his gaze. "And what family business is that?"

"One that requires a tail and an escort from Blue Larkspur into the compound."

"You give me too much credit. I'm just looking out for my little girl."

"Like you have for the past decade?"

Dom didn't want to blow this gig but he wasn't inclined to give Mike too much leeway, either. The man had left his daughter vulnerable. Likely the only good thing he'd done was get out of her life. But an enterprising thug with revenge on his mind could easily have come after Sami.

Hell, look how easily he'd sidled up to her.

At the thought of the lies he'd told to get into her good graces, a shot of something dark and sour swirled in his stomach. He'd done what he had to do, but that didn't make it right. Nor did it make him feel a hell of a lot better about any of it.

"My relationship with my daughter is my business."

"And now it's mine."

Whatever else he'd come here to do, Dom wasn't backing off that point, and it was essential Evans knew that.

He'd take whatever initiation was required into the Warlords. He'd do what he had to do in order to gain Lone Wolf's trust.

But Sami's safety was nonnegotiable.

Mike considered him across the expanse of the coffee table that separated them before nodding. "Come back Wednesday night. My guys have some work to do and they could use an extra pair of hands."

"I'll be here."

Sami chose that moment to come back in, a beer for her father in one hand along with a few sodas for her and Dom in the other. "What's happening Wednesday?"

"Dom offered to help out with some work here around the house. You both can come back then." Mike kept his attention on Sami, his smile broad. "It'll give us a chance to get to know each other better."

"KNOW EACH OTHER BETTER?"

Dom had barely cleared the compound when Sami started in. She'd recognized she was going to get little out of two close-lipped men inside Mike's home, but she'd expected better of Dom once they left the cabin. Only he had a sour look on his too-gorgeous face, his mouth turned down, indicating he had no interest in answering her question.

It was only as he glanced in the rearview mirror and, satisfied no one was behind them, shook his head, mouthing, *Not now.*

If not now, then when?

She nearly asked him that when she caught the shake of his head before he smoothly answered her question with vague platitudes. "I'm looking forward to getting to know your dad a bit better. After all, I am marrying his daughter."

The sweet tone of his voice shot straight to her head, even as she tried to keep herself in line.

It's not real.

But the sweet line did have its desired effect, some semblance of understanding dawning. She dug her phone out of her purse while making small talk about their lunch and the afternoon. It was only when she held up her phone, letters typed across the face, that Dom nodded, recognizing she understood.

YOU THINK THE TRUCK IS BUGGED?

He nodded before mouthing, *It's possible.*

One more unexpected treasure in a week full of them. Had those goons who stood outside her father's home really bugged Dom's car?

And what if they had?

What if they'd done more than that?

Suddenly, the haven she considered her own home took on a new dimension.

Had her father been following her? Keeping tabs on her all these years? Here she was, blithely assuming she was free of that influence for nearly a decade, and all the while he might have been aware of all she did through some sort of weird, grasping secretive over-sight.

It was worse than knowing that he was a criminal, and that was no freaking picnic.

But to think that it was possible she'd never really had any privacy?

She shivered at the thought, disappointed in her dad *and* in herself.

Had she been living in a fantasy world all these years?

The drive back to Blue Larkspur felt endless, but Sami filled it with odd snippets of conversation about work and a relatively boring string of questions about roofing she wasn't all that interested in but passed the time.

Dom seemed to understand her strategy because he peppered his answers with some silly anecdotes about nearly falling off a slate roof and about rescuing a cat the prior summer that she figured were made up. But as she pictured the one-eyed, three-legged pet he described, she couldn't hold back her amusement.

The man could tell a tall tale, that was for sure. A side effect of being one of twelve children? Or a talent all his own, regardless of circumstance?

She let out her first easy breath when Dom pulled into her driveway, already leaping out of the truck as Dom put it into Park and had her front door open before she heard the truck fully turn off.

Home greeted her. The familiar walls and the specific arrangement of her throw pillows and the light scent of pumpkin spice from the fall-scented candle she loved too much not to burn year-round.

They were all there, waiting for her.

Even if those unsettling thoughts continued to trouble her. If they were worried about listening devices in the truck, was it possible her home was bugged, too?

She didn't know what to believe anymore but she also hadn't gotten any sense from her time with her father today that he knew things about her.

Dom stood beside her, his arm on her shoulder gentle. "Are you okay?"

"Good. Fine. I'm—" The stress of the day and the frustration and fear she'd harbored the entire ride home—exacerbated somehow by the risk that her father's thugs might have bugged Dom's truck—rose up and grabbed her by the throat.

Instead of strong, confident, competent words, all that came out was a harsh sob.

Dom pulled her against his chest and she took solace in his solid form and the ready press of his arms around her body.

Here was safety.

And here was an escape from the fear that had suddenly consumed her, altering the way she thought of her only remaining parent.

Because that was the real rub of this whole thing.

The mental truce she'd managed to erect in her mind—allowing her father to do his thing and believing that she could do hers—had all been a farce.

A lie she'd told herself over and over to be shielded from the truth.

Mike Evans was a bad man who'd made bad choices at every opportunity. Choices that had killed her mother, even if that was by association. And choices that had ensured she'd never really be free of the dark miasma that shrouded his life.

Her grandmother had tried to safeguard her from it all. With the small inheritance that provided for her home and her business, she had done the best she could to see that Sami had a future.

But even Gram couldn't have predicted just how close the past was now—and had always been—nipping at her heels.

"Hey there. It's okay now." He rubbed large circles over her back, his voice soothing as he gave her the time and the space to cry it out. "It's a lot to take on, I know. But you did great today. You were so amazing the entire time."

She heard the words and felt the comforting touch, but it was the steady beat of his heart beneath her ear that did the most to calm her.

And in the quiet calm, standing there in his arms, Sami recognized the truth. She was falling for him. It wasn't the best idea, given the circumstances, and she had no reason to feel the way that she did.

But smart or not, it didn't make her feelings any less real.

Which made them dangerous.

So she'd have to channel them in order to convince her father and his crew how she felt about Dom and then turn it off when she was with him. It was the only way to preserve some semblance of her heart for when this was all over.

If she'd questioned that at all over the past week, since discovering whom Dom really was and the fact that her father wanted her back in his life, she didn't any longer.

The Feds were on to Mike's games and his days committing crimes were coming to an end.

Soon.

Dom was committed to that outcome and, by joining up with him, she'd committed herself to the same. A part of her—a very small part— questioned if she was a bad daughter. But the bigger part of her—the part that had lived for years without a mother—knew the truth.

Her father needed to be stopped.

Her interest in and attraction to Dom might be misplaced, but her belief in his ability to get the job done and infiltrate the Warlords wasn't.

She just had to hold on to that faith a bit longer.

And do everything in her power to keep her heart safe.

DOM WAS STILL rattled by Sami's response to their trip to Warlords territory a few hours later as he ran a debugging device over his truck. He hadn't wanted to leave her, but after ordering in a pizza and debriefing on the day, she'd seemed to find her equilibrium again. Add on the need to use the equipment at his own home and to pack to move in with her, Dom had headed back to his rental.

The house was still larger than he'd needed, but he hadn't wanted to be in an apartment as he did his work in Blue Larkspur, nor was he willing to go to his mother's home, since he was working a job. The risks to civilians was limited, knowing how far out the War-lords stayed in their attempts to keep to themselves, but he'd still wanted something that was an individual dwelling in the event things went sideways.

His neighbors were a bit too close for Dom's comfort, but there was still a fair amount of space between the properties and the FBI kept it regularly mowed, using two undercover agents posing as lawn maintenance to maintain perimeter checks and proper surveillance set on the house.

And he had a garage.

The two-car garage was windowless, which was perfect for what he needed to do now and what he'd need to do each and every time he came back from Warlord territory. He couldn't risk keeping anything in the truck that might tip Mike's goons off, but he couldn't rule out the continued possibility of electronic surveillance, especially after seeing how sophisticated the setup was out at the compound.

As he turned off the small hand-held device— one he'd run throughout Sami's home earlier—and shifted to one last visual check, Dom considered all he'd learned today.

The hi-tech electronics were only the start. Regardless of how Mike Evans had gotten his motorcycle club back in business, the fact remained the MC had laid low for many years. In order for their set up to be as slick as it was, they either had a lot more cash rolling in than the FBI suspected to date, or they'd been set up from the jump.

For his money, Dom was betting on the latter.

A point he felt even more confident about when the bug check confirmed he hadn't driven home with an electronic tail. One more point of proof that they might have an impressive tech setup but using them wasn't second nature yet.

What he had driven home with was the knowledge that this job was going to take a lot more emotional fortitude than he'd anticipated.

Sami's response once they got back to her house had been the pure let down of adrenaline. A fact reinforced when she'd sat yawning on her couch after they'd finished a pizza. He knew it himself and often slept like the proverbial dead after a mission wrapped, the need to recharge something that happened on a cellular level.

If it were only that, he could see past it. But in this case, he recognized there was more at stake. Whatever she might feel—and her willingness to help the FBI against her father was a pretty serious sign of her commitment—Mike Evans was still her dad.

And as he'd discovered dealing with his complicated feelings about his own dad, nothing about this op would be easy.

His phone buzzed and Dom saw his older brother's name on the readout. He picked up, offering a brotherly "Yo" when Caleb answered.

"Where are you?"

"In the garage."

"I need to talk to you."

"Meet me at the Corner Pocket. Fifteen minutes."

At Caleb's quick agreement, Dom opted for the motorcycle tucked away in the garage. He wasn't a big rider, but the FBI had added the sleek ride to augment his cover story and give him a more seamless in with the Warlords. Since it was pointless to put a listening device on a motorcycle, Dom figured it would give an added layer of protection if Evans's goons decided to make another run at him tonight.

Even if things had been suspiciously quiet since he and Sami had driven home from the compound.

In less than fifteen minutes, Dom had settled himself in one of the Corner Pocket's back booths, the dim lighting giving him a bit more peace of mind about being out. But it was Caleb's grim face when he slid into the opposite side that had Dom wondering if *peace* was quite the right word.

"What's with all this?" his brother started in.

"I can't tell you much, but I'm on a job. No one can see you at my house."

Caleb shot an uneasy glance around the bar. "And this is better?"

Dom shot him a wry grin. "I can say you're my lawyer if anyone asks."

As alibis went, that one actually wasn't half bad.

The crowd was quiet and Roman DiMera, the owner, came over himself to see what they wanted. Dom wasn't familiar with the man, but Caleb greeted him warmly before extending a hand to Dom. He kept up the ruse, introducing himself as Dom Conner, unsurprised when the stoic DiMera shook his hand with a promise to pull the draughts and no small talk.

"What did you need to talk to me about?"

"What do you know about Ronald Spence?"

"That guy exonerated as part of the Truth Foundation's last case?"

"The last case involving Dad," Caleb corrected, lowering his voice on the last word.

"Right. Sure."

His brother and sister felt strongly about their work. But it was still a surprise that Caleb came out this late to discuss it with him.

"What's this all about?"

"Rachel had a case prosecuted through the DA's office. Guy was ultimately convicted of the crimes Spence was in jail for."

"So he got off."

"Only—" Caleb broke off, thanking Roman for the two draughts before the owner disappeared as fast as he'd arrived. Once he was out of earshot, Caleb added, "Only Morgan and I are starting to wonder."

"You think he's guilty?"

"I think the guy's still suspicious. Even more so now that I've done some off-the-record digging all afternoon."

"You aren't one to miss the big stuff. Why'd you take him on in the first place if you had concerns."

"That's the problem. It seemed open-and-shut. Another one of Da... Judge Colton's messes. Either I was off my game, believing the context over the substance of the case, or I missed the signs. But the guy who is now doing time went awfully willingly when there was already a warm body sitting in jail for the same crimes."

Dom listened as his brother walked him through the rest of it and let a few ideas of his own play out.

If Spence wasn't innocent and had been working from the shadows all this time, was it possible he was the ringleader Dom kept wondering about when it came to the Warlords?

The startup costs to get going again.

The ready access to supply that just sort of started again, without any word of gang violence or turf wars.

And then that tech piece that Dom had puzzled over all night. Was Spence a wiz there?

Even if the guy had tech skills, he'd have to be pretty charismatic, too, to get someone else to take the rap for him. Either that or more powerful than Caleb and Morgan had thought when they were reviewing his case.

"I'll have someone on my team look into it."

"You won't?"

"I'm a bit busy for the next few weeks."

"What's going on with you?"

Caleb missed nothing—it was what made him an outstanding lawyer—but Dom had spent a long time avoiding familial scrutiny. Like a slippery eel, he knew when and how to evade.

"My job."

"Dom—"

He waved a hand, cutting his brother off before Caleb could get a head of steam. "I'll keep you posted on what I find out. But you need to give me space. And don't come over to my house again."

Caleb nodded, his features drawn and, Dom recognized, tired. Caleb had always carried a sizeable workload, but now that he'd found Nadine and was engaged, Dom had figured his brother had found some balance in his life.

"Why are you here with me instead of home with your fiancée?"

"She understands." Caleb shrugged and took one last sip of his beer. "She knows what drives me because it drives her, too. That's why she fought for justice for her father and she knows I need to find that for others. Why she continues to advocate for others, too. That's a gift, you know."

Dom knew that. What he hadn't realized was just how much still weighed on Caleb's shoulders.

One more gift from their father that kept on giving.

Here Caleb was, trying to do right by Ben Colton's victims, only to find out he might have made a mistake. That was a heavy load to bear—both as the righter of wrongs and as the one responsible for parsing through the bad to try and find the good.

"Get out of here and get home. The beers are on me."

"I can wait."

"Get out of here. And you came to the right place. I can do some digging and see if your gut is playing fair or just giving you cold feet about your upcoming nuptials."

Caleb grinned and for the first time since they sat down, Dom saw a shimmer of the boy he remembered growing up with. Although he'd always had Oliver and Ezra, Caleb was only three years older than the three of them. The four of them had made a merry crew more often than not.

The weight of their father's crimes had hung heavy on them all, but heavier than most on Caleb, who had felt the additional responsibility of helping raise his younger siblings. So it was good to see him light up.

"My feet are very, very warm."

"Then get out of here and go kiss Nadine. I'll let you know what I find out."

"Deal." Caleb nodded and slid to the edge of the booth before seeming to think better of it. On a last note of caution, he added, "I know you don't need me to say this, but watch your back."

"Consider it done."

Caleb said nothing more, just headed for the exit. As covers went, they'd certainly looked deep in conversation. But again, other than the two beers, Dom figured he could spin a story if one was needed as to why he was meeting with a lawyer from Blue Larkspur on a Monday night.

What struck him as the real surprise in the whole meeting was the way he was still thinking about his brother's besotted grin when Caleb spoke of Nadine. Had Dom ever felt like that for anyone?

When Sami's face filled his mind's eye, he surprised himself even more by not shrinking away from the sudden heat that filled him. Although he wasn't a particularly big believer in happy ever after, he had to admit that she was the first woman he'd ever spent time with who made him understand why it was a possibility for some.

Waiting another ten minutes, Dom tossed a twenty on the table and stood to leave. He nodded at DiMera, who still stood behind the bar, then walked out into the night air.

It might have been May, but at this altitude there was

still a decided chill in the air and he shrugged into his coat before climbing on the back of his bike.

It was only as he lifted his foot to hit the starter pedal that he felt the distinct shape of metal against his lower back.

And the second distinct click of a gun safety being removed a few feet away.

Chapter Ten

Dom cursed himself a million ways to Sunday before turning to look at the jerk who had a gun pressed to his side. He kept his movements slow, his hands firmly on the motorcycle's handlebars, as he took in one of the goons from earlier that day outside Lone Wolf's house.

"Well, what have we here? You guys sure are spending an awful lot of time keeping an eye on me. Your boss give you the orders to play babysitter?"

The barb appeared to meet its desired mark; the weapon at his back was dropped. "We ain't no babysitters."

"Could have fooled me."

"You're a party of interest." The one with the unlocked gun made a show of putting the safety back on. "That's all."

"Because I'm marrying the boss's daughter."

"Because the boss don't like lying weasels."

"What am I lying about?"

The goon who'd already popped the safety back on used the tip of his gun to tap at Dom's forearm, clearly focused on something beneath his jacket sleeve. "The tat you're sporting says you've done the work. Boss isn't so sure."

"If he's so concerned about it, why doesn't he ask me himself? I already volunteered for duty."

That tidbit seemed to catch both of Evans's thugs off guard. The one who'd stood behind him came around to face Dom from the front of the motorcycle. "Volunteered?"

"Yeah." Dom shrugged, playing it casual but intrigued by the obvious lack of detail Evans had shared with his henchmen. "I'm marrying in. I want to give my time to the family business. Spending my days walking around on people's roofs isn't a hell of a lot of fun. And drywalling in the summer's like working in hell."

The bigger of the two laughed. "Did a few summers working construction when I was a kid. It sucked."

Dom stared the guy down, then the other one. "You let Lone Wolf know you paid me a visit and that I'm all in, just like I told him today."

The other thug brightened with an idea before his gaze turned dark. "Who were you in the bar with?"

Dom considered how to play it, knowing he could still fall back on the lawyer angle, but curious if they'd cased the bar or not. He didn't recall seeing them inside and there was no reason to overplay his hand and lead on he was with someone if they hadn't noticed.

"Myself."

"Why you doing that when you have a sweet fiancée at home?"

He hunched his shoulders but shot a dark look at the question. "Why do you care?"

"Just asking."

"I've got business in town and I needed to see to a few of my interests."

"Boss isn't gonna like it if you're two-timing his daughter. Or two-timing his business, either."

Dom sensed the man's interest—and his eagerness to trip up the boss's future son-in-law with whatever he could find. It was yet another show of the hand and more insight into what Evans did—and didn't—share with his employees. He puffed up his chest and moved a few steps closer. "I got nothing of interest that'll affect him. And I'm not two-timing his daughter. Anyone who says otherwise goes through me."

"She's a sweet piece."

He needed to keep his head. Realistically, he might need to *act* like a hothead, but actually behaving like one would get him nowhere.

But the derogatory mention of Sami had Dom seeing red.

Without care for the gun or his own safety at that point, he pushed himself right into Evans's thug, getting up into the man's leering face. "She's my fiancée. You'd do well to remember that."

"Whoa!" The guy lifted his hands before he seemed to realize he had a gun glinting under the lights of the Corner Pocket's parking lot. He tucked his weapon back into the holster under his jacket before lifting his hands. "Calm down."

"Not about her. I'm not calm about her. You get me?"

"Yeah, pal. I get ya."

Dom held his ground, a wash of red still hazing his vision.

This might be a job and he might be undercover, but Sami was *his*. There was no room for negotiation on that.

The response was elemental and sometime later he knew he might think about how quickly his emotions escalated, but in the moment, all that mattered was sending a message.

One that Evans's goons responded to.

The bigger guy moved back first before laying a hand on his buddy's chest, the two of them taking a couple of clear steps back from Dom's bike.

The thug spoke once more. "Boss said you're coming back out on Wednesday. I'm Bryce. This is Neal."

Dom nodded.

"We'll see if there's a place for you in the Warlords then."

Dom said nothing else, just kept his gaze firm and steady as they climbed back into the sedan that had followed him and Sami.

He was still standing there five minutes later, long after the car had left the parking lot of the Corner Pocket. As he breathed in the cool mountain air, that haze finally receded from his vision. Dom let the other impressions of the night flow back in with his now-even breathing.

And recognized he was in a hell of a lot deeper than he'd ever imagined.

SAMI ROAMED AROUND the house, restless after waking up from a nap on the couch. The day with her father had been overwhelming on every level, and after the emotional stress and strain, she'd fallen asleep with little difficulty.

Only now, wide-awake, any sense of peace she'd found had vanished.

Dom had left over three hours ago to go to his house

and get his things for their fake living arrangements and he still wasn't back. She'd finally given in and texted him about an hour before, but nothing had come winging back, his standard cheeky mix of reassurance and flirty undertones absent.

Where was he?

His job had a lot of facets and it was very possible he was working, talking with his team and game planning the next few weeks. He hadn't given her a specific time he'd arrive home and besides, he was a grown man, well able to take care of himself.

Even if her continued mental admonitions that he was fine hadn't brought a lick of peace.

Had her father interfered again?

Sent more of his thugs to harass Dom?

At that thought, she'd casually hovered near her windows, peeking around the edge of the curtains to see if anyone was visible outside.

But her repeated inspections as she paced the living room hadn't turned up anything on that front, either.

And what about her father?

He said he was looking forward to seeing them again on Wednesday. It would hardly make sense to send someone to hurt Dom when they'd promised that they'd both be back. But could she trust anything when it came to him?

The day hadn't been what she'd expected, that was for sure. After the initial shock of realizing that her dad had aged, she'd settled into the flow of conversation. He'd asked her about her work and how her business was faring and seemed genuinely impressed when she talked about her job and her profits from the past few seasons.

He'd seemed proud of her, too, which had set heavily on her shoulders.

Was it okay to feel good under that attention?

Wasn't she spending time with him solely because she believed that his crimes needed to stop? Feeling good about his praise flew in the face of that in every way.

Besides, she mentally groused to herself, it was confusing.

The distant roar of a motorcycle grew louder, ultimately resolving in her front driveway. She raced to the door and nearly threw it open in relief before remembering to stop and check the windows.

Dom!

She hadn't seen him on a motorcycle yet and while it wasn't entirely a surprise he had one, she hadn't expected that warm shot of attraction as he lifted his powerful body off the bike, one jean-clad leg firmly planted on the ground as the other came over the seat.

As she gave that attraction a few more seconds just to be—as she was secretly looking at him through the front window—she recognized the truth. If she questioned her emotions over her father, the ones she had for Dom were abundantly clear. They were misplaced, with no room to explore them as they navigated this tense time with the Warlords, but they were as clear as freshly cleaned glass.

And they had to stop, no matter how good the man looked on a motorcycle.

Or any other place for that matter.

It was funny, she reflected, as she dropped the curtain, unwilling to be caught peeping. She kept coming back to the physical, likely because he was so *pres-*

ent. But the physical was only a small part of what attracted her to him.

There was a core of honor in him that tugged at her. Deeply. There was also a kindness, one that wasn't readily apparent in the gruff demeanor he was able to slip into so easily for his job. But it was there all the same. She'd seen flashes of it but had seen it most readily the other night when they were with his sister. He'd carried an indulgent smile for Aubrey throughout the evening that spoke of deep care and affection.

Even if what tugged at Sami the most about Dom was the lingering loneliness that swirled in his bright dark blue gaze.

A loneliness that had drawn her from the first, because in it she sensed the familiar. Someone who, like her, understood what it was to spend long hours and days alone. More, someone who understood what it was to face life armed with little more than their own moxie and determination.

She'd always believed it was her lot in life because she was an only child. But as one of twelve kids, Dom had given her a new perspective. Maybe her life and her choices were a product of her and her view of the world, not her circumstances. She depended on herself and, on pretty much every level, she liked it that way.

Even if she'd reveled in opening up and sharing some of the current load with Dom.

She also couldn't deny that feeling of kinship at knowing they'd both survived life-changing disappointments from a parent. Her father's behavior was always something she'd tried to ignore, but it was a stark realization to see the same lived experiences in someone else—and come to understand much of her view of the world had been shaped by her father's actions.

The knock on the door, followed by a shout announcing himself, had her flinging open the thick oak. Without checking the impulse, she pulled him close.

Because someone might be watching?

That thought crossed oh so briefly through her mind before she admitted that it really didn't matter. He was here and she wanted the reassurance that he was safe and whole and in her arms.

Dom's lips found hers and what she'd intended as a greeting that reinforced the roles they were playing turned immediately into so much more. Hot liquid heat curled in her belly at the hard press of his mouth, the urgent and sexy play of lips and tongues taking her under.

Had she ever been kissed like this?

Like she was consumed by fire and a delicious sort of electricity all at once.

Her entire body responded, lighting up her nerve endings with pleasure and an urgency that tempted and teased, even as it left concern swirling in its wake. Temptation because it made her want to throw all her cautions to the wind and sleep with him again. And concern because that temptation was steeped as much in a physical need as an emotional one.

Not quite ready to choose a path, she gave in to the kiss instead, taking what he offered and forcing herself to accept it was enough. Because right now, in this moment, it had to be.

As if he sensed they should go no further, Dom lifted his head. "Hi."

"Hey."

Suddenly conscious they were, once again, standing in her front doorway, she moved around him to close the door, giving herself a bit of distance from all those swirling emotions.

And don't forget the sex, those small-but-powerful urges screamed through her. They only served to irritate her even more as her gaze lingered over the broad lines of his back. Oh, how easily her traitorous body was willing to override her mind on that. Even her steady reprimands to herself that he'd lied about who he was had lost its luster.

Yeah, fine, he'd lied to do his job. She now knew who he was, and he'd shot straight with her ever since. Continuing to hang on to her ire with a tight grip felt useless.

Especially since you'd rather be hanging onto him.

Since she was doing a very poor job of talking herself out of dragging the man to her bedroom, she figured she'd better start talking to distract herself. "Everything okay?"

"Yeah. Fine. Sort of." He ran a hand through his hair before dropping it back to his side. "No."

"Tell me about it." She gestured him toward the couch in the living room, deliberately taking the seat that cornered the couch instead of sitting directly beside him.

In a matter of minutes, she understood what had taken him so long, between gathering his things at his own home, the conversation with his brother and then the reality of her father's thugs following him once more.

A reality that only added to her own conflicting feelings about Mike Evans.

"Do you think they were acting alone? Or at my father's command?"

Dom shrugged. "It wasn't clear. I think they're still pissed I shook their tail last night and they're trying to make up for it. Show the boss they know how to do their jobs."

"By following you around town?"

"By getting as much intel on me as they can to feed back to him. A ploy to get back in his good graces."

"Your offer of joining up with the Warlords wasn't enough?" While she hadn't spent much time in her dad's orbit these last ten years, she knew enough about human nature to know that people reacted poorly when pushed into a corner. Dom's ability to lose the two gangsters on the road when they'd been given direct orders to follow after her and Dom likely had caused trouble for them with her father.

Which meant it was now going to cause trouble for Dom.

"I can do something about this. I can tell my father he needs to call them off."

The alarm was clear in his eyes but it was the fierce tone of his words that pulled her up short. "You don't need to do that. In fact, don't do that. I can handle this."

"Sure. Right. By having guns pointed at you outside a bar?"

"I handled it, Sami. That's what I do."

All that anxiety she'd woken up with found a place to land. Leaping to her feet, she paced in front of him. "Don't dismiss this out of hand or use your job as an excuse. Two men held guns on you, one against your back. This isn't just some job, Dom."

She stressed his name, just as he'd done with her, desperate to make her point.

"It's still *my* job and not for you to interfere with."

"I have some leeway right now. My father wants a relationship with me. I should be able to use that to my advantage—" She flung out a hand. "To our advantage! To reset the expectation of how things will be between us if he wants a relationship with his adult daughter. He's not treating my fiancé that way."

An expression crossed his face she couldn't quite place. Was he amused? Angry? Something else altogether?

It would be so easy to chalk this fight up to frustration—a tension that was built on a lot of levels, from the circumstances with her father to the still-lingering sexual awareness that swirled between them—but for some reason she sensed there was something more there.

Something a lot like hope.

Or was she just seeing what she wanted to see? That each time she used a word like *fiancé*—even if it was tied to wildly fake circumstances—she couldn't deny the quick tug of happiness that filled her at the thought.

And all for a man she'd known—what three weeks at most?

How had it all twisted up so quickly? Their lives had become intertwined so fast and so tightly that it was hard to remember she ultimately had a real existence waiting for her.

Something she'd go back to when this charade was complete.

She dropped back into her chair, irritated to see a

grin tugging at the corner of his mouth. "What are you laughing at?"

"I'm not laughing."

"Could have fooled me."

"It's just—" Despite what looked like a mighty strong attempt to stop it, that grin grew wider. "Is this our first fight as a couple?"

"Fake couples can't have fights."

"Seems like we just did."

"Then it was a fake fight."

The conversation was ridiculous in the extreme, but in her arguments was a desperate desire to protect herself.

Because it was way too easy to see him as a permanent fixture in her life.

And it was even easier to enjoy the weight of the engagement ring on her left hand and the way the word *fiancé* tripped off her tongue. They were things that meant promise and permanence, and she'd had little of that growing up.

"What, exactly, is a fake fight?"

"It's one where each party is mad but doesn't have a say in what the other one does."

Although she'd improvised, she wasn't entirely sure that was the right description. Did a promise of marriage—even when real—not include a continued independence for each party? Yet, didn't you have a say, too? Wasn't that the great juggling act of binding your life with another person?

And wasn't that the real betrayal of her father to her mother? And, by extension, to her?

"Sami?" Dom's smile had faded, an earnest look filling his eyes. "Are you okay?"

"Sure. I'm fine."

"Why don't I believe you?"

He'd sworn to her that he wouldn't lie. Could she really offer him anything less? "Our fake fight got me thinking, that's all."

"About what?"

"We're on weird ground because we technically don't have a say in one another's lives." She saw him about to make a point and rushed on. "Beyond the confines of your case, we really don't. You have no claim on me and I have none on you."

He nodded, considering. "Okay. I think I'm following."

"But I guess I'm also getting tripped up on that idea of a claim overall. I mean, I realize commitment has a lot of facets. And it means that someone does have a right to be concerned about you and you have the same right in return.

"But the possession part of it all bothers me. That claim on another person. It makes me think of my mother."

"That your father controlled her somehow?"

"Yes and no. That by virtue of them being together, her life took such an awful turn. That making a commitment and expecting something of one another broke her."

A tightness filled her—was it because she was finally talking about this?—but she pushed on, even as the words seemed to cut her throat like glass.

"Didn't he have a responsibility to her? To be better? To do better? If you love someone and commit to someone, isn't that required? Yet, his life and his choices didn't change. They still haven't."

"I think I know what you mean," he said. "My father's choices were similar. What they did to my mother. What they did to me and my brothers and sisters. It's hard. It's like we want the people in our lives to be better. To be more. And whether it's beyond them or it ends up getting beyond them, they can't do it."

That same desire that had filled her as she'd stared at Dom through her front window reached up, nearly smothering her with its intensity.

Her feelings for him *did* go beyond the physical. Way beyond, actually. And with each moment she spent with him, she knew it was going to be harder and harder to go back.

Back to a life that didn't include him.

And back to a life when she could choose to ignore all these realities that she'd pushed away and refused to think about for a decade. Each of them—her father, her mother, even her own view on the world—had suddenly reared up, forcing her to look at them.

To consider them.

To *feel* them.

She might not have a claim on Dom Colton, but she knew with undeniable certainty that her troubles would be far easier to face with him by her side than without.

RONALD SPENCE CRUMPLED the empty pack of cigarettes, frustrated he'd forgotten to grab a fresh pack out of his coat pocket before he sat down. Now he had to get up and he'd just hit a particularly viable vein of information on the dark web.

On a heavy exhale, he read a few more details on a high-profile drug-smuggling ring operating out of southern Wyoming and considered how he might put them out of business as he got up and crossed nearly the entire width of the small apartment he was holed up in.

Hardly a fine set of digs, but appropriate for who and what the world thought he was right now.

A man trying to get his life back.

What a freaking joke.

He tore at the plastic wrapper on the cigarettes and resettled himself in front of the laptop. A few smokes later and about twenty minutes more digging had netted him a name and a contact point.

Evans could handle it.

More, Spence dragged on his cigarette, Evans *would* handle it. Guy had been more than pleased to get his old gang back and become king of Colorado again when he'd reached out. They'd gotten off to a bit of a slow start, but things were moving now and through Lone Wolf and his boys, Ronald now had nearly all the activity west of the Rockies in Colorado locked up. He wasn't ceding an inch of Wyoming or Utah, either.

No use having the Warlords on his payroll if he couldn't count on them to do cleanup when needed. Take the territory and either recruit those who could be remolded to the motorcycle club or get rid of them.

On that thought, Spence laughed to himself, stabbing out the nub of his cigarette in his ashtray.

Gotta love living in a state with such wide-open places. Hiding a body was almost so easy as to be laughable. And Mike "Lone Wolf" Evans knew how to hide his tracks. It was how he'd gotten his name and how he managed to keep his reputation intact, year after year.

Spence considered the man's resilience, even as he did wonder about his few years when he'd stepped outside the business. It had been the only thing that had worried Spence about getting the guy back on the payroll. He never quite trusted the dudes who tried to go straight, even if the guy had claimed that lingering feelings over his wife's death had been the cause.

Evans had done some time on a commune of all places, burying himself in plants and some crap like that. He'd dusted that off his boots after a year or two, then drifted to a small meth business in eastern Utah, just cooking, never leading a crew or anything. Dude must have gotten sick of how things were being run because by the time Spence had reached out to him, Evans was nearly begging him to come back.

Said he was ready to run his gang back and had been in touch with some of the old members, also ready to come back.

So Spence had taken a chance. Not like he had a hell of a lot of choice. A man couldn't be too careful in prison and you needed to depend on the guys you knew on the outside.

But still, he worried.

Because nothing could bring Evans's wife back. And nothing could change the fact that, while it hadn't lasted, the guy had flirted with going straight.

Ronald lit another smoke and tapped out his orders on a burner phone. That small-time racket in Wyoming needed to be handled. It was time to see how Lone Wolf did on cleanup duty.

Chapter Eleven

Dom glanced at Sami. Her eyes were on the road straight ahead as she sat in the passenger seat. He wondered yet again what he was doing bringing her back here, to Warlords territory. He'd considered the job ahead and knew he could brazen his way through any protests from Lone Wolf if she'd stayed behind. Knew even more that he could use whatever danger Mike Evans was surely going to drag him into as an excuse to keep his daughter safely ensconced in Blue Larkspur.

But she'd hear none of it.

He hadn't even tried bringing it up the other night. The strain had gripped them both—from recounting his exchange with Bryce and Neal to the mind-numbing kiss she'd laid on him at the door to the strange twists and turns, and yes, the near fight. When they had spoken, it all coalesced into a fraught exchange that finally ended with him heading off to her spare room to start a fitful night's sleep.

Yesterday hadn't gotten much better, but he had broached the subject of her staying behind and gotten the exact response he'd anticipated.

A *hell no*, followed by a serious freeze-out for the rest of the day. When he did finally get her talking over a peace offering of meatball subs for dinner, a sort of odd wariness still hovered between them.

And none of it could keep his mind from traveling, over and over, down that difficult conversational path they'd walked, discussing marriage and, by extension, her parents' relationship.

It wasn't a surprise this time with her father was stirring up memories she'd likely have preferred to keep buried. And based on the timing of Mike Evans's call, coming as it did so unexpectedly, she'd be dealing with this situation, whether or not Dom and his FBI mission had come into her life.

What he hadn't quite reconciled for himself was how much of this job was messing with his own memories of his family.

My father's choices were similar. What they did to my mother. What they did to me and my brothers and sisters. It's hard. It's like we want the people in our lives to be better. To be more. And whether it's beyond them or it ends up getting beyond them, they can't do it.

While he wasn't actually defending Mike Evans, he was surprised by how quickly he'd associated Evans and his own father in his mind.

Because no matter how much he tried to deny his own feelings, he couldn't deny that lone truth that had whispered to him throughout his adult life.

He *did* want his father to be better, even though that was impossible now.

The expectations he'd always carried, in his mind and in his heart, of the man Ben Colton was had been wrong. And maybe he shouldn't have seen it as a betrayal, but no matter how much he told himself that, he'd never actually believed it.

Because Ben had betrayed him. And his mother. And Caleb, Morgan, Oliver, Ezra, Rachel, Gideon, Aubrey, Jasper, Gavin, Alexa and Naomi.

He'd also betrayed the good people of Lark's County. Those who'd believed the justice system was there to protect them. Only, in his father's hands, it had done the exact opposite. It had preyed on them, taking its toll out on those with the least ability to fight back.

"We're almost to the turn off." Sami's comment broke the silence and the repetitive ground his thoughts seemed determined to travel. "I wonder if we'll get an escort this time."

"I don't see why we won't."

"No, I suppose you're right."

He heard the resignation and wanted to find a way to reassure her. Even if he had little reason to think her disappointment wasn't well placed, he couldn't ignore it, either.

"We're going to get through this, Sami."

"I know you think so, but I'm not so sure he's going to let you walk away, Dom. That's my biggest fear, you know. That even if I did interfere, it's not enough to save you if things go sideways."

It was his job to assess risks, to prepare properly and to recognize that going into any sort of undercover work had the possibility of a poor outcome. He trained for it, with an exacting sort of discipline that required his full focus on his work. Because he'd also accepted long ago that he was best suited in roles that took his own natural capability for leadership and his deep desire to work independently and combined them into work that mattered.

Work that proved he was nothing like Ben.

And if it meant that he had a lone wolf streak inside of him to rival Sami's father, well…he'd have to live with that uncomfortable similarity sitting on his shoulders.

"You don't have to worry about anyone letting me walk away. I'm trained for this and I *will* walk away. So will you."

"Is it wrong that I feel bad about what I'm doing?"

The question was spoken in almost a whisper, even as it echoed through the car like a gunshot. A gunshot that suddenly put the past two days and her cool distance in vivid perspective.

"You're human, Sami, not a robot. It'd be worse if you felt nothing."

"It'd be easier if I were a robot. Then I could walk into this without emotion or care for what happened." Her voice grew stronger, a fierce tone in every syllable. "For what has to happen. Because I'm doing what's right. I know that. I just wish I could put my brain on hold and the voice that keeps telling me I'm betraying my father."

His boss had pressed Dom for over a week now on whether or not it made sense to bring Sami fully into the op, questioning Dom on how much he was sharing about the Warlords. The opportunity she provided into the MC was invaluable, but the big brass had worried that her family connection with Lone Wolf Evans—no matter how estranged—would end up carrying weight.

Despite his conviction this was the right path forward, his boss's questions had sown doubt.

Yet, as he listened to her—more, as he heard the genuine anguish in her voice—he recognized just how much they'd underestimated her.

How much *he'd* underestimated her.

And with that knowledge, it was deeply important to him to provide comfort and the very real affirmation that her ability to remain human in all this was a gift and not a shortcoming.

"Your brain's working just fine. It's your heart giving you the challenges."

"Stupid heart."

"Dumb emotions," he added, trying to lighten the load.

"Idiot feelings." She sighed, a ripping sort of sound that tore at him. "By a stupid, dumb, idiot kid who still wishes her father was like everyone else."

That tear in his chest widened, splitting wide open.

Because in that assessment—one he refused to believe fit her in any way—he recognized his own lingering emotions.

And knew them for a perfect fit.

One that was a reality that had haunted him for twenty years. One he now had words to match to the feelings.

Because he, too, thought he was a stupid, dumb, idiot kid who just wanted a father like everyone else's.

SAMI TOOK HER first easy breath as they crossed the threshold into Warlords territory and didn't suddenly acquire a tail. It was silly to think this might be a portent of better things to come, but it did offer a small moment of ease that her father might be willing to give Dom the benefit of the doubt.

A limited benefit, to be sure, but she'd take what she could get right now.

Especially with Dom's words ringing in her ears like bells.

Your brain's working just fine. It's your heart giving you the challenges.

It was an astute assessment that had—oddly—settled her for what they had to do.

As part of Dom's *initiation*, they'd be staying on the property through the weekend. She'd juggled things at work to take a few days off, even with being in the midst of her busiest season, and Dom had gotten the time off from his crew boss.

This five-day stretch was the lynchpin of their act and meant to cement her father's belief that this was the start of a new relationship between him and Sami and, by extension, Mike and Dom. For that reason and the broader issue of making a convincing act, she and Dom needed to be in sync. Even with the strain that had hovered between the two of them these past few days, it was amazing to her how quickly he put her at ease with a few simple words.

And how comforting it was to look across the small cab of the truck and see his face.

He calmed her. Reassured her. And made her feel that the thoughts in her head were both valid and listened to. The only other person in her life she could compare with any degree of similarity had been her grandmother. Their time together had been too short, but what they had shared had been mutually respectful and supportive.

"Do you have any idea what you'll be asked to do?"

"I'm expecting a few tests of my loyalty."

"You've done that sort of thing before?"

"Yes."

"Oh."

She tried to come up with something that didn't sound nearly as naive as she felt when Dom pressed on. "I am trained for this sort of thing. And I have a certain amount of latitude to make necessary decisions to stay in character, while trying to preserve peace. Besides, your father doesn't want to kill me."

"What!"

She felt the strangled squeal come out of her throat; heard the sound that was part barking seal, part shocked innocent.

Kill Dom?

No, no! That clanging voice in her head corrected her. *The very real idea that her father might murder Dom.*

"I mean it. I'm not saying there's no danger in the next few days, but your father isn't incentivized to kill me, Sami. I'm too important to you and having a relationship with you is too important to him."

It made an odd sort of sense, even if the cavalier way he spoke of being killed was a shock to the senses.

"So you think you'll be okay?"

"Yeah, I do. I'll take the tests and prove my loyalty and my value, all at the same time."

She didn't think any of it was as easy as he tried to play it off to be, but as the shock receded, she had to admit he had a point. Her dad's first call, reaching out with a desire to renew and repair their relationship, had happened independently of Dom's investigation.

The timing was odd, but still a coincidence.

But if something happened to Dom, it was going to make renewing their father-daughter relationship nearly impossible.

It was that truth she had to focus on each time her nerves spiked up or she worried about the ultimate outcome of their attempts to infiltrate the Warlords. When she added in that training he spoke of with such assurance, she figured it might be time to give credence to his words.

He was well-trained and he had the federal government backing him up, aware of where he was, what he was working on and what he faced. Dom might be in a position where he was handling this on his own, but he wasn't without resources.

And he wasn't without her.

Even if she'd already been told that she'd be staying in the cabin for the evening. It chafed to be left behind, but it might give her a chance to think about her own plans and how she could help Dom.

She might not have the same training, but she had eyes and ears, and she knew what she was watching for.

The question was how much Mike would give away in front of her.

Growing up, those details had been naturally kept from her.

But now?

Would he still see her as a child? Or would he recognize that if he took her fiancé into his confidence he sure as hell should take his daughter in, too?

DOM HADN'T MINCED words with Sami, but he hadn't elaborated, either. This trip to Warlords territory was about his testing into the organization. He needed to prove his talents and his loyalty, and of the two, the Warlords would put the most weight on loyalty.

For all the purported strength of the Warlords—or

any other similar organization—Dom knew that success was predicated on a very specific social order. It was one steeped in fear and hierarchy, and Mike Evans seemed to have a steady hand on that front.

Hadn't his late-night visit outside the Corner Pocket with Bryce and Neal suggested that?

Both men had seemingly been seeking a way back into the boss's favor. The fact they had only tailed him to the parking lot—and hadn't come inside to investigate what he was up to—suggested their ambition was minimal but their fear was strong.

A fact he now understood as he braced himself for another slam into his rib cage with the sap. He wasn't exactly sure what they'd filled the small pouch with but his money was on bullets.

The initiation had been limited to a few strategic hits, but Dom recognized the glint in Mike Evans's eyes. The man wasn't enjoying himself so much as testing Dom's fortitude and it wouldn't do to give in and beg for mercy. Even if his ribs were screaming from the force of the bag of heavy metal pieces Evans wielded with precision.

"You claim to be committed to my daughter."

"I am. Sir." Dom avoided the temptation to spit on the ground, instead taking a minute to ostensibly catch his breath, all while eyeing the interior of the facility Evans had driven them to. The high-ceilinged warehouse was about forty-five minutes from Evans's house, a fact that could be significant or could also indicate Dom had been driven in circles for some amount of that time. He'd figure it out on the drive back.

For now, he needed to get as much intel as he could because there wasn't a Warlords warehouse on the

FBI's radar. Their drone detail had secured imagery of several outbuildings on the compound property, but nothing that had the scope and scale of this place. Dom got the sense there was a loading area, which further suggested a location closer to the highway.

Easy in and out.

Which is what he needed to do with his breathing. *Easy in. Easy out.* Even if each inhalation felt like a white-hot poker was stabbing in between every single one of his rib bones.

Standing back up to his full height, Dom kept his gaze steady on Lone Wolf. "I love her, sir. I am committed to her. There're no buts about it."

"And you think this is a life for her?"

"I can provide for her. And I will take care of her. She won't want for anything with me."

"By coming to work for me?"

"If you'll have me."

Evans pulled his arm back once more, swinging the cotton bag by the tip of his fingers before tightening his grip. Dom eyed the sap, both out of the very real anticipation of the pain to come, as well as because he knew it was expected of him.

His future father-in-law—and that was the headspace Dom needed to maintain, to stay in character—was looking for something very specific in this exercise. He wanted obedience but Dom sensed the man recognized some spirit was needed to properly take care of his daughter.

Dom was determined that all the man would see was a perfect fit.

Which was why his arm snaked out at the very last

minute, wresting the bag from Evans just shy of it striking his body once more.

The move was enough to bring shouts of surprise
from the small cadre of men surrounding Dom and
Mike in a circle, but it was Mike's quick lift of his hand
that had them all stilling, returning the guns each carried back to their sides.

"You got a problem with me?" Dom gritted out the
words, the small bag still firmly gripped in his fist.

"I'm a man who's looking out for his daughter."

"And I'm the man marrying that daughter. That has
nothing to do with working for you." He hefted the cotton sack and gave it a sharp shake. "This has nothing
to do with working for you."

Mike's hazel gaze, so like Sami's, was calculating
as it roamed over Dom's face. He wasn't backing off
but he hadn't wrested control back of the weapon, all
suggesting Dom's own calculations had paid off.

And further suggesting the first test had been
passed.

"Why don't you come over here? We have a new job
I could use your help with."

Mike had gestured toward a far corner of the warehouse, and as Dom turned, he could see a conference
table set up and what looked like maps spread over
the top. It was the one part of the room he hadn't been
able to take in during his initial surveillance and now,
looking at it, it was clear there'd been some prep work
put into place.

He was sore and already anticipated the bruises that
awaited him tomorrow. They would look like large
purple eggs covering his midsection, but it was a small
price to pay. He'd had bruised ribs before—hell, grow-

ing up with six brothers had ensured he knew how to take a few hits—and since that part of the initiation was over, he was now finally in a position to learn something.

Like just how deep the Warlords had penetrated the western part of the US.

And who, exactly, was pulling their strings.

MIKE STARED AT the man sitting across the conference table, all the questions he had about his future son-in-law threatening his focus on this job. Spence had been very specific on his call the night before. He wanted this other drug-smuggling ring in Wyoming taken out, post haste.

Mike hadn't disagreed with the strategy—they needed to run the west, free and clear—but the snapped-out orders suggested Spence was running out of patience.

And an impatient man was one who made mistakes.

But could Mike really blame him? Spence had spent the past six months playing the repentant dupe, looking for all the world like a man who was on the straight and narrow. But with the guys in Wyoming moving in like they were, it suggested Spence's little act carried more believability than the man had actually wanted.

There was a time no one would have considered moving in on Ronald Spence's territory. But how things had changed.

This was the biggest test the Warlords had faced since restarting operations. And now he had a wild card in the mix with Dom Conner.

Did it mean he had a new recruit, one who was eager and willing to get things done? Or was he taking a risk with an unknown entity who could blow everything sky-high?

There was no freaking way of knowing. It was just a matter of going with his gut and taking advantage of the manpower he had at hand.

Conner was motivated, that was for sure.

I love her, sir. I am committed to her. There's no buts about it.

He'd also taken the hits without flinching and Mike knew for a fact they hurt like hell. He'd faced a sap more than a few times in his life, which was why that particular weapon was a key tool in his arsenal.

What he hadn't banked on was the sincerity that came off Conner in waves.

As far as Mike was concerned, Sami would be his baby girl forever. They might have been apart for the past decade, but no man was good enough for her and that was a damn solid fact. But Dom Conner?

He loved Sami, of that Mike had no doubt.

As a father, could he really ask for more?

He'd toyed for a while with the novelty of going straight but didn't have it in him. His only regret had been losing Sami. But now? With her in love with a guy who clearly had the knack for the work?

It felt like he might finally have a legacy.

Because whether he wanted to admit it or not, time did keep marching on. He'd seen that clearly enough in his own life and in the long years he'd already lost with his daughter.

He wasn't willing to risk losing any more.

So he'd go with his gut. Include Conner in on this job and see how the guy did. He was big and strong—

an intimidating son of a bitch—and Mike figured he'd do well on this Wyoming gig.

It was why he'd wanted to stop with the hits. No use messing up his new workhorse and putting him out of commission before he was needed. Conner's convenient display of dominance had helped them end the little show. And truth be told, he admired that bit of fire.

Conner had toed that line between taking his lumps and showing his chops, which had nearly had Mike grinning. He admired a bit of piss and vinegar, especially when it was coming from someone he could mold and, ultimately, use to great effect.

And he already had.

That little play with the sap—both giving it and Conner's grab—would have an impact on the rest of the crew. A little competition was healthy. Good for morale. Add on Conner had dropped the tail—twice—and Bryce and Neal would be running scared of their own shadows.

So yeah, some fresh blood could be good.

And since it gave him another angle in with Sami, it was even better.

Wasn't that why he'd agreed to working with Spence in the first place? He'd passed the point in his life where he needed the adulation of running the show. Now he could sit back and reap the benefits, allowing the younger generation to take some of the hits. It was a good plan.

A damn good one.

Chapter Twelve

Sami flipped another few channels on the TV, not actually seeing what was playing on the screen. If she thought she'd been worried the other night, it was nothing compared to the increasing terror that filled her as each hour ticked by on the clock.

Where was Dom?

The interior of the home that she and Dom had been given for their stay—several acres away from Mike's house—was cozy and welcoming. Not what she'd expected upon arrival and definitely not something she'd expected to find on the Warlords compound.

She'd anticipated they would spend their time at her dad's home, but he'd surprised her with the offer of the guest cabin on the property and the reassurance that a young couple didn't need to be under her father's thumb. It was…normal?

Almost normal.

Unless you counted the fact that she and Dom needed to worry the property might be bugged, as well as under video surveillance. And that she also had to worry that Mike had taken Dom who knew where to rough him up and initiate him into the Warlords.

Would he make it back?

Had she been wrong about her dad and his intentions? Did something go wrong with Dom's cover? And worst of all, what if she had truly underestimated her father?

The fact that thought even crossed her mind was indicative of just how messed up her relationship was with her own parent. Her endless suspicions about what he'd potentially known that had led to her mother's death. The questions about what illegal activities he was involved in now. And even her doubts about what he might be doing, at this very moment, to Dom.

What kind of a life was this?

And what did it say about her ability to love?

She had spent a lot of time over the past few weeks thinking about her feelings for Dom Colton. Her interest in him and her attraction. Even the little fantasies that had tugged at her at odd moments as she thought about what it would be like if their fake engagement was something real instead.

What she really should have considered was if she was actually cut out for a relationship. And maybe why all her prior ones hadn't worked out.

How did someone learn how to be in a relationship if they were raised with an absence of warmth? Raised by someone who didn't only subsist on the shadow side of the law, but who operated their entire life there.

The door to the small cabin they were staying in opened, and Dom walked in. Keen, aching relief swept through her, nanoseconds before she registered the pain in his eyes.

"Are you okay?"

"Yeah, fine." Exhaustion laced his voice, leaving a small ache for him in her chest.

They had already discussed the potential that their sleeping quarters could be bugged, so Sami focused on playing her part and hoped all the things she didn't say were reflected in her eyes.

"You were gone a long time. Did everything go okay?"

"Yeah, babe. Your dad's cool."

"That's good." She felt stupid, pattering out these idiot comments, but knew there was no help for it. They'd already planned out a lunch trip tomorrow so they could talk in private and she recognized any and all questions had to wait until then. In the meantime, she had a part to play.

"I think he likes you."

"The man who's marrying his daughter?" His mouth quirked into a wry smile. "You might be overestimating my charm."

"I don't think so." She forced a smile, hoping it translated into the pride she pumped into her voice for anyone who might be listening. "I think he sees himself in you."

It was impossible to miss the way his mouth turned down into a frown and something in that quick nearly reflexive reaction buoyed something inside her.

Something that flew in the face of the dismal thoughts that had gripped her before he'd come back.

She was in this with Dom. As partners. And she knew what an honorable man he was.

Maybe she did recognize the qualities that made up a good solid relationship.

And maybe she could take that as her biggest gift out of this whole escapade. A level of confidence that while her attraction to him would never have a future, her experiences with him could pave a path *to* her future.

One that included love.

Even if everything inside of her rebelled at the idea that she'd ever meet another man as good and decent as Dom Colton.

Resolved to think about that at another time, she continued to trowel on the compliments in the event of any listeners. "You both have the qualities of a leader. And I think he's secretly impressed with your lion tattoo."

"You might be on to something with that." The frown vanished and Dom's eyes lit up before he shot her a wink. "I think it's why your dad's underlings don't like me."

"What do you mean, don't like you?" She heard the affront lacing her words and couldn't claim that the reaction was totally for show. Of course, she knew the henchmen didn't like Dom, but what had they actually done that evening?

"I think they see me as a threat."

Sami searched Dom's face for any clues on how to play this. When he nodded and gave a small hand motion that suggested she should keep the ploy going, she picked up the thread. "Well, of course, they do. You're impressive. You're physically powerful, you're a natural leader and you know how to keep your head. You are, after all, a man that walks roofs for a living."

"I think they care more that I'm with the boss's daughter."

"No, baby, that's just an excuse. It's you. You were the impressive one. And you probably scare the hell out of them."

His smile was broad, encouraging, and Sami knew she had hit all the right notes. Riding that wave and going only on instinct, she went for broke. Stepping up and wrapping her arms around him, she pressed her lips to his jaw line and purred. "You're a badass, Dom Conner."

The fake name rolled off the tongue, a seamless reminder that no matter what they did, they needed to keep their cover. Even if it did creep her out that someone might hear the two of them kissing.

But the way his arms tightened around her made her forget the game all too quickly.

Her lips drifted from the line of his jaw toward his mouth, encouraged when he opened for her, drawing her hard against his chest. It was only as she ran her hands over his shoulders, down over his chest that she heard his sharp intake of breath, just as she felt him wince against her lips.

"Dom?"

"Hmm?" His voice was distracted, the tone similar to other times they'd kissed, but his body language was all wrong. He was pulling back from her, the move clearly instinctive, even as his voice suggested he wanted to remain close.

She fully stepped back then, her hands reaching for his chest, surprised when he danced out of her reach. His expression was serious as he laid a finger over his lips and shook his head.

Sami nodded, even as her pulse spiked, her heart hammering in her throat. What was going on here?

The long-sleeved black T-shirt he'd worn for his outing with her father was already hanging over his jeans, untucked, and he reached for the hem, lifting the shirt.

As he did so, she recognized his careful movements, a stiffness there that, now come to think of it, he'd exhibited since walking into the cabin.

But it was the tight expression on his face as he lifted the shirt up, up, up and over his stomach, then his chest that had her eyes widening.

And bugged living room or not, she refused to remain silent when he gingerly pulled the garment off over his head.

"What in the hell happened to you?"

DOM KNEW THE unveiling of his ribs wasn't going to go down very well, but he had no idea how to let her know what was going on with their subterfuge of speaking without actually talking.

So he'd gone with instinct and shown her instead.

And was now the innocent bystander of a tongue lashing that sort of made him wish the house definitely *was* bugged.

"Who did this to you?"

"No one, babe."

"Don't give me that BS. What the hell was this? Some sort of ridiculous male initiation?"

"It's not like that."

She eyed him darkly, and for the moment Dom wasn't sure if he was dealing with the real Sami or the consummate actress he'd witnessed for the past few days. "Then tell me what it's like."

"It's guys, you know. It's what we do."

"A black eye is guy stuff. A few bruised knuckles is guy stuff. This —" she shook a hand at his torso. "This is criminal. I'm calling my father."

"No, you're not."

It was a risk, in all ways, but Dom went ahead and played his odds on this one. "This is him and me."

"You've been hurt. Mauled, more like."

"Nothing that hasn't happened to me before. I'm fine."

He might have been worried that Actress Sami had vanished, but if he were honest with himself, Actor Dom had vanished as well. This was what he'd signed up for.

This is what he did.

She could take it personally because it involved her father, but it didn't change the work.

Nor did it change the part that he had to play in order to further infiltrate the Warlords.

If she needed physical proof to understand that, then so be it.

They stood there for a few beats in locked silence, neither backing down from the other. But with one final dip of her eyes over the bruising on his body, Dom saw the moment his point fully registered. Her anger changed—there was still an unholy fire in her eyes, but he did see resignation beneath the flames.

And in the resignation, for the first time, Dom saw real fear.

From the beginning, this job had pulled at him, testing him in ways he had never imagined. From his initial attraction to Sami, to making love with her against his better judgment, to taking her into his confidence regarding this job with the Warlords, nothing had gone to plan.

And nothing—no amount of self-recrimination or a solid mental talking-to—could make him walk away from her.

She was the variable in all this. The wild card.

And staring into that fear, Dom had to acknowledge he had plenty of his own. Not for himself, but for her.

All for her.

He extended a hand, please when she extended hers in return. As their fingers met and linked, Dom did all he could to hold that fear at bay.

They could do this. Together.

He had the full weight of the federal government behind him. More, he had the conviction that what he was doing was right. That what they were doing— this deception that was a necessity—would lead to the desired outcome. That this charade would put a much-needed dent in the drug trade in this part of the country and well beyond.

Cutting one node off the many-headed hydra that was the criminal underworld often felt useless. But since receiving this assignment, Dom had felt that he could make a real impact. The volume of drugs moving through the Warlords was significant. The International Corruption Unit knew it and the small pieces of information he managed to glean tonight over the Warlords conference table reinforced that fact.

It was why he had to keep pushing forward.

He stared down at their hands, joined together, and understood the task before him.

Because all the forward momentum in the world wouldn't mean anything if he lost her in the process.

So he'd keep her close and protect her with his life.

SAMI FOLDED HER MENU, already decided on a burger and fries. She and Dom had eaten breakfast with her father but it had been a half-hearted exercise, with overbright smiles and tense conversation.

And while the question of whether or not the cabin was bugged was still outstanding, she had no doubt that Mike knew *she* knew who had put those hideous marks on Dom.

The whole subject still infuriated her. And while Dom had technically prepared her for the scenario where he ended up hurt, she hadn't really believed the outcome would be that awful.

The bruises that were red and tender last night had grown purple overnight. His motions were decidedly stiffer this morning as he moved around the bedroom getting ready. It broke her heart, those stilted movements he seemed to accept as his due and which she couldn't look away from.

Even the night before, she'd barely slept. Partially because they'd shared the same bed and she'd wanted to give him plenty of space, worried she'd hurt him if she rolled over during the night.

And also because she couldn't stop looking at him.

He'd put a T-shirt on to sleep, but she could still visualize the exact placement of each bruise. Could still see the way he'd instinctively pulled back from her touch because of the pain.

Although they'd planned to get out for lunch all along to talk, the tense situation had made her ploy to run into the nearest large town for a few items likely more plausible than she'd have expected. Mike made little argument and even asked them if they'd pick up a case of motor oil for him at one of the big-box stores.

She waited until Dom closed his menu before diving in. "What did you learn last night?"

"There's a lot of movement right now. And an upcoming job in southern Wyoming. We're headed out tonight."

"And it took you this long to tell me?"

Dom shot her a dark look. "I'm telling you now. We agreed we couldn't talk in the cabin."

"And how are you supposed to go out on some job with my father with broken ribs?"

"Bruised, is all."

"Come on. You know what I mean."

"I'll be fine. Besides, it's worse when you wake up. I'm looser already."

Empirically, she knew this needed to be done. They were here so he could get evidence and get the case wrapped up. But she still couldn't get over the sheer shock and horror at those raw marks.

"What did he do to you?"

He was prevented from answering by their waitress who walked up, so they each ordered their burgers and waited until she was back out of earshot.

"It's a sap."

"A what?"

"A bag with items in it. You hit someone with it."

If she was horrified before, this only made it all worse. It was one thing to throw a punch. There was something personal in that and it required an individual to get involved in the activity. Although she had blessedly few problems with her crew, her guys got into fistfights from time to time. Tensions ran high, especially in the dog days of summer, and it had been known to happen when tempers flared.

But this?

This took someone—*her father*, Sami mentally

forced herself to acknowledge—to fill a bag and me-
thodically hit another person. It was torture and dominance all rolled into one.

"What was in the bag?"

"Bullets, I think."

The urge to scream filled her but it was only looking at his calm visage across the table that had her
catching herself.

That and the strange sense of acceptance he had
about it all.

"You've been through this before?"

"We're trained for a lot of things. This isn't my first
initiation, Sami."

She'd known what Dom did for a living was dangerous. Realistically, she'd understood that. But now?
To understand the layer of brutality that settled over
all of it, she was nauseous.

Worse, to understand that her father was the type
of man who'd utilize that brutality only reinforced all
those awful thoughts she'd had the night before while
waiting for Dom.

What was she to come from a monster like this?
What lived inside of her, in the strands of her DNA?
In the forces that had shaped her personality?

And worse, she had to admit as an image of her beloved grandmother's face filled her thoughts, how had
Gram lived with this?

She felt like she should be asking questions, but all
she could do was sit there with her thoughts running
through her mind over and over on a loop. And despite her hunger when they'd arrived, she could only
pick at a few French fries after their waitress had de-
livered their lunch.

For his part, Dom dug in with gusto and she was happy that his bruises weren't so bad he couldn't eat. That had to mean he didn't have internal damage, right? But maybe she could persuade him to see a doctor when they got back to Blue Larkspur. And she was going to watch him like a hawk until then for any possible changes.

"How long will it take you to heal?"

He grinned at that, wiping his hands on his napkin. "No time at all, once we pick up that aspirin on our trip to the store."

She wanted to be mad. But that coursing anger and frustration and shock that had started with her father's call a few weeks ago and had only escalated through each thing she'd learned couldn't withstand the grinning face of Dom Colton.

"You look too damn cheery."

"I am. I have a plan. And a way into the Warlords tonight. We should have this wrapped in a matter of weeks."

Weeks.

Which meant they'd have to continue on with this charade for some time more. They'd escape back to Blue Larkspur for a few days—she did legitimately have a job—but there was a sadness in her to think they'd still have to come back. That she had to keep facing, over and over, the truth about her father.

Yet, wasn't that a part of this whole journey?

Dealing with her past.

Although she hadn't really considered this situation in that way, now that the thought landed, Sami had to admit it was spot on.

For ten years, she'd walked away from him and her

past and done her level best to forget either existed.
Only they *did* exist. And ignoring things—even for a
decade—hadn't made them go away.

Perhaps this whole experience wasn't just about
rooting out Mike Evans's criminal enterprise and taking it down. Maybe it was also about healing. Personal
growth. And putting the past behind her because she'd
truly done the work to put it there, rather than trying
to ignore it ever existed.

Although she wasn't all that hungry, she ate a few
bites of her burger and nibbled on her fries. The burger
was fortifying, the protein making her feel a bit less
peaky than when Dom had explained how her father
had tortured him the night before.

"You about ready to go?" Dom laid enough cash
on the table to cover their food and tip when his gaze
caught on something through the wide window of the
diner.

"What?"

"Let's get out of here. Your father's minions are out
in the parking lot and I want to know why."

"Did they see you?"

"No. But it looks like Bryce and Neal are in conversation with someone I don't recognize."

"Another Warlord? You might not have met everyone yet."

"I guess I'm going to find out."

In minutes, they were in the parking lot. Dom kept
her firmly behind him as he strode up to the trio of men
standing a few parking spaces down from their truck.

"Bryce. Neal." Dom nodded, his voice carrying
deadly calm notes that sent a chill through Sami.

How did the man do it? Every time she thought she

had a handle on Dom, she realized yet another facet. And suddenly, she realized why he'd gone through an *initiation* in the first place.

Other men instinctively recognized the power in a man like Dom Colton. It wasn't just his physical presence, though that was impressive. It was an innate quality that rolled off him in steady waves.

A message to others that said he was the leader of the pack. That he knew how to defend and protect himself and anyone he cared about.

"What are you doing here, Conner?" one of the men Dom had recognized—Neal?—asked.

"Having lunch with my fiancée. You?"

"Having a meeting."

Dom's voice held distinctly taunting notes. "Is that what we're calling it?"

"Who the hell is this?" The third guy between Bryce and Neal cocked his head.

Dom reached out behind him, his hand going to her side. Although she remained behind him, she couldn't deny how good it felt to have that reassuring touch. The power play might have irritated her under normal circumstances, but now, in this moment, it felt good to have that distinct show of protection.

Really good.

"No one for you to worry about." Bryce bit out the words before shifting his body to shut Dom out of the conversation.

The third man was undeterred by Bryce's attempts to shift his attention. "I still don't have an answer to my question."

"He's a new guy in the club," Neal chimed in, seeming to improvise. "Boss is testing him out. You don't need to worry about him."

"Since when does the boss let new guys in? Especially ones who don't know their place and go around sticking their noses into personal conversations?"

It was like some tableau out of a gangster movie, yet Sami instinctively realized it was 100 percent real. All those roiling thoughts that had been her constant companion for the past few weeks were a testament to that fact. Every time she thought she had a handle on the events unfolding around her, she felt the ground shift beneath her, a new reality forcing its way to the surface.

Her father made his life with men like this.

Hell, he *was* a man like this.

"Conner, get the hell out of here and take Evans's daughter with you," Bryce hissed.

The third man's eyes widened. "She's Lone Wolf's kid?"

"He's her fiancé," Neal added, oh, so helpful with the introductions.

"What meeting is this?" Dom reiterated his question. "What's going on?"

Sami heard a distinct click mere moments before a low voice rasped out instructions behind her.

"Whoever the hell you are, this doesn't involve you. Or Lone Wolf's kid."

Sami felt Dom's hand tighten on her arm, his press against her flesh steady as he turned around to face their new threat.

But before he could push her behind him, the new arrival with the gun snaked out a free hand and tugged Sami's other arm, catching her off balance so that she tumbled into him.

She crashed into a large body, one nearly as powerful as Dom's, her cheek smushed against his chest before she could catch hold of herself.

That low voice pressed on, rumbling through the chest she hadn't yet disengaged from.

"Now. I think you all owe my partner here an answer."

Chapter Thirteen

Dom cursed himself a million ways and beyond as the situation rapidly spiraled out of control. He hadn't carried a gun with him, his government-issued piece still locked safely in his rented home and the unregistered one entrusted to him on this op was still on the floor of his truck, beneath the seat.

Stupid amateur move, Colton.

Several ripe curses floated through his mind as he sized up the new entrant into this strange power play.

Who were these guys?

While Sami's question about just how many members of the Warlords Dom had met was an accurate one, this tête-à-tête in the parking lot smacked of subterfuge. Add on the clown with the gun who had his hands all over Sami and Dom wasn't inclined to wait and ask questions.

But if he acted too fast his rash actions might get her hurt.

"I'll give you exactly three seconds to get your hands off my woman."

Although he'd never thought of a woman he'd dated as *his*, Dom hoped like hell the dark possessive tone would get through to this meathead.

"Those are big words, brother." The guy shifted his gun away from Sami so it pointed toward the ground but his free hand hadn't yet lifted from where he held her possessively against his body.

"Two. O—"

Dom nearly had the last word out when the man lifted his hand from Sami, shoving her hard enough with the other to send her careening into Dom. He'd braced for the dick move and was already cushioning her against his chest, his arms quickly wrapping around her.

With a press of his lips against her head, Dom kept his gaze steady on the intruder. "What the hell do you want?"

He ignored Dom's question, instead tossing a dark look toward Bryce and Neal. "Who is he?"

Bryce spoke first. "Told ya. Boss's daughter's fiancé and the newest Warlord. Name's Dom Conner."

"Like hell he is."

Dom had braced for any number of ways his cover could get blown, but this was a surprise. He didn't recognize either of the new players in this little game and he'd been briefed on every known criminal west of the Rockies.

"He is," Neal added with a nervous laugh. "Boss initiated 'im himself last night."

Dom felt Sami tense against him at the reminder but she didn't say anything.

The nameless thug pressed on, undeterred by Bryce and Neal's endorsements. "He's buttering up the boss. Thinks he can jump the line and go straight to the top because he's marrying into the family."

If you only knew, you bastard, Dom thought grimly.

But he held back from saying anything more, the underlying menace beginning to make sense.

There was some turf war going on here, but Dom wasn't being singled out because someone had blown his cover. Nope, he kept his focus steady on the various players, all standing there in varying stages of agitation, the situation growing clearer with each passing moment.

This was about who wanted to make a move for the top.

One more clue Mike Evans had a challenging situation on his hands. A shadow player in the background running the show, someone that the FBI couldn't find. Possible dissention in the ranks. And now his minions having meetings out of the boss's line of sight.

It was a powder keg, Dom realized, and one that might blow sky-high before he could figure out who was running that show in the background.

"You guys in the Warlords?" Dom finally asked. "I haven't seen you around."

"That makes two of us."

So the one with the gun was the talker. Based on the puffed-out chest and the weapon that, while now at his side hadn't been actually stowed away even while standing here in a public parking lot, Dom recognized his most likely problem for the next few weeks.

"I'm Dom Conner. This is Mike's daughter, Sami." He made no move to extend a hand, nor did he release his hold on her, but he did force a steady, easy tone.

"I'm Edge. That's Drew." The guy nodded toward the other man still standing between Neal and Bryce.

Edge.

Dom avoided saying anything—Edge *was* sporting

permanent ink in an effort to sway these guys into believing he was legit—but knew the name was made up. Made up and off the FBI's radar, which was going to require some digging after this.

"Any reason you are meeting out here instead of back at the compound?" It was a gamble but he needed to know what he was dealing with. Besides, Edge might not mind waving a gun around but the likelihood of him shooting the boss's daughter was extremely low.

Dom knew it and Edge knew it, too.

Clearly, Edge knew it well enough that the ass finally tucked the gun back into his waistband. Yet another bonehead move that indicated his approach was a mix of bully and bad TV criminal he was obviously looking to emulate.

"I could ask you the same."

Dom glanced down at Sami at the same time she looked up. Something lodged in the center of his chest, the tense situation they were dealing with unable to fully kill that spark of awareness that always flared between them.

Swallowing back the sudden dryness in his throat, he refocused on Edge. "We're out for the day. Running errands and enjoying lunch together."

"There's lots to do. We are getting married in a few months," Sami added, a layer of steel threaded through her words.

Edge eyed them both, a knowing look painting his features. "I'll bet."

He then looked to the other three, something flashing between all of them before he shifted his attention back to Sami and Dom. "See you around, Conner."

"Count on it."

EDGE GOT IN his car and made a great show of pulling out of the parking lot of the diner. He hated when things didn't go to plan and lately it felt like something was simmering under the surface.

For a year they'd moved drugs around Colorado freely, his work as Ronald Spence's go-between with the Warlords an easy job. *Maybe too easy*, Edge considered.

Evans had his men under control and he was committed to the work. But this new addition was a concern.

Did Spence know Evans had a kid?

He probably did, Edge figured. Guy knew everything else.

And she was hot, he'd say that. The guy with her sure seemed interested. And it was that guy who made Edge itchy.

New additions to the mix always made him itchy, but this dude just showing up suddenly was a question mark. He hadn't missed the tat on the guy's forearm, too. He looked initiated. But when? And for what gang?

Lots of questions, Edge thought as he hit the highway. A hell of a lot of questions.

And all details Spence needed to know.

SAMI PUSHED THE big cart through the cavernous rows of the warehouse club, barely seeing the items on the shelves. Images of what had gone down in the diner parking lot refused to leave her mind's eye and she couldn't shake the bone-deep cold that had settled beneath her skin.

Dom had tried to engage her in conversation a few times, but after her one-and two-word answers, he'd seemed to understand that she needed some space with her thoughts and he'd stopped talking.

So here they were, just aimlessly roaming the aisles. They'd picked up the case of motor oil her father had requested as well as various oversized boxes of dry goods when it struck either of their fancy. Which meant they now had— she glanced down into the cart—sixty packets of instant oatmeal, forty-eight fruit cups and more pretzels than she could eat in a year. It was only as Dom reached for a triple package of high-fat sandwich cookies that she laid a hand on his arm.

"What are we doing?"

"Comfort shopping?" he asked, the stark lines of his face suggesting anything but.

"I'd call it avoidance shopping."

"What are you avoiding?"

Although she suspected he already knew, Sami decided right then and there that it was as good a time as any to talk about this. And while she hadn't imagined baring her soul in a large aisle full of shipping pallets, the car and the cabin they were staying in had proven ill-equipped for a serious conversation.

And she suddenly couldn't hold it in a moment longer.

"Is this my father's life?" The words ripped out of her, even as she tried to keep her voice low. The store wasn't that crowded, but she didn't need or want any attention.

And damn, she hated crying in public, but based on the tight thickness in her throat, she likely wasn't going to be successful on that front, either.

"Because all these years, I've managed to put him in a box in my mind. One where I could say *yeah, he's not a good guy but he's out of my life and it's not my problem.*" She swiped at a lone tear that had managed to escape the corner of her eye. "But he's a monster. What he's involved with is horrific. And all I've done is close my eyes and try to pretend it doesn't affect me. Or that it doesn't matter so long as I'm away from that."

She did brush at her eyes now, the hot tears splashing over her cheeks. "But it is about me. And closing my eyes has only been selfish."

He stood there, his expression quiet and serious, as she spilled both her guts and her tears. And once she stopped talking, her last words rushing out on a hard exhale, he only continued to stare at her with those steady deep blue eyes.

Until something shifted in those depths, like he'd done some sort of calculation in his head and the answer added up to yes.

A yes that became clear as he began to speak.

"I've been running from my father's memory for a long time."

"What do you mean running? You're in law enforcement. I'd say you embraced the situation and have chosen to actively spend your life doing something about it."

"It might look like it, but it's not true."

"You can't think this is the same? You've done something with your life. As your profession. You help people, Dom."

"By hiding out and surrounding myself with missions and ops, doing my level best to keep distance with my family? That's *doing something*?"

She didn't understand his push back or why he didn't see that he was actively trying to make the world better. But before she could press her point, Dom kept on going.

"And what could you have done? Your mother paid a price for remaining too close to your father. I'd say you got out and the only decent thing your father has done was let you go."

"I should have done more."

"At the risk of your life? Of your happiness?"

Recognizing their surroundings, his voice remained low, but power punched beneath each and every word.

Although she wasn't anywhere close to letting herself off the hook, the sad reality of his comments wasn't lost on her, either. There was a risk being with her father. It was real now and it had been real then. Not understanding the full depths of what Mike Evans was involved in—more, not wanting to know—hadn't changed the fact that remaining in his orbit did risk her life.

Then and now.

What surprised her in all this was Dom's feelings that he'd run, too.

"Why do you think you've run away?"

"We all have, my siblings and I, on some level. I can't speak for my brothers and sisters and it's not fair to try, but look at all of us. A couple of our lives are about avenging our father's bad choices, but there's guilt there, too. Guilt that underpins all of it because we were the beneficiaries of his greed for so long."

"You were children."

He shrugged, his gaze drifting over stacked-four-high packages of peanut butter. "I was sixteen when he died. So were my triplet brothers. Morgan and Caleb were nineteen. We were old enough to see that we lived a privileged life for a family with twelve kids."

"I think you're putting way too much on yourself with this. How would you have known? How could you possibly have known? Your father's crimes were hidden from everyone, including the very community he served."

It was obvious she wasn't making a particularly large dent, but she refused to back down on her point.

"It's easy to look back on something and say you should have known. But you're not omniscient and you're not a bad human because you believed in your father. He was the one who betrayed you, not the other way around. But looking at my father's life. And at my own?" She shook her head, the resonant guilt that had grown and evolved over the past few weeks wouldn't be silenced. "I can't say the same. I knew exactly what my father was and is, and I've hidden myself away. Physically and emotionally, I've lived my adult life pretending he doesn't exist."

"Seeking safety isn't pretending."

"It isn't living, either."

Sami had no idea why it was so important to her to get this out or why she wanted to make him understand, but she wasn't giving in on this.

Nor was she giving herself an easy out.

"Are we actually having this discussion in front of peanut butter and jelly?"

"Yeah, we are."

"I'm not going to change my mind and say you're right."

"I'm not going to change *my* mind and say *you're* right."

"Does this mean we're having another fake fight?"

A lopsided grin tilted the corner of his lips, as if he couldn't quite hide his amusement at his own joke.

An answering grin tugged at her own lips, even as she tried to remain firm in her resolve. "I guess we are."

The humor in his gaze winked out as he moved closer and Sami turned away from the shopping cart to face him. The air heated between them, an incendiary charge sparking in the too-wide aisle, under garish fluorescent lights and pallets of boxed food.

It was the most romantic moment of her life and she had no idea how that was possible, only that it was.

Because under those bright bulbs, she had nothing to hide. She had no more excuses and no ability to run.

Or maybe, Sami acknowledged, she had no desire to run.

Whatever had led her to this moment, she was here and in it. She'd see it through.

And if it meant that she had to put her heart on the line to do it, then she'd face that, too. Because whatever else she wanted to fix about herself, she knew she didn't have the ability to resist Dom Colton.

And she'd be damned if she was going to run from what she could have for the next few weeks for fear of what her future held.

She'd run long enough.

It was time to live in the present.

No, she amended to herself, as she lifted her arms to wrap them around his neck, it was time to *live*.

DOM WASN'T SURE how it happened, but one minute he was *fake fighting* about something that felt entirely too real and the next he had Sami Evans in his arms.

All the emotions he kept trying to fight—about her, about his past and the strange way those two things seemed braided together—wouldn't be denied.

Nor could he deny this desperate attraction to her that seemed to grow stronger by the minute.

He pressed his lips to hers, the motion tentative and almost reverent at first. Without a doubt, this was the worst idea of his life. He'd already gotten in way too deep with her and continuing down this path couldn't lead anywhere good.

But as her lips opened beneath his, their tongues meeting in an urgent, needful joining, he couldn't deny what was between them. This nearly overwhelming want that he'd never experienced before.

That he'd never wanted to experience before.

And wasn't that the real crux of it all? He'd dated before and engaged in mutually enjoyable adult activities with mutually interested women.

But he'd never felt this need to protect and defend. To hold and cherish. He'd never felt the deep-seated desire to put himself on the line.

Whether it was the betrayal by his father at an impressionable age or a personality flaw, he wasn't sure, but he kept others at a distance. His family were the only ones he let get close and even there he often kept a physical distance to avoid that intimacy. His job was busy, yes, but it could be an incredibly handy excuse not to be around, too.

And he'd used it without remorse.

But now. Here. With Sami...

Dom didn't want distance, either physical or emotional. It was as scary as it was invigorating, all while being wholly unexpected, but he wanted her.

"Dom. We should—" The whisper against his lips faded away as her hold tightened around his waist.

They should...

Should do what? Stop? Leave and go somewhere more private? He should back away?

He should...

Dom stilled, lifting his head, his vision full of her. The pretty hazel of her eyes, currently smoky with need. The light sweep of her hair, that fiery auburn as it swept behind her ear. And the delicate dusting of freckles over her nose, a sweet side effect of all the time she spent in the sun.

She was gorgeous.

And she had a vibrancy he couldn't ignore.

But he still needed to stop.

It was one thing to pretend in front of the Warlords. It was the task at hand and they were both committed to seeing it through. But right now, this was just the two of them, alone, acting on this stunning attraction that wouldn't be sated.

He kept his hold on her shoulders but put some physical distance between them. "We should stop."

"Yeah." She nodded, but that hazy need still filled her gaze and it would be the work of impulse to slide right back into that intoxicating place, where nothing existed except the two of them.

Which is why he needed to step away.

She turned away from him then, making a show of looking at the shelf of peanut butter. He gave her a minute, moving a few cart-lengths away to peruse the vast array of jelly brands that still only seemed to come in grape or strawberry, trying to get himself under some semblance of control.

His body throbbed for her, an insatiable, aching need that seemed to have taken him over. His thoughts were too full of her and that was dangerous.

"Can I ask you something?"

Although it hadn't proven much distraction, he had gotten himself focused on the ingredient list on an odd, slightly gross jar of peanut butter and jelly—already mixed together—when her question registered.

Turning to her immediately, he nodded. "Always."

"A few weeks ago. After our date. Did you stay with me because I was the job?"

"No." The denial was out, real and absolute, even if the lingering remorse he felt over misleading her was equally real.

Equally absolute.

He'd ultimately acquiesced to the very real, very demanding urgency of his body staying with her that night, because he'd been weak. He'd given in and sacrificed the principles he'd vowed to uphold always.

"Is it why you tried to leave after dessert?"

"Yes."

His mind flitted back over that night. Had it really only been a few weeks? It seemed like so much longer.

"What changed your mind?"

"I didn't want to leave. I wanted you and I have from the first moment I talked to you, that day on the Traverson job. But my real job demanded that I do the right thing."

"The right thing? There are right and wrong things when you're undercover? That seems odd, considering the illegal run you're going out on tonight with my father."

"It's not like that. I mean, you do what's needed

but—" He broke off, trying to come up with the right way to explain himself.

Because like it or not, he did lie for a living. It was couched in the excuse of undercover work and catching the bad guys, but it also covered any manner of sins with a sort of de facto excuse that people were just supposed to buy and say they were okay with.

But was he?

He had a personal code of honor. It was something he'd determined for himself even before he signed all the paperwork to join the FBI. He understood what he was choosing to do for the government and he knew that his job had a lot of fuzzy edges to it.

But he also had his convictions and the lines he wouldn't cross. Taking advantage of unsuspecting women was one he'd vowed not to go against.

One of many, really. Because once you broke your own standards, there was nowhere to go but down. Hadn't that been lesson number one from Ben Colton's big disgrace?

"I execute my profession to a personal standard I can live with. Spending the night with you was the first time I've betrayed that. I'm sorry. That I shared that level of intimacy with you without you knowing who I really was."

"It's... I mean, it's fine. I'm over it."

"I'm not."

Her eyes widened at that. "You're not?"

"Not really. It's not who I am and it's not how I choose to live my life. I hated lying to you and I should have walked away. But there's something about you, Sami. Something about this attraction between us. I tried, but in the end I failed miserably at staying away."

"I think it's time you moved on from the guilt. I shared that night with you freely. I wasn't sorry about it then and I'm not sorry about it now."

He wasn't looking for absolution but recognized the gift all the same.

"I'm not sorry for sharing the time with you," he said. "It was the most amazing night of my life. But I'll be forever sorry that hurting you was any part of that night."

On some level, it felt hollow and empty to say it. He'd still made the choice. Still gotten her into this mess.

But on another level, an apology was everything Sami deserved and more.

Now it was up to him to prove that he was worthy of her forgiveness. Even as that attraction continued to swirl around them both, swamping them with endless waves of need.

He wanted her. He had from the start.

But he had to keep that at bay.

She deserved a man who could give her everything. And while there hadn't been a woman up to now who had captured him like Samantha Evans, Dom still knew himself.

Knew who he was to the core.

Remorse for Ben's sins lived with all his children and each had reacted to the truth of their father's lies with choices of their own.

Dom was a loner, and he was good at it.

And when this was all over and Sami's father was behind bars, Dom would go back to his job at the International Corruption Unit.

He'd go back to more undercover work.

And he'd go back to being the lonely man who buried himself in work to avoid facing the risk that came with loving another person unconditionally.

Chapter Fourteen

The high desert spread out around Dom in majestic quiet as they drove north. The sun had descended twenty minutes ago as he and several of Lone Wolf's men rode in an SUV caravan toward Wyoming. The dying light was a warm red, bathing the craggy land with a beauty that hurt his chest.

A visual reminder of how even the most pristine landscapes could be ruined by crime and other nefarious deeds under their vast cover.

An endless sort of waste that sickened him.

Had he ever hated his job before?

The thought had struck him as he'd put on his night gear in the cabin, after he and Sami had returned from their outing, and stuck with him ever since. They hadn't said much after that electrifying kiss in the wholesale club next to the peanut butter and, really, wasn't that a picture unto itself?

Or maybe proof that their *relationship* was as fake as the need to hide out for the day.

The woman he had a blazing attraction to—one he was increasingly worried contained a hell of a lot stronger emotion than simple desire—had been the object of his lust in the same aisle parents the world over shopped for their kids' lunch fixings.

Peanut butter and jelly and French kisses. He sounded like some horny teenager who was desperate to get his girlfriend alone, anywhere he possibly could. Even if his and Sami's outing had been a strategic attempt to avoid detection and listening devices, it only punctuated the strange backdrop that made up their courtship.

Or fake courtship.

Or maybe it was a real courtship, but an impossible relationship.

Dom wasn't sure any longer.

And in the end, did it matter? Whatever either of them wanted to call it couldn't change the reality that there was no future for them.

"You ready for tonight, Conner?"

The guy asking—Zeke—looked mean as a snake but he'd been strangely helpful since Dom joined up with everyone for the briefing around five thirty. A big guy, Zeke clearly saw it as his duty to look out for the crew. It struck Dom, not for the first time, that even in bad circumstances, there were still natural leaders. Protectors. Alphas and betas and those who were trying to skate by.

Sort of like all people everywhere.

How much different could their lives be if they'd chosen a different path? One where those talents were used for legal purposes and the betterment of society, not its demise.

Which was all to say that it was one more layer of melancholy and that strange ennui that had gripped him since he and Sami had arrived at the Warlords compound.

It was also yet one more thing to screw with his focus and he had to buckle down. Had to keep his wits about him.

Especially since he'd seen no sign of Edge since that meeting in the parking lot after lunch. Who was the guy? And what was he to Mike Evans?

"I'm good, Zeke, thanks."

"Lone Wolf likes his team prepared."

"I got that from the briefing." Dom realized Zeke's papa-bear routine might work to his advantage. "He's thorough. And he leads his men. It's a refreshing change."

"Change from what?" Bryce asked from the front where he drove the SUV.

Bryce and Neal had stuck close to him all through the briefing. To keep an eye on him or make sure he didn't mention seeing them that day in the diner parking lot, Dom wasn't sure. But he hadn't been surprised when he'd been directed to ride in their SUV for the evening's job.

"Change from those who don't," Dom finally said, curious to see if Bryce picked up on his actual lack of an answer.

It seemed to work when Neal spoke up. "How didn't we know about these dudes in Wyoming cutting into our territory?"

Zeke shrugged. "It hasn't been our territory for all that long. And we've been focused on pushing west, not north. It gave an opening."

Dom considered the large maps they had up in the war room back at the ICU. Aerial maps with detailed photographs as well as more basic road maps and standard highway renderings. None of those had shown a group in Wyoming encroaching on Lone Wolf's team and it gave even more credence why the FBI had put Dom in place.

The fraudulent senator who had started this whole investigation hadn't shared much information, claiming any number of governmental privileges he didn't possess, ones which they'd still hadn't fully worn down with his lawyers. And nothing beat the intel they could get on the ground, no matter how many drones they sent up or how many aerial photos they managed to get.

"You been part of the Warlords for long, Zeke?"

"Since I was young. Floated around a bit when we disbanded but am happy to be back on Lone Wolf's crew."

Yep. Intel on the ground beats all every time, Dom thought. They'd believed the Warlords had disbanded for a time but Zeke's comments now affirmed it.

Dom made a show of looking out the window, the day's light nothing but a small line at the horizon. "It's a lot of area to cover."

"And it's ours," Zeke said proudly. "We run this part of the country."

"This group in Wyoming's not the only crew sniffing around," Bryce argued as he turned off the highway behind the other two SUVs. "I've heard rumors."

"Where?" Neal asked.

It was Bryce's turn to be evasive and he simply pressed on with his points. "The Dragons MC has been pushing south out of Idaho and the Saints are making inroads out of California. It's a lot of land but everyone wants more territory."

"We'll handle them," Dom said, adding a hard grunt to punctuate his point before an idea struck just as they crossed the Wyoming state line. One designed to test the team and see if his instincts from earlier in the parking lot were spot on or not. "The Warlords aren't ceding ground to any of them. I'll talk to Mike about it."

"Whoa, cowboy," Bryce glanced at him in the rearview mirror. "Mike talks to us."

"Yeah, sure." Dom acted casual. "But he's going to want a plan of attack. I can make us one of those."

Dom's approach seemed to agitate Bryce, who suddenly went quiet and shared no further gossip. Neal appeared to sense his partner's mood and they all quieted for the last fifteen minutes of the ride to the watering hole the Wyoming gang was purported to hang out in.

As lights came into view about ten minutes later, Dom saw the SUVs ahead put on their blinkers, Bryce following suit. A field of motorcycles filled the parking lot and all Dom could think was, *Bingo.*

They'd found the Wyoming gang.

Now it was time to show Mike, Bryce, Neal and everyone else he was committed to the Warlords.

Committed to taking them down, Dom reiterated in his mind, buoying himself in the face of what was to come tonight.

Because even when that bit of news came later, that Dom Colton of the FBI was their great betrayer, it didn't matter right now. For now, all Lone Wolf Evans and his men needed to know was that Dom was 100 percent committed to them.

SAMI WORKED THE ground in front of her father's house, the cool dirt an emotional balm as she tilled a small patch underneath the front picture window. The last rays of day had fallen behind the horizon about fifteen minutes before but she had plenty of light from several outdoor house overhead lights. Add on that digging was a mindless exercise—one she'd done hundreds of times before—and she took comfort from the feel of the earth between her hands. It soothed her in ways nothing else could.

And she needed some measure of comfort to give herself the mental space to think.

She had a decision to make.

Her day with Dom had only added to the running confusion in her mind. Confusion that had grown deeper and stronger when she and Dom had returned to the Warlords compound with their shopping haul. They'd brought the motor oil over to her father, dropping it off where he worked on an old muscle car in a freestanding garage halfway between his home and the cabin she and Dom were staying in.

"Thanks for picking this up for me," Mike nodded toward the case of oil as he pulled a rag out of his pocket to wipe at his fingers. "What do I owe you?"

"Nothing." Dom waved him off. "It was our pleasure."

"Nah, I—" A funny expression came over Mike's face before he nodded, solemn. "Thanks for that."

Yet again, Sami sensed more in what wasn't said than in what was. A strange sort of shorthand to avoid all that *needed* to be said.

"I'm going to head over to the cabin and wash up," Dom said, his gaze moving between both of them. "Give you a bit of time to catch up."

She hadn't known what to make of the gesture, but

also recognized that avoiding her dad wasn't going particularly far to create a relationship with him. Nor would it put her in very good stead if things did hit rocky ground. She needed some relationship with her father to press her agenda, namely keeping Dom safe, no matter what.

It was impossible to do that if they didn't speak.

Only now, when they were left alone with one another, the words wouldn't come. Anger and frustration and a raw sort of fury over her life and her choices so far practically consumed her and Sami had no idea what to do with any of it.

"I like your man, Conner. He's solid."

"He is."

"I wasn't sure at first, you know. A father's prerogative and all." He smiled and she recognized the tug that pulled at his upper lip as one she saw in the mirror every day.

Just like the same hazel eyes they shared.

And just like the same small furrow between those eyes when they were thinking through a problem. His was deeper, honed through the weathering of age, but it was a match for hers.

How odd, to look in someone's face and see herself. What should have been a comfort, to recognize family, only punctuated more of that smothering frustration that had ridden her earlier. The anger over why her father felt the need to live a life based on violence and dominance and crime. Why he couldn't be the man she needed him to be. Or her mother and grandmother had needed.

Why he chose this life over them, day in and day out, year after year.

"I love Dom. And I am glad to hear you like him."

The words were simple but, oh, wow, they packed a punch. Especially because they were true, Sami admitted to herself around the sudden tightness in her chest. For all the other subterfuge and hidden agendas, this one thing was true.

She and Dom might be pretending to have a relationship, but her feelings were real. And no matter how many times she scolded herself to keep things light and not commit emotionally, it was far too late for that.

She was in. All in.

And no amount of telling herself how difficult it would be later when he was gone had worked.

She loved Dom Colton.

"I know you do. Look." Her father pulled that rag back out of his pocket, twisting it in his hands. "I know I don't have a right to ask this. And I don't really know what you're planning for the wedding. But I'd like—" He broke off again, twisting even harder on the rag before seeming to catch himself and shoving it back into his pocket. "I'd like to be there. I'd like even more to walk you down the aisle."

Like the aftereffects from a punch to the face, his words lingered there, swirling around her without having any place to land. The proverbial cartoon birds were flying around her head as she sought to regain some measure of equilibrium.

"You want to do that?"

"If you'll have me."

The self-righteous anger she'd held onto like a vivid

burning coal flared high and bright and she wanted to cry with the sudden rush of emotion.

How could he stand there and ask her that? This man who'd beaten Dom? The same man he wanted to walk with her to meet at the end of a wedding aisle.

How did those two ideas even live in the same breath? The same thought?

"Look." He waved a hand. "Think about it. I know we've only just seen each other again and I know it's a lot to ask."

"It's not a lot to ask."

The words were quiet, nearly so caught in her throat as to be unintelligible. Only Mike did hear them and he took a few steps closer. "It's not?"

"It's what a father does." She shook her head, aware she was about to tread on dangerous ground. Even more aware Dom had told her not to. But try as she might, she couldn't hold this back. Couldn't pretend it didn't matter.

Because it did.

"I guess I'm just surprised, is all."

"About what?"

"You beat Dom last night. Hard enough to leave marks and bruise his ribs. Now you want to give me away?"

She'd always hated that image, for herself and for any other woman. She wasn't a piece of property to be handed over. Yet, even as she hated the idea, she'd always loved the sentiment. It was amazing how those two convictions could live so closely together, but somehow they did. The idea of standing on her own two feet, all while desperately wanting a relationship with her parent.

Wanting that sense of security that came from someone who loved you unconditionally.

Wanting. Needing. Aching for it, yet knowing it couldn't exist.

Something played across her father's face, a level of remorse she didn't expect. "I did it *for* him."

"Excuse me?"

Mike looked around, his gaze settling on the car before he turned back to her. "Dom's an impressive man. A bit like this car here. No one underestimates a muscle car, no matter how mild-mannered it looks."

"Dom's not a car."

"No, he's not. But the men on my crew, they respond better to actions than words."

"So beating Dom was for his own good?"

"It sent a message. And when he handled it, that sent another message."

"What message is that? Brutality as a form of advancement?"

Once again, Dom's words rang in her ears to leave it alone, but she couldn't. She'd lived with the reality of her mother's death for too long. A death that had been wholly preventable if her father had engaged in a different life.

Made different choices.

If her mother hadn't been collateral damage in Mike's endless gang warfare.

"I wish it weren't like that, but it is. And yes, Dom's ability to handle it all reflects well on him."

Even as it left her with the knowledge that Mike's view on the world, no matter how much she wanted it to be different, was tied to some sort of animalistic show of strength and dominance,

He led his *crew*, as he called them, that way.

His wife had been killed because of those warfare politics.

And even in his need to regain a relationship with his daughter, Mike Evans still couldn't walk away from who he was, as evidenced by his treatment of Dom.

It was a particular sort of madness and no matter how desperately she'd fantasized about having a father to walk her down the aisle, she couldn't help but recognize how hollow it all was.

She might biologically have a father but he wasn't whom she actually needed in her life. Nor would he ever be the man she needed him to be.

But she didn't say any of that. She'd given a lame, "I'll think about it," before making an excuse that she needed to call her own crew chief to see how her business was running.

That conversation had run through her mind since, endlessly looping through her thoughts. Even hours later, she couldn't shake the emotional ache that discussion with her father had left inside of her.

What she was doing here, now—Sami looked around at the now-weeded earth in front of her father's house—she had no idea. But she'd instinctively known that she needed to touch something in her father's life that she could affect positively. When that matched well with her own need to find solace and comfort—something she always found in the dirt—it had felt like the right thing to do.

It had also kept her mind off where Dom had gone tonight.

Because layered underneath the pain of her conversation with her dad was that other reality that had hit her today. The one that flowed through her, gaining power by the second.

She loved Dom Colton.

And she'd be damned if he was going to die because of her father. She'd lost one person that way and watched another—her grandmother—die with a soul-deep grief over her son that had never left her.

There was no way Sami could lose Dom, too.

Dom stood in a line of men, Warlords to his right and left, with Mike Evans standing point in front of them. Out in front, alone, living up to his moniker of Lone Wolf. Because despite having a cadre of men behind him, he was responsible for facing down the threat of the encroachers making inroads up in Wyoming.

It was something Dom understood about this mission and he knew enough about gang politics to sit back and wait for the proper signal. Mike was in charge and Dom left him to it.

A large man with a scar bisecting his left cheek moved up to the front of his own group of men. Dom cycled through the photos he'd reviewed at the ICU, finally settling on the name of the other gang leader.

Joseph "the Blade" Drummond.

The man had a rep a mile wide and, up until five months ago, had been in federal prison.

Which helped explain the timing.

What it didn't help was the speed with which he'd managed to set up his organization once again, running hard and fast enough, he was giving the Warlords a solid run for the region.

That same lingering anger that had draped over his shoulders all afternoon and on the drive here spiked once more. The absolute weight of it all and the endless miasma of crime and drugs that the FBI battled.

Five months.

This guy had been out of federal prison for five months and he was already running a major job in southern Wyoming.

Prison hadn't reformed him and clearly the government's efforts to minimize his influence by locking him away hadn't worked very well, either. Again, Dom couldn't quite fight the feeling of wondering what it was all for if this was the outcome.

Over and over, it was the same. The same crimes. The same mess clogging the streets and killing people as the drugs circulated through communities like wildfire.

The same endless war they never seemed to truly advance in. Oh, sure, the FBI and its fellow agencies globally made inroads. Won a few battles. But the problem never really went away. Nor did they make near enough of a dent to see things improve.

"This is taking too long," Neal muttered beside Dom and he glanced over at the man. Sweat beaded the back of his neck, despite the cool desert air, easily visible in the overhead lights of the bar parking lot.

Dom kept his voice low, quiet. "It takes as long as it takes. We wait for Lone Wolf's signal."

"Yeah, but something's up. The longer we stand here, the more we're sitting ducks."

Although he hadn't gotten the sense that Neal was much of an original thinker, the guy had street smarts in spades and he wasn't wrong about this. The longer they stood there, out in the open, the more risk they ran of having the underlying tensions spill over into violence. The only thing in their favor, Dom considered, was the fact that they were out in the open and at a public place. Even if this was the other gang's territory, a fight like this would draw police attention.

Something neither party wanted.

Dom was also pretty sure the ICU had eyes on this place, even if they didn't have anyone embedded. He'd already scanned the wait staff and those assembled in groups on the wide patio in front of the bar and hadn't seen anyone he recognized but that didn't mean they weren't here.

In the briefing meeting, Mike had shared that the objective of the meeting was to warn the team off or invite them to join up under the Warlords' guidance, but no one was under the delusion it would work.

Which left the reality that they were going to need to employ proper enforcement.

What Dom still didn't know was who was pulling Mike's strings. Mike didn't want the Warlords competing against another group this close but the drive to Wyoming had taken them an hour and a half across barren stretches of land. Were the territories between the two groups really that overlapping?

Or was it the puppet master behind Mike that wanted the competition gone?

He'd considered the Ronald Spence angle off and on, keeping his attention peeled for any mention of who could be directing Mike's actions. Caleb's thoughts on Spence had gone a long way toward forming Dom's impressions on the matter, but nothing he'd seen or heard suggested the leader behind the scenes was Spence. He had managed to get a message to the ICU on an encrypted file before he and Sami left Blue Larkspur,

but he had no ability to check for a reply while they
were here.

He had an in-case-of-emergency-break-glass way of
reaching out to the ICU, but it wasn't for routine email
monitoring. Which meant it would have to wait until
the weekend when they headed home and any news of
Spence along with it.

*Spence or not, you haven't gotten a real handle on
who's behind the scenes*, he reminded himself. Evans
had been quiet as a tomb about it and his team didn't
let on that they had any idea anyone other than Lone
Wolf was in charge. He hadn't wanted to stand out by
asking too many questions, but the few he had managed to ask had all turned up a general consensus that
Mike ran the Warlords and Mike was the leader.

And the men who made up the motorcycle club
seemed content to take that on faith.

Even if the arrival of Edge and his buddy the day
before at the diner still gnawed at Dom. Who were
those guys? Bryce and Neal seemed more than willing to fall in line with Mike. And while it might be an
act, it didn't explain why they were there, hiding out of
sight of the compound, versus conducting their business in plain sight.

One more weird thread to tug in a tapestry that was
far more tangled than Dom had anticipated.

The Blade finally spoke. "You're awfully far north,
Lone Wolf."

"Just keeping watch on what's mine." Mike's tone
suggested there wasn't anything unusual about his trip
to Wyoming.

"Then you'd better get out of here and go back to Colorado. It wouldn't do to turn your back on what's yours."

"I protect what's mine."

Blade took an imperceptible step closer. "So do I."

A war cry echoed off the side of the building, floating up into the night as the throng of men behind Blade charged forward. Dom had braced for any eventuality, but he'd anticipated it would take a bit longer to get to violence.

Major miscalculation, Colton.

It was the last thought he had before he rushed ahead into the throng.

Chapter Fifteen

Dom threw himself forward, his only focus on protecting Mike Evans. The man was the leading witness the ICU needed to keep their case alive and there was no way he could let anything happen to him.

And if the fleeting thought also struck him that Lone Wolf was Sami's father and he didn't want her to go through that loss, well, he'd worry about it later.

Right now, they had a battle on their hands.

Various members of Blade's team brandished knives or switchblades, a match for the same on the Warlords' side. What became apparent quickly, though, was how many fewer men Blade had on his side than the Warlords had on theirs. Several grunts and screams drifted up to the sky but Dom ignored it all, the hand-to-hand battle with Blade taking all his focus.

Mike managed to get a few kicks in but Dom had Blade on the ground in a matter of minutes, his only goal to subdue the rival leader and, by doing so, get his men to fall in line.

If he had his way, they'd do that all while having a minimum of serious injury.

The punch to his ribs was swift and hard and, coming on top of the bruises from the night before, had him seeing stars as he twisted to the side to protect himself from another hit. That movement was enough for Blade to shift loose but Mike was on top of Blade immediately, covering for him and holding the man down while Dom caught his breath. It was only the flash of a blade in the overhead lights that had Dom moving again.

He leaped on Blade, taking the swipe meant for Mike across the fleshy part of his upper arm. He didn't even feel it as adrenaline pumped hard and fast through his system and he used that to his advantage, holding Blade firmly to the ground, his hands at the man's throat.

The fight was over nearly as fast as it began but Dom never let up on the pressure.

It was only as Zeke came up beside him, pulling Dom bodily off of Blade, that Dom saw what had happened. The swipe of the knife he'd taken had continued on its trajectory.

And now stuck out of Mike's chest at an odd angle.

SAMI HAD IMAGINED any number of scenarios to end the night, but a caravan of SUVs racing into the compound was even more than her fevered brain had thought up.

A fact that seemed increasingly irrelevant as Dom fell out of the back of the car that pulled up to the cabin before he reached back in and dragged Mike out with another large man she hadn't met yet.

"Dom! Dad!" Sami ran toward the car and the group of men who were climbing out of the other cars as well. All looked bedraggled and in varying states of hurt, but none of them had a blood-soaked rag bunched up against their chest like her father did.

"What happened?"

"Let's get him inside." Dom barked out orders and she raced up the steps of Mike's cabin, leading the way through the door.

Dom and the other guy got her dad inside the house and on the couch, Dom's hand pressed hard against the rag. He instructed the other guy to hold it in place before turning back to Sami. "I need you to get some stuff out of my truck."

He instructed her on the location of a first-aid kit and she took off at a run for the cabin where they were staying and the truck parked out front.

The next hour passed in a blur, the rush for the kit and the run back, with any number of thoughts racing through her mind. Even as one kept coming to the forefront.

Would Mike Evans die?

Her frustrations earlier that day and into the evening felt irrelevant now. Murmurs of a doctor they could call kept coming up but there was also a genuine appreciation for Dom's skills. After thoroughly cleaning the knife wound, Dom expertly sewed stitches to close it up.

Although her father was groggy and out of it, he'd screamed at the first touch of the needle before one of his guys plied him with whiskey to calm down.

And then it was done.

One more cleaning of the wound, about four aspirin and one last shot of alcohol and Lone Wolf was settled on the couch in a pile of blankets, snoring.

"We'll stay with him, ma'am." A guy Dom had called Zeke sat on a chair across the room. "You should get some sleep. We'll call you if we need you."

A mix of emotion welled up and swamped her, at odds with the lingering thoughts of earlier and the very real fear that had come over her as she'd watched Dom work over her father. His choices sickened her and made her question everything about her life.

Yet, seeing a knife wound high up on his chest, not all that far from his heart?

It shook her.

What if he'd died?

He still could, she admitted to herself, unleashing another roiling wave of confusion. Dom must have sensed her wavering because an arm came around her back, pulling her close to hold her steady. "Thanks, Zeke. We'll take you up on that. Come get us if you need anything."

The big man eyed a snoring Mike once more. "Will do."

Sami stayed like that, wrapped up with Dom, all the way back to the cabin. She kept wanting to say something, but nothing came to mind. All she could see was her dad, laying on the couch with a gaping wound. All she could think was that he could've died tonight.

Don opened the cabin door and escorted her inside. He settled her on the couch and headed out to the kitchen. She heard a bit of clinking against the counter and in minutes he was back, two glasses of bourbon in hand.

"Here. This will help settle you a bit."

"I don't care for liquor like this." Her voice—the one that croaked out of her throat—sounded small, and very far away.

"I didn't pour very much. But take a sip or two. You'll feel better."

Sami wasn't so sure about that but he seemed insistent enough so she took the glass. Without thinking, she drank it down, choking on the contents as fire burned a path from throat to stomach.

"Whoa. Whoa." He took the glass from her and set it on the coffee table, sitting down beside her on the couch and rubbing her back. "I said sip it, not wolf it."

He continued the motions, big soothing circles designed to calm her racing adrenaline.

She allowed his touch to lull her, but even with his nearness and those big hands moving over her back with such care, Sammy couldn't settle.

Because they still worried the cabin was bugged, she couldn't tell him what was really wrong. Or why the panic flooding her in great soupy waves refused to calm.

But she knew.

And she had to hold it tight inside because it said terrible things about her.

Awful things that, as she stood there in her father's home, hovering over his wounded body, she'd fantasized that he would die. That Dom's amateur medical skills wouldn't be enough and this entire problem would vanish. Like the underbrush and weeds she regularly removed from poorly tended landscapes, she could rid herself of her only living parent and move on.

Because that's who she was.

Way down deep inside, when she stopped running and faced her demons, she had to acknowledge the truth.

She was just as bad as the person she was running from.

Dom wasn't sure how to console Sami. He'd sat with her for a while on the couch. He would have stayed there all night, but for the first time since they'd met, he sensed that she didn't really want to be around him. So after giving as much comfort as he could, he excused himself and went to clean up.

With the continued worry that the cabin had ears, he wasn't able to do anything about calling into his team, so he opted for a hot shower, an inspection of his own wound up on his upper arm and one more glass of bourbon.

By the time he came back into the living room, Sami was curled up on the couch into a small ball. He settled a blanket over her and stood there for a long time, just staring down at her.

And in the quiet, he acknowledged that it was all a lot.

From the first moment he'd come into her life, he had upended it. Yes, Mike played a role in that, but Dom knew he had been the catalyst. And for all the change that had come since, he had started it all into motion the day he flirted with her on the job they were both working.

Those feelings from earlier came on again. The idea that he hated his job spiked its edgy truth once more.

Did he hate it? Or had he finally passed the point where he no longer cared? Where he no longer wanted to prioritize the work and make it the focus of his life?

There was a time he would've said he *was* the job. The hard work, earning his place in the FBI, running ops with his team—that had meant everything to him.

But now? He wasn't so sure. Because now he'd seen glimpses of what it would be like to truly have something that meant everything.

And his job felt hollow and empty because of it.

His arm throbbed, and Dom looked longingly toward the kitchen and the lure of a third glass of bourbon. He wasn't prone to heavy drinking, and he needed to keep his wits about him, but damn his arm burned from the knife slash.

Since oblivion wasn't in the cards tonight—both for the need to keep watch over Sami as well as any possible attention Mike would need if infection set in—Dom remained where he was. In a small uncomfortable chair opposite the couch, watching over Sami.

He'd take the pain in his arm as a sort of penance. And he'd stay right where he was, close enough to touch Sami, yet willingly giving her the distance she needed.

And he'd do his level best to figure out who might be working behind the scenes.

His actions tonight should put him in good stead with Mike and the rest of the Warlords. Maybe it would be enough to earn Mike's trust and a name. He could work with a name. The FBI could work with a name.

And, if his brother was right, a name might lead them to a clue about Ronald Spence.

Dom let it all run through his mind in a steady cadence, twisting and turning each fact as he knew them. It was only as he twisted and turned his way through each data point for a third time that Dom felt the room dim around him.

And fell asleep on the thought that Sami's father really needed to make it through the night.

SAMI WOKE ON a hard start, the sensation of being pulled fully out of sleep jarring. The room around her was unfamiliar and so was wherever she was laying, a blanket twisted around her. She struggled to sit up and then took a moment to reorient herself.

And saw Dom sitting across the way, his large body looking especially oversized in a too-small chair. His neck bent at an odd angle but the steady breathing and light snore indicated he was sound asleep.

It was amazing to her, she realized sitting there, looking at him—how powerful he still looked, even in sleep.

He was formidable. It was the only word that really suited. She'd known that from the first but last night only showed yet another facet of the tough, impressive man that was Dom Colton. He'd carried her father into the house, took over the handling of Mike's injury and kept his head from start to finish, doing what had to be done to save him.

Although she believed he'd been successful—assuming they could keep infection at bay—she couldn't deny how scary it had been. The cloths pressed against her dad's chest had proven just how much blood Mike Evans had lost.

And with that image came all she hadn't wanted to talk about last night.

The idea that her father would just slip away.

Live by the sword. Die by the sword.

Hadn't she heard that through the years, a colloquialism that was also a cautionary tale? Mike Evans made his choices every day and they had consequences.

Terrible ones, if the memory of that blood spread across his chest was any indication.

But what did it say about her that she'd rather he was no longer with them?

Regardless of what it all meant, she *had* thought

those things and even now, in the bright light of morning, she couldn't deny the feelings. Complicated and complex, just like her relationship with her dad. And a sad reality she needed to bear alone.

Because ignoring him all these years hadn't made her feelings any less complicated or complex. So maybe what she needed to do was use this time to find a way forward and ask the questions she'd never wanted the answers to.

Assuming he made it through the night, it was time to ask him all the things she'd left unsaid after her mother's death.

And all her fear about his answers?

It was time to face that, too.

RONALD SPENCE LISTENED to the cryptic message on his burner phone, well aware of what each word meant. The Wyoming threat had been dealt with. There was likely still a second round of cleanup required, but the group there had been brought to heel and several of the men had already sworn their allegiance to the Warlords.

"Bastards know a good deal when they see it," Spence muttered to himself.

He used the same burner phone to dial the man at the other end, pleased when the sharp voice answered, despite the early hour. "Good morning, sir."

"Got your message." Spence wasted no time. "You follow through on what we asked?"

"I did. Blade's dead. He was beaten up pretty bad after the fight at the bar with Lone Wolf's men. He wasn't too hard to handle. I left him in a stretch of woods off the highway near Cheyenne."

"Good." Spence mentally calculated the time it would take for the body to be found. Considering nature and the fact that Blade's gang had broken up, there wouldn't likely be a big rush to look for him.

"What about the other thing. In your message?" Spence asked, already dismissing Blade from his mind.

"I got news on Lone Wolf."

"Yes?"

"He's not quite the loner we thought. He's got a daughter."

Spence had known that but the kid hadn't been a part of Lone Wolf's life for a long time, and never part of the Warlords. "He doesn't care about her."

"I think that's an act. She's back and my intel says she's there because Evans wants her there."

"Yeah?"

Spence weighed the new information with what he knew about Mike Evans. The guy had been loyal to a fault, handling whatever Spence had tasked him with and doing it with a cool efficiency that kept the Warlords off the radar. He was a good ally and hell, the man had to be at least sixty. It wasn't a big surprise he had a kid.

"I've met her."

"What? Where?"

"Yesterday. She's back in Lone Wolf's life. Got herself engaged, too, and has brought the fiancé around with her."

"Evans okay with that?"

"Don't know." Ronald could practically hear the shrug through the phone, "but I don't get the sense his loyal followers care for the newbie too much."

Spence had instructed his inner circle to keep a

pulse on some of the more high-ranking Warlords. Evans couldn't be everywhere, and he had a hierarchy in his crew. Spence figured the same ambition that had put those guys into positions of command would make them ripe for some off-the-record conversations.

But this was an interesting new development.

A new son-in-law meant competition.

And a new son-in-law meant whoever was second-in-command risked getting a demotion.

"This is good work, Edge."

"Thanks, boss."

"Keep me posted if you learn more."

"Will do. Oh, and, boss."

"Yeah?"

"Daughter's name is Sami. Her new bruiser of a fiancé is Dom. Dom Conner."

Once again, Edge had come through.

"Right."

Spence hung up, staring down at the phone as several thoughts flashed through his mind. He lit a cigarette and fired up a web browser, typing Sami Evans into the search bar. Several results came back, at the top a listing for Evans Landscaping. Clicking in, he got a standard small business site. There was a main page, a Contact Us form and a series of before and after pictures full of now-lushly landscaped homes in the height of bloom.

But it was the About the Owner section that caught his attention. Clicking in again, Spence saw a pretty young woman with long red hair, a big smile and a fit attractive body, still hot underneath a shapeless golf shirt and work shorts.

He didn't miss the resemblance to Mike Evans, especially around the eyes and mouth. Nor did he miss just how close she'd been all along.

The subline above the header stood out like a headlight: *Blue Larkspur's only residential landscaper.*

What the hell were the odds, Spence thought, that all his own problems, all stemming from Ben Colton, had started in Blue Larkspur, too.

Playing a hunch, he typed Dom Conner into the same search bar, a few links coming up. They were limited but he saw a guy who had a few social media pages he used occasionally and a notation in an online community site in Blue Larkspur for a charity home build he worked on. Spence looked at the photo, something snapping into place in his mind.

He hit the search bar one more time, typing in Judge Ben Colton family.

And there it was.

A family photo of the Honorable Benjamin Colton of Lark's County with his wife and twelve children. A dozen kids would get attention no matter what, and as part of a prominent public figure's family, that went double. Ronald scanned the footer, naming each child based on where they stood in the image. And right there, three from the left, was a gangly teenager with the name Dominic Colton.

What were the odds?

As he flipped to the other open window and looked at the adult in the photo mentioned as Dom Conner, Ronald realized the odds were very clearly in his favor.

"The world's too damn small," he growled to himself as he lit a fresh smoke off the first. But his gaze never left the screen or the bright, happy family smiling back out of it.

"Too damn small."

SAMI STOOD OVER her father's stove and scrambled up eggs. The task was mindless and it had diverted her from the strange, rather bedraggled welcoming committee that had greeted her at the door. She recognized several men from the night before, many of whom looked like they hadn't slept. All had stayed with and watched out for him.

It was a special sort of loyalty and only added to the endless questions that had haunted her for days now.

If a man could engender that sort of loyalty from others, what was he doing running a gang? What could Mike Evans have been if he'd chosen a path that didn't involve living the life of a criminal?

She finished up the eggs, transferring them to a large bowl just as the oven dinged, letting her know the bacon was ready. The toast slices she'd managed between cooking the eggs were all set out on a plate and while it was hardly a feast, everyone could make a breakfast sandwich or two.

She plated up one for her father, heading out to where he still sat on the living room couch. After encouraging the rest of the men to head in and get food, she handed over the plate.

"You're looking a lot better this morning."

"Good." Mike grinned, even if the cocky smile couldn't cover the pain in his eyes. "Because I feel like hell."

"You're lucky you're doing well enough to feel like hell."

"Don't I know it."

Unbidden, tears welled in her eyes. Sami wanted to believe it was the stress of the past few days, coupled with the bigger pressure of the entire charade her and

Dom were perpetrating, but as her father patted the seat beside him, gesturing for her to sit down, she realized she wasn't quite sure.

Were the tears nothing more than stress-induced release?

Or was she sad over Mike Evans's brush with death?

The hell of it was she had absolutely no idea. But as she sat down beside him, his arm going around her, she figured she'd take the moment.

It felt slightly traitorous, but she also couldn't deny the opportunity to sit quietly with her dad for a few minutes.

She still remembered snuggling up to him when she was small. The way she could press herself up against his side, totally fitting in the crook of his arm. It wasn't something she'd thought about in years.

But now?

Here?

Sitting beside him?

The memories swamped her in waves.

Her tears fell silently, hot tracks down her cheeks, as they sat there. He didn't say anything and neither did she. They just sat like that, next to each other.

And as she gave her emotions free rein, refusing to check herself or question the moment, she realized something else.

In a few short weeks, there'd never be an opportunity to make a memory like this again. It had nothing to do with death and everything to do with the op Dom and the FBI were running.

The op she'd willingly chosen to participate in.

There'd never be another opportunity to hug her

father. To snuggle into his side. To hold his arm as he walked her down an aisle.

She'd believed that she'd given those things up years ago. That when she'd walked away, she'd chosen a future without him.

But now? Sitting here with him?

She had to admit just how wrong she had been. Because for all her conviction when she'd walked away ten years ago, she'd made a choice that could still be reversed.

She no longer had that option.

And no matter how comforting the memories of her childhood, snuggled tight in these same arms, Sami well knew that she wasn't a child any longer.

Her decisions had become irrevocable.

Chapter Sixteen

Dom had sensed the change in Sami from the moment they'd hit Warlords territory on Wednesday evening and she'd only grown more and more distant as the days wore on. She played her role for others to absolute perfection. In front of her father or any of his men, she was the picture of a woman in love. She was affectionate, passionate and very clearly excited about planning her future.

And in his company, when it was just the two of them?

She was like a ghost. There, but not really present. He sensed her but any attempt to engage her was brushed off or dismissed after the most perfunctory of answers.

And there wasn't a damn thing he could do about it.

She wasn't his fiancée and he also couldn't say she wasn't fulfilling her side of the bargain. The FBI had nothing to worry about having Lone Wolf's daughter in on the op. Because while he sensed her slipping away from him, he realized it was also tied to her very evident need to put emotional distance between themselves and what they were doing.

She'd chosen a role that would put her father in

prison for life. She knew it. Dom knew it. And it was like a mountain that stood between them, as immovable as the situation.

Mike Evans had no real future and she was actively contributing to that outcome.

So why was he so frustrated by that distance?

If he were smart, he'd embrace it for all it was worth. The possibility of an inconvenient attachment was virtually nonexistent with a woman who didn't want anything to do with him. And wasn't that what he wanted?

Dom Colton, loner FBI agent, didn't do attachments. He didn't envision his future attached to anyone. And he liked it that way.

Only now that he'd spent all this time with Sami, he was coming to realize that he didn't like his life that way. Or he didn't any longer.

He liked life with her.

The drive back to Blue Larkspur was quiet, more of that endless silence between them. They'd spent the past few days since Mike's injury keeping an eye on his healing wound, and Dom had spent the rest of his time working on plans with the Warlords for their next big job. The Wyoming situation had given the Warlords the regional dominance they'd wanted and the indoctrination of several of Blade's men had already begun.

They'd pay their dues—nothing quite as painful as Dom's initiation—but they were being tested. Dom saw it in some of the tasks they were given as well as several questions about Blade's operation.

And although he needed to get confirmation and proof from his colleagues at the ICU, Dom suspected Blade had been handled in some way. Mike hadn't mentioned any sort of specific operation to remove the man, but Blade hadn't resurfaced since the fight at the bar, nor had he contacted any of his former gang members.

As planned, Dom and Sami were now heading back to their respective jobs for the next week and would return again to the Warlords compound on Friday. It wasn't ideal—and at this point, Dom would rather close out the op—but there wasn't anything to be done for it.

He took the last turn off the expressway into Blue Larkspur and considered the town he'd grown up in. It certainly had changed since he was a kid. And in the decade and a half since he'd been in Denver, Blue Larkspur had both modernized and expanded. People built lives here. Had families. And they had a thriving community around them that supported all they wanted to do.

For the longest time, he thought of Blue Larkspur as the place he'd left. It had been home, but that was when he'd believed his father was a good man and the security of being with his family was all he needed in the world. It was only now, as he looked around, that Dom admitted he'd not only abandoned his past, but he'd rejected the place *and* the family who'd raised him.

It was a stark admittance and one that sat increasingly uncomfortably on his shoulders.

Had he failed the Coltons? Or perhaps more to the point, had he simply abandoned them?

It had been so much easier to stay away. Because coming here—coming to Blue Larkspur and spending time with his family—meant he had to acknowledge the one member of their family who wasn't alive any longer. The shadow that loomed large over all of them.

Dom pulled into Sami's driveway and cut the engine. "Back home."

"Yep."

"Go ahead. I'll get our bags."

She sat there another few beats, staring at the house with an inscrutable look on her face. And then on a small sigh, she seemed to nod to herself and get out of the truck.

Dom watched her walk up to a small pad installed on the side of the garage, the door going up after she punched in a few numbers. And then she disappeared inside, leaving him to those endlessly roiling thoughts, a witch's brew of emotion and anger and disappointment.

And layered underneath were all the things about his life he refused to acknowledge.

Gathering up their bags, he followed the same path she took into the house, closing the garage door after he got inside. He set their bags down and went looking for her, finding her in the kitchen. The water ran as she scrubbed her hands vigorously.

"You okay?"

Sami slammed the faucet off, reaching for a towel hanging off a nearby rack. She didn't turn around, but she did acknowledge his question. "Just trying to clean the stink of the past five days off my hands."

"You're home now and we can talk freely without worry there's anyone listening. Do you want to talk about the past few days?"

"No."

"Your father's okay but it could have been worse."

"I know."

"And you don't want to talk about it?"

Dom had no idea why he was pressing this or what point he was possibly trying to make, but something kept pushing him forward.

His own feelings of guilt at what the FBI and, by extension, he were putting her through? Or his own personal feelings about his father and his family that were all jammed up in his chest?

Or maybe it was just that damnable frustration that she wouldn't talk to him about what was bothering her.

Sami spun around at the counter. "No, Dom, I don't want to talk about it! I don't want to share the bs rolling around in my head with an FBI agent. And I don't understand why you keep pushing despite my clear body language that says I'm not at all interested in this conversation."

"Maybe it's because I want another fake fight."

The joke fell flat—*very* flat if her frown was any indication—and suddenly he realized he didn't want to make a joke. And he didn't want anything about what was between them to be fake.

Not their relationship.

Not their feelings.

And most definitely not this fight.

Which was why he pressed on before she could get another word in.

"I understand you've had to deal with a lot the past few weeks."

"You understand?" She moved toward him, her expression a stark mix of fiery passion and ice-cold fury. "You think you understand what it is to live with the reality that your father isn't just a criminal, but one who runs an entire organization? That you have to live with the fact that he's responsible for putting drugs on the streets that kill people? That *he* kills people?"

Before he could protest or even give a bit of insight into all the things he'd begun to realize about his own life, she rushed on, that cold heat seeming to catch fire.

"Do you understand what it is to stand over your injured parent and think they should just die so it would be easier for everyone?"

And there it was. The ingredients bubbling under that witch's brew that he understood better than anyone.

"Actually, I do. Because mine did die and it wasn't actually any easier."

A deep flush covered her face and he saw the way her heart beat overtime by the pulse in her throat. But it was the remorse that filled her hazel eyes, turning them nearly green in the bright sunlight coming in through the window behind her, that made him realize he needed to say some things. All the details he refused to even discuss with himself needed a place to land.

And beyond all understanding, he suddenly knew Sami was the perfect place.

"My father's crimes were uncovered when I was sixteen."

She nodded, that gaze unwavering on his face. "You told me that the other day. And I still say sixteen is too young to have known."

"His corruption couldn't last forever and an investigation by a keen reporter and a family whose son was wrongly imprisoned uncovered Ben's misdeeds."

He told the tale, of what was uncovered and how the ensuing state's investigation had ultimately taken over the work for Ben Colton's other victims. His father's work for years with private prisons and juvenile detention centers to put innocents away all came to light as a result.

And after, that shocking embarrassment that had befallen Dom's family when they realized their house and the lifestyle they lived was funded on the backs of those innocents.

"What did you do?"

"What could we do? Morgan and Caleb were nineteen and me, Oliver and Ezra were sixteen. The rest of the kids were all younger. We weren't in a position to do anything. Then," he added, thinking of all they'd done in the years since.

"I'm sorry you went through that. In every way, I am. But I still don't see how it compares to my wishing my father would die."

"You didn't wish that."

"But—"

It was suddenly important that she understand this. That strange, swirling, mixing set of human emotions they all carried were complicated but they also weren't rational.

Moving forward, he took her hands in his, willing her to grasp all he needed to say to absolve her of that raging guilt that just waited to move in.

"Sami, all you said was that his death would be easier for everyone."

"Right!" She twisted her hands in his but he held tight. "I wanted him to die."

"Wanted him to die or wanted to be rid of the pain of who he is? Because they're not the same."

"Of course, they're the same!" What came out on a

shout coalesced quickly into a sob, her stoic face and hard attitude shattering all at once. "He's my father!"

On some level, he'd sensed the storm coming, but had no idea how hard it would break when it finally did. So Dom did the only thing he could do.

The thing he somehow now understood only he could do.

He pulled her close, holding her tight against his chest. And let every one of those complex and confusing emotions pour out of her in heavy, heaving sobs of pain.

SAMI FELT EVERY single one of those sharp, stabbing emotions working their way out of her in the thick hiccupping sobs that wracked her body. It was nearly uncontrollable, the sobs only coming harder when she tried to hold them back.

So, as Dom held her close, she finally gave in and let them go. Let all the hurt and guilt and anger and pain flow out of her on those wrenching exhales of breath and tears and vivid, violent emotion.

Yet, even as she cried, Sami knew there was something more. Something about having that strong, warm body holding her as she let it all go.

She wasn't alone.

The wild storm subsided, a needed moment in time that did, finally, fade. And when it was done, Sami understood the gift he'd just offered.

Not only wasn't she alone, but he'd stayed and seen her worst. And despite it all, he hadn't run away. Or hidden. Or dropped excessive platitudes, telling her that everything would be okay.

It wouldn't.

But she would be and maybe that was the reality she was actually coming to terms with. The choices she'd made—and would continue to make until the FBI had Mike Evans in custody—were difficult. But she stood behind the decision and, more, she stood behind the inevitable outcome.

"You okay?" Dom tilted back so he could look down on her.

"Yeah. I've soaked you and for that I'm sorry."

"I'm not. You needed someone and I'm glad I could be here."

"Dom, I—" Sami stopped, considering her words. She what? Was sorry for shutting him out? Sorry for crying? Sorry for just wanting it all to end?

Or maybe there was something else. Something that had grown stronger, even as she'd done her level best to push him away.

"I want you to stay."

If he sensed her intention, he didn't show it, his response simple, easy even. "I'm not going anywhere."

"I know. You're my fake fiancé until this is over. But I want to be with you. I'm attracted to you and I care for you. And whether it's a good idea or not, I want you in every way."

And I'm going to keep on wanting you, even once this is all over.

And wasn't that the real pain in all this? Weren't those unfortunate emotions also layered beneath the storm inside? Yes, her situation was upsetting in the extreme, but if that were the only problem she was dealing with, she'd attempt to compartmentalize those emotions along with the reality of why she'd made the decision to work with the FBI in the first place.

No matter the complexity of her emotions for her father, he was a criminal and she had the power to do something about that.

But Dom?

Nothing about those emotions could be compartmentalized. And damn it, hadn't she tried? All week, she'd attempted to walk away from him. To put all that much-needed distance between them to keep her heart safe.

And in that same time, all she'd realized was how futile it was to try.

"Sami. I want you. You have to know that. But our circumstances just aren't right. And now, with you upset? I'd just be taking advantage."

"It's not taking advantage if I'm asking."

"Why are you asking?"

It was a loaded question and she knew it. Was he trying to understand if she was in too deep, her feelings growing bigger than the op? Or was he testing her to see if she gave an answer that only proved his point—that she was in a bad place emotionally and he'd only be taking advantage of that if they had sex?

So she went with as much as she was willing to share.

"I'm attracted to you. More than I should be, but I'm not going to makes excuses for it. We've spent a lot of time together and you're not easy on a girl's heart, Dom Colton."

"I don't want to hurt you, Sami. When this is all over—" he trailed off before taking a deep breath. "When this is all over, we both have to go back to our lives. What I do for a living puts those around me at risk. That would go doubly so for a woman I was in a relationship with.

"Because of that, I can't take advantage of you."

She cocked her head, fascinated that he only saw this through that one small dimension. "Why isn't this me taking advantage of you? Taking what I want while I can still have it."

At the confusion that rode in that compelling blue gaze, she pressed on. "I know we don't have something that will last. I'm okay with that and I've accepted it. What I'm not so willing to accept is having you right here, in my home, and not enjoying the time we have left. Unless you're not interested."

He pressed against her, locking her between his body and the sink. In the movement, she sensed she'd gained some serious ground, but it was the deep husky timbre of his voice and the insistent press of his body against hers that sealed the deal. "You know I am."

She ran her hands over his chest, then up to his shoulders, threading her fingers through his hair. "Then why are we standing here, talking in my kitchen?"

"I have no idea." Dom bent his head and laid his lips gently against hers. "I really have no idea."

Sami gave in to the kiss, this one totally different from all the touching and kissing they'd done in character over the past week. Because this was real.

Gloriously both-of-them-in-the-moment real.

They'd left the parts they were playing at the door— Dom Conner, thug-in-training, and Sami Evans, dutiful-loving-daughter-seeking-a-reunion—and were now just Dom and Sami.

Together.

She knew it wouldn't last. On some level, she tried to reason with herself, maybe it shouldn't.

But right here, right now, he was hers. And she was going to take full advantage of the opportunity.

With one last toe-curling kiss, she took his hands in hers and walked backward toward her bedroom. They stopped every few feet to either embrace or remove an article of clothing, and by the time they'd completed the trip to her bedroom, they'd shed everything, leaving the last few days and the lingering stench of the Warlords behind them, firmly outside the bedroom.

Sami was surprised by the shot of comfort that warmed her as she looked around her room. She was *home*. A fact that only added to her desire, the increasing ardor building in every nerve ending. She made a quick stop for her end table drawer, pulling out the box of condoms she'd bought a few weeks before, and setting them down within reach.

And then he was there with her, pressing her body into the thick duvet over her bed and kissing every inch of her. Sami reveled in the ease with which they touched each other, pleasure sparking with an electricity that flowed only between them.

She knew this was just sex. Good sex, but still just an act between consenting adults. But as she and Dom kissed and touched, pleasure flowing between them in mutual waves, she knew in her heart that it was more.

That it meant more.

Even if it was something she'd carry forward, a secret inside her that was all her own, what was between them meant something.

Which made her next move that much more deliberate. Shifting so that she was on top of him, she used her position to work her way down his body, kissing a path down his neck, over his chest. She stilled at his ribs, the bruises her father had placed on him had faded slightly, the initial harsh purple turning a muted shade of yellow.

"I'm so sorry." She whispered it against his skin before she continued on her path, caressing each bruise with tender softness. It was at odds with the increasing need that built between them, but she couldn't move on until she'd done her best to erase the pain and replace it with something warm and caring.

With something that wasn't rooted in ugliness and malice.

But as that urgency finally pushed her on, she moved lower, her tongue finding the small divot of his navel, the light dusting of hair over his chest growing darker as she kept on. And then she'd reached her destination, taking him into her mouth and using her tongue to paint everything she felt inside over his body. It was erotic and sensual and she knew there was nowhere else she wanted to be; no one else she could ever imagine wanting this more with.

"Sami—"The sound tore from his throat in a mix of agony and supreme pleasure, the husky tones both needful and satisfied, all at once.

Before she could take him to completion, he had her shoulders in his powerful hands, uttering her name again and pulling her gently to his side.

"I want you. Now." He pulled her close so they lay side by side, his leg going between hers as his fingers found the most intimate part of her.

She stilled briefly, about to protest that he'd stopped her when her own train of thought abruptly vanished, replaced by the building, increasingly insistent pressure of his clever fingers.

"Dom!"

She clutched at his shoulders, anticipating what was to come. And when the pleasure broke inside her, the exquisite pressure of a million shockwaves throughout her body, she refused to ride it alone.

"Dom. Now!"

Body still quaking in release, she pulled him to her. A shock of sensation whipped through her as their bodies met and merged, a shining reward for all they'd survived so far and a very real, tangible reason to keep surviving.

To keep each other safe.

A second, impossible wave of ecstasy crested through her body just as Dom shouted his own release.

With her arms wrapped around his midsection, her hands firm on his broad back, she fell into the abyss right along with him.

Dom kept his face buried in Sami's neck, not entirely sure he could move. The slight twinge of his still-healing ribs was the only thing that got him shifting, and that was likely only because it reminded him that he was crushing her into the mattress with the weight of his body.

As he shifted his weight off her, pulling her close against his chest, her words from the kitchen echoed in his mind, just as they had virtually since the moment she'd spoken them.

You're not easy on a girl's heart, Dom Colton.

All he could think was, *Right back at ya.*

He'd believed he'd had good sex in the past. But

in that moment, laying there with her, he couldn't remember another sexual experience in all his life. It was like every memory of how to be with a woman had faded away until it simply vanished, like his will-power around Sami Evans.

Oddly, he had no energy to care. Nor was he interested in the effort required to remember.

All he could remember was her.

All he could think about was her.

And in the aftermath of what they'd shared, Dom knew the truth. He hadn't just fallen for her, giving in to the attraction that had sparked between them from their very first moment.

He loved her. Not because of the sex, even as he knew the mutual pleasure of making love with her had only enhanced the feelings. But he was *in love* with her.

He had no idea how he knew, not being remotely acquainted with the emotion, but at the same time he was certain with a level of clarity that was almost frightening.

Over the past few months, he'd seen some of his siblings fall in love and on some level, he now acknowledged to himself, he'd believed them foolish. That the rush into a relationship with someone was only one more way to make yourself vulnerable. That the ability to fall for another person was a gift promised only to those who hadn't suffered such pain and loss and betrayal as the Coltons had.

Oh, how misguided and shortsighted he'd been.

And how much had he underestimated the power of love.

He glanced down at Sami, suddenly anxious to tell her, when the insistent ringing of his phone went off.

The FBI-issued cell, assigned to him for the op with the Warlords, had been programmed with a few key details, one of which was a specific ring that would register on a blocked number.

With that obvious signal going off, he reluctantly left Sami's side and climbed out of bed to get his phone, hunting up his jeans just outside her bedroom door.

"Hello."

"Colton. It's Manning."

Before Dom could say anything, the head of his ICU division in Denver began barking out orders. The agent they'd planted in Blade's organization in Wyoming had moved with the other new recruits into the Warlords and he'd been made.

"Made? How the hell did that happen?" Dom realized he was shouting when Sami stirred in the bed, sitting up with a confused expression on her face.

"We don't know but we need you in there with Lone Wolf. You need to talk him down and you need to keep Kent alive until we can get there."

"He doesn't trust me enough yet."

"You saved his life, Colton. He trusts you."

"How the hell do you know that?"

"Kent got word out to us. We think that's how he was discovered. I've got a team headed that way now and I need you as eyes and ears inside. We're closing this out tonight."

Everything inside of Dom rebelled, but he had a job to do and he knew it well. "I'll be there in less than two hours."

"Take the daughter."

"No!" The denial was out before he could stop it, but Dennis Manning wasn't amused or willing to back off.

"She's in this, Colton, and she's the only backup you've got right now."

"No." Dom's mind whirled with another way. With any other way until he finally settled on the answer. He wasn't taking Sami back in there, unaware of what they'd find when they arrived back at the compound.

"It's the only way."

"I'll find another way. I'm leaving now." He disconnected before Manning could bark out any further orders. He might not like his boss's perspective but he had no doubt the man had his back and would have their team at the compound as soon as they could finalize tactics.

In the meantime, he was off to play mediator.

As he turned, it was to find Sami, fully dressed and standing with his clothes in her outstretched hand. "Get dressed. We're leaving."

"You can't go."

"I'm sure as hell not staying behind."

Chapter Seventeen

Sami stared at the now-familiar roadside as Dom drove west. She was still semi-surprised she'd convinced him that she was coming along but had refrained from saying anything, well aware he was operating on the most tenuous of threads, as the worry for his colleague had to be overwhelming.

Well, hell, so was she.

Although they were in a hurry, Dom had driven over to his house for a quick stop. He had equipment there to determine if the vehicle had been bugged and he ran the device over the truck stem to stern before moving on to the undercarriage and then inside, ultimately satisfied they were bug-free.

She was glad he'd done it so they could speak openly on the drive. Even if she was still trying to come up with something to say.

Dom had also stowed a few of his FBI comms devices in the glove compartment, unwilling to leave her without some level of protection in the event something happened to him. He'd explained his password on the phone and how to contact his team. And he'd also showed her where he stowed a gun and a small tracking device, along with that phone, under the truck's manual.

It wasn't much but it was something and she was grateful he'd taken her even more deeply into his trust.

And that what was between them had deepened back there at her house.

They might have been interrupted by the call from Dom's boss from talking about their decision to be intimate again, but Sami couldn't stop thinking about it.

Nor could she come up with any sense of regret that she'd wanted to sleep with him again.

The late-afternoon sun glinted off her diamond and she glanced down at her engagement ring. This had all started out as an exercise in pretend, from his initial outreach to her under the guise of Dom Conner to their fake engagement to the act they'd been perpetrating for her father.

When had it all become so real?

On paper, there was nothing about this experience she should want to carry forward. Men who lied weren't redeemable—hadn't she seen that with friends through the years? Yet, with Dom, she felt differently. His job and the requirements to keep others safe had necessitated a set of decisions.

No, she mentally shook her head. *Actions*. A man in his position had to act in ways designed to capture criminals.

But ever since she'd discovered who he was, he'd stood by his word. He hadn't lied to her and he hadn't kept her in the dark about her father or his actions. This had been a difficult time, having to fully acknowledge who Mike Evans was down to his core, but Dom had been there for her every step of the way.

Now she had to worry that she could be there for him in the same way. That she could protect him through whatever they faced when they got to the Warlords compound.

She also had to think about who she was going to be when this was all done. Because the past few weeks had proven that she'd been living something of a falsehood herself these past ten years. Running from the knowledge of who Mike Evans was had been bad enough. But telling herself she was okay with it—compartmentalizing the emotional work she truly had to do in order to live with the reality of his life—had been the real lie.

And she'd told it to herself, over and over.

"Those thoughts are awfully deep." Dom's voice penetrated the interior of the truck cab. "I can hear their echoes from over here."

"Just thinking."

"Want to share?"

She glanced toward him, his gaze briefly leaving the road to capture hers.

"Just thinking about what we're facing. What I've chosen to do by working to capture my father."

"It's hard."

"It should be easy."

"I don't know about that." His gaze was firmly back on the road but she sensed his deep attention on her. That present awareness that always seemed to hover around him and, when directed her way, was so all-consuming.

Dom *listened*. He paid attention. And when she was with him, she felt that he really saw her.

"You think I should make a different decision?"

"Not at all. But that doesn't mean it's easy." His jaw

hardened as he seemingly considered his next words. "I'm so proud of what you're doing. Precisely because it isn't easy. It's really brave, actually."

"Oh." Sami struggled with what to say, his words so fervent, and again that word popped into her head— *real*—that she was taken off guard. "Thank you."

He reached out and took her hand. "I mean it, Sami. What you're doing is brave. We love our parents. It's part of who we are."

"Based on his behavior," she whispered the words at the heart of what troubled her so deeply, "he doesn't deserve my love."

"Maybe not, but you deserve to give it. And that's why what you're doing here truly is selfless."

Her throat tightened at his conviction and unwavering support. Since she had nothing to say, she swallowed hard around that lump and squeezed his hand.

And prayed he was right as they drove through the entrance to the compound.

Dom considered how to play his and Sami's returning so soon after their departure and opted for the closest to the truth he could get. He'd heard through a contact back in Blue Larkspur that there was an interloper in the mix.

All he needed was enough time to keep his colleague safe so the FBI could get in place. Manning would get a team in—they'd been planning their strategy for weeks on how to get in with minimal collateral damage—and they could end this in a matter of hours.

All of it.

He pulled up in front of Lone Wolf's cabin, the air eerily quiet as he and Sami stepped from the truck.

Where was everyone?

Over the past several days, Dom had gotten the rhythm of the place. Those on watch. Those who managed the night shifts. And the general air of busyness that pervaded the Warlords camp like an underlying hum. The men were consistently trafficking large caches of drugs and there was always something to be done, from managing drops to counting and dividing a shipment to shipping out to their distribution network.

Which again, made that silence so startling.

"Where is everyone?" Sami asked, her fingers threading through his.

"I'm not sure."

They walked up to Mike's front door and knocked. Although Mike had warmed to Dom and said repeatedly he wanted Sami to feel at home, neither of them were willing to walk inside without an invitation.

So they waited, even as the house carried that quiet stillness where you just knew no one was home.

"Where do you think he is? When we left this morning, he was looking better than he has for the past few days, but he's still moving slow from his wound."

Dom shook his head, moving to look in the front window. The living room was empty and the place had a darkened quality that reinforced their assumption no one was there.

"Let's go look for him. He has to be around," Sami said, turning from the window, her voice stilling midturn on a hard catch. "Someone has to be—"

Dom turned immediately, his training and deep attunement to her kicking in double-time.

And came face-to-face with Edge, the surprise guest at lunch a few days before.

"What the hell are you doing here? What's going on?"

"I could ask you the same." Edge lifted the gun in his right hand, leveled on the two of them. *"Colton."*

IT WAS THE man from the parking lot the day she and Dom went to the diner for lunch. He'd looked mean then and even meaner now.

And he knew who Dom was.

Sami fought the shiver but stepped right up, well aware everything hinged on what she said next.

"What the hell are you talking about? Who's Colton?"

"He is," the guy said and gestured with his gun. "Your man here is FBI."

"What!" Sami pushed every ounce of shock, surprise and disdain into her words. "He's my father's newest employee and I've been working with him for weeks. His name's Dom Conner and I'm marrying him."

Edge's grin was sharp and dangerous. "That's what he wants you to think."

"Why the hell would he be anyone else? And what makes you think he's FBI?"

Edge just laughed, but she saw the slightest flicker of surprise shimmer in his eyes. He might be sure in his knowledge of who Dom was, but she'd done enough to raise his suspicions that *she* didn't know that. "Oh, sweetheart, you've got a lot to learn."

Maybe she did but she wasn't backing down and she wasn't leaving Dom hanging out to dry. Staring Edge down, she kept her tone low and even. "And you're holding a gun on Mike Evans's daughter. I suggest you stop if you have any hope of keeping the peace with my father."

Edge didn't seem impressed by the bravado but he did lower the gun slightly. Still held high enough to do damage if either she or Dom attempted to rush him, but not directly pointed at them, either.

"Your father's dealing with a few things at the moment. Walk in front of me and I'll show you."

"Enough of this. Where the hell is Lone Wolf?" Dom demanded.

"Nope." Edge shook his head. "Walk. That way." He gestured with the gun. "Everyone's having a party over in the packing house."

Sami didn't know every building on the compound but Dom had given her a sense of the basic layout. The packing house was a large outbuilding where the Warlords sorted drugs, put them together in shipments and then got them out into their network of distributors and dealers. The very idea of it made her sick, but Sami recognized that this was the reality of what her father did.

Both the proof of his crimes and the very real physical requirements of moving thousands of pounds of illicit substances.

She and Dom walked, perp-style, in front of Edge to the packing house. It was about four hundred yards away, over a small rise that made it nearly invisible when parked in the cabin's driveway. Close but not really visible if you didn't look too hard.

Like your life, Sami-girl. Pretend it's not there and—poof!—it isn't.

The thought was depressing but true and it hardened

her resolve. That and the very real knowledge that the FBI *was* coming. She and Dom just had to manage this very delicate dance until help arrived.

The three of them navigated their way across the vast expanse of land. As she took each step, she had to acknowledge how each footfall took her farther and farther away from the support tech Dom had shown her in the truck's glove compartment. A reality she'd have to face, and where she'd need to run if things went sideways.

They made it to the packing house, and as they got closer, she could hear shouts coming from inside as well as an agonized scream. That had to be the agent Dom's boss had called him about.

That tormented shout was enough to push the bravado back in her tone but even as she whirled on Edge to confront him, Sami had to admit there was also a genuine desire to help the man inside. "What is going on? Why is someone screaming?"

"Punishment." Edge licked the seam of his lips as his gaze flicked to Dom. "Undercover agents might walk into this territory but they don't walk out." He tilted his head toward Dom, and Sami saw the clear avarice and excitement gleaming in the man's eyes. "This one sure as hell won't."

"Why do you keep saying that? He's a construction worker and a new employee of my father."

Edge lifted the gun higher. "You keep telling yourself that, girlie. Whatever gets you through. But your fiancé is a Fed and he's going to pay for it."

She moved closer to Dom and took the hands they'd already held clasped and put them behind her back. With her free hand, she laid it against his chest, felt his

heart beating strong and firm and at a clearly accelerated rate. Since it matched her own, she was gratified
to know that his strategy of keeping his calm was just
that—a strategy to handle this situation.

"You're the one who's going to pay for it. Just as
soon as my father sees you for what you really are.
A traitor to the organization, holding secret meetings
with other Warlords out of his sight."

Edge laughed at that, throwing his head fully back
as if she'd just told the best joke he'd ever heard.

"Those bumbling idiots in the parking lot the other
day? Even Lone Wolf wouldn't be dumb enough to
put his faith in them." Edge laughed again, the sound
even more eerie than the quiet cabin they'd discovered upon their arrival. "He was too busy putting it
in other places."

Where *was* Mike Evans putting his faith, then?

Although she hated to break the physical contact
with Dom, she was unwilling to stand there any longer.
With a swift turn on her heel, Sami pushed through the
door. They weren't getting anything out of Edge and
the continued screams from inside curled her stomach.

But it was only as she crossed the threshold that she
realized just how bad it really was.

The man she assumed was the FBI's other undercover agent was strung up by chains, his face beaten
and bloody, two Warlords standing on either side of
him.

And then there was her father, standing a few feet
away, his legs splayed and his arms crossed.

Something dark and absolutely painful covered his
face as he caught sight of her before he bellowed out
orders. "Get her the hell out of here! Now!"

"I don't think so, Dad." Her gaze darted to the man strung up in chains, an awful tableau that she knew she'd never forget. "It's time you recognized what I actually know. About you and about your business."

"Sami—" Dom's voice was urgent beside her. But before she could say anything, he was wrenched from her side, two more men dragging him bodily away.

"Dom!" She whirled on her dad. "Leave him alone."

"I can't do that." Mike shook his head. "He's in on this."

"No, he's not." She pushed every single ounce of fear and disbelief she could possibly muster into her voice. The fear was easy, but the disbelief she knew was a sizeable stretch. It would take every ounce of acting talent she possessed to convey that.

But she *had* to convince him of Dom's innocence. And she had to make this stop before anyone else was hurt.

"He is and he's got to be punished."

The two guys who grabbed Dom shoved him over toward the other agent, another stepping up with a matching set of chains in his hands. She screamed and pushed forward toward Dom, but Mike grabbed her before she could get very far, his grip strong despite his recent injuries.

"This isn't for you to deal with and it's not for you to see. I want you out of here."

"But I love him!"

Those words seemed to reverberate off the walls of the large outbuilding, and she felt their impact down to her soul. And unlike her fears that Mike Evans would see through her ruse of ignorance over Dom's real job, she knew this plea was 100 percent real.

She loved Dom.

And she couldn't bear to see her father harm him.

"Dad. Please." She stared up into the eyes so like her own, pleading. "Don't do this. Please don't break us completely."

Mike stared down at her, his face set in hard implacable lines. And in that moment, Sami desperately sought some small measure of the man she'd once known.

The father she once loved.

"Please. We were a family. Before mom died. Before this." Her gaze darted around the room. "Before this became your entire world."

He continued to stare down at her, that inscrutable focus never shifting away from her. It was only when he spoke that she felt the tiniest bit of hope spear through her. "No, Sami. You're my entire world."

"Then please. *Please.*" She wanted him to be different. Wanted to believe he could be different. "Don't hurt Dom. Don't do this anymore. I can find a way. I'll get you out."

When she'd agreed to this op, she'd done it with the sole belief that her father needed to pay for his crimes. That he needed to be off the streets and under federal custody so that he could no longer perpetrate the crimes that ruined families and sent others spiraling into addiction.

But here. Now.

Now she finally understood the bargaining stage of grief. If only he would come with her.

If only he would take that single step, she could make it right. She knew she could.

"Please."

"Sami. I—" Mike glanced around, remorse filling his eyes. "I'm in this. I'm in so deep."

"So we dig you out. You can be better. You can do better."

"It's too late for me. I love you, my Sami-girl, but I'm in too deep. The man I'm in this with will never let me out."

"No, Dad, it's not. It's not too late."

"He effectively owns me, kiddo. And no one goes against—"

One minute Mike was standing upright and the next Sami saw him clutching his chest as shots rang in her ears like a reverberating gong. He stumbled into her with the full weight of his body.

"Daddy! No!"

Yet, even as she heard herself pleading, even as she felt herself balancing his weight in order to lower him to the ground, Sami knew the truth.

There wasn't anything left to bargain for.

IN THE MELEE that followed the shots fired inside the packing house, Dom moved on instinct. He elbowed the guy who held him in place at his left and swept his leg into the knee of the man on his right. All of it was simply to launch himself at Sami, dropping over her and shielding her with his body.

Shouts echoed through the room and he could only focus on keeping her safe when some of the yelling finally registered in his mind. His colleagues had arrived, their instructions resonating out of a bullhorn as several officers moved in to subdue the Warlords.

Over the top of Sami's head, he saw them cut down Kent from the chains, someone ready to catch his limp body as he fell into the rescue team. Manning kept his gun firmly trained on several men and it was only as he saw Edge slipping through the back of the packing house that Dom squeezed Sami before gently letting go. "I have to—"

"Go!" Tears ran thick tracks over her face but her order was firm. Unbreakable.

He raced after Edge, determined to get the man and get the truth of what he knew. But as the cool spring air greeted him at the door, the compound now bathed in darkness, Dom knew it was a lost cause.

Whoever Edge really was, he was working for the enemy. And he'd been the one to pull the trigger, ending Mike Evans's life before he could utter the name of the man he was working for.

Dom gave chase a couple hundred more yards, but he knew the chase wouldn't bear fruit. Edge had an exit strategy. He'd had one all along.

Racing back inside, he went straight to Sami. She still held Mike's body but a medic had come over to remove her father, gentle but firm as he requested she let go. With searching eyes on Dom, the guy glanced down at the daughter still locked tight to her dad before lifting his eyes once again.

Dom got the message and dropped down beside her. "You need to let him go, baby."

"But he's—" Those tears continued to fall, hot trails of grief coursing down her face. "He's gone, Dom."

He promised her he'd never lie to her again and he had no other words other than the truth. "He is."

"He's not innocent, but he was going to tell me. Tell us," she corrected as she glanced back down at her father where he lay in her lap. Slowly, she released him, the medic there to take the weight as Dom pulled her slowly to her feet. "He was going to tell us who he was working for."

"He was." A final act of decency from a man who'd showed little of it in his life.

But he would have for his daughter.

"He loved you, Sami. You have to believe that. No matter what comes next, you need to hold on to that."

"He loved me." She repeated his words, a sense of wonder permeating the grief that still held her in a tight grip.

"Hold on to that and keep it close. He meant it and it was his last gift to you."

Dom pulled her close, wrapping her in his arms and letting her cry it out on his chest.

"Please. Let me take you away from this. Let me take you home."

Without turning back to look at the room, she sheltered herself in his embrace and allowed him to do just that.

SAMI STARED DOWN at the landscaping renderings she'd pulled together for an upcoming job, surprised to realize they were wet with tears. Disgusted with herself, she ran her forearm over them, smearing the tears along with the graphite from her pencil.

Oh, what was wrong with her?

She slammed back out of the chair at her kitchen table, sick of her endless thoughts and the tears that came at odd moments and the maudlin way she'd walked through the past three weeks.

She was stronger than this.

And she wasn't one to sit around pining for a man.

Even if that man had to go back to his job in Denver—
just like he'd told her from the start—and taken on his
next assignment.

Just like he'd also told her from the start.

She knew the consequences of her undercover ad-
venture with Dom Colton. She just hadn't believed how
hard it would all be after he left.

After they both went back to their lives.

After she had to find a way to move forward.

It was a difficult, sad reality but she'd had a long
time to recognize that her father's life choices were
not only dangerous, but they could have deadly consequences. As a fresh set of tears pooled in her eyes,
she knew she had to get out for a bit. She'd go for a
drive or head into town for ice cream or even go do
her grocery shopping.

Anything but sitting here.

She had her keys in hand and was nearly to the door
that led to her garage when her doorbell rang.

The rush of curiosity and a strange shot of anticipation propelled her forward before she thought better of
it and went to answer the door.

And opened it to find Dom on the other side, his
large frame filling the doorway.

"Hi."

"Hi."

There was a haggard edge to his features—as if he
hadn't slept—and a few days scruff on his face.

He'd never looked more gorgeous.

She wanted to ask why he was here but that would
lead to the other whys. The ones she hadn't stopped
asking herself for three weeks.

Why had he left?

Why couldn't he be a part of her life?

Why was she so stupid to go and fall in love with him?

"I came to tell you that I made a job change today."

Whatever she was expecting him to say, that wasn't quite it. "Where are you going?"

"It seems that my superiors are concerned that I'm a bit too noticeable."

He *was* noticeable, but she didn't think the problem was his bosses at the FBI thought he was hot.

"They're concerned by the number of thugs I spent time with on the Warlords job. And they're especially concerned someone made me as a Colton which, you know, is sort of like a red flag here in this part of Colorado."

"What are you going to do?"

"I've been thinking about a desk job in Denver. That maybe it's time to put my talents to different use. I was also thinking…"

He stopped, his gaze capturing hers.

"Yes?" she asked when his words still hovered there between them.

"I've been thinking that my last name has caused me a few other problems, besides blowing my cover."

Sami had no idea where he was going with this, but she desperately wanted to find out.

"I had this ridiculous notion that if I didn't love anyone or let anyone into my life, I'd be safe."

"Safe from what?"

"From being hurt and from putting my trust in the wrong person."

"You mean the way you put your trust in your father?"

"Something like that." His gaze found hers again and something solidified in those deep pools of blue. "Actually, yes, exactly like that."

Her heart broke for him. Broke because she knew how hard it was. How difficult it was to move past the hurts that came from the very people who were supposed to protect you.

Who were supposed to put you first, always.

"What are you going to do about it?"

"I'm going to stop running. And I'm going to give you this." He dug into the pocket of his jeans, producing the engagement ring she'd insisted he take back.

"Even though all I can really offer you is myself. And my pledge that I'm never leaving your side."

She allowed him to slip the ring on her finger, barely able to breathe she was so stunned that he was actually here—right here—with her.

"I love you, Sami Evans. If you'll have me, I can promise you that I'm not leaving you. Ever."

She laid a hand on his cheek as she stared up at him. "You love me?"

"I do. Real love, not that fake stuff we've been peddling. The kind that sticks around."

The grief that had been her constant partner for the past three weeks vanished, slipping away for another time.

Because here. In this moment. She had all she'd ever wanted.

And all she'd ever need.

In the man who stood before her, she saw her future.

"I love you, too, Dom. Real love. Forever love."

As his lips met hers, their hands locked tight between them, Sami knew true joy. And as Dom's lips met hers, he whispered a promise against her lips she knew he'd keep.

"Always."

Epilogue

Dom had an arm around Sami's shoulders as they stared out over the dance floor. The Gemini Ranch had been transformed for Caleb and Nadine's nuptials. Dom had wondered what they'd done with the cows, but since he never underestimated his sister Aubrey when she got an idea in her head, he had to figure they were stashed safely somewhere.

In the meantime, he was in the bosom of his family, laughing and toasting and enjoying his own time with the woman he loved.

He and Sami had faced a few challenges since wrapping up the situation with her father and the Warlords, her grief still coming in hard waves most days. But they had each other and he was there to see her through it.

He'd also found an exciting distraction to keep them both focused on the future. When it became evident his cover had been blown to bits, he had a choice to make. The International Corruption Unit still needed him, but he was going to focus more on a desk job instead of out in the field undercover. He liked Denver and after he and Sami made their fake engagement 100 percent real, she made him the happiest man alive by telling him that yes, she'd happily relocate her business to Denver to be there with him.

"Sami, dear, you look gorgeous." His mother swept up to them both, a happy lightness Dom hadn't seen in her in far too long seeming to make her float. "I'm so happy you're here. And I'm elated you and my Dom are going to settle down in Denver. Thank you for being there for my sweet boy."

Sami hugged his mother before stepping back. "I'm lucky my business is one hundred percent portable. And while I've always thought of myself as a bit of a country girl, I can't deny how much I'm enjoying exploring the city."

"The city is a fine place for young lovers." His mother winked before her gaze alighted on Aubrey and Luke standing across the dance floor, laughing and clapping. His sister Rachel and her fiancé, James, stood nearby, their baby daughter, Iris, in James's arms. The little girl laughed, waving her fists in time to the music, and Dom had to admit Iris had a surprising amount of rhythm for not even walking yet.

"Your granddaughter looks like she's waving at you, Mom." Dom tilted his head toward the baby.

"Oh, my sweetness, look at her."

His mother was about to head off when the chief of police, Theo Lawson, came up to them. "Mind if I steal your mother for a dance?"

"She was just saying how much she wanted to cut a rug." Dom practically pushed his mother into Theo's arms.

"They make a cute couple, Cupid," Sami teased him as she pressed a kiss to his jaw.

"She deserves to be happy."

"Everyone does," she agreed.

A point that had him shifting slightly, turning so they faced each other. With that, Dom bent his head, pressing his lips to hers.

The kiss was soft, warm and quickly went to his head, but he hadn't been able to stop himself. He'd run from love for so many years. Now that he'd found it, he was loath to let it go.

"Just whose wedding is this?"

The voice registered just before Dom totally lost himself in the kiss with Sami and he surfaced to find his brother Gideon grinning at him like a fool.

"Way to intrude, Gid."

Even though he'd have happily kissed Sami for the rest of the wedding, he couldn't deny how good it was to be with his family. Gideon's fiancée, Sophia, had already pulled Sami close in a warm embrace. Sophia had been one of the first members of his family to reach out to him after the events at the Warlords compound. She'd shared several articles on how to deal with grief and had already taken Sami to lunch a few times, offering a warm, safe place to share her sorrows.

Dom had already grown attached to his future sister-in-law but he loved her even more for her kindness and understanding. And it was wonderful to see how much her presence eased Sami's emotions, her smile brighter and softer spending time talking to her new friend.

"Everyone's here except Gavin," Gideon said, standing at Dom's side. "You, Ezra and Oliver get your fill of one another yet?"

"Never," Dom said, thinking of the late night he and his triplet brothers had spent the evening before, shooting the breeze and discussing life over beers.

"I'm glad Ezra's here for the month. It's good to have him home from his tour of duty."

"That it is," Dom agreed. It was better than good, he actually thought, and hoped Ezra reconsidered leaving the country again. He'd done several tours at this point and was well within his right to begin thinking of retiring from military service.

For now, though, he'd just be happy to have his brother home.

Keeping Oliver in place might prove harder, since he was already planning his next business enterprise in Malaysia, but Dom knew there was little that stopped Oliver when he got his mind set on something. So he'd just have to live life vicariously through his triplet brother, since it looked like Dom was going to be in Denver for the foreseeable future.

A state, he thought as he looked at Sami laughing with Sophia, he could absolutely get used to.

"It's time!" Alexa's shout from the opposite end of the dance floor caught everyone's attention. "Nadine's going to toss her bouquet."

Sophia shot Dom a smile before reaching for Sami's hand. "Mind if I steal her for a few minutes?"

"You promise to bring her back?"

Sophia winked. "For a hottie like you? I don't think she'd stay away."

He wanted to be embarrassed, but the whole day was just too damn happy to do anything but smile.

Had he seen his family like this? Ever?

As Dom took in the room, his gaze tripping over each and every Colton, he realized that so many of them hadn't been this happy. Not like this.

Not for a long time.

Not since *before*.

The thought nearly popped the delightful bubble of happiness that floated around him until he caught sight of Sami. Lined up in the half circle around Nadine, she was laughing and smiling between Sophia and Aubrey, miming a baseball catcher's stance to catch the bouquet.

And in the brightness that was her smile, Dom realized the truth.

They would all live with the legacy of their father's betrayal, but it was up to all of them to move on and *live*. To embrace their futures with an expectation that they could make the world better. That they could have better.

And, if someone was as lucky as he was, to share that future with a woman as amazing as Samantha Evans, well then, wasn't that everything that really mattered in life?

The band played a quick riff on the drums, a crescendo on the cymbal that resonated in a crash as Nadine's cue to toss the bouquet. And Dom laughed as he saw it was his Sami that came up with the pretty bundle of roses.

A cheer went up from everyone and in a matter of moments, people had dispersed back to the dance floor for the next song. Sami ran up to him and he pulled her close, staring down at the bouquet. It hadn't escaped his notice that she'd continued wearing the engagement ring he'd bought her, even though the two of them hadn't discussed whether or not they'd get married anytime soon.

But in that moment, her arms full of roses and his arms full of her, Dom knew it was time.

He didn't want to take anything away from Caleb and Nadine, so he took her hand and pulled her to a small alcove where they could talk.

"You were victorious. That catcher's stance must have worked."

"You saw that?" Her eyes widened even as her smile remained.

"Of course I did. And I thought it was a brilliant strategy."

She stared down at the bouquet before lifting those vivid hazel eyes back up to him. "Five years of girls' little league ought to count for something."

He lifted her left hand, pleased it wasn't the one currently wrapped around the stem of the bouquet. Pressing his lips to the top of the ring, he kissed her fingers. "There's something I want to ask you, Samantha Evans."

"Oh, Dom." She glanced around, checking to make sure they were out of earshot. "We don't have to do this now. It's Caleb and Nadine's special day."

"And it will be theirs. I'm doing this for us. Just us, right here, away from the whole blooming lot of prying Colton eyes."

"They're loving eyes."

"Loving, prying eyes," he amended with a smile. "And I'm not doing it because you have a ring on your finger or a bouquet in your hands, but because I can't wait a minute longer."

"You can't wait for what?"

"Marry me, Sami. Become my wife and make a life with me. I love you, and for the first time I can ever remember, I'm excited about my future. Excited because I know you'll be a part of it."

"Yes. I will. Because for the first time, I'm excited about my future, too."

"We're a pair." He bent his head, kissing her once again with all the passion and fire and need he had for this woman.

This wonderful, amazing, strong, sexy woman.

If anyone had told him even three months ago he'd be out of undercover work and happy about it, Dom would have said they were wrong. But now, standing here with Sami, hidden away in their little alcove, Dom knew the truth.

The past that had haunted him no longer held the same power it once had.

And he'd never been happier in his life as he now faced forward, ready to embrace forever with her.

* * * * *

MILLS & BOON

THE HEART OF ROMANCE

A ROMANCE FOR EVERY READER

MODERN

Prepare to be swept off your feet by sophisticated, sexy and seductive heroes, in some of the world's most glamourous and romantic locations, where power and passion collide.

HISTORICAL

Escape with historical heroes from time gone by. Whether your passion is for wicked Regency Rakes, muscled Vikings or rugged Highlanders, awaken the romance of the past.

MEDICAL

Set your pulse racing with dedicated, delectable doctors in the high-pressure world of medicine, where emotions run high and passion, comfort and love are the best medicine.

True Love

Celebrate true love with tender stories of heartfelt romance, from the rush of falling in love to the joy a new baby can bring, and a focus on the emotional heart of a relationship.

Desire

Indulge in secrets and scandal, intense drama and plenty of sizzling hot action with powerful and passionate heroes who have it all: wealth, status, good looks…everything but the right woman.

HEROES

Experience all the excitement of a gripping thriller, with an intense romance at its heart. Resourceful, true-to-life women and strong, fearless men face danger and desire - a killer combination!

To see which titles are coming soon, please visit

millsandboon.co.uk/nextmonth

LET'S TALK
Romance

For exclusive extracts, competitions
and special offers, find us online:

MILLS & BOON
Desire

Indulge in secrets and scandal, intense drama and plenty of sizzling hot action with powerful and passionate heroes who have it all: wealth, status, good looks…everything but the right woman.

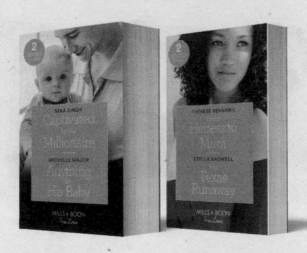